RETURN
TO
ENCHANTAS

Corey M. LaBissoniere

Martin Sisters Publishing

Published by

Martin Sisters Publishing Company

www. martinsisterspublishing. com

Copyright © 2014 Corey LaBissoniere

Martin Sisters Publishing Company
ISBN: 978-1-62553-083-7
Young Adult/Fantasy
Printed in the United States of America
Martin Sisters Publishing Company

DEDICATION

I dedicate this book to my father, William LaBissoniere. His guidance, wisdom and love has steered me throughout my life. His guidance helped me be the boy I'm proud to have been. His wisdom has made me the man I am today, and his love continues to make me strive to be better every day.

ACKNOWLEDGEMENTS

A sincere thank-you to Chandra Murrell for helping me keep the dream of Enchantas alive and for always being there for me. Your love and encouragement kept me going when at times I faltered and struggled to continue.

A special thank you to Cyndi Perkins for her support in my writings and help in the initial edits of this book as well as my first book "Land of Enchantas."

I also want to express my sincere gratitude to all the fans of my first book "Land of Enchantas". A heart felt welcome to all my new readers to the glorious world of Enchantas. I genuinely hope you delight in reading my creations as much as I enjoyed writing them. May your imagination never diminish!

PRELUDE

The cold cellar was dark and dreary. The smell of must, mold and mildew surrounded the young blonde girl as she sat on a torn dirty mattress. The floor was drenched from the water dripping through cracks in the cement walls. Hot wax sizzled from a tiny candle when it hit the wet floor.

She cowered in one corner of the mattress wrapping her skinny arms around her knees and covering her bare legs with her shirt. She was very pretty, but her bruised face and dirty body concealed her beauty. Her body shivered and rocked as she wondered how long she had been there. Footsteps from above terrified her, and at each step she feared they were headed for the stairs and ultimately to her. Her eyes had adjusted to the darkness after the first day of her imprisonment. She had lost count of the number of days she'd been there. At first she wondered why her father had imprisoned her, but now it didn't seem important. Now she only cared about her freedom.

Wiping a tear from her cheek, she thought about the night her loving, caring father changed into a frightening monster. She was sleeping peacefully in her warm bed, snuggling with her favorite doll. Her dream was invigorating and blissful, though now she couldn't pinpoint what it was actually about. That fateful night, her father stormed into her room, picked her up and carried her down the stairs. His forcefulness was uncharacteristic; he was always a loving father who constantly spoiled his little girl.

"Father!" she had pleaded and begged. "What are you doing? Let me go!" She had kicked and wiggled free for a moment, but he was too quick and too strong. He grabbed her ankle as she tried to crawl away, pulling her toward the basement door.

"Father! Please!" she kicked again. He let her loose, but only for a second.

"This is for your own good Alexis!" he growled, clasping his hands around her ankles again and tugging.

"Let me go! Please!" she pleaded.

"Alexis, this is for your own good!" his voice was frantic, even insane. "You'll be safe! We'll be together!"

"Stop it!" Alexis tried wiggling free again. "Please! Why are you doing this?"

"She's coming!"

"Who's coming?" Her nails scrabbled on the floor but she couldn't dig in, couldn't break free.

His father stared at her, his eyes transmitting horror. He was more terrified than she had ever seen him before.

"It's you!"

"What? What's me?"

"You're the one! I have to protect them all!"

"Father! Let me go!" she pleaded again as he opened the basement door.

Her father did not stop dragging her as they went down the stairs. Her head slammed into several step on the way down, blood trickled down her back. Though still conscious after the first couple steps, she didn't feel pain.

"Father! Please stop this!"

Passing the furnace, then the washer and dryer, they reached the far wall.

"Where are you taking me?"

Her father didn't answer; his silence was scarier than his ranting.

"Father!" The wall opened outward revealing a hidden room. "What is this?" Her panic banged in her skull, thumped at her heart. "Where did this come from?"

He pulled her in easily, tossing her to the floor like a doll before stepping out. She was too weak to fight. She laid face down on the damp floor sobbing as her father slammed the door shut without a word, leaving her alone in the dark.

"Father, please!" she begged again, crying. "Let me out!"

But there was only silence – cold, black silence.

She was jolted back to the present by a voice overhead. It was her father. She couldn't make out the words but it sounded like he was either on the phone or talking in person to someone.

If she were bolder she would scream, but she knew all too well what that would bring. She moved her hand to her lower back, rubbing her fingers over the scars. There were other welts, higher up. If she made a sound he would use the belt on her, or worse. He had used a club twice before, before she learned about the consequences of disobedience. He would break her if she broke the silence.

She wondered why he was doing this to her. What does she mean to him? What changed? Time was all she had now, time to wonder, time to try to remember the good times and how safe she used to feel when she was with him.

There was the day he took her fishing. They woke up around five in the morning, making hot chocolate and packing an enormous lunch in the big blue cooler that they loaded along with the old blue metal tackle box, poles, net and neon orange lifejackets. Everything fit neatly into the little red boat as they towed it on its trailer to Clear Lake.

She remembered the earthy smell of the fat, fresh night crawlers as she managed to bait her own hook with careful instructions from her father. She remembered his smile when she got a tug on her line. "I think I got one!" she hollered as he happily advised her on how to set the hook and reel in her catch of the day, a small-but-plump bass. Not a keeper, but that didn't matter.

Happiness was no longer part of her existence. The worst part was having no idea why. Their relationship would never be the same. That much-loved little girl in the boat was forever lost.

The muffled voice upstairs stopped. She heard footsteps moving toward the basement door. She trembled, braced herself by pressing her back harder against the far wall of her prison. The door opened and the footsteps on the basement stairs made her heart skip and body stiffen.

She squeezed her eyes shut, hoping it would all go away. The jingling of keys sent violent tremors up her spine and through her body. She instinctively tried to scoot back farther, but there was no more room to retreat. The cold, wet wall felt oddly soothing against her wounded back.

"Alexis," her father said calmly. His beard was unkempt, and there were greasy smears of dirt spattered on his gray shirt and sweat pants. His partially bald head was filthy. His potbelly protruded slightly, even though he was skinny everywhere else. "I have food."

She remained silent, still, fearing a trap to lure her closer so he could beat her again.

"Come on, Alexis," he coaxed softly. "I won't hurt you."

She moved her hands from around her knees and placed them on the nearby pillow, almost leaning toward him. Weak with fear, she couldn't sustain her momentum and again crouched into her defensive position thinking how crazy they both were.

"Alexis!" he bellowed, accelerating back to the authoritative, angry tone that had become his new normal. "Get over here right now!"

Alexis slowly stood up and tentatively made her way toward him, arms limp and head down.

"That's better," he cooed. "That's a good girl."

What am I now, a dog? She was about to ask the question aloud, but thought better of it and took the plate instead.

"I made your favorite, grilled cheese," he smiled again. "Hope you like it."

Alexis replied with a short grunt and turned away.

"Don't you turn your back on me, young lady!" His mood changed as if someone flicked a switch. "I taught you to be respectful!"

Alexis leaped to the mattress and hovered over the plate.

"Alexis," his demeanor was again soothing. "I'm not going to hurt you."

She noticeably tensed up again.

"Alexis!" He was back in rage mode. "I said-"

The doorbell rang. Stunned, her father stood up quickly, moving from the secret room faster than she thought possible for a man his age.

"Shut up, and don't say a word," he hissed through the closed door. The lock clicked; she could hear him swiftly stomping up the stairs.

Alexis ran to her prison door. Dumping the water from the drinking glass he'd handed her she put it against the door and held it against her ear. She couldn't hear distinct words with the old-school spy method, but could distinctly make out a second voice. The wooden door was a decent conductor. She moved the glass more toward the middle of it seeking the ideal spot. There!

"Kevin, I know she's here." Alexis recognized the stern voice. It was Uncle Brad. "Where is Alexis?"

"Brad — she's really sick," her father was trying to sound caring and concerned. "I've called the school all week to let them know, keep them posted."

Alexis smiled. The relief was intense. As long as she could remember, her uncle had been a kind man who always loved and cared for her, but then again, so had her father.

"Well at least let me go look in on her," Uncle Brad insisted. Footsteps moved upstairs toward her bedroom.

"No," her father's voice sounded nervous now. "She's trying to rest. And she's contagious."

"I'll be fine, Kevin." She blessed her insistent uncle as he moved closer to her bedroom. How she wished she was there, resting! Then the footsteps stopped.

"What are you doing? Let me see her."

Alexis heard a small scuffle before the door to the bedroom banged open hard enough to hit the wall. "Alexis? Where are you? Where is she, Kevin?"

"I'm down here!" Alexis screamed. "Uncle Brad! Help!"

"What the hell?" Uncle Brad had heard her. He was coming. Two sets of footsteps barreled downstairs, echoed more loudly as the men approached the basement door.

They were fighting, full out. Alexis heard the sound of fists clubbing and bodies bouncing into walls. Finally, someone hit the floor.

"Kevin! What the hell are you doing?" Uncle Brad was panting, shocked and exhausted.

"I'm saving everyone!" her father yelled. "She's evil! Just like her mother!"

After the loudest thud of all, the basement door opened. Alexis scuttled to the far corner unsure who was coming for her: demented father or savior uncle.

"Alexis, it's me."

"I'm in here, Uncle Brad!" She ran toward the door, wincing and laughing as she banged on it with her bruised arm. "I'm here, I'm here!"

"I can't see how to get in. Where's the door?"

"It's hidden." Alexis couldn't stop crying. "It's there, right where you're standing."

"Yep, there's a door. But you'll need these." The keys jingled as her father dangled them, teasing.

"You locked her down here? Why would you do that? What is wrong with you?" Brad couldn't hide his outrage and alarm. "This is your daughter, Kevin!"

"She's evil Brad! Just like -"

"Kevin. You're not rational. This is your little girl." Her uncle spoke in a calm-down tone that she knew would only set her father off.

"She's evil!" Kevin was frantic, wild-eyed, and insistent. "Just like her mother! I saw the signs!"

The rant used up the last of Brad's patience. He spoke in clear, slow, harsh words designed to snap Kevin back to sanity. "Kevin. Listen. You're talking like a crazy man. Her mother isn't evil. She left you. I'm sorry, Kevin. She left you and it's really sad, but this is not right. Now give me those keys!"

"Why aren't you listening to me, Brad?" Kevin moved closer to him. "Did you see what she did to me?"

"My God, that was years ago." Brad shook his head. "That life is over now. You need to move on."

"You're wrong! It'll come back to haunt us Brad! You'll see! She's just as evil as her mother!"

"Give me the keys now," Brad demanded.

"No. Try and st-"

Alexis was startled by a bright flash of blue light that briefly beamed through the cracks of the wall.

In the silence that followed she heard the sound of her father's key chain, a sound that rattled her heart, ramming her entire being back into a dark place of fear. She cringed as the key turned in the lock, not daring then daring to hope.

"Uncle?"

"It's me, sweetie. It's Uncle Brad." He stepped from the shadows, arms wide, inviting her in. "You're safe now."

"Oh my God!" Alexis threw herself into Uncle Brad's secure, enfolding hug, weeping. "I thought I was going to be down here forever. I thought I was going to die in there."

"It's okay." He held her tight. "I'm here now."

Her father was face-down on the cement floor.

"What happened?"

"I just knocked him out," her uncle reassured, as he patted her back as rhythmically and soothingly as a father burping his baby. "No lasting damage. He'll be fine 'til the police show up."

The hours after her rescue were a blur of flashing red-and-blue emergency lights from the police cars and emergency vehicles surrounding the house, their beacons shining into every window. The vague, murmuring dark humps of concerned and curious neighbors just beyond the yellow police tape made her wonder, briefly, what stories they were telling themselves. She didn't really care because they couldn't come up with anything worse than what really happened.

"She's evil!" Alexis saw her still-spewing father being escorted by three officers to a patrol car. "You'll see! I'm trying to protect everyone! Kill her! Kill her now before-" the closing door turned his rant into soundless babbling. Alexis watched, bewildered, as her father bounced around the back seat in a series of wild contortions despite the handcuffs, banging his head against the side window-glass and security cage separating him from the front seat.

"Uncle Brad," she asked, eyes still trained on the police car, and neither of them able to stop watching the insane performance, "What's my father talking about? Why did he do this to me? What is he saying about my mother? I thought she died when I was born."

"Your father's been sick for many years," her uncle told her. "Your mother isn't dead. Sweetie, she left you when you were a baby." He gave her another hug.

"Why didn't anyone tell me?"

"He didn't want you to know. None of us wanted you to be hurt by it. You see how it's hurt him. He didn't want that for you." He squeezed her a little more. "I am so sorry, Alexis. I never thought he would resort to this."

14

Alexis had no words. How many levels of shock can there be, she wondered.

"Alexis." Uncle Brad gently clasped her shoulders, looked directly into her eyes. "For now all you need to know is that you're safe and you're going to stay that way. Let's find you a spot to rest away from these lights. They'll be coming in again soon to examine the crime scene. You're going into shock. I've got a sleeping bag in the Explorer that we can wrap around you."

Uncle Brad led her to the large black Explorer parked just off the driveway leading into the garage. He opened the seat flat, shaking out a navy-blue bag lined with soft red-plaid flannel.

"Here, sweetie. There's a pillow, too. Just go ahead and snuggle in. Everything will be all right now. You're with me."

"But I don't know if I can sleep," she protested.

"Just settle in, Alexis. It's fine. It's really all right. You're safe. You're with me. I'm not going anywhere."

Alexis obediently closed her eyes, but relaxing, let alone going to sleep, was easier said than done. The questions rushed through her mind in a continuous stream. What would drive her father to lock her in their basement and beat her time and time again? Who was her mother? Why would she leave them? What was the evil her father both hated and feared? She needed the answers. She would find them when the time was right.

Chapter I
Becky

The setting sun gleamed over the pine forest as a young girl sat on the warped wooden steps of her old ramshackle trailer. Even with closed eyes it would be clear that no one bothered with lawn care in this neighborhood. The strong scent of dead wet leaves and fermented rotten apples smelled like neglect. Only half of the trailers in the twenty space park were occupied. Although the girl's trailer suffered from torn siding and a leaky roof it was superior in comparison to the rest.

Becky wasn't just attractive; she was a strikingly beautiful girl with black hair so dark that it glimmered with natural navy-indigo highlights in direct sunlight. Her startling sky-blue eyes mesmerized boys who dared look into them. She wore tight-fitting blue jeans with artfully slashed vents in the thighs and a brand-new black long-sleeved shirt with sequins that sparkled like her eyes. The snug top revealed a figure too mature for her age. Not one to shy away from make-up, her bold, crimson-traced, lush lips popped wetly into ripe contours. Her eyelashes, winged and shaded with many coats of mascara and artfully applied liner were designed to flutter and flirt with skill. A temptress at heart, Becky enjoyed the effect she had on the boys at school and didn't feel the need to hide her beauty, making her all the more mysterious and desirable.

Becky counted on precious moments alone, eager for coveted alone time while her dad was away. When he was home, life was uneasy, unproductive, unhappy, and only slightly unpredictable: he was either drunk and short-tempered or drunk and passed out.

Becky took a drag from her cigarette and sipped on a can of warm beer as she thought about what her night entailed. She was going to her brother John's football game, of course. She never missed a game. After that, her night was open. She would most likely hit a party with a of couple friends — as long as she didn't get too wasted before the night started.

Becky thought about the recent changes in her big brother, who was a little over two years older in age, but only one grade ahead of her. She had always looked up to him; attitudes expressed loud and clear in her rebellious antics.

But John had changed. Since school started in the new year, he'd been living that self-improvement cliché 'turning his life around'.

If only her dad would do the same.

John started working for good grades and earning them. He joined the football team. As his attitude changed, he both attracted and found new friends. His old friends, of course, were angry and disgusted. Now Becky hung out with most of them, although it bothered her when they made fun of him behind his back, calling him *traitor*, *preppie*, or *jock*. Mostly she ignored it but every now and then the trash-talking got to be too much and she was drawn into standing up for John. Knocking back-stabbers down to size with a cutting comment, a scolding or a rare and thus unexpected punch was usually her style.

She loved John. She really would do anything for him. The shift was weird; it felt lonely, missing the tough guy that influenced her own cocky, outrageous persona. She wasn't ready to follow in his most recent footsteps now or ever. She'd never admit it publicly, but she was proud of him, all the same.

Becky poured the last of the foamed beer onto the gravel driveway. Standing, she teetered, but quickly regained her balance. Normally she didn't drink alone. But her dad had been gone for five days and yesterday the power company had shut off the electricity. She figured his beer wasn't going to get any colder.

Dad's job at the mill, the town's main way to make a living, tied him up all day. Released from hard labor, he immediately headed downtown to the local pubs. If he ran out of money or was close to passing out he'd often sleep in his old battered truck. Still, there were too many nights to count when John would ride his bike to whatever watering hole his dad was getting wasted at, just to drive his drunken butt home. The bartenders knew who to call. But there hadn't been any late-night calls in more than two weeks – unlike the electricity, their phone bill wasn't past due.

Becky had a feeling that it wasn't just her brother's behavior that had changed. For as long as she could remember, dad's behavior ran in predictable seasonal cycles. For a few weeks he'd stick to going out with friends for a few drinks after work. The friends, he went through a lot of them, would either tire of the routine or tire of him. He'd turn to partying alone, drinking himself into oblivion in one pub or another, trying to buy new friends with cocktails. Until he'd run a bar tab so high he would be kicked out and not allowed back in until the debt was paid. Then there would be weeks where he lounged in the tatty brown fake-leather living-room recliner watching re-runs of old TV Westerns or worse, sporting events that he barely pretended to be interested in. It was all about betting on any game available with the local bookie.

After this phase of his binge drinking, her father would sober up, go back to work and begin the daunting task of slowly paying off his delinquent bills. In a matter of weeks the cycle began again.

This time, however, the cycle was off. He just kept drinking downtown, showing no desire to lick his wounds at home, gather his strength and begin again the process of getting his life together before his next binge.

John had helped with his bills the previous summer before he lost his job at the Pizza Shop. Football and schoolwork didn't leave time for a job. He didn't have any time for Becky, either. She told herself she really didn't mind; she enjoyed her time alone. She also liked to watch him play football even if she didn't like the game itself.

Becky handled her concerns using the traditional family method. She went inside and grabbed a quick shot of dad's bottom-shelf whiskey then pulled the last warm beer out of the silent fridge. She flopped back down on the steps and took a swig of the bargain-brand brew.

A crisp breeze ruffled her shiny black hair, flattened the lighter flame as she stoked another cigarette, drawing smoke deep into her lungs and coughing slightly. It felt more like summer than fall. She wished she could relive the past summer, between seventh and eighth grade. It had been the best summer yet. The beginning was boring, but her best friend Jessica had introduced her to *high-school-boys* and *high-school-parties*. She'd never understood the fascination for finding a remote field, beach or forest, fueling a large bonfire with wood and tires, drinking, fighting and generally being obnoxious. Her low opinion of these activities changed when she got drunk for the first time.

That was the legendary night that she went skinny dipping in Clear Lake, emerging on the beach next to a teacher's house. She, of course, didn't remember, but everyone at the party did. Her nickname for the rest of the summer was *Little Guppy*. Rather than being embarrassed, she enjoyed the attention and she was too thick-skinned to let a little teasing bother her.

Becky was surprised her brother never mentioned her summer escapades. If he knew, he never let her know it. She avoided trouble even when the police busted the parties and scattered the panicked teens. Her first raid was hilarious; she found it highly amusing to watch all of her peers scurry into the woods. They looked like a flock of gazelles running from a pride of lions, only not as fast or as gracefully. To her it was uncool to run away. She sat next to the beer keg, nonchalantly sipping her drink. No one ever got in trouble anyway; the police just ordered them to go home. She figured it was their way of avoiding late-night paperwork hassles, and a good way of getting free beer for themselves.

The best summer so far also had some love drama. Becky fell hard for the first time with, of all things, a senior. She knew that if her brother found out she was involved with an older guy he would beat him up, so she was trying to keep the relationship as secretive as possible in certain circles where John might pick up on it.

Carl was a partier, too. Becky thought it quite the achievement that Carl was an upperclassman. All of her other friends were dating freshman or sophomores. She would brag about it every now and again; nothing good or special ever happened to her, so she felt entitled.

She met Carl after the first few parties. Becky, Jessica and a few other girlfriends had decided to compete with each other to find out who could kiss the most guys by the end of summer. Becky was on ten going for eleven when she met Carl at yet another outdoor kegger. She was trying to get a beer but the hand-tap wouldn't work. Carl helped her out. At the time, she believed it was love at first sight. He was so handsome with his long curly light-brown hair; she had a weakness for curly hair, and romantic blue eyes. But by the end of summer Becky saw that it wasn't love at first sight. It was drunken lust at first sip.

The relationship started out as perfectly as a teen love movie. They took long drives in Carl's yellow Mustang through the hilly and mountainous countryside, passing large lakes hidden in thick forests. They ran in the waves at Clear Lake and lay, warmed by the sun, on an old blanket spread on the sand. They even hung out at his house with his parents. She lied about her age; she didn't think they would take too kindly to their almost seventeen year old son dating a thirteen year old eighth-grader, even if she was turning fourteen soon. Make-up, hair, and clothes, along with her womanly figure, helped her look older. Her friends all agreed she could pass for at least seventeen.

Her first love ended on Mid-Summer Blast, a party that coincided with her fourteenth birthday. Becky discovered Carl and her best friend Jessica making out in the Mustang. *Little Guppy* no more, Becky pulled Jessica out by the hair, punching her repeatedly. The partying kids enjoyed the show, many chanting "chick fight, chick fight" as Becky bloodied an unresisting Jessica. The boys cheered themselves silly; the girls tried to jump in, siding almost evenly between Becky's and Jessica's. Eventually some of the boys decided to pull Becky off before she did more damage. Becky, still unmarked and furious, turned on Carl. Like her brother and father, her short-fused temper and fast reflexes made her a feisty scrapper.

Not surprisingly, Jessica and Becky were no longer friends after the incident. Becky debated continuing the kissing competition and decided she didn't want to go back to school with a reputation of being the summer skank, or something worse. She didn't really care what others thought about her, but to keep her "don't mess with me" reputation, she'd have to beat up everyone who'd call her a bad name. By the end of the school year, she wouldn't have any friends because everyone would be too afraid of her.

Becky was heartbroken for the first week or so. The bloody lips and black eyes on her ex-best friend and ex-boyfriend may have made her feel better for a moment, but it didn't alleviate the sadness or stop the tears from flowing. John noticed her crying a few times at night. He would ask who the guy was that hurt her and threaten to beat him up. Becky would smile, knowing that was how John showed his love; protecting his little sister. She would always tell him to forget it and that she'd already taken care of it. John usually laughed lovingly and they'd each have a beer. She really enjoyed those bonding moments with John and kind of missed them too. It was always her and John taking care of each other.

Coincidently, she had heard that Carl and John had been butting heads ever since John was bumped to the varsity football team. She wondered if the summer fiascos had anything to do with it.

Becky moved on, in her own way, but never found another serious boyfriend. Not because she couldn't, but because she wanted to be independent and not need someone by her side to be happy. There were many boys who flirted with her since the breakup. She loved the attention and flirted back just like any normal girl would, but she refused to date anyone who was immature. Her standards were very high, which made her realize that since she was in eighth grade; she'd be single until college. Becky's ideal guy was someone who was cute, but not all into himself, had a quirky sense of humor, and not a cheating lowlife like Carl. Until the day came where that guy walked into her life, she'd keep to herself and do what she enjoyed doing.

Since the breakup and her new outlook on boys, Becky found a new thrill; shoplifting. Becky found herself stealing from stores more and more. She had done it a few times in the past year, but never made a habit of it. Over the past few months, she had gotten pretty good too. She'd steal anything shoes, clothes, cigarettes, liquor, and food. Shoes, clothes, and food were a necessity because her father never bought new clothes or kept the trailer stocked with anything to eat. The cigarettes and booze she took were for her and her friends. John hinted that he knew what she was up to. He'd joke around, saying "nice new shirt" or "it's my birthday soon; you want to *buy* me some new clothes?" He would never rat her out, especially when he knew they were going through some troubled times.

Becky was not a bad girl. After all, she did very well in school. She had the best grades in her class and she had a very high IQ. She hid that fact because she was sure her classmates would treat her differently and probably even cheat off her if they knew. Her teachers loved her as a student, but Becky didn't want them to discover her other side, her rebellious side. If the teachers knew about her partying, stealing and other mischief, they might not respect her for her intelligence. It was quite an accomplishment to keep her secrets from everyone. Becky knew all too well the fallout of stereotyping. Her brother was a great example.

John was once a good kid, but then got caught doing some things that were unacceptable. Becky knew that if you did something wrong and people heard about it, that was what they would remember about you, forever. Even if you did a million good things, that one bad thing would brand you for life. Even with this in mind, she could not stop her unruly ways. She was just having too much fun.

Becky took another drag of her cigarette and a big swig of beer, grimacing at the taste of the bitter, unrefreshing liquid. A police car cruised slowly up the drive. Its flashers were off but she still felt an impending threat. They were looking for her. She knew it. She tossed the half-empty beer can under the trailer and stamped out her cigarette as an officer pulled up and parked. He walked toward her with a purposeful stride.

Becky tensed. He could be here for her, her brother or her father. A few days ago she and a couple of friends had stolen what they could from a block of unlocked cars at the mall, netting a carton of cigarettes and more than one hundred dollars.

"Hello there," the officer said in a deep, scratchy, authoritative voice.

"Hi," Becky replied, her attempt to be cocky minimized by her inability to make eye contact. "Can I help you?"

"I hope so," the officer stepped closer. "I'm Sergeant Greg. I'm an old friend of your dad's. Jim's your father, right?"

Becky nodded.

"Would you happen to know where he is?"

Becky couldn't help herself. Cops got her snippy up. "Well if you were such a good friend, wouldn't you know where he is?"

"I never said I was a good friend. I'm an old friend. We used to work together a long time ago."

Becky could tell she was ticking him off. It was a dangerous time to be a smart mouth, considering the beer on her breath and the lingering stench of cigarettes.

"Umm, I haven't seen him for a while," she said, making an excuse for her rudeness. "Sorry for being short with you. Not knowing where my dad is worries me." *Good one Becky*, she thought to herself. "Did you try all the pubs? Bar-hopping seems to be his only hobby."

"I just came from them before I came here."

"Ha," Becky snorted. "You do know him well then."

"Well, if you see him," Greg handed her a card, "Could you have him call me right away?"

"Sure," Becky's unease, that feeling she'd had all afternoon that there was more wrong than usual, intensified. "Is everything all right?"

"I hope so, there was a hit-and-run the other night," Sergeant Greg's expression turned even more serious, watching her for a reaction. "Your dad's truck may have been spotted."

"Oh no," she said, wide-eyed. "Is anyone hurt?"

"Not too bad," Greg sighed. "Luckily it's just a broken leg. The victim will heal, but of course he wants to press charges."

Becky buttoned her lip. Her dad probably did it. Usually when he screwed up bad or was hiding from whoever he owed, he'd retreat for a few days, drinking his problems away at a secluded hunting camp. If this was like the other times, he'd come back pretending nothing had happened. She and John always knew better.

"I want to get to him before anyone else," Greg broke the silence. "The sheriff wants to put him in jail. She has it out for your father."

"Doesn't everybody?" Becky mumbled to herself.

"Well, I'd better go. Aren't you going to your brother's game tonight? I heard he's doing real well this year. I never knew he played football. You know, he's the talk of the town, right?"

Becky gave him a big smile. She was so proud of her brother. "Yeah, I'm going, I just need to get ready."

"Better hurry. It's already started."

"Are you sure?" Becky glanced at the clock inside the window, but realized – again – that it wasn't working. "Crap! I didn't realize what time it was."

"If you leave now, you'll be there for the second half." Sergeant Greg nodded goodbye as he walked back to his car.

Becky lifted her foot to check the condition of her cigarette, demolished, to her dismay. Cursing out loud again she rooted through the crumpled-foil lined pack. Empty. She bit her lip, debating. She could go to the store and steal a pack, but the easiest store to steal from was on the other side of town. It was too late to ride John's bike there and still make it in time to watch the end of the game.

Then she remembered. She rushed into the trailer headed for John's room. It hadn't changed that much since the beginning of the school year; clothes were still scattered over the floor. The only obvious improvement was the unknown rock band posters covering the holes he'd previously punched in the walls.

Becky started digging, rummaging through his dresser drawers, closet, under the bed. No cigarettes, darn it! He'd quit a little over a month ago. How could she have forgotten? He'd been the crabbiest person alive for at least two weeks. Disappointed that he hadn't overlooked at least a stray butt with a couple of puffs left in it, she sulkily walked right over the piles of clothes before brightening again as she moved to the hall closet. There it was. John's old black leather jacket. She dug through two pockets with no luck. But in the inside vest pocket her searching fingers clasped around a cool metal circlet. She pulled it out, closely examining the plain, gray metal bracelet. She was about to put it on when she noticed a rectangle, like a cigarette-pack box, in the other interior pocket. She smiled victoriously.

"Thank God," she said aloud, easing the jacket off its hanger and extracting the miraculously unopened cigarette pack. She went deeper into the pocket for his Zippo lighter. Becky tossed the bracelet aside and slid into the jacket. She surveyed herself in the smudgy full-length mirror on the back of the closet door. Other than the too-long arms, the jacket fit. "Not bad," she said, examining her bad-girl look from all angles.

Outside the cracked living room window she could see the sun had almost set, long evening shadows overtaking the bright afternoon. The lights would have kicked on over the football field. She needed to hurry to catch the second half.

She checked her make-up, applied more lipstick, sleeked a dime-sized dollop of argan oil over the shiny curtains of hair framing her face. She blew a mocking kiss to her image. "Here we go, girl."

Standing on the threshold, considering whether to lock the door or not in case dad came home, she took in the battered trailer and another mood passed through her like skidding, shredding, fast-moving clouds on a windy day. Tears welled. She was ashamed of where she lived. What a dump. What a life. It wasn't the first time she'd thought about running far, far away from her drunken father's cruddy trailer. She would find somewhere she and John could have a better life. Her brother was doing it, but she couldn't start fresh here.

Before those useless, cry-baby emotions could really kick in and ruin her make-up, she took a long swallow of the cheapest and easiest medicine she knew, her father's half-empty whiskey bottle. She had found it lying neglected next to the peeling-laminate end-table which was next to ugly stained pea-green couch. She wrinkled her nose and shuddered, both hating and savoring the hot, harsh burning liquid as it moved down her throat all the way into her belly. Even with an alcohol buzz she skillfully rode John's bicycle, pedaling as fast as she could with a cigarette in her hand.

"Homecoming victory, here we come," she declared. "Go John!"

Chapter II
Homecoming

Sally's mom pulled the brown station wagon into the gravel parking lot next to the football field. "Is this fine, dear?" Her mother smiled but didn't take her eyes off the fan-crowded throughway as she inched a few feet closer to the main ticket gate.

"This is perfect." Sally smiled back and opened the door. "Thanks for the ride, Mom."

"No problem. Are you late?"

"No, I think I'm just in time to kiss him good luck before he runs out on the field."

"Aww," her mother chuckled, crinkling her eyes. "That's so cute. I really like Ryan. He's a nice boy."

"I know Mom," Sally laughed and stepped out. The breeze had picked up slightly, gently fanning the delicate layers of the skirt on her bluish-green dress. "Remember he's mine, though." she joked.

Around her streamed throngs of fans in a festive, rowdy mood as they moved toward the entrance. It was the biggest game of the season. Sally was already nervous for Ryan. Ever since Ryan and John were brought up from the freshman team to play varsity, the

29

pressure for them to do their very best was intensified. The community closely followed their Willington Panthers hometown football team. They knew everything about the players, especially the star quarterback and wide receiver.

The bump to varsity wouldn't have happened if Ryan's brother Ben and Todd the wide receiver hadn't been hurt earlier in the season in freak accidents on the same play. The tackles took both of them out for the year. Todd needed knee surgery and Ben broke his wrist in the brutal pile-up.

Neither John nor Ryan wanted to move up to the high school big leagues. They were having a great JV season, enjoying the camaraderie of players their own age. Their advanced skills put them at the head of the pack. The varsity coaches hounded them for days until they agreed.

Sally rarely got to spend time with Ryan after that. She'd gone to practices, thinking if she couldn't talk to him at least she could watch him and he could feel her support, but after a few days Ryan asked her not to come, saying it was a distraction. Sally knew he was too nice to tell the truth; she was sure it was because the older players teased him about his girlfriend being at his practices. Even though he was younger, he was supposed to be the team leader. He needed to establish authority and respect to boost morale and get the Willington Panthers back on a winning path. The injuries had kicked off a string of defeats.

Sally was proud of her boyfriend. It was thrilling to see him finally being recognized for his achievements and talents. The down side, besides having less time with him, was the extra female attention he was getting. Except for practices and games it seemed like the girls didn't leave Ryan, or John, alone for even a moment. It was super annoying. She wasn't jealous of Ryan's popularity. Through her own personal development she'd acquired a happy, supportive circle of fun friends and her own popularity too, well before Ryan became the biggest man in school. But the girls panting after Ryan like hyper, overexcited puppies brought back all the insecurities stemming from her schlumpy-klutzy Sally past. She just couldn't shake the irritation and the fear of losing him, even though she knew she'd found her spirit-mate and he felt the same.

The jealous, angry, frightened feelings kicked into overdrive whenever Ryan walked the halls in school. The girls swarmed him, hugging him, even kissing his check despite school rules that banned public displays of affection. He didn't invite it; in fact it felt like an ambush to him every time it happened. It almost always caused an argument. Ryan would brush it off, saying they were just silly girls looking for attention. She would remind herself that the two of them were meant to be together and nothing could change that. Sometimes it worked. Other times the emotions were so upsetting that she went as far as wishing they were back in Enchantas, where there weren't any annoying girls around. She had wanted desperately to come home, but now she sometimes wished they'd both stayed with Mel.

Life had evolved for Sally since her time in Enchantas. Apart from coping, or not, with flirtatious girls hitting on her boyfriend, it had mostly changed for the better. Even life at home actually felt normal. The magic spell her parents cast upon their return made everyone in town forget the circumstances surrounding their supposed death. The wide-reaching spell was so powerful it had started to rub off on Sally even though she knew the truth.

There were nights when Sally dreamed of doing things with her parents during the time of their disappearance. Normal stuff, like going on picnics, grocery shopping or once, hunting for colored eggs and spotting a giant rabbit in the yard that they told her was the Easter Bunny. She knew the dreams weren't real, but they felt like memories. It was confusing. The times when strangers would approach her in public and casually talk about her mom and dad as if they'd never disappeared also weirded her out.

Especially her uncanny ability to join in the discussion of situations or events that she rationally knew had never occurred. The magic was astounding in its strength. And really, what harm did the pretending do?

Sally's mother leaned over, as always tender and protective of the daughter she'd done without for so many years. "Are you going to be too cold wearing that dress? I have a sweater for you."

"Eww. Mom." *A ratty, raggedy, homemade brown sweater. She couldn't be serious.* "That ugly thing?"

"Think about what you're saying, Sally," her mother replied. "Your grandmother made this for you."

"I know." Sally turned away, flushing slightly at her unkind remark. She was very grateful for her grandmother and of course loved her. But her former wardrobe choices had been one of the reasons she'd never had friends. It was a shallow way to look at things but it did affect her status. She didn't want to be seen in public as the star quarterback's girlfriend wearing something that could damage their reputation.

"Will you need a ride home after the game?" her mother asked.

"No thanks, Mom. Ryan has his brother's car."

"Does he have his license?" Mom looked worried.

"Well, not yet, but he does have his permit," Sally said, truthfully, as always.

"I don't feel safe with you riding with someone who doesn't have a license."

"Oh, mom," Sally used her most persuasive tone, her most pleading expression. "Please stop being a worrywart. I'll be fine. He's had lots of practice hours. He won't drink, I promise, and we aren't driving that far."

"I'm sorry my dear," the sadness of those missed years were in her mother's tear-glistened eyes. "I just don't want to lose you again."

"You won't, Mom," Sally shut the door, resting her elbows on the frame and leaning in through the open window. "If Ryan has the strength and smarts and courage to fight in a battle for Enchantas, he's totally capable of safely driving me home."

Sally's mother didn't respond. She shut down whenever Sally brought up anything about Enchantas. As if silence could erase the guilt for not being in Sally's life during her crucial years growing up. The regret was at times unbearable for both her and her husband. They were the only townspeople for whom their spell didn't work. Erasing one's own memories was impossible, even in the awe-inspiring realm of Enchantian magic. They were doomed to remember that wicked, wounded past.

"I'm sorry for bringing it up, mom."

"It's all right, dear. It's not your fault. Our curse is memory, memory of how horrible we'd become. Desperation can lead many to dark paths."

Now it was Sally's turn to wish for a subject change. "Um, yeah." She withdrew from the window. "I'll be home sometime after the game. If we win we'll be going to a party at Carl's."

"Sally, I've heard what can go on at those parties. I don't think you should go."

"Mom, you really do worry too much. Ryan's expected to go. It's for the team. I won't do anything stupid and neither will Ryan. I promise."

"Sorry for the paranoia. I just want you to stay safe. Promise me you'll leave if it gets wild or there's drinking or anything. I don't want to give you a hard time. I love you."

"I love you too, mom. I promise. I'll be fine."

Sally's mom clearly still had doubts, but she eventually put the car in gear. Sally merged into the crowd and headed for the clubhouse locker room. She could hear Coach Klein barking out a rousing pre-game pep talk.

Good, I didn't miss him, she thought. She'd managed to give Ryan a good luck kiss before every game he'd started and she wasn't about to miss the ritual on Homecoming night.

Sally walked down to the player's entrance of the field where the cheerleaders held aloft the flamboyantly decorated blue and white break-away Willington Panther banner. The banner was a team ritual that dated back to before her parents' time. Before every game the players barreled straight for it, ripping it open triumphantly. It was said that if a game starts without the time-honored tradition, the Panthers would lose for sure. Sally puts more faith in her lucky-kiss ritual and thought Ryan probably did too. His first run through the banner was embarrassing. He and John led the team, but since they'd never had any practice and were understandably nervous and excited, they misjudged their footing. They never figured out whether Ryan tripped John or vice versa, but it was an embarrassment they both wanted to forget. The laughter and jeers of the crowd was forgotten by game's end, though. Respect was earned in full after Ryan threw six touchdowns and John caught four of them. Numbers Twenty-Two and Eleven became instant stars, admired and applauded on and off the field.

Sally didn't really pay much attention to rules of the game. She would just kiss Ryan's cheek or nod approvingly as he explained plays or strategy, understanding his need for competitiveness but supremely uninterested in the sport. Sally's interests lie more along the lines of hiking, reading, and watching movies with Ryan.

The door of the locker-room clubhouse opened and thirty players sporting Brandeis blue and white jerseys trotted toward the banner. Sally searched intently for twenty-two, the mob around her blocking the view. She jumped up and down several times trying to see over the crowd before she spotted him.

"Ryan!" Sally yelled, but the crowd was too loud. She squeezed, elbowed and prodded her way through the packed-in revelers as fast as she could, but was too late. By the time she was in range of her spirit-mate, two bleached blondes had closed in on Ryan and John, squealing like adoring, hysterical groupies at a boy band concert: "Ryan! John! Ryan! John!"

Sally's chin dropped. Her shoulders slumped. She scowled as she watched the cooing duo hug and kiss and hang all over the guys. "Good luck! We love you!" the girls screamed as the lined-up team proceeded along the chanting tunnel formation of pom-pom waving cheerleaders, bursting through the banner onto the field.

Sally swore. She wasn't normally one to cuss, but she'd learned a few choice words thanks to John, and frustration brought out the potty mouth in her.

Normally she'd be mortified by the adults showering her with disapproving looks and the little kids staring at her curiously after her outburst. She was too blood-boilingly angry to care what anybody thought was unpleasant. Unfamiliar feelings of aggression and rage whipped through her mind and body. She would never act on her rage. The negative, repressed emotions could only damage their trembling host. Her eyes watered, her dress blotched by an escaped tear as she put her head down and blindly let the crowd push her toward the bleachers.

How could they do that to her? Sally thought to herself. What witches! This was *her* time to wish *her* boyfriend good luck, not time for snotty little prissy girls to push their way in where they weren't wanted.

When she gave way to the runaway train of hateful thoughts, her emotions betrayed her and she was on the brink of being uncontrollable. She had heard that expression "can't think straight," but never knew you could actually feel that way. Depression and loneliness made themselves at home with her rage;

she lost track of where she was and what she was doing. The team was already on the field and she'd somehow found a seat in the back row of the bleachers. Ordering herself to focus, she looked away from the field to orient herself. She swore again, under her breath. Somehow she'd managed to sit right behind the two blonde girls who had just kissed her boyfriend.

"Oh my god Jessica!" one of them squealed. "I cannot believe we actually kissed John and Ryan!"

"I know, right?" Jessica was even giddier. "They are so hot! This is our night, Amber!"

"I've got a plan," Amber said. "At Carl's party let's invite them into the basement." She giggled and tossed her hair.

"Girl, you read my mind!" Jessica smiled, lowering her voice seductively. "You know what happens in Carl's basement."

"Shush!" Amber's surveyed the bleachers to see who was around them. She was still whispering loud enough for Sally to hear the overworked, inappropriate cliché. "What happens in Carl's basement..."

"Stays in Carl's basement!" they finished in unison, whinnying like ponies as they brought their red beverage cups together in a celebratory toast. "I can't wait!" Jessica said.

Sally had completely tuned out the game as she eavesdropped on the self-proclaimed seductresses. Teeth clenched, hands fisted, she pierced them with imaginary eye darts. *If only I had magic*, she thought, her anger revving back into high gear, those manipulative, conniving wenches would have nothing to smile about. Her plan to go to Carl's with Ryan was ruined. She couldn't stand to watch any more of Amber or Jessica's disgusting, disrespectful behavior. But how could she let him go alone?

***

The roar of Panther fans hungry for Homecoming victory echoed and hummed on the field below. The game had been a pushing-and-shoving match on both sides. Neither team was able to gain more than a seven-point lead over the course of the game. With ten seconds left the Panthers were losing to the Bloomsfield Bears twenty-one to sixteen.

Ryan led his exhausted teammates to another huddle.

"All right guys," he huffed, drawing in deep lungfuls of oxygen. "We have time for one more play and we *need* a touchdown to win."

"It's impossible, kid," a large line-backer gasped, hunched over, hands on his knees. He turned his head from the huddle and spit. "Their line is solid. No openings."

"I know, Tank," Ryan smiled. "But I've got an idea."

"Well, I hope you're calling in a miracle," another player said, panting. His face was dripping with blood.

"Oh yeah. That's what it is. A miracle. And now we're gonna pray." Ryan dropped to one knee, looking up to make contact with every pair of eyes he could reach. "So, Coach wants us to run it through the middle, but I know it won't work on that brick wall."

"I hear ya!" Tank hollered, sounding interested in spite of his deeply pessimistic attitude.

"Ryan, I don't feel comfortable going against the coach's orders," another player stuttered.

"You don't feel comfortable?" Ryan mimicked. "Where are we, in gym class? Come on man, what's Coach gonna do? Bench us?" He smirked. "This is our last game, our last play, *our* Homecoming. Let's win it for us!"

"You heard him," John chimed in. "Sometimes the rules don't get you where you need to be. Let's take this to the end zone!"

His battle cry was pierced by the referee's whistle. A yellow flag hit the ground.

"Crap. Delay of game," John mustered the strength to maintain momentum, pulling from deep inside to portray calm even as he heard a furious coach throwing a tantrum on the

37

sidelines. The outburst was more colorful than the half-time show. The ruckus featured wildly inventive cussing as well as a thrown clipboard that unfortunately hit an injured player smack in the forehead.

"Okay. Let's do this." Ryan snapped back to the job at hand. "We're setting up in 'I' formation. After I say down, I will move into shotgun. Smiddy and Shooter will move to each side of me. I will hand it off to Smiddy. Smiddy, you run left and reverse it to Blake. Blake I want you to run back to the right and line; I want you guys to screen him until he gets about ten yards. Blake, then I want you to lateral it back to me and then," he stares into John's tired but determined eyes. "I want you to run fast and as hard as you can and I'll Hail-Mary it to you."

"Why does the scrub get the touchdown?" Carl whined.

"Drop it, Carl," Ryan sighed. "In fact, that's what you're best at. Now who's ready to win this game?"

"Thanks Ryan," John whispered. "I've been waiting all season for you to say that."

"Thank me if this works." Ryan stiffened and put his arm out, "All right. Let's do this. Ready…"

"GO PANTHERS," the huddle clapped hard before breaking into position.

Sweat and blood dripped from their limbs. Their breath steamed in the cold night, bodies burning with exertion even as the temperature on the field dropped.

Ryan looked right, then left. Slowly squatting, he set the magic in motion:

"DOWN!"

The players were swift, certain in their positioning as Ryan took a few steps back into a shotgun position.

"SET…" Ryan glanced around. He saw Coach Klein and the secondary coaches freaking out. The offensive coach was pulling what little hair he had left. A grin bloomed and widened behind his facemask. The Panthers were at that very moment putting the F-U-N back in football. He yelled so hard he could feel the pressure behind his eyes.

"HIKE!"

The moment the ball left the line everything moved into fast forward. Bodies banged and tripped as Ryan handed off the ball to Smiddy. Ryan headed to the right of the line to wait for the lateral from Blake.

The once-thunderous crowd became silent, anxious, waiting.

Blake grabbed the ball from Smiddy.

The Bears' sideline began yelling "REVERSE! REVERSE!" trying to get their teammates' attention.

The Bears altered positions and clumsily slipped on the field as they responded to the unexpected play. Blake broke a quick tackle and got behind the screen of Panther linemen. He made a quick shuffle to his right until he met a line of Bears ready to annihilate him. He passed the ball backward to Ryan. It was almost too high to catch, but Ryan managed to grab it.

He looked for John down the field. He was wide open.

"PASS! PASS! PASS!" the Bear's sideline chanted, trying to warn their teammates of the trick play, but it was too late. Thanks to the confusion, the safety and cornerbacks had already left John alone.

Such an easy throw; a gift, Ryan wasted a few precious seconds second-guessing himself with the normal human doubtful questions: *Can I throw it that far? What if I lose control?*

Finally, murmuring one of his favorite football prayers: "No guts no glory," Ryan wound up and let the ball glide gracefully off his fingertips. No more than a second later, he was tackled and slammed to the ground. But in that moment before the stadium lights blinded him and his head smacked the ground, knocking him out cold, his eyes fixated on the ball sailing through the air like an unstoppable force of nature. The glory of that perfect pass would stay with him long after the bruises healed. It was embedded in his soul for eternity.

***

Sally found no pleasure in this game. She tried to watch it, but Jessica and Amber wouldn't stop talking and the more she listened the more she balked at going to Carl's party. She obsessed over Ryan's imagined reactions when she said she didn't want to go. She did not want to leave Ryan out of her sight, ever.

The blabby blondes had no qualms about discussing in detail all the guys they'd been with. Sally lost track of the number but it was at least a dozen apiece at the end of the first quarter.

She thought about moving to another section, but the bleachers were really crowded and for some dumb reason she worried that changing seats might make her look weak. Sally made up a lot of stories in her own head. Did Amber and Jessica know that she was behind them? Were they purposely discussing their booty calls and boyfriends just to psyche her out?

She was distracted from her interior monologue by a beautiful dark-haired girl making her way up the bleachers, stumbling slightly but quickly regaining her balance. When she looked around to see if anyone had noticed Sally felt a twinge of empathy. She knew what that felt like. She also recognized the girl, who at first glance looked older than she was, but she wasn't sure from where. Now that Sally was fairly popular in school she assumed that she knew everyone. But she still couldn't place her, even as she enjoyed watching the girl glare at the gossipy pair in front of her.

"Anyone sitting here?" the girl asked.

Sally looked around and the spots next to her were depressingly empty. She realized that for the first time in a long time she felt alone. She'd regressed to her old, outcast ways. It was time for a quick reversal.

"Nope, there's plenty of room." Sally replied a bit sadly.

"Well, if you don't mind," the girl flopped down with easy grace and a quirky, endearing grin. She caught herself from losing balance and toppling backward by grabbing Sally's shoulder.

Sally smelled the alcohol, an actual reek. That explained a lot.

"Are you okay?" Sally didn't want to be rude or uncool; she didn't know what to say.

"I'm fine, girl; thanks for the hand, or should I say shoulder?" the girl laughed. "My name is Becky, by the way."

"Hi, I'm Sally." She put out her hand.

"No, no, no, I bump," Becky stuck her fist out. "Like this."

Sally made a fist and touched knuckles with Becky. It felt awkward for a minute, then it was funny.

"Okay." Sally wanted to keep the conversation going. Anything was better than listening to those two in front of her. "You look really familiar. How do I know you? I've seen you somewhere. I know I've seen you at the games, but that's not it."

"Uh, duh." Becky's eyes sparkled with fun. Then she awkwardly hugged Sally. "You still don't recognize me?"

Sally shrugged, embarrassed that Becky so clearly had placed her.

"Enough with the guessing games. You give up?"

Sally nodded.

"You're friends with my brother John. At least I see you hanging out with him and that other guy, Ryan, I think his name is."

"Yeah, that's me," Sally said. "Sorry I didn't recognize you. I'm sort of surprised we've never met. Ryan and John are good friends."

"It hasn't always been like that. John dumped most of his other friends when he started playing football. Don't get me wrong; it's all good," Becky said. "But we hang out with different crowds now. No offense. You're all fine. I just don't see him much anymore."

"John told me about you," Sally said, remembering their talk in Enchantas. "It's nice to finally put a face to the name."

"Yeah, well, I don't know any of his new friends. I think I met Ryan once. He's the cute quarterback right?"

"Yep, that's my boyfriend," Sally said, a little edge to her voice.

"No worries, girl." Becky put her hands up, surrendering and laughing. "I don't need to steal boyfriends. I can get my own, thank you very much. Not like some other girls I know. Desperate, skanky girls with no morals, 'cause no decent guy wants to be seen with them."

Sally cringed, but she was also smiling. Becky was loud and she was directing her general insults at the back of Jessica's and Amber's heads. They didn't turn around but Sally could tell they heard every word.

Sally laughed out loud. Becky wasn't bad at all, even if she did smell like liquor, which come to think of it, the scent reminded her of the Husky Sled Saloon in Enchantas.

"So why the late entrance? Did you just get here?"

"Yep. I had a few beers at home. Just to put things in the right perspective."

Sally didn't want to get into anything too heavy. She'd had enough drama to last her a lifetime. "Oh?"

Becky lowered her voice to a conspiratorial whisper. "Let me be honest. I'll admit it. I don't really like football. My ex-boyfriend Carl is on the team. John is the only reason I'm here. I'm here to support."

That Carl? Sally thought, but decided not to mention the party. Sally always believed that there are times when silence truly was golden.

"Oh my God I can't wait to see Ryan at Carl's party. He told me he'd be there," Jessica gushed in a malicious way, seemingly to boast in front of Sally.

"I know. I can't wait!" said Amber. "John is in for the night of his life!"

"Screw that!" Becky muttered. She leaned in toward the pair. "Hey, I'm not sure what your plans are for tonight. But if I were you, I'd think twice about bothering my brother or my girl's man!"

"Oh yeah?" Jessica whipped around, eyes bulging with outrage. "And what are you going to do about it you scrawny little brat?"

"If you lay as much as a sneeze on either one of those guys, I will beat in your faces so bad you'll forever be named *elephant girls*." Becky leaned in closer and continued. "No one, not even your own parents, will recognize you. Did you forget how I kicked the living crap out of you when you messed around with Carl? If you mess around with my brother I can guarantee you'll never see the light of day again!"

Jessica grinned but there was no smile in her flinty eyes.

"You know," Becky continued proudly. "I'm kind of hoping you won't listen to me. I'm actually looking for a good reason to land my fist on your ugly face again. You're such a disloyal piece of work."

"You wouldn't," Jessica fluttered nervously. "I'll press charges."

"And where would that get you?" Becky scoffed. "You know I have nothing to lose. So if I were you I'd get the hell out of my face before I lose my temper."

Shocked speechless Jessica and Amber rapidly moved out of range, hurrying down the row of bleachers to another place to sit far, far away from the fearsome Becky.

Sally laughed again. Finally, someone stuck up for her. She'd always been soft spoken, held back by her own passive nature more than anything else. This girl had something to teach her about dignity and self-defense.

"I hate those witches." Becky swore. "They have no life, no self-respect. And to think Jessica used to be my best friend."

"They both kissed John and Ryan before the game."

"What? Are you serious?" Becky stood up, ready to go after them. "Why didn't you tell me?"

"I was trying to forget it." Sally sighed. "I was way too pissed off. It's stupid to get that angry."

"Did you do anything about it?" Becky looked at her alertly, hands on hips, ready to set things straight.

"No," Sally lowered her eyes, looking at nobody, ashamed. "Not my style. What could I have done, anyway?"

"Beat them up, of course," Becky said briskly.

"Yeah, with these ginormous pipes? Sure." Sally flopped her thin arms like she was doing the chicken dance. "I don't beat anyone up. And I don't want to learn how. It just gets you in trouble."

"Whatever. Who cares? I beat up Jessica this summer for making out with Carl. It was very satisfying. Fun, even."

A burst of static from the loudspeaker startled them to attention. Then came the announcement:

"Ten seconds left, last play of the game, Panthers have the ball."

Becky glanced at the scoreboard. "Wow. We could win. We're only down by five."

"So is that one touchdown?"

"Yep. Six points is all we need." Becky chuckled. "Geez, girl, you know less about football than I do — and you're going out with the quarterback! What's up with that?"

Sally shrugged. "It's not that interesting to me. I mostly worry about him getting a concussion or a broken leg or something, so I don't watch too closely. It makes me too nervous. And I know

44

when he's doing well because they call his name over the loudspeaker."

"I picked up quite a bit from watching football with my dad. It's actually the only time we hang out," Becky said. "Let's go down there for a closer look." She pointed to a spot near the Panther players' sideline.

"By the bench?" Sally was aghast. "You could get hurt if you got too close. Coaches throw things. Players crash into spectators on the sidelines all the time."

"Come on. We'll hang by the end zone," Becky urged. "If we score, everyone rushes the field. Trust me, it's a blast!"

"All right. I guess."

They made it down for the final play. The crowd was silent. She heard Ryan yell something; the players jumped as if shot out of a cannon, moving frenetically. Sally had no idea what was going on, but suddenly there was Ryan with the ball. He threw it and was immediately slammed into the ground.

"Ryan!" Sally screamed and then out of the corner of her eye she saw a player run passed them. "Is that John?"

Becky whooped. "Yes! Go Eleven! Run, John, run!"

The ball spiraled through the clear, icy air, landing gracefully in John's hands.

"Touchdown!" Becky, and most of the crowd, screamed. She and Sally hugged, jumping up and down with excitement.

True to Becky's word the elated crowd took over the field. Sally ran with the fans, losing Becky in the process. She cheered with people she knew and hugged complete strangers, caught up with everyone else in the pure joy of the moment. The Willington Panthers had just won Homecoming.

Chapter III
Enchantas

Celebrating fans slowly passed Becky as she sat next to a cedar tree outside the clubhouse locker room waiting patiently for her brother, her mind still slightly groggy from the alcohol she'd consumed earlier.

She stepped back into a copse of pines in the slightly wooded area adjacent to the locker room, lighting another cigarette to help pass the time. She could hear the sounds of celebration in the locker room. She smiled at the cheering, singing and jubilant shouting, happy for the team and especially John. Her brother had been working hard the past few months and deserved to have things go right for once in his life. With a wistful sigh, exhaling a ribbon of smoke, she wished the same for herself. The excitement of sneaking into the game, meeting Sally and joining the happy mob on the field dimmed.

Behind her the metal door slammed shut. She quickly but carefully pinched out her burning cigarette, saving the rest for later.

"Little Guppy?" a familiar male voice hissed behind her.

Her spirits dropped even further as Carl stepped in front of her, shirtless.

"For heaven's sake, Carl, what do you want?" Becky exclaimed. "And please don't call me that!"

"Pretty good game, huh?" Carl smiled. His light brown curly hair blew in the wind. "Were you waiting for me?"

"No," Becky said, annoyed. "I'm waiting for my brother. Why would I wait for you?"

"I don't know," he said. "Maybe 'cause you're going to my party and need a ride. You *are* going to my party, right?"

"Probably not," Becky looked at him with loathing. He was so full of himself "You don't deserve my presence."

"That's too bad."

"Why's that?"

"Because, I know you'd have a good time," he tried to grab her hand, but she quickly slapped his away. "What's your problem?" he asked.

"You're my problem, Carl," she stepped back. "Remember, we broke up. Is that a big enough hint for you? I don't want to be with you."

As she said the words she meant them, but deep down she knew he was her weakness; if she wasn't careful she could be persuaded to go back to him. She knew all too well that would just lead to another broken heart.

"Come on Becky! I miss you so much and I know you feel the same."

"No, I don't, Carl! So shut up!" She took a few steps back. "Get away from me."

"I am so sorry that I hurt you Becky," his eyes were sincere. "I truly am. I would do anything to take back what I did." He pleaded. "I love you so much and I never wanted to hurt you."

"Bull!" Becky swore again. "You knew she was my best friend and I caught you!"

"I was so drunk that night, I probably could have kissed your brother and not have known."

"Let's not even go there."

"I'm just making a point Becky," he chuckled for a second and immediately became serious again. "I want you, please take me back. Come on, Lil Gup." Carl stepped closer to her, swiftly laying his lips on hers.

Becky's heart fluttered, or was it her stomach, or both? She stopped thinking for a few seconds. As Carl continued to kiss her, consciousness returned. She reminded herself how much his cheating hurt. Resurrecting all her strength, rage, and passion, she landed a gut-wrenching punch to his stomach that sent him flying to the ground. She snorted at the stunned look on his face as he landed on his backside. Looking down on him was so gratifying.

"What the heck was that for?" He gasped out the words. She'd knocked the wind out of him.

"Don't ever touch me again, Carl. I thought you learned your lesson when I kicked your butt this summer. But I guess not. This is the second time. Don't go for the third. Because I'm warning you. It's not the charm!"

Grinning with satisfaction, she decided to move along before he could get up. She'd wait for John in the parking lot.

***

Excited voices and honking horns resounded through the parking lot. Sally leaned up against Ryan's blue convertible Corvette, her brown hair flowing artfully in the wind. Her lucky diamond earrings glittered, casting sparkles as the lights of the football field gleamed over the trees. She hadn't been able to see Ryan face-to-face after the game; it had been bedlam as he and John were carried off the field. But she was still riding high herself on the thrill of the win and the exhilaration of running onto the field with her classmates. She was calm, joyful, smiling, the antics of Jessica and Amber slowly fading from her mind. They didn't matter. She was excited to see her spirit-mate and congratulate him herself.

She waited patiently as the parking lot emptied. Out of the shadows came the two tall, strong, smiling, well-built young men. They wore matching tan khakis and blue dress shirts. Their ties hung loose around their necks making them look even more carefree and handsome.

They shoved each other, jesting as they approached.

"My best game yet." John tossed a football into the air and Ryan caught it.

"Yeah, you did an awesome job!" Ryan tossed it back to him. "That was a phenomenal fifty-yard throw that I tossed to you for the winning touchdown." Ryan wasn't trying to sound conceited; he couldn't help but brag. It had been a tough game. He was proud of himself.

Sally shook her head and opened the door to the corvette. "You boys should get over yourselves."

"I think Ryan should get over himself," John said, grinning. "He's afraid I'm gonna take away all of his glory."

"Hey!" Ryan shook his head, disagreeing. "Not at all. I'm really glad you decided to join the team."

"Well, I wouldn't have if I didn't quit smoking."

"Johnny!" an excited voice cried out. Becky ran to him, giving him a hug. She wobbled slightly, clutching him tighter. John could tell she was under the influence of something.

"Hey, sis!" John was pleasantly surprised. "I didn't know you were here."

"Yeah! You were great out there," Becky pulled back slightly, hoping that he wouldn't smell her beer-and-whiskey breath.

"Hey, John, we gotta get going." Ryan kissed Sally as she moved to the passenger side, moving a couple jackets out of the small back seat. "You two want a ride?"

"Sure," John replied. "C'mon, Becky!"

Becky hesitated, hoping they weren't planning to go to Carl's.

Ryan was about to open the car door when he noticed a peculiar, bright, apple-sized, blue light approaching from the direction of the field. They all stared in wonderment as it floated toward them, calling out, "Humans! We need your help!"

"What the heck?" Becky whispered, squinting as the light continued its approach. Close up it was blindingly bright. "Are we all seeing this?" Becky looked around, but no one heard her.

The light drew within a few feet from them and dimmed slightly, revealing a distinct profile within the sphere: A tiny, sparkling ebony-haired girl with butterfly wings. Becky rubbed her eyes in disbelief as the creature rhythmically opened and closed its flapping wings. Was she hallucinating? Maybe there was something stronger than alcohol in dad's whiskey.

"Dyad!" John was beside himself with excitement. "What are you doing here?"

"John?" Becky gave John a sharp look and then looked back at the tiny little creature. Why was John so excited? What was this thing? Her eyes quickly darted back to John and then again to the others and back again to the creature. "What in the heck is that?"

"It's a fairy," John replied nonchalantly, laughing.

"A fair–" she began in disbelief, but she was interrupted by the frantic Dyad.

"Professor Mel is in trouble," Dyad fluttered hysterically, her movements as frantic and rapid as a moth drawn to a flame. "Enchantas needs your help."

"Professor Mel?" John asked.

"Yes," Dyad said urgently. "It has been many cycles since your departure from Enchantas. Much has changed. Mel is the Professor of Advanced Potions at the Enchantian Institute of Magic."

"Wow, much *has* changed," John repeated.

Becky's mouth was wide open and her eyes moving ceaselessly from person to person and back to the fairy-creature that her brother apparently knew. She still could not reconcile what she was seeing with reality. She found it funny that the others didn't seem particularly shocked.

"Let us hurry," Dyad said, glowing brighter. "Time is of the essence. Remember that time is different here than Enchantas."

Sally had been taking it all in. "Let's go!" she urged. "We can't let anything happen to Mel."

"Enchantas?" Becky managed to asked, still puzzled and reeling from what she was seeing and hearing. "What's going on here?"

"Becky, there's a lot I need to tell you, but it looks like I have to go." John put his hand on her shoulder. "There's something I need to do."

"John," Becky took a huge breath, exhaled and stared into his eyes, trying to focus and concentrate. "I'm coming with you."

John thought for a moment, contemplating the alternative, their dad, who was still an unpredictable abusive drunk. John knew Becky wasn't safe without him here protecting her. He didn't want to leave his sister behind.

"She can come, John." Dyad fluttered urgently, but her words were welcoming and reassuring. "But we must hurry. Every tick counts."

"All right," John told Becky. "You can come with us."

"Where is it we're going?"

"I'll explain everything when we get there. Just close your eyes."

"Okay," she mumbled, not believing that what was happening was real. Eyes shut tight, she whispered to herself, "If only I could get more of whatever was in that whiskey, I could play along better."

The other three also closed their eyes, shielding them from the brightness of Dyad's intensifying light. They didn't see the small gray-and-white rabbit watching them from the shadows behind the car. Its eyes opened wide as it recognized the Enchantas fairy. The rabbit smiled, showing its buck teeth and happily hopped toward the group as fast as it could.

"Ready?" Dyad lifted her arms and intoned:

"Fairy games, playful fun,
To Enchantas, here we come!"

The bright blue light wrapped around and consumed them as they instantaneously disappeared. The gray-and-white rabbit thumped a not-so-lucky foot in frustration. He'd been too late. Mumbles was once again trapped in this still-unfamiliar world.

***

Dyad and the four teens materialized in an empty field surrounded by a forest of leafless trees. The lightning-white sun was about to set over the pale-green horizon. The purple grass beneath them was frozen. Rainbow-colored, star-shaped snowflakes began to flutter down from the sky landing gently on the ground as well as on their heads and shoulders. The brisk Enchantian air was thick with moisture, tantalizing their senses with fresh flavors and smells of bubblegum, cinnamon and blueberry. The others took it in stride, somewhat desensitized to the magnificence by their previous adventures. Becky was astonished.

"What is this place?" Still under the influence, Becky tried to separate the real from the imaginary. It was impossible. The colored snow, falling faster, had begun to cover the valley floor, coating the bare tree branches as well as the vivid red, green and blue pines interspersed in the landscape outside of the main forest. Massive walls of dark-blue mountains could be seen in the far distance. "This isn't Willington, that's for sure," Becky muttered.

"This is Enchantas," Sally told her, brushing the colorful snow off Becky's shoulders.

"But how did we get here? How does this place exist?"

"Dyad brought us," Sally continued.

"Just believe it, because it's real, sis," John smiled, patting her arm reassuringly. "We found this place by accident one day after school. I couldn't believe it either when we first got here."

"This place is so strange," Becky lifted a hand allowing the snowflakes to settle gently in it. "These snowflakes look like Frootie Flakes cereal." She licked her palm. "Holy crap, they taste like them too!"

"I would not eat the black snow, dear." Dyad warned nonchalantly.

Becky only looked at her inquisitively, without word. Was she really talking to a fairy?

"Yeah, Enchantas is bizarre, but in a very cool way," Ryan added, almost as if he enjoyed showing the place off to a newbie. "Every day we were here we learned something new and encountered the most peculiar creatures. You can't begin to imagine how Enchantas will surprise you, day after day."

"Every day?" Becky questioned.

"Don't even ask, sis," John chuckled. "Just take everything as it comes and expect the impossible. The more you question, the more confused you'll become."

"All right, I guess I'll take your word for it," Becky continued to inquisitively scan her surroundings with a sense of bewilderment and awe. She saw a neon-green stream flowing down a hill, with abnormally large animals drinking from it. She pointed at the group of colored creatures, about to ask another question, then reminded herself to take her brother's advice.

Meanwhile, Sally was questioning their fairy guide. "What's wrong with Mel, Dyad?" Sally asked. "There doesn't seem to be anything going on here that needs our attention."

"I agree," Ryan held Sally's hand, glancing around at the seemingly peaceful scenery. "I was expecting devastation, burned towns, you know, World War Three."

"Well, my friends," Dyad hovered, circling them slowly to make eye contact with one and all. "Enchantas is doing fine. Thriving, you could say. There is peace in most of the territories, finally, and it has happily been so now for many cycles.

"But, Sally, the threat from your stepsister remains." Dyad hovered in front of Sally with a grave expression. "She is still at large. She has declared herself as 'The Empress of Enchantas' and there are rumors now that she is building an army on the other side of our world. Her delusions have become more apparent these past few cycles as she believes she is the ruler of Enchantas. When in actuality, the Knight's Council is now governing most of the lands of Enchantas."

"What about Mel?" John chimed in. "I don't know what's crazier: that he's a professor or that he's in danger."

"Neither seems strange to us, given our history," Dyad said kindly but sternly. "There have been multiple assassination attempts on the professor as well as other council members. My sisters and I urged him to seek refuge or more protection, but his stubbornness has not lessened. He treats all dangers as a joke and does not take anything seriously. We thought it best to bring you three, his friends, here to persuade him to take refuge."

"That sure sounds like typical Mel." John laughed.

"Not funny, John." Sally frowned. "If Mel's in danger we have to help."

"I know," John drew his eyebrows together, his expressive face telegraphing sincere concern. "But what makes you think he'll listen to us? He probably thinks he can protect himself and he's probably right. I'll bet he's learned a lot of magic by now."

"Indeed he has, John," Dyad verified. "But these assassination attempts keep happening. All it takes is to be caught off guard one time."

"Why does Lexis want to kill Mel?" Sally asked. Knowing that the evil Gypsy was her stepsister really bothered her. They weren't truly related; her parents were godparents serving as adoptive guardians. She was dismayed to learn that Lexis hadn't settled down or just gone away, but instead was proclaiming herself Empress, ruler of the land.

"Be warned," Dyad said. "Since the battle for Enchantas, she has become more twisted and evil. Her anger and resentment towards the four of you has grown immensely and revenge is on the top of her list of priorities."

Sally gulped, remembering how betrayed Lexis felt when Sally had reunited with her parents. She'd been furious. "Ryan, are we safe here? Do you think we should go back?"

"Not without Mel," Ryan looked at Dyad. "Maybe we can persuade him to come back to our world with us. Then he'll be safe. We will all be safe."

"Safe for now, my friends," Dyad replied dryly. "It would only be a matter of time before she would seek you out in your world."

"I agree with Dyad." John crossed his arms with resolve. His experience in Enchantas the first time changed his life and made him very protective of his friends. His sister's safety wasn't his only concern. "We can't just leave Enchantas when it's on the brink of another war and that crazy Gypsy-Empress or whatever she calls herself now is still out there roaming freely."

"John's right," Ryan agreed. "Let's talk to Mel first and figure things out. Which way, Dyad?"

"It is this way, I believe," Dyad moved to their left. "Using magic to come back from your world can be a little unpredictable, so I am unsure of our exact location. But we are close to Gumbo Fields, by Cropville."

"Huh. You can transport us across worlds but you don't have a GPS?" Becky had remained quiet for a while, taking it all in. Empresses, magic and confetti-colored snowflakes were a bit much to handle; but she couldn't keep her blunt honesty under wraps for more than five minutes.

Dyad greeted her comment with a moment of dignified silence before zipping forward to lead the way, intent on the business at hand. "Let us hurry! We are only a few tocks away."

"What?" Becky tossed her head as if trying to shake off her confusion. She didn't understand anything this fairy was saying.

"Hang in there, sis. I'll tell you on the way." John took her hand.

***

The white sun had finally set. The rainbow snowflakes glowed in the darkness, spectral glimmers coloring the sky like ethereal fireflies. The purplish-blue valley with the bare trees and luminescent candy-colored snow above and below was enchanting to Becky, who wondered if that was how Enchantas got its name. But the strangest thing of all was how John, Sally and Ryan took it all in stride. She couldn't believe they were acting like this was normal.

She listened as her brother and the others told the story of their first visit to Enchantas, beginning with how they met. She laughed at the prank Mel pulled during the first day of school a couple months ago. She couldn't wait to meet him.

She shared their sadness over the horrible death of Gitchy and was horrified by the mere thought of screaming vegetables. She wanted to ride on the magic carpet and sail through the sky in those flying pirate ships. Unlike her brother, Becky enjoyed the thrill of heights. It didn't matter if it was a cliff or a skyscraper.

One of her favorite summer activities was cliff-jumping and rope-swinging at Clear Lake with friends. She never missed an opportunity. John, who balked at heights, would only sit and watch.

All in all, Becky seemed to take the tales of their previous journey quite well. Becky could tell her brother was surprised and relieved by her reaction, but then, she had been drinking, so maybe that made it easier for her to believe.

"The thing I don't really get is this passive-aggressive Lexis chick. She liked you, she hated you, then she liked you again. And then she wanted to kill you. Or she was just pretending to like you and wanted to kill you all the whole time," Becky pondered. "What's her deal?"

"We don't know," the others said in unison, laughing at the inadvertent chorus.

"She's just crazy," John added.

"Yes, insanity describes it." Dyad flitted and twirled around Becky's head as if trying to get to know her better. "The self-proclaimed Empress is now our only threat to widespread peace in Enchantas."

"Well, I wish I could meet her," Becky said, catching herself as she stumbled over a rock. "I'd show her what I'm made of!"

"I'm sure you would, your grace," John chuckled, steadying her with a hand on the small of her back. He tried to keep his tone light. "How much have you had to drink today?"

"Not much. I'm sobering up now, bro," she said, wondering if he'd heard her hiccup slightly when she tripped. She quickly changed the subject. "Oh by the way, the police came to the house looking for dad today."

"What? Why?"

"There was a hit-and-run. Dad's a suspect."

"What the hell," John shook his head, ashamed that he hadn't given his father the Bracelet of Hope. The bracelet given to him by the gargoyles would have turned his father's life around. John could finally admit that he hadn't given it to him because he'd hoped his dad would be strong enough to do the right thing by himself, for their family. But that was a misguided hope. "Why can't he just stop?"

"He's getting worse, John." Becky said sadly.

"Is he? I guess I couldn't tell."

"Of course you can't tell," Becky's voice became deeper and a little louder, showing her irritation. "You're never home."

"What are you talking about? I'm always home."

"You know you're not," she said. "Since you've joined football, you're never home."

"Becky, I've been busy." John was defensive. "Who cares if I'm home all the time or not?"

"I do, John. I'm your sister. We're family. You probably didn't know that dad's been hitting me more lately!" She surprised herself as well as John by bursting into tears. The repressed memories of her father's beatings during the last couple of months overtook her; the bottled-up pain fizzed and bubbled furiously out.

"What the hell are you talking about?" John stopped, thunderstruck.

The others walked ahead, respectfully leaving the two alone.

"While you were off turning your life around, making it better, I was home alone! With dad!"

"Why didn't you say anything?" John began to feel even worse about not using the bracelet.

"And what? Ruin everything for you?" Becky buried her face in her brother's chest and wept. "I couldn't do that to you!"

"I'm so sorry, Becky," John grasped her tight. "I had no idea. You should have told me. You are never a burden in my life." John smiled and lifted her chin. "You know, I didn't tell you this, but I could have stayed here in Enchantas. But I came home. Want to know why?"

"Why?" she asked softly, wiping away her tears.

"Because of you, goof-ball!" John squeezed her hard. "I love you, sis! I wanted to be home so I could be with you and protect you."

"Oh, John!" Becky squeezed him tighter, feeling loved. John had never been so affectionate with her and it made her appreciate this moment that much more. "I love you too!"

"You still should have told me about dad."

"I know," Becky wiped her smeared make-up from her eyes.

"Becky," John whispered to her. "Is that my leather jacket you're wearing?"

Becky looked down and giggled. "Yeah, did you want it back?" She waved both her arms out as the ends dangled slightly from her fingertips. "See it fits perfectly."

"No, that's fine, sis," John rubbed the top of her head like he used to. "You can wear it, but don't lose it. There is a Leprechaun here that wants it."

"Ha!" Grinning, Becky put up her fists. "Bring it on!"

A few yards away next to one of the bare trees, Sally, Ryan and Dyad sat on the ground watching the siblings.

"You know Dyad," Sally whispered. "John still has feelings for you."

Dyad looked at her, smiling sweetly without saying anything, Sally knew Dyad felt the same.

"He talks about you every day."

"Well, if he cares for me half as much as he cares for his sister, I can safely say that I am the luckiest fairy in all of Enchantas." Dyad winked and then slowly fluttered ahead. "We should keep moving. We need to cross the Beaverton Bridge. It's just up here."

The four visitors followed Dyad, climbing over a small ridge. They reached a large cliff overlooking the bridge. Its stone-and-concrete surface was as wide as two freeways back home. The fortress-like supporting cobblestone walls of the structure were similar to a castle, as were the two imposing, stone towers framing the entrance at both ends.

Behind the bridge to the left, they could see a spectacular large waterfall glittering electric blue where the moonlight pierced the water. As the torrent joined the pool, water below it foamed and roiled, transformed to rapids flowing down into the indigo valley. The moonbeams created a rainbow mist, hazing the view of the empty canyon surrounding the city underneath the bridge.

Beaverton City was unlike any other settlement ever seen. Buildings hung from the bridge, upside-down skyscrapers in an upside-down town. The creatures who dwelled here roamed the city using stairways, rope bridges and balconies, a network of handholds and stabilizers that safely transported dwellers from building to building. Ryan, Sally, and John, who'd thought there was nothing new in Enchantas to astonish them, watched the busy city in awe.

As they moved closer to the bridge, the array of creatures became identifiable. Many were small, about shoulder height to the teenagers, with wide, flat, paddle tails. Obviously beavers. There were some other, more gruesome-looking inhabitants three times as tall as the beavers. Dark, wooly fur covered their entire bodies. Their legs were much shorter than their arms; they walked like gorillas. Their snouts were pointy. A short, spiked antler-type horn jutted from each grotesque forehead.

"Here we are," Dyad motioned toward a small green-stoned trail. "Beaverton Bridge and Beaverton City."

"Dyad," Sally's voice quivered in fear. "What are those ugly things with the Beavers? They look as if they are going to eat them."

"Do not worry, my dear. Trolls are not the most beautiful or graceful of creatures, but they make remarkable guards of the city and are very stubborn when it comes to collecting the tolls to cross the bridge."

"They do look fierce." John approached Dyad, happy to be near her. "I'm surprised they're getting along."

"This was not always the case." Dyad noted. "The trolls were once slave owners of the beavers, forcing them to build this bridge and the city underneath."

"What happened?"

"When the prophets of Enchantas brought liberty to our lands it changed everything." Dyad sat on his shoulder. "Please, do not be alarmed if you are referred to as prophets or saviors here."

"That's embarrassing," Sally chimed in. "I have no idea what to say to that."

"I think 'thank-you' would be a good start, sweetie," Ryan smiled.

Becky remained silent, listening to the conversations and taking in this new world. As they approached the tower, she noticed the attraction between her brother and Dyad. There was something about their connection that seemed right, even though they weren't the same size. Becky was happy for him. She couldn't remember John ever having had a real girlfriend.

Snarling troll faces glared at them, peeking over windowless ledges. Dyad brightened her glow three times, apparently a sign of friendship and request for admittance. It was a nifty trick that reminded Becky of a dimmer switch on a light fixture.

"Who goes there?" a deep, eerie voice demanded from behind the door.

"I am Dyad, the fairy. We are kindly requesting safe passage."

"We?" the voice became more unyielding. "Who is *we*?"

"I have brought four humans from the otherworld." Dyad explained. "We wish for safe passage over your bridge and to travel to the Institute."

"Toll?"

"Yes," Dyad sounded irritated. She was not must use to being questioned or asked to pay tolls. "We have payment."

"Mr. Troll," a soft, sensual voice interjected behind the door. "Please don't be rude. Open the door."

"Yes, madam," the troll responded obediently.

As the door rose a teeny emerald-green light zipped from underneath, transmitting eager excitement as it whipped around checking out the visitors.

"Hello!" the light trilled, moving too fast for anyone to see the possessor of the voice. "Why, Dyad! I did not know you would be coming this way."

"Hello, Nymph." Dyad floated slowly to her. "No need to be so excited."

"Excited?" Nymph bubbled laughter. "Of course I am excited! It is not every day you meet new humans."

"Everyone," Dyad put up a tiny hand, admonishing her sister to calm to a hover and lower her light. She adjusted her own dimmer down so the quartet could see. "Please meet my younger sister. This is Nymph."

"Pleasure to meet you!" Sally said moving closer. She noticed a similarity between Dyad's and Nymph's facial features, although in contrast to her dark-haired sibling, Nymph had strawberry-blonde hair complemented by a pale-pink dress.

"You must be Sally, I've heard all about you from Mel." Nymph gave her a dainty wave before floating nearer to John. "And you must be John," again the laughter bubbled. "I've heard a lot about you from Dyad."

Becky was amazed at Dyad's reaction. Who knew fairies could blush?

"I'm John's sister," she said.

"Glad to meet you, John's sister," Nymph said, eyes twinkling as she made her way to Ryan, slowly surveying him from the top of his head to his feet and back up again. "Holy lixy dust! You must be Ryan."

"That's me." Ryan was a little uncomfortable as Nymph fluttered around him.

"How gorgeous this one is, sister!" Nymph turned to Dyad. "Can I have him?"

"*Have* him?" Sally was stunned by the blunt request.

"No, Nymph," Dyad answered softly. "You cannot."

"But I want him!"

"He is already taken, dear," Dyad gestured. "By Sally here. He is hers. She is his."

"Oh," Nymph pouted prettily, flying close to Ryan's ear. "I still think you are very handsome, Ryan," Nymph pronounced, kissing his cheek.

Ryan flinched slightly, biting the inside of the kissed cheek as he tried not to show any emotion. He was painfully aware of Sally's frustration with how females interacted with him so he was very uncomfortable with Nymph's assertiveness towards him.

"Nymph, please come over here," said Dyad. "And stop being flirtatious."

"Yes, sister." Nymph responded obediently and cheerfully, but couldn't resist a teasing look over her teensy shoulder. "Bye, Ryan."

Dyad and Nymph led them onto the empty, quiet bridge. Trolls and beavers below stopped what they were doing briefly to watch the travelers walk by, but quickly turned back to their chores.

"What was that all about?" Sally demanded.

"What?" Ryan was bummed. He'd been hoping she could just let it go. Though nothing had happened, he felt himself getting defensive. "With that fairy? Nothing. It's not my fault she kissed me. To tell you the truth, it caught me off guard."

"You could have at least pushed her away when she kissed you." Sally clenched her teeth as well as her fists. "Just like those two girls you kissed before the game."

"What?" Ryan had forgotten about that. Their pre-game fussing over John and him hadn't left a lasting impression. It took him a moment to remember them. "They're just a couple of silly little girls. It didn't mean anything. I'm not interested. You should know that. I think you're blowing this all out of proportion."

"Blowing it out of proportion? I am sick of-" She raised her voice. Ryan sighed.

"Sally, please." He tried to stay calm. "We can talk about this later somewhere in private. We're making a scene."

Sally looked around, realizing that everyone, even the trolls and beavers, was watching the one-sided argument. Embarrassment consumed her instantaneously. "I'm sorry. Yes, you're right. We can talk about it later."

Sally hated letting negative emotions get the better of her. She didn't want to nag or whine, but she also didn't want to be the doormat she used to be, allowing everyone to put her down. Old habits as well as habits new to this relationship were proving difficult to get rid of; if only Ryan didn't attract so much female attention. She had the right to be angry and annoyed when other girls were hanging all over him, kissing him, following him around. *They had no right*, she thought, adamantly shaking her head. *No! It wasn't right. He was hers and she was his!*

Sally was so preoccupied with her anger she didn't realize they had stopped to talk to the mayor of Beaverton. He was taller than most of the beavers, formally clad in a long, buttoned-up blue coat and black top hat. He carried a carved-wood handled cane.

"We are very honored by your presence, young prophets," the beaver bowed, removing his hat with a flourish. "My name is Toggle and this here is Hunglebee," Toggle gestured to an oncoming troll who like his beaver counterpart was a little taller than the usual troll. He also had a larger rack of antler-horns. "We are the elder chiefs of Beaverton Bridge and Beaverton City." Hunglebee grunted.

"Don't mind the trolls," Toggle grinned, his buck teeth jutted out. "They know the common tongue, but prefer their own language. Hunglebee passes his greetings."

"Pleasure to meet you," Ryan stated formally. "And I must say, this bridge and the city underneath are fantastic. Very well constructed."

"And the view is marvelous!" Sally added.

"Why thank you, both." Toggle replied. "We take much pride in our accomplishments here."

Hunglebee grunted again.

"Pardon," Toggle interpreted. "Hunglebee says 'thank you' also." He paused for a moment and asked. "Would you like a tour?"

The four looked at each other, uncertain of the proper response. They needed to get to Mel but they wanted to avoid offending the leaders or townsfolk. Dyad replied with perfect composure and diplomacy.

"Thank you Toggle, that is much appreciated. However, these four are quite tired and we must decline. We have quite a way to go before we reach the Institute."

"Of course. But might I say, dear Dyad, the old Minerton Castle is at least fifty sprints from here. Unless you can travel 100 dashes per tock – an amazing feat indeed – you would not get there till morning."

"Dyad," John stifled a yawn. "I have no idea what you're talking about, other than it sounds like a long way. Will we make it tonight?"

"I do not know, John. We may need to rest half way."

"I'm getting tired," said Becky. John's yawn was contagious. "I really would like a warm bed."

66

"I have an idea, young Knights." Toggle conferred in whispers with Hunglebee. The troll grunted, seemingly in complaint, but moseyed away. "We can provide you with safe travel," Toggle continued. "From an old friend, might I add."

A wavy blanket-like shape zipped from underneath the bridge, twisting and turning about. It flew up high and darted low, circling the four with excitement.

"Gusto!" Sally ran to it eagerly. "Oh my gosh! Have I missed you!"

"Oh no," John moaned. "I thought you said 'safe travel'."

"John?" Becky asked. "What is that?" She pointed to the animated maroon rug, admiring the intricate teal colored designs on its body.

"Meet Gusto, the magic carpet," John replied, giving her a panicked look. "I tell you, I was fine during the battle with the flying pirate ship, but waking up on that thing with a massive hangover has scarred me for life!"

"Oh come on." Becky grabbed his hand and pulled him to the spunky rug. "It can't be that bad."

"If only there was a seat belt." John yanked his hand away, but he'd given in to the inevitable. It was the fastest way to get to Mel. "I call the middle!"

"What's wrong buddy?" Ryan slugged John's shoulder. "Still afraid of heights?"

John narrowed his eyes. "Lay off." His fear of heights embarrassed him enormously.

"Thank you for this kind gesture, Toggle." Dyad said. "I did not know Gusto was in these parts. This makes their arrival much more pleasant."

Gusto nodded his top half in agreement before descending low and hovering in place so everyone could climb on.

"Yes, sister," Nymph floated back with Hunglebee. "Gusto came with me to secure our alliance with the Trolls and Beavers."

"Then you were right." Dyad looked sorrowful. "War may soon be upon us."

"We do not know for sure, but our Sage had asked us to travel and reassure alliances."

"I see," Dyad came closer to her. "Will you be coming with us to the Institute?"

"Not now. I must travel to a few more villages to meet with leaders. I should be back before the festival."

"Is it that time of cycle?" Dyad questioned.

"What festival?" Ryan asked, clambering onto Gusto.

"It is our annual festival, celebrating the rebirth of Enchantas. 'Prophet's Day'."

"Cool." Sally smiled.

"It is destiny that you have come during this time. It has been more than fourteen cycles since your departure."

"Fourteen?" John was astonished. "Wait, Mel has been only gone for like two months back home. So it's been that many years over here? Mind boggling."

Dyad settled on his shoulder. "Remember, John, time works differently here."

Becky curled up on the rug while the others talked about the mechanics of this strange world. Sobered, she was more tired than she could remember being in a long time.

As she closed her eyes she heard Sally bellow, "Go Gusto Go!" the sound echoing through the ravine as they sped off past the waterfall and up into the sky, heading to yet another strange place in the curious world of Enchantas.

Chapter IV
The Reunion

Gusto descended from the navy blue, star-lit sky. Becky, awake from her nap, joined Sally and Ryan in staring intently ahead. John remained face first on Gusto's textured back, unable to look up because it would make him motion sick. The pale blue moon set, disappearing as they flew through thick red clouds. They emerged into an open valley scattered with maple, oak and willow trees. A small bluish lake could be seen in the distance. An enormous forbidding gray castle rested as pompously as a self-important dignitary atop the tallest hill. Small granite buildings were scattered around the great castle, positioning it at the center of the small village.

"Welcome to the new Minerton Castle," Dyad proudly announced.

John sat up to look, his fear and motion sickness temporarily quelled as he gazed in distracted awe at the extravagant castle. Every window glowed with soft lights shining outward. The torch-lined roof provided a guiding beacon for wayward travelers.

"Man, this place has changed since the last time we were here." John exclaimed. "It was nothing but a large pile of rubble."

"Yeah," Ryan agreed. "I can't believe it's the same place."

"The Knights and Professor Mel agreed that in order to start our society over correctly, Enchantas required a new center capitol, a new foundation to build from," Dyad explained. "Previously the castle served as a protective fortress, used for war. Now it serves as a school for learning and advancement. Education is the heart of Enchantas now, education and magic."

"What about preparing to defend yourselves, just in case?" asked Ryan. "If Lexis or some other enemy is building an army against you, wouldn't it be wise to be ready?"

"This has been our ongoing fear. We have an academy for our military forces. Those who don't wish to or cannot train in magic are offered the opportunity to perfect military skills at a training center for that purpose. It's in the old Witch's and Warlock's castle, which you may remember."

"How many attend the schools?" asked Sally, quickly wanting to change the subject. She did not like being reminded of who her parents once were.

"There are more than a thousand Enchantians enrolled at the Enchantian Institute of Magic. There are a few hundred Enchantians training at our military academy as we speak. However, I do not know how many are enlisted in the new Enchantas Army."

"Fascinating," Sally leaned over Gusto's edge, peering at the scurrying Enchantians below. "Everyone looks so busy."

"Yes," Dyad laughed. "This is the end of their exam period. Many are stressed."

John harrumphed under his breath.

"Pardon me, John?" Dyad floated back to his shoulder. "Did you say something?"

"No, I was just thinking that it sucks to be them. I can relate. I hate studying."

Ryan nodded in agreement.

Gusto slowly flew over the school buildings then climbed upward toward a large clock tower.

"What time is that clock showing?" Becky studied the curious circular clock. There were ten rather than twelve numbers on the face.

"It is three-quarters after midnight or ten seventy-eight, if you wish to be precise," Dyad responded briskly.

Becky gawked at the clock face, raising her eyebrows. "Ten seventy-eight?"

"Becky," Ryan laughed. "Time works differently here. Dyad can explain."

"Tickity Tock goes-" Dyad was about to recite the verse when Sally stopped her.

"Wait. I apologize for interrupting you, Dyad." Sally smiled kindly. "But believe me, I know. The verses will just confuse her more. It took me a long time to figure it out. My parents helped me while I was helping them transition back home. They were used to Enchantas time; I had to reteach them how to tell time in our world when they returned. So I had to figure out an easy way to translate Enchantas time to our-world time." She scooted closer to Becky. "Now instead of hours, here in Enchantas, they call them tocks. Minutes are ticks and seconds are tacks. You still with me?"

Becky nodded, watching John as he oh-so-casually moved closer to listen to Sally's explanation. Sally also noticed. She was glad he was tuning in. They could all use a brush-up on the way things worked in this world.

"As you look at the clock tower over there," Sally pointed, "You can see that ten numbers circle it instead of twelve. That means there are only twenty tocks, rather than our twenty-four hours, in a complete day-and-night cycle. Each tock, or hour, has one hundred ticks, or minutes, and each tick has fifty tacks, what we would refer to in our world as seconds. Does that make sense?"

"It's still kind of confusing," Becky said. "But I get it. I feel sure they do their time like that here because the hours of daylight are different."

"That is correct, Miss Becky," said an approving Dyad as Gusto gracefully floated down to a parking area atop one of the towers in an admirable display of stability and equilibrium.

Gargoyles stood proudly, honor in every line of their noble postures. Several were stationed on each tower, a beefed-up detachment guarding the castle until first light. John hastily stepped off Gusto as soon as he could, sighing with relief. If it wouldn't have looked so wimpy he would have knelt down and kissed the landing strip.

Becky, who had disembarked, with a pet to Gusto's soft nap and a sincere thank you, tapped her brother on the shoulder. "Hey, what are those tall gray creatures with wings? They look like statues, like from an old church."

Observing the dignified, vigilant, well-mannered gargoyles, John thought about the night he'd spent with a very different group of the creatures. Those gargoyles drank Rottin Ale with him until nobody could stand or talk. It was on that night that this miserable bunch of Enchantians faced their demons and depressions head on and found hope again. Something he wished for his father.

"Oh those are gargoyles. They guard this place."

"We are the night-watch guardians, Master John," a commanding voice, familiar to John from his previous visit, reverberated behind them.

The four teens spun around, as a large figure approached from the tower. As he came closer, the torchlight revealed his identity. It was Bion, Dex's former right hand.

John remembered his last, intoxicated conversation with Dex. The details weren't so crystal clear thanks to his inebriated state at the time, but the feeling he'd had as they'd talked about his dad had stayed with him. Before his death, Dex asked his ex-fiancé

Brista, the Griffin princess, to give John the Bracelet of Hope. John was to give it to his father to relieve him of his drinking problem, but John had been too stubborn and vindictive to use it. Now, thanks to Becky, he was facing the fact that their father was getting worse, not better, and deeply regretting his selfish, immature decision. His resentment could cost his father jail time, or worse, prison, if there were felony charges. If Becky's suspicions — not to mention the police department's — were correct, the hit-and-run could leave them essentially parentless. Then what? Their mother had left them when John was only eleven, and Becky was eight. They would surely be sent away to some foster home, and could possibly be separated.

"Bion!" Ryan walked up to the gargoyle and heartily shook his index finger. Bion's fist was as large a Ryan's upper body. "How have you been? It looks like everything is under control."

"That's certainly so, Master Ryan," Bion patted Ryan on his back unaware that he almost knocked the wind out of him. "Every night, this castle has been safe, just as it once was, many ages ago. Thanks to you." Bion turned to Sally and Becky. "How are you Miss Sally?"

"I'm doing great!" Sally jumped up to give him a hug. "I am so happy to see you, to see all the gargoyles."

"Oh my, thank you," Bion, flattered and stunned by Sally's obvious affection, turned to Becky. "And who is this beautiful young lady?"

"This is my sister Becky," said John, standing next to her.

"Well, I'll be," Bion shook her arm gently. "It is my pleasure to meet a sister of John's." Bion smiled and whispered. "John is a hero, you know, to all gargoyles. You should be very proud of him."

Becky smiled. "Thank you," she said quietly. "I *am* proud."

73

"Why, this calls for a celebration. How about I break out a bottle of the old Butchbark? Or some Rottin Ale, huh?" Bion rubbed his giant hands together in anticipation.

"Not today, my friend," another familiar voice joined the conversation: Mel stood in the doorway. His demeanor had dramatically changed from the nerdy class clown, he was clearly more confident, mature, even sophisticated. He wore dark blue pants and a creamy white shirt topped with a light brown vest. The brown leather satchel strapped crosswise across his torso accented his professorial silhouette. His hair, grown longer, was pulled back in a well-groomed ponytail landing in the middle of his back just past his shoulders. He looked quizzically at Bion. "I thought you all were 'on the wagon'?"

"Pardon my slip, Professor," Bion bowed. "Old habits die hard."

"Understandable, dear friend," Mel winked. "And please, just call me Mel. Especially since my old friends have finally arrived. I don't want them to feel intimidated."

"Mel!" Sally's eyes opened wide as he walked up to her and gave her a hug. "What did you do to your hair?" Sally grabbed his ponytail, gave it a playful tug and giggled, "Stylish."

"There you are, old buddy!" John gave him a big hug. He also couldn't resist a tug at Mel's ponytail.

"Oh boy," Mel said, arms still open wide. "Everyone is so *touchy-feely* today."

"Ryan!" Mel shook his hand, patted his back and gave him a quick side hug. "How have you been? How's football?"

"Things are good," Ryan said, grinning at Sally and remembering the prank Mel had pulled on the two of them, a stunt that inadvertently kick-started their relationship. "Football is great. We just won Homecoming. I convinced John to join the team and even though he's still a pain in the be-hind I've got to admit he's an awesome player."

"Did you really join the team and put that temper — or should I say athletic talent — to use?" Mel cocked his head, giving John a thumbs-up. "Good for you!

He glanced back at Ryan. "And I see you're both modeling the off-the-field Panther uniform tonight. Charming. Speaking of which, I hope John's delightful charm hasn't rubbed off on you, Ryan."

"Not me," Ryan replied, as always taking Mel's jokes in stride. "But Sally's expanded her vocabulary. You should hear her cuss."

"That's hard to believe." Mel shook his head in mock disgust.

"Hey guys," John was insulted. "I'm standing right here."

"No offense. You know we're just kidding around." Ryan assured him. "Check it out Mel: John scored the winning touchdown tonight. He's the true-blue Homecoming hero."

Mel shook his head in amazement. "As we say here in Enchantas, much has changed."

"I know," Sally added. "Some pretty amazing events have happened in the last two months."

"Really? Only two months?" Mel responded. "Oh, right. I almost forgot. It's been roughly fourteen and one-half cycles since you guys left, though I have only aged two months. Humans age our-world-time, not Enchantian-time."

"Cycles?" Becky was still getting used to Enchantas lingo.

"A year in Enchantas," Sally whispered to her.

"Wow!" John exclaimed. "You must have learned a lot by now."

"I sure have," Mel smiled, lifting a shirt sleeve to show off a hand-crafted bracelet that, except for a flaring purple diamond, closely resembled the V-shaped persona bracelets they'd used on their last trip. "This is one of the first magic pieces I made here. Every student is required to create one before graduation. I have four persona weapons now, although I still prefer my boomerang

75

over all the others. Oh and I can muster up a ton of spells, too. It's so cool."

"Well Mel," Ryan smiled. "It sounds like you made the right choice staying here."

"Yep." Mel grinned. "But I do wonder how my parents are doing. Any news?"

"I think they're okay," Sally said. "You put them through the wringer, though. They posted 'MISSING' flyers all over town. Horrible picture of you on it, by the way."

"Yeah," Ryan chimed in. "Besides calling the police your mother practically did a one-woman house-to-house search. I wasn't home when she came to our place, but my brother was. She left a flyer. Sally's right. Horrible picture." He grinned, then frowned. "But seriously, man. She's really been upset."

Mel didn't respond. He didn't know how to handle the sudden guilt pang. He knew the decision to stay in Enchantas was the wisest choice for his own well-being. It had never occurred to him that he was loved and missed and that his selfishness would hurt his mother.

"That's where I know you from!" Becky broke into the conversation as events clicked into place. "You're that missing kid who was all over the news. You've been here the whole time?"

"Whoa," Mel said under his breath. His eyes widened as he stuttered out loud, "Y-yep, that's me. And you are?"

"Oh sorry Mel," John put his arm around Becky. "This is my kid sister, Becky."

Mel nervously extended a hand. They shook. He held on. "So you're John's sister?" *Nice going, Captain Obvious,* but he didn't know what else to say.

"Yeppers," Becky laughed, trying to pull her hand away. He had a firm grip. "That's me."

"Ah, Mel?" John snickered. "Can you let go of my sister's hand? I don't really want to hurt you, but I will if I have to."

"Oh, sorry, John. Sorry, Becky." Mel let her go. It was for the best anyway. His palms were sweaty. "So. Okay. Please follow me you guys. Everyone is waiting."

"Everyone?" Ryan asked.

"Yes. We're having a council meeting with the Knights," Mel was walking fast; it took a moment for everyone to catch up. "After the meeting we'll have dinner."

"Great," Becky tapped her belly. "My stomach's growling."

The quartet followed Mel through a large archway leading to a set of multiple stairways and corridors that extended throughout the castle. Becky's curiosity and interest increased as they went along. She longed to explore, but knew now was not the time.

"This is one of our lecture buildings," Mel briefly pointed to the classrooms lining the hall, right and left. Peering in, Becky saw they were set up all the same with the desks arranged in a circle. "We offer many majors of study here. Classes such as basic spell casting, luck charms, potions, lixy dust, curses, voodoo, herbs and remedies, martial magic — that's self-defense — crystal balls and much more. We also teach about the art of the five natural elements: earth, water, fire, wind and space. Advanced classes are offered in each field. To graduate, each student must pick a field of study and finish the curriculum. They must also, as I mentioned, create their own persona bracelet."

"What classes do you teach?" Sally wondered, forgetting what Dyad had told her earlier.

"I'm the professor of advanced potions."

"Very fitting," Ryan said, smiling.

"I know, right? With my love for chemistry it was the obvious choice."

"Chemistry?" Becky chimed in. "That's one of my favorite subjects, too! I've got a few Chemistry books at home I look over. Too bad they don't offer it until high school."

"Really?" Both Mel and John blurted.

"I never knew that." John was dumbfounded; he thought he knew everything about his sister, but apparently not.

"John, come on." Becky giggled. "How would you know anything about my love of science? You were too busy getting drunk or stoned for most of last year and the year before. And now it's all about football and your own schoolwork."

She tried to keep her voice light, but John felt the pain. He rode the wave of guilt on an uneasy laugh. "I guess you're right."

"Well let me tell you, Becky, I'm pumped to have someone to talk to who's into chemistry, too." Mel's heart skipped; he felt an unfamiliar giddiness, a new sensation that led him to believe he was actually flirting, and not doing too bad a job at it. "You're welcome to come and sit in on one of my lectures. That is, if you want to." He trailed off with a weird croak; there was a frog in his throat. He didn't know if girls liked it if you were too transparent. To avoid further embarrassment he cleared his throat and quickly continued, "You're all welcome to sit in on any class you like while you're here. Just let me know and I can set it up."

Sally, fascinated with history, perked up at the opportunity to learn more about the Enchantas of yesteryear and how it evolved through the cycles. John's interest was piqued by the martial magic. Learning how to fight with magic would be exhilarating. Ryan couldn't pick a favorite. They all sounded interesting.

"I'm intrigued," Becky told Mel. "Count me in."

Her eyes met Mel's and in true love-story fashion his heart skipped a beat. Becky's quick smile was a mystery; he couldn't tell if she was as affected by him as he was by everything about her, from her lively eyes to the rich, slightly teasing tone of her voice.

"So how is everything else going here in Enchantas?" asked Ryan, snapping Mel back to the business at hand. "If they were able to restore this castle to its original state I can only imagine what the rest of the world looks like."

"Enchantian society is blossoming in every community," Mel said, his delight apparent. "We've fully recovered from the battle for Enchantas. Ruphport has cleaned up its act. It's strictly a shipping and trading port. There are still snuffball races, but only for recreational purposes. Gambling is illegal. And you won't believe it, but Foxtown has become a theme park with games and rides. The Duke wanted to make up for all the past cycles of abuse and torment. He figured this was a way to bring joy and excitement back to the citizens. You know the foxes, though. Not all of them went along with the change. Some are roaming the countryside, finding food and shelter wherever they can." He paused, checking to make sure they were all keeping up with his rapid stride. "Rabbit City is the same."

They passed through yet another archway, this one leading into a vast courtyard dotted with artfully landscaped yellow-and-green pine trees. Shining moonlight twinkled and sparkled on the rainbow-hued snow. Becky was so hungry she was tempted to grab a handful. As they made their way across the yard she noticed the bare vines on the walls were also lightly covered with fluorescent snow. She decided it might be more hygienic than eating it off the ground. She trudged on, not wanting to fall behind. Soon, they arrived at another building.

"I can't believe how much this place has changed." John said.

"This is the dormitory," Mel lowered his voice. "We need to keep it down. Most of the students are sleeping. Or studying."

"Gotcha," John whispered. The rest of the group nodded.

The halls were darkened for rest period. Mel raised his hand; a blue torch appeared from his bracelet.

They turned a corner off the corridor; Mel opened the door to a large, round, dome-ceilinged room. The brightly lit ceiling and walls were covered with intricately detailed paintings featuring the entire history of Enchantas. There were portraits of the first miners meeting a group of Enchantians, war scenes and landscapes and tableaux showcasing the building and rebuilding of all the major villages and cities. The visitors almost forgot their hunger as they gazed at the wondrous, immense, creative artistry and another, equally impressive sight: the knights seated at a massively built round table centered in the middle of the opulent chamber.

"Welcome, young Masters," Brian's greeting rang out from the far side of the table, his voice as deep as they remembered. He wore a regal midnight-blue robe embossed down the front with a light purple stripe. His crystal-balled scepter stood propped behind his chair, emanating a soothing blue glow. Looking virtually the same as in the previous visit, Brian showed no signs of age as he sat up straight with imperial bearing. His dark-brown hair and beard long enough to pool on the table top, resting silkily on the flat surface like a soft kitten curled in its favorite napping place. "Please sit wherever you'd like." Brian didn't rise, but conducted the normal courtesies by waving one arm with a practiced flourish. The empty chairs moved a foot away from the table.

They took their places, but not soon enough for a few of the knights who were visibly irritated and impatient with the delay. It seemed the newcomers weren't the only ones who had worked up an appetite.

The huge table sat twenty-five comfortably. At Brian's left sat Firp, a frog attired in the same style: pointy purple hat and long, swirling robes that he'd worn when they met all those cycles ago. His moist green skin shimmered in the light of the overhead chandelier. When the teens had last seen him, during their time trapped on a cursed island, he'd been an apprentice to the Knights. Firp must have moved up in rank, Ryan thought, as there was no other explanation for why he'd be sitting with the council.

"Almost everyone is here. Just a few more ticks," Brian said cheerfully, his smile wreathed by his ornate mustache as well as his beard. "While we're waiting, please share: How was your trip back to Enchantas – and who is this exquisite young newcomer?"

"This is my-" John's introduction barely started before Becky interjected. Slightly hungover and hungry enough to eat her own arm, she was not in the mood for formalities.

"I'm Becky, John's sister." She boldly glanced around the table with challenge in her eyes, making eye contact with each and every Knight, even uncomfortably nodding at the weird frog.

"Welcome," the Knights said in unison, taking her bold initiative in stride.

"Yes, Becky, you are very welcome." Brian expounded on the greeting. "It's a surprise to see an unfamiliar face at this table. A very pleasant surprise, I might add."

"Well thank you, sir." Becky hesitated with the "sir", but it seemed the easiest form of address since she didn't know his name – or anyone else's, for that matter. "It has been," she paused, again searching for the right word, "*mesmerizing* so far. I'm looking forward to learning more about your world."

Brian nodded approval. "Many have been captivated by the tranquil and mystical world of Enchantas. It has been so for many, many cycles, or how do you say it? Years?" Brian chuckled. "It has been a long time since I last visited your world. Much has been lost in translation. Refresh my memory, please Mel, if you haven't forgotten yourself: How many *hours* in a day?"

"Twenty-four, sir," Mel immediately responded. "With sixty minutes to an hour and sixty seconds to a minute."

"Odd," Brian replied. "I find the units bewildering. Our way is much easier. Everything is *even.*" Brian considered this silently for a moment before continuing, "Let's complete the introductions while we wait, shall we? This will benefit more than the beautiful Becky. I don't believe any of you have received a proper introduction to our esteemed council members. There was never an opportune time during your last visit."

Brian took a deep breath and turned to the frog. "This is Firp, who has acquired the position of Herald since you three last visited. He has done quite well with his added responsibilities, documenting much of our evolving history as well as cataloging our school library. Very well done, Firp."

"Thank you, sir." Firp smiled, and licked his own eye with his abnormally long tongue. "Hello again," Firp bowed to the visitors, who nodded in return.

"Next we have David. David is in charge of our criminal investigations unit. Like any society, Enchantas needs to be policed. David runs this division and its subsidiaries." David nodded his bald head in greeting. The red-bearded top cop with the piercing gray eyes looked intimidating. Then he smiled and his entire demeanor changed, making the visitors feel warmly welcomed.

"Next to David we have Rory, who holds the title of Minerton Prison Warden. As a side note, the island where we all were once cursed now serves as the new Enchantian Prison." Brian chuckled again. The jovial leader seemed to enjoy being the center of attention. "We thought it would be fitting."

"Well, that's one way of looking at it," Rory rumbled in a deep, daunting voice that emphasized his authority. Well over six feet tall, the heavy-boned man's hair and beard were a similar shade of brown but much shaggier than Brian's and his dirty face a reminder of his miner's legacy. "Personally, I think I had enough of that island."

"Rory," Brian replied, raising his eyebrows as both chastisement and warning. "You wanted the job."

"Yes, but I didn't know-"

"In any event," Brian interrupted. "Let's move on and save the debates for later, shall we? Next to Rory we have the Honorable Judge Casey." Casey inclined his dark blond head. He also sported a well-trimmed beard, also dark blond. He wore a rich forest-green robe, the hood cowling around his sturdy neck.

"This is Phillip, dear friends. He's with public relations." Phillip flapped a skinny arm in their direction. It was difficult to imagine him working in a Willington mine. He didn't look strong enough to carry rocks of any size, or wield a pickaxe for that matter. The clean-shaven Phillip wore a sky-blue robe that set off his short, bright-white hair.

Brian continued the round with a nod toward the next Knight. "Russell, is our Intelligence Director." Russell avoided their eyes, his blank, emotionless gaze remained focused on Brian. Also clean shaven, he sported the shortest haircut at the table, his black hair trimmed perfectly to the shape of his small head. He was dressed in a dark black formal dress shirt crisscrossed with a silken sky-blue sash. "Russell, say hello to our guests," Brian's suggestion went unanswered. Before the silence could become any more uncomfortable the leader rapidly picked up where he'd left off.

"Moving on to our military contingent," Brian gestured to an attractive man with long blond hair. "We have Robert, Commander of Air Combat. Next to him is Randall, Admiral of the Sea Armada. Daniel," The aforementioned Daniel saluted the newcomers, "is our Infantry General. Finally, we have Major Matthew, who takes full charge of our academy training programs." The uniformed men with their regulation haircuts and hairless faces briefly acknowledged Brian and even more briefly nodded to the visitors. Their stone-faced silence was as off-putting as Russell's taciturn manner.

"Here we have Mark," Brian looked down the table to the third tall skinny man to his right. Becky gave up trying to keep track, barely registering that the guy had a neat, short haircut, no beard and wore a forest-green robe similar to the judge. She stifled a yawn. Sally, Ryan and John also looked like they were fading fast. It had been a very long and emotional Homecoming night. Whizzing around on a flying carpet and walking for miles through candy-colored landscapes and massive castle corridors had taken their toll. Food and bed. That's what she needed. That's what they all needed.

Brian seemed to sense the lagging energy level. "These men are worth their weight in gold, my friends!" he proclaimed, slightly raising his voice to convey enthusiasm for the prestigious gray-haired financiers. "Mark is in charge of the Enchantas economy. He runs the trade and banking industry. Next to him is Treasurer Christopher and finally, William, our Head of Magic Research and Development." All the men nodded in a friendly way, looking almost royal in their matching eggplant-purple robes.

Mel cleared his throat.

"Oh, and how could I forget? Perhaps you aren't yet aware that Mel serves on the council in the vital role of Honorary Secretary. Though he is not fully knighted yet, we expect he will become an enduring member of our governing body in the near future."

Only Ryan and John noticed Mel's momentarily frustrated expression before he quickly masked it with a neutral smile.

Two large arched doors swung open behind Brian. The Knights quieted as the newcomer slowly entered the space. His magnificent head reached the tall dome ceiling; his chestnut-feathered body streaked with silvery-gray plumage was as wide as the table. Becky's eyes widened with amazement, it was a giant owl! No chance of her falling asleep while this intimidating creature was hovering over her. She gulped audibly.

"Please rise for the Grand Sage, the Great Owl!" Firp declared in a trumpeting cry as he stood up in stiff attention. The rest of the council followed suit.

"I am very sorry to be late," the owl apologized in a calm, unruffled, kingly baritone. "I had an urgent meeting with the Representative Committee."

"Does this concern the rule of business that is on our agenda this evening?" asked Brian.

"Yes." the owl nodded.

"Excellent." Brian sat back down. The visitors jumped when he produced a gavel, loudly pounding it on the table. "Let us begin this meeting of the council with an update from our Grand Sage, the Great Owl."

"Thank you, Sir Brian," the owl moved to the opposite side of the room where he could survey the group. "As we all know, the god-daughter of the Witch and Warlock has continued to be aggressive and hostile as she searches for supporters of the old faction in an attempt to build an army."

"These are only rumors," barked Intelligence Director Russell. "There is no validity to this claim."

"True, Russ," Brian agreed. Sally was surprised he used a nickname for the super-pompous bureaucrat. "But there is danger in writing this off; many rumors begin with a grain of truth. Please continue, Honorable Grand Sage."

The owl went on, "Our emergency meeting encompassed every representative of the villages, towns, ports and cities of Enchantas. We have not had a gathering of this magnitude in many cycles. I'd say not since the birth of the new committee."

"This is unheard of. Why was I not made aware of it?" asked PR Director Phillip.

"We did not think it was a public relations issue, Sir Phillip," the owl continued. "Reports of the Banshee's, AKA the Gypsy's, AKA the Empress' recruitment tactics have originated from areas including Foxtown, Rabbit City, Gnelfton, Cloud Island, Ruphport, Enchantic Mines and many smaller villages in between including communities beyond the Grand Enchantic River."

"Has she herself been spotted recruiting?" Brian asked.

"Yes, but my guess is she only goes where she feels safe," the owl took a deep breath. "The Banshee has been wreaking havoc all over Enchantas. Uncooperative villages are being raided. She has also allied with the chameleon gangs."

"This makes sense," David, the Criminal Investigation Director, piped in. "It was a chameleon who made the assassination attempt on Professor Mel."

"Yeah Mel! An assassination attempt is nothing to be taken lightly!" Sally burst out.

"I'm fine Sally." Mel turned to her, his eyes asking for her silence. "Really."

"Mel," Brian looked serious. "You weren't injured, but it was a close call. If you had been alone the chameleon might have succeeded. You are vulnerable. That is why we agreed with the fairies when they strongly recommended that your friends return to be your companions."

"Are you serious?" Mel's erupted. "That's why they're here? Are you kidding me?"

David firmly interjected. "We cannot protect you twenty tocks a day, young Sir. It was Nymph's and Dyad's idea to search out and bring here your most loyal companions, those most able to safeguard your work and your life. The only drawback that gave us pause was the Banshee's extreme hatred for the four prophets of Destiny."

"Banshee?" Ryan looked at Mel. "Are they talking about Lexis?"

"That witch has too many names," Mel replied quietly. "Banshee seems to be the preferred term around here. In the outlying villages she's still known as the Gypsy. Everyone in her presence is expected to address her as Empress — and they do, if they value their lives."

"Thank you again for coming, Sally, Ryan and John." Brian's sincere gratitude showed in his eyes. "Thank you for coming on such short notice."

"We'd do anything to help our friend," said Ryan.

"Yeah," John patted Mel's back. "We're here for you, buddy."

Mel grumbled under his breath. Sally was just about to ask for the details surrounding the attempt on his life when Ryan's keen sense of logic prompted an urgent shift in the conversation.

"If we're going to help we need to know the full story. Maybe I'm wrong to assume this, but I have to ask. Are we being used as bait?"

"No," Russell replied quickly, but after a momentary pause admitted reluctantly, "Sorry, I mean, yes. You are being used as bait. The intelligence committee figured-"

"What the hell? I'm nobody's sacrificial lamb." John butted in. He didn't like being set up. And that was only the start of his objections.

"Our intelligence committee determined that the Banshee is too clever to stay in one place long enough for us to find her," continued Russell. "They recommend luring her instead. Once word of your arrival reaches her it will only be a matter of time before she makes her approach."

"She's a lot of things, but stupid isn't one of them. Of course she'll figure out that angle. Of course she'll beef up her attack. She won't back off. She'll just arrange to have assassins on hand for all of us." Ryan spoke forcefully but quietly, his apparent calm betrayed by his tightened fists and clenched jaw.

"That may be true," agreed Infantry General Daniel. "But we are willing to take that chance."

"And you just assumed that we were willing to go along with this?" Mel was obviously just as irate with the plan.

"This is bull," John swore. "I'm willing to go on the offense and fight, but I'm not gonna just sit here and do nothing. Find us? No way. Let's go find *her*."

"We don't want to send her into hiding, John," Brian countered. "Better to flush her out and deal with her now, before she gains any power or does more damage. Please understand that you are not the proverbial sitting ducks. This school contains specific design features that function as a trap for unwanted visitors. I am sure she will come." Brian gave Sally a look of reassurance. "And when she does, you will all be as safe as you are right now."

"Okay," Sally said, somewhat relieved. She decided to withhold judgment for the time being.

The other three boys and Becky also stayed silent.

"Excellent! And not all is dark and dire." Brian tried to lighten the mood. "The annual Prophet's Day festival is taking place all week. There will be many events; Enchantians from all around the land are coming. Word of your arrival should quickly spread."

"Prophet's Day?" Ryan mouthed at Mel. John gave Mel the side eye, hissing, "Explain."

Mel moved closer so he could fill them in while other council members continued the general discussion. "It's kind of like Christmas, New Years and Thanksgiving, all rolled into one. There's a parade, races, and gladiator games."

"Gladiator games?" John felt the nervous excitement that always accompanied any mention of fighting competition. It was truly his passion.

"Not what you think, John." Mel snorted. "Oh, and there's a fancy Enchantas Ball. It should be fun."

"So, it is settled," Brian rose, gavel in hand. "We shall make preparations to lure the Banshee to the school."

"We will arrest her when the time comes," David finally smiled, a mean, hard grin that was almost a grimace.

"I've got a special prison cell, just waiting for her." Rory bragged.

"I declare this council session closed." Brian slammed the gavel again. "We meet again next week." Brian looked askance at Mel. "How many days is that in the otherworld time?"

"Seven, sir." Mel reminded him.

"So odd. Literally." Brian shook his head as he gathered his scepter and swept out of the room. Some of the council members approached to shake hands and offer personal greetings before slowly clearing the room. The five young people and the owl remained.

"It has been a pleasure to see you three again," the owl pronounced. "I'd nearly forgotten what you look like. The statues of you in the library do not do you justice."

"There are statues of us? How embarrassing." Sally blushed, but she was intrigued and in truth could not wait to see them.

The owl hooted in response, a rolling, trilled, almost dovelike cooing noise that made them all laugh along with the kind, wise Sage. Still in good humor the owl bowed slightly. "Well hello, Miss Becky. It is quite delightful to meet you."

"How do you know my name?" Becky was awed.

"It is my job to know things, my dear," the owl turned briskly toward the door. "I must be off now, my young prophets. This body is not getting any younger, and I must retire to sleep."

Rotating his head all the way around to look over his back and blink a final orb-eyed goodbye, the owl exited and the doors shut of their own volition.

"He said he was old the last time we were here," Sally mused out loud. "He must be ancient by now, but he moves well. And he's funny."

"That's how he concludes almost all of his conversations," Mel said, smiling. "It gets him out of a lot of useless conversations." Mel sat back down. "Who's hungry?"

"Oh my gosh, I'm starving!" Becky flopped down next to Mel, companionably resting her petite, slightly pointed chin on his shoulder. "What's for dinner?"

"Umm. Uh," Mel was trembling. The contact was vibratory, a tingly, amazing feeling that took his words away.

"What's the matter?" Becky jokingly smacked his back. "Are you so hungry that you can't even talk? I could eat my own arm, I swear."

"I think you make him nervous, sis." John winked.

"What? Me? Bull. I'm just trying to be friendly." Becky kissed Mel's cheek, a perfectly innocent smooch that made him break out in a sweat. "Sorry, I get a little loopy when I'm hungry."

Mel was paralyzed; it was the first time he'd ever been kissed by a girl. Other than his mother, of course, but that wasn't even close to the same thing.

"Burf should be in soon," Mel finally got out the words just as the doors on the opposite end of the room opened and a disgruntled looking fat brown rabbit wearing a food-stained white apron stormed into the room. He was holding a large silver pot by its black handle in one paw, juggling a stack of bowls and spoons in the other, and balancing a long, skinny loaf of bright yellow bread between his ears.

"Dinner is served!" Burf announced grumpily. Without further ado he slammed the pot on the table hard enough to spatter the contents as he slid the bowls across to the other end of the table and dealt out the spoons, slapping one in front of each diner. "You'd better like it! Making me slave over this in the dead of night of all things! You know, Professor, I do have a bedtime! I have a life! And I'm sure everyone expects a good breakfast in the morning too."

"I'm sorry, Burf. We appreciate your culinary efforts," said Mel, trying to keep a straight face as the huffy chef aired his grievances.

"I should say so! I want it on the record right now that if breakfast is not up to everybody's specifications or standards in the morning I am personally blaming you."

"That's fine," Mel really did feel bad. "But this is a special dinner for my friends and they just got here after traveling a long way."

"Yeah, yeah," Burf said dispassionately as he hopped away. "Prophets, flopits, I don't care. I've got a festival crowd to cook for and I'm already in the weeds with too much to do in too short a time. They may be the stars of the show but nobody's happy if they can't eat!"

"Sorry again, Burf." Mel was truly contrite.

Burf wasn't finished. "One more thing. You all better like what I made!" He pointed at each individual kid. "Otherwise, I'll make you do dishes all week. And don't think I can't. I have allies you know."

Everyone stared silently at their one-spoon place setting as the door slammed behind him.

"My God," Becky held back a giggle. "Is he always like that?"

"No, not all the time," Mel replied. "He's usually crabbier. Sorry."

"No, don't be sorry, I kind of like him. Are all rabbits here like that?"

"Nope," Mel smiled. "Burf is one in a million." Mel grabbed the pot, scooping stew into bowls. "Let's eat."

When he was finished dishing up the main course Mel set to work cutting the bread. Becky, tentatively sniffing her stew, watched the others eat. It smelled good, like old fashioned vegetable stew but with a sweet curry flavoring.

"This is really good," said John, too hungry to care about talking with his mouth full. He bit into his bread. "Wow, what kind of bread is this? It's delicious. I'm getting sweet, but a little spicy, too."

"It's gnye bread." Mel's mouth was also full. "The gnomes and elves make it. The gnye grain comes from the yellow plains where Lexis cursed us."

"Let's not go there," said John. "You'll ruin my appetite."

"Why, what happened?" asked Becky. Gathering her courage, pushed by extreme hunger, she took her first bite. A jolt of amazing flavor instantly hit her taste buds. She moaned. "This stuff is fantastic!"

"Pretty good, huh?" Mel gleamed with pride. The crabby rabbit was a culinary genius. There was a reason everyone he cooked for put up with his abrasive personality.

As they ate, Ryan paused between spoonfuls to bring Becky up to speed. "Last time we were here the Gypsy, real name Lexis, also called the Banshee – the one everyone is talking about – cursed us. She paralyzed me. Sally was blind. John's mouth disappeared and Mel lost his hearing."

"That's horrible. How did you get away?"

"Luck," Sally said. "I tripped over a bottle which broke. Then a bus-sized blue worm came out of it and granted us wishes."

"Wow! If I'd heard that yesterday I'd have said you're all crazy. But not anymore." Becky spooned into her stew. "Is there enough for seconds?"

As Mel refilled Becky's bowl Sally started in on the questions that had been collecting in her brain since they arrived.

"Mel, did you say there are elves here?"

"Yeah," Mel passed Becky her bowl. "Believe it or not, the elves, gnomes, dwarves and leprechauns are cousins by race."

"What do you mean?" Sally was intrigued, excited to hear her first Enchantas history lecture.

"Well, when Enchantas was founded, there were human-like beings here that the miners called 'munchkins.' The name began as a joke in reference to the 'Wizard of Oz,' but over time these little beings began to separate into groups. Not as enemies but because

92

they chose to live different types of lives. Different factions formed unique and diverse societies. First there were the elves. They mostly lived on top of the trees and build vast cities in the forest canopies. Elves are adventurous and outgoing. They are hunters and gatherers — of vegetables, mostly. They maintain a friendly relationship with the gnomes.

"Gnomes are usually scholars and historians. Unlike the elves they live secluded, quiet lives in small villages. Their homes are underneath the trees amongst the root structures. Both species are hospitable and friendly. There is even a conjoined city, Gnelfton. But the elves and gnomes seldom visit their cousin dwarves. And they despise the leprechauns. You can distinguish elves from the others because they normally wear blue. Gnomes can be identified by their long, stiff, pointed hats, like Gitchy's. At least that's how I can tell the difference."

"That's really interesting," said Sally. "What about the dwarves and leprechauns?"

"I really don't want to know about leprechauns." John remembered his interactions with Liddy the leprechaun the last time he was in Enchantas. "Feel free to skip that part of the lecture."

"But you need to know about them, John." Mel looked concerned. "There are *so* many dangerous beings here. When we were here the first time no one warned us what to watch out for. I'm really, really surprised that we survived."

"Fine," John sighed.

"Well," said Mel, relieved to continue covering the safety basics, "Dwarves are easy to deal with. They're very plain folk, cranky and unsociable. They just want to be left alone in their mines and caves. They operate a vast transportation system of underground tunnels and roads far larger than the networks of rabbits and prairie dogs but serving the same purpose: to isolate them and keep them safe from predators. Though the dwarves are incredibly touchy and normally quite antisocial, they can't help but be hospitable when visitors arrive." Mel smiled slightly. "They always want to figure out what they can get from you. But if you hang around long enough, your 'welcome' becomes very thin.

"Leprechauns are disliked by basically everyone in Enchantas, especially by their three cousins: the elves, the dwarves, and the gnomes. They are the disliked and distrusted, black sheep of that family, if you will. The leprechauns didn't leave on good terms when they started their own society. Actually they didn't leave of their own free will. The original founders were banished for stealing gold and lixy rock from the miners. Since then they've upheld their reputation for being tricky, sly, and greedy thieves who steal from their own kind and anyone else who has something they covet. It's been difficult for the Knights to keep the peace."

"Are there any good leprechauns?" asked Sally.

"Yes. There are a few, and in our commitment against prejudice we try to give them the benefit of the doubt. We have a leprechaun attending the institute. He's a troublemaker and I don't trust him; although he's an academically superior student."

"It's a shame they can't work out their differences," Sally said. "After all, they come from the same family tree; it's just the branches that are different."

"It is a shame," Mel agreed. "Especially since leprechauns and dwarves do have one thing in common: Their enthusiasm for doing the dirty jobs that no one else wants to do. If they united, they could be a true economic force."

It wasn't long before everyone else finished first helpings of stew and gnye bread. Mel obligingly served seconds – and thirds, to Becky. She looked around the room, less hungry after the filling meal and able to better process the tremendous amount of wonderment invoked by this new and totally alien place. She was still astounded by how comfortable John and his friends were in this strange world. They didn't appear to see Enchantas as all that different from their world. But she knew that it was, although she could tell her opinion and comfort level was already changing.

Sally was enjoying the exhilaration and excitement coursing through her veins as the realization that she had returned to Enchantas clicked in. The events of her previous visit had forever and drastically changed for the better who she was and who she would become. The petty jealousy that had consumed her earlier in the evening had completely transmuted and transfigured into a steady, confident sense of belonging and well-being. She would never forget what this land had done for her, how it had given her back her parents and restored her self-esteem. Enchantas would forever be her home away from home.

Ryan was feeling jumpier than usual. He didn't want to be used as bait. He trusted Mel but otherwise questioned the council's motives and judgment. He struggled to believe that they would not put him and his friends in harm's way. In his gut, he also had doubts that the council could protect them if they were put in harm's way. Looking at John, who was clearly protective of his sister, Ryan wondered if he was as worried about the girls as he was. Sally wasn't a fighter. Becky acted tough, but she didn't understand the no-holds-barred battle rules of this ever-changing land. She'd never met the evil Gypsy, quick to befriend but even quicker to brutally reverse. What would they do if they lost them?

John cleared his mind as he ate his food, savoring the flavors of the delicious meal. For the time being he was free of worries and enjoying the moment of peace.

The doors opened again, admitting young female fox wearing a long, flouncy purple skirt and holding a serving plate.

"I almost forgot about dessert." Mel sat up excitedly. "The bad thing though; we only have three. I wasn't expecting Becky to be coming." Mel gave her a mischievous wink.

"Thanks anyway, Mel. I'm stuffed. Couldn't even think of having another bite."

"Thanks Mel," John said, sniffing the aromatic pie the smiling fox placed in front of him. "Becky, that's too bad. Are you sure I can't save you a bite?"

"This looks great, Mel," Ryan added. "Cherry, right? I know you didn't make it yourself but please pass on our thanks to the chef."

"No problem," Mel bit his cheeks, trying not to laugh. "Let me know how you like it."

Sally, Ryan and John took their first bites in unison and instantly squealed like agitated pigs.

Becky watched her brother's head jerk back and forth. His chin dropped to his chest and back up. His eyes squeezed shut and his cheeks sucked into his mouth. "Mel! What did you do?"

"They'll be fine," he laughed, watching Sally and Ryan go through the same gyrations, their faces so severely puckered, they resembled shriveled prunes.

Becky was at a loss for the right adjective as she stared at Sally's wrinkly raisin of a face, eyes only slightly open, mouth nose, chin and cheek pushed together. "Why are they all squinchy?" she finally hollered. "What did you do?"

"It's my puckerberry pie!" Mel bent over laughing.

"Yur wat?" John could only open his mouth as wide as a dime. "Wut the hall was tat?"

"My goosh!" Sally's face was just as scrunched together, if not more because she'd taken a bigger bite than the guys. "Tat wuz the must sour ting I huv ever had!"

"Wut the heck, Mil," Ryan crossed his arms. Trying to look angry and serious, but his scrunched up face was much too funny to take seriously. "I'm pished."

"Oh come on guys," Mel laughed and stood up. "It was just a joke!"

"If it wush jusht a joke," John mumbled. "Why wasn't my shister in it?"

"We actually only did have three pieces left," Mel looked at Becky. She was laughing so hard her eyes were watering. "You're welcome to have some, Becky."

"No thanks," Becky wiped at the tears running down her face. "John, you have to look in the mirror."

"Even ish I had a mirror, I can't shee out of my eyesh!"

"Oh don't be a baby, John." Mel laughed again. "The affects will only last a few tocks; you'll be sleeping before then."

"Others actually eat thish pie?" asked Sally, trying to open her eyes. She pushed the plate away in annoyance.

"Not exactly." Mel gathered the plates. "I actually invented the puckerberries." Mel pulled one out of a piece of pie and showed them. Becky, however, was the only one who could see it. The grape-sized bright purple berry was shaped like an octahedron. "During my first couple cycles here I had a craving for sour food. The lixy fruit just couldn't cut it. I wanted something more sour and tart. It took some time, but I came up with these puckerberries. Pretty good huh? I was striving for the sourest food in both worlds."

"They are sho shour!" Ryan tried prying his eyes open with his fingers. His mouth and cheeks were beginning to hurt.

"Oh, my," Sally began touched her face anxiously. "I can't feel a shing!"

"Sorry about that. The paralysis is a temporary side effect. Trust me, you'll be back to normal in the morning." Mel went to the door and called. "Buttercup!"

"Yes sir?" the fox-maiden returned.

"Please show our guests to their rooms. Before long, they won't be able to move, so it'd be best to get them to bed right away." Mel looked at his friends. Their contorted faces were difficult to read but the body language spoke volumes. He

97

wondered if the anger would last longer than the paralysis. "They must be very tired," he told Buttercup.

"Yes, sir," she agreed.

"Urineusshole," Sally swore for the first time in front of him.

"Hey, just a gag for old time's sake," Mel said, barely controlling his smirk. "I didn't mean to make you so mad, just figured you might have missed my practical jokes."

Becky exited last, making sure the others didn't see as she leaned in, whispering, "Good one!" They exchanged a congratulatory high five. "See you in the morning," she said.

He could hardly wait.

"Well, well," Mel whispered to himself. "I'm glad someone here appreciates my work."

With a quick flick of his wrist, Mel extinguished the candles in the council chambers, retiring to his room for the kind of good night's sleep you can only achieve with a clear conscience.

Chapter V
Breakfast

The smell of rotting onions stung John's nostrils as he strained to open his aching, bloodshot eyes. He tried to rub his throbbing temples, only to discover his hands were behind his back, chained to his legs. He was kneeling on a small wooden trolley which appeared to have been pulled by an over-sized turquoise rabbit. The rabbit was lying on the ground covered with blood, its left ear nearly cut in half. It gasped for air, desperate to breathe.

John cautiously took in his surroundings. He saw packs of orange furry animals that looked like overgrown foxes. Their yellow eyes scowled with hatred as they revealed their sharp fangs in anticipation of a hearty feast. Many wore yellow, green, or blue sashes; a few were clad in silver armor. An unbearable stench emanated from each grotesque beast, wrapping him in a nauseating rotten-meat-and-manure-sweat cloud that made him gag every few seconds.

Further covert inspection showed he was in a gray cobblestone paved courtyard encircled by brown and gray mud colored buildings. The town itself seemed to be drooping and lopsided, full of crooked angles and uneven surfaces, probably due to poor design and engineering. Every window was either broken or severely cracked. The narrow streets exiting the courtyard led directly to a small castle in the center of the town.

"Hear ye, hear ye," a familiar voice shouted. John looked quickly as a leprechaun wearing all green except for John's black leather jacket walked towards him. "Hello to all citizens of Foxtown. Me's come, yet again, to sell me current stock."

John swore, realizing that this was the leprechaun who had tricked and drugged him back in the forest after he'd left Ryan, Mel and Sally to go off on his own. Oh, how he'd hated being in this whacked-out place. He'd been stupid to fight with Ryan. If he'd backed off, just walked away, neither one of them would have fallen into that treacherous well. His aggressive, irrational behavior had landed them here, in Enchantas, trapping them in an unsolvable predicament. Then he made matters worse by abandoning the only true friends he'd ever had. Ditching Ryan, Mel, and Sally in the valley had created the perfect opening for this crazy, conniving leprechaun to rip him off.

"Let me go!" John demanded, tumbling over as he tried to get up without having arms for balance. "Give me my jacket back, you ugly little half pint!"

A few of the hideous fox citizens squealed with laughter.

"Can't do that. Me selling ye, me lad," the grinning leprechaun sniffed, helping the boy back to his knees.

"Selling me for what?"

"Profit, of course," Liddy looked over to the restless crowd. They had been anxious to see what their friendly leprechaun had brought to them today.

"What is it Liddy?" A curious fox growled from the crowd. John noticed that all the foxes suffered from a terrible lisp.

"My dear friends," Liddy waved his tiny arm gesturing to the boy. "This here is a human-being!"

100

The crowd gasped a mixture of stunned fright and bloodthirsty excitement.

"Three buttons." A fox wearing a green sash bartered.

"Three buttons?" Insulted, Liddy mimicked the lisping fox as his face turned a rage-infused red-purple beet color. "That is outrageous! When is the last time ye seen a human? They all but extinct in these here parts."

"Does it know magic?" A female fox asked rather curiously. She wore a brown, floral-patterned dress, her fluffy white-tipped tail wagging free like a decorative plume outside a cleverly designed vent. "Yes, Liddy," the female's husband came up behind her. "It won't be any use to me if it can vanish with the use of magic or use it against me."

"Don't ye think if it knew magic, it had done it by now?" Liddy smirked proudly. "It tis in chains and yer all safe fer now."

"Good point," the fox nodded "Five buttons."

Liddy became a little more furious, blurting out, "Aren't ye listening? This is a human boy! Come now, someone be want him fer a good price?"

"TWENTY golden buttons!" a one-eyed fox snarled, walking confidently and deliberately out of the crowd. A young female fox kit peered shyly from her hiding place tucked against her father's hindquarters.

"Much better," Liddy murmured to himself. "Ahh, we gotta winner! Me old friend, Trox!" He walked up to him shaking his paw. "Still running the games, me sees."

"Yes, old friend," Trox smiled after taking a large bite out of a red rabbit's foot. "And with this human here, my profits may triple." Trox rubbed John's cheek.

"Don't touch me!" John swore and spit in the fox's face.

"Ha!" He laughed. "A feisty one, eh? Perfect. The feisty ones make excellent gladiators."

"I'm not a gladiator." John spit in his face again.

"Oh, yes!" Trox nibbled on the rabbit foot in delight. "We will make you into a fighter soon enough!"

"Let me go!" John yelled at Liddy.

But Liddy had already snatched his bag of money. "Sorry friend. Ye have been sold!"

"What? No! You can't do this! This isn't right!"

"Oh yes, me lad!" Liddy shook the bag of buttons. "Me can and me did! Now yer fun begins!"

"I'll get you for his Liddy!" John screamed. "Just you wait! I'll get you back!"

Liddy only chuckled as he counted his gold buttons.

"All right, let's go, you mangy rabbit!" Trox whipped the beaten turquoise rabbit. It slowly rose and pulled the trolley from the courtyard and up the spiral streets of the town.

"You're mine now, human!" Trox began to laugh, a very sinister and demented sound that seemed to last forever.

Panicked, John struggled to move, to break free, but the more he tried the more restricted he became. There was no use, his fate was sealed.

John abruptly woke in a dark room, disoriented and sweaty. He watched as a stream of light pierced the floor-length curtains and realized he was safely in Minerton Castle and just awaked had a nightmare. He spotted movement in the far corner of the room. Whatever was moving; moved closer.

With the Foxtown nightmare fresh in his mind, John was ready to jump out of his skin, heart racing and fingers quivering. Even his eyebrows felt twitchy. He sat up swiftly, groping for a weapon as the curtains smoothly slipped open, as if on casters. Bright sunlight suddenly encased the room. John's eyes took a moment to adjust and when they did he saw Buttercup approaching slowly, stalking like a huntress, a wickedly sharp serrated bone-handled knife in her hand. She snarled, bearing pointed, with razor-sharp yellow teeth. Completely unprotected, John was convinced he was doomed.

Surprisingly, the young fox greeted him with a cheerful smile and said, "Good morning Master." She was prettily clad in a long, sandy-colored tan dress with no menacing teeth in sight. "I've brought your breakfast." Her voice, soft and gentle, was the opposite of what John had learned to expect from foxes. "Snuffball egg omelets are my favorite. I hope you like them, too. Burf fixed them up special."

John kept quiet. He hated to be so suspicious but friendly foxes were an anomaly and with assassins loose, none of them could be too careful. "Try it," Buttercup urged, holding a forkful up to his mouth. "Trust me. It's really good."

The aroma was rich and inviting. John instinctively opened his mouth. "It *is* good. Thank you," he told her. "I'm wondering something, no offense." Buttercup nodded for him to proceed. "You don't have a lisp. I thought all of the foxes had a 'lithp'."

She handed him a full plate, along with silverware. "Since education has come to the forefront of life in Enchantas we've benefitted from speech therapy. And I'm so glad you like the food! My name is Buttercup, I don't think we were properly introduced last night. Anything that's needed, please let me know."

They shook, hand to paw, before John dug into his nourishing breakfast. His taste buds had recovered but his face still felt slightly numb from last night's puckerberry trick.

"Professor Mel never tires of his puckerberry prank," Buttercup remarked as she watched him feel his face to ensure it was still there. "Everyone at school, from professors, to students and staff – even the Knights – has experienced the puckerberry prank. Ever since he invented those berries, it's been the traditional orientation dessert for all incoming students and visitors." Brandishing her tail, Buttercup began dusting the room.

"Yeah, Mel's a real prankster. He's been that way for as long as I've known him. But sometimes the joke's on him."

John recalled how Mel's love-spell had backfired on Ryan and Sally. Eventually they got payback using a love spell of their own, but unfortunately John was caught in that crossfire and Mel was temporarily fixated on him, very embarrassing for both.

He chuckled, shrugging his shoulders. "He's usually harmless. And he has a good heart."

"That's true," Buttercup agreed, casting her long-lashed eyelids down demurely before adding, "I must say that after hearing of your arrival – you and the other prophets, I mean – you were the only one I wanted to meet. I've seen you before. I was very, very young. But I've never forgotten. You were being sold by Liddy the leprechaun in Foxtown. Trox was my father."

John was stunned. He remembered Trox well. He and Ryan had battled her father in the gladiator cages beneath the Foxtown dungeons.

They had killed Trox during the battle of Enchantas.

"Please, don't worry John," Buttercup smiled. "No hard feelings. My mother asked me to pass on a message. She thanks you for saving our world. My father was, let's say in bland terms, a real big jerk. He was cruel to everyone. He cared for no one but himself. Our lives are better now. And without the help of you and your friends, I would never have been able to go to school, to learn magic."

Speechless at first, John just smiled. Then he realized what he wanted to say. "Thank you, Buttercup! I'm glad to hear that we made a difference. But it's all of you living here who have really made the changes for the better. Enchantas has changed a lot since we've been gone." A moment of silence came over him, trying to imagine what Foxtown looked like now, as an amusement park. "How is your mother? What does she do now?"

"My mother is still in Foxtown," Buttercup said, smiling. "It's a theme park now, you know. Professor Mel's and the Duke's idea. A good one too. Foxtown has become one of the richest cities in Enchantas and by honorable means, not by stealing, or slavery or gladiator fights. We just sell family-oriented fun at a reasonable price."

"Wow, that's wonderful."

"Mother used to do laundry for all of the gladiators and soldiers. But now she owns one of the largest gaming circuits in the city." Her chores complete, Buttercup shook her tail out the open window before heading to the door. "Well, I'd better get going. There's a lot to do before the festival begins. Your clothes are on the table over there. I'm sure I'll see you later."

"Thanks so much, Buttercup." John went back to eating his omelet. After he'd cleaned his plate, he hopped out of bed and glanced around the room, ten times larger than his bedroom at home and much tidier, but then, he didn't have a fox-maiden to pick up after him at home. The serene purple-and-gold décor, from plush tapestry rugs to the opulent comforter, made him feel pampered and comfortable.

John put on the black pants and slate-green shirt Buttercup had left for him. As he buttoned the shirt he looked at the view out the window, down onto a spacious, fully enclosed courtyard, apparently at the heart of the castle. Enchantian students carrying books hustled and bustled below, hurrying to their next lab or lecture.

As John scoped the busy scene below more closely he noticed something startling: Becky and Mel holding each other's hands.

John cursed, flying straight into protective brother mode as he stormed out of the room.

***

Becky slowly opened the door leading from her bedroom into the hall. She hoped it wouldn't creak. She took a quick look in both directions to make sure no one would see her, then dashed to the nearest stairwell. Nothing would deter her from her morning ritual of having the first cigarette of the day.

After tip-toeing down the stairs as fast as possible, she'd almost reached the exit when a harsh voice startled her, bringing her to a frozen halt.

"Where do you think you're going, little lady?" It was Burf, that fat brown rabbit. He had a cigar clamped between his teeth, a pot in one paw and a dripping spoon in the other, as if his stirring had been interrupted. He was wearing the same, stained apron he'd worn the night before. "Isn't it a little early to be running off?"

Becky saw no reason to fib to a fellow smoker. She pulled out the cigarette pack and Zippo from her inherited leather jacket. "I was looking for a place to smoke a cigarette."

"A cigarette? What's that?"

"Kind of like your cigar, but smaller."

"Ahh," Burf's ears twitched. "Well, you're talking to the right rabbit. I'm one of the few smokers around here. And those of us who do smoke, do our smoking in the kitchen. Come, please have a seat." Burf pointed at a stained bar stool across from him.

"Isn't that a little unsanitary?" Becky came into the adjacent room and sat down. The kitchen was filthy, from the dirty floors and greasy walls to the mounds of unwashed dishes covering nearly every surface.

"Unsanitary?" Burf snorted, flicking cigar ash into the pot he was still holding before slapping it down on a crusty burner atop a humongous wood-burning stove. "That's what gives the food I serve the real flavor. What rubbish that you'd think otherwise! Clearly you know nothing about the culinary arts."

"No offense," Becky lit up, taking a huge drag on her cigarette. She exhaled gratefully, "I was just saying."

"My cigar ash is what imparts that wonderful smoky flavor in my special stew you enjoyed last night."

"Oh, really?" Becky didn't know what else to say. The stew had been delicious, but the thought of eating ashes was nauseating.

"Yes sirree, young lady, I've got a million chef's tricks and secret ingredients you've never heard of," Burf said, retrieving a plate from the oven. He handed her the slightly warm crockery filled with what looked like pancakes. He fiddled in his apron pocket, producing a fork which he wiped with a corner of the fabric. "Ah, here we are."

Becky shrank from the proffered utensil, looking for an empty spot to set the plate down. "Thank you, but I don't usually eat breakfast."

"Don't eat breakfast?" Burf was outraged. "That's the craziest thing I've ever heard. It's the most important meal of the day. It's the greasiest!"

Becky gave in, accepting the fork while putting the cigarette down in an ashtray. Becky slowly took a bite of the pancake-like food.

"I wouldn't eat that," Burf said casually. "It's supposed to be used for fertilizing the veggies." He slowly turned around giving her a blank stare.

Becky emptied her mouth cautiously by scraping her tongue. She grabbed a glass of what resembled orange juice and put it to her mouth to wash it down.

"I'm only kidding. The fertilizer is what you are about to drink."

Becky quickly put the glass down.

"You're horrible, Burf! Worse than Mel." Becky declared, then smiled. "I like that."

"Why thank you," he said, furiously stirring the now-bubbling concoction in the pot. "So how are you liking your stay here in Enchantas?"

"It's going pretty good," Becky said. "You know, this was the last place I ever thought I'd end up when I was drinking alone on my porch last night. I mean, come on, there's a fantasy world underneath my home town. Who knew?"

"Ah, but what if you're only dreaming?" Burf asked mischievously as he disgorged a heap of dishes from under a water pump in the crowded sink, proceeding to fill another larger pot with water.

"Trust me, I've wondered. I tried pinching myself awake last night. I've got bruises all over myself to prove it."

"And I'm sure talking to a fat old rabbit like me isn't helping your sanity, either." He laughed uproariously, sprinkling powdery green flecks of seasoning in both pots.

"Not at all," she chuckled.

Burf bent down to open a basket, pulling out a potato, carrot, onion and mushroom which he forcefully held down with the weight of his furry arm. "Well brace yourself. This isn't likely to help your frame of mind, either."

Becky took a closer look at the vegetables and wondered if she was hallucinating. They had little arms and legs which were moving frantically, as if they were trying to escape.

"What the heck," Becky felt woozy. She jumped when the carrot screamed.

"Ahh! Let me go!" its voice was as ear-piercing and it appeared to be angry as well as horrorstruck. "Let me go you fat, ugly rabbit!"

"That's it! No one calls me fat but me!" Burf raised his butcher knife, slicing off one of its arms and both legs in two neat passes.

"Aaaahhh!" the carrot shrieked even louder, pleading, "Why did you do that? Are you mad?"

"Oh my God, Burf!" Becky stepped away from the table in shock. "They're alive!"

"They are," Burf confirmed, clamping down on his still-smoking cigar as he concentrated on the necessary slaughter. "But only until I kill them. There," he said. "Got it!" he tossed the remaining arm in the pot along with the other limbs.

"Oh please, stop the pain!" the carrot moaned pathetically.

"At least be humane and put him, it, whatever, out of his misery," Becky pleaded.

"Nah. The more they scream and wiggle, the better they taste." Burf finally tossed the carrot into the stewpot. "You'll know the stew is done when the screaming stops. When they're nice and chewy, with a pleasantly nutty undertone."

"I'm burning!" the carrot wailed. "Stop the pain! Stop the pain!"

Burf proceeded to the onion. "No, please! I have family! Please don't do this," it begged, but with another two swipes of the knife it too was helpless and in pain.

"Sorry, Burf," Becky stepped back in shock. "I don't think I can handle this horror show."

Becky was about to stub out her cigarette when Burf stopped her. "Here. Gimme that real quick." He gestured imperiously.

She handed over the half-finished cigarette.

"Perfect," smiling demonically, Burf slowly lowered the burning embers toward the onion, thoroughly burning the surface. It screamed piteously. "Just a hint of crisp," the torturer proclaimed. He was enjoying his work.

"Don't go, little lady. You haven't finished your breakfast."

"That's quite all right, Burf," Becky started toward the door. "I've lost my appetite."

"I do apologize," Momentarily distracted, Burf unconsciously lifted his arm. The potato scurried off the table, shooting past Becky out the door to freedom.

"Too fat to catch me, rabbit!" the potato squealed victoriously as it made a triumphant escape.

"No matter, there's always one that gets away." Burf snarled at the panicked mushroom, who was pacing the cutting board urgently seeking a way out. It was too small and fragile to make it to the floor. "And where do you think you're going, my little mushroom?"

"Please, please, let me go," the mushroom was in tears.

Burf only smiled viciously, his knife raised high.

Without hesitation and with nowhere else to turn the desperate mushroom spun around and jumped, inadvertently landing in the steaming stew pot.

"Owwww!" the mushroom futilely scraped its little fingers against the inside of the pot, trying to climb out. "Wrong way! Wrong way!"

"Stupid 'shroom!" Burf cackled. "Of course that was the wrong way."

The screams from the kitchen echoed through the castle corridors. Becky moved away somewhat dazed from the shock of watching the slaughter. Students began to pass her, laughing and smiling with one another as they carried on normal friendly conversations. All were seemingly impassive of the vegetable massacre that was occurring in the *kitchen of death*. She was outraged by the indifference. No one came to the defense of the poor little veggies.

"Good morning, Becky," Mel smiled brightly as he greeted her where she had stood frozen in the hallway, numbed by the lack of concern for the wholesale slaughter. "How are you? Did you have breakfast yet?"

"Don't you hear that?" Becky shouted. "Don't you care?"

"Hear what?" Mel asked, sincerely confused.

"The death screams of those vegetables!"

"Right," Mel could see her anxiety mounting. "Of course, follow me," Mel took her stiff hand, pulling her away. "We hear it every morning. I call it the '*wake-up call.*' "

They walked out to the interior the courtyard and sat on a bench underneath a yellow-and-blue maple tree. Becky was shaking with revulsion and rage.

"That is so – so ... disturbing," she managed to get out.

"Yeah," Mel put his arm around her shoulders. "I thought so too at first, but then I got used to it."

"But they're just dying in there," Becky turned toward the kitchen door. They could still hear the agonized screams. "They're being tortured."

"Becky, I'm truly sorry you had to see that. It is hard." He wondered how long it would take her to get used to the idea of eating them. "How can I help you relax?"

Becky silently pulled out another cigarette and lit it, but somehow each drag reminded her of the singed onion.

"Oh, you smoke?" Mel pulled out his pipe and sparked a match. "I don't do tobacco. I'm into this wimple weed. It tastes better and calms the nerves. Try it."

Becky took a long toke of Mel's pipe, closing her eyes. "It's all right. I'm not a fan of toffee flavor." Her nerves began to cool.

"Not everyone is," Mel said, taking a puff, and changing the subject, trying to lighten the mood. "You're in eighth grade, right?"

"That's right." She usually lied about her age but for some reason it didn't feel right. Not here. Not with him.

"I remember you from last year in middle school," Mel didn't expect her to remember. "I talked to you once."

"Really? Sorry. I don't remember."

"Didn't think you would," Mel took another puff. "We were in the office waiting to talk to the principal. I think you were there for skipping class. I was there because I exchanged Miss Philips' hairspray with homemade hair dye."

"That was you?" Becky laughed. "She had blue hair for like a week!"

"Yeah, I knew it would work because she sprays her helmet-hair incessantly," Mel giggled.

"Right," Becky smiled. "You can't get within five feet of her without gasping for air."

Mel nodded, remembering that day. At the time, he was excited to have the chance to talk with Becky. He didn't mind that she was a grade below him. He just thought she was really pretty. He was grateful he'd gotten in trouble at the same time she did. He would have never had the courage to talk to her otherwise.

The courtyard of the Institute was vibrant with a light base of snowfall on the ground. Paw tracks of rabbits, foxes, dogs, cats, skunks, squirrels, chipmunks and other Enchantians tracks like gnomes, elves, dwarves and turtles scattered the square.

Becky looked up at the clock again. It was 8:65. She was still fascinated by the time difference. "So what time is it back in our world?"

"Depends on when you left," replied Mel. "To be specific, what I've learned is that one Enchantian day is about fifteen minutes in our world. So one day back home is ninety-six Enchantian days."

"So you've been here for about two months, which is," Becky paused to calculate. "Something like 5,760 Enchantian days. You look so young!"

"Yeah," Mel was surprised at her quick math. "A little over fourteen Enchantian years, or cycles. But I still only aged about two months in our world. So technically, I'm still fourteen."

"That must make you almost an immortal here right?"

"Kind of. Most of the Knights have been here from the beginning. I'd like to say that was around twenty years ago or so in our world. But I'm not too sure." Mel gave a little snort. "I'll let you do the math on that."

Becky stood quiet for a moment, calculating the math, but quickly gave up and said, "What an amazing experience!"

"Tell me about it. I've learned so much during my time here," Mel smiled. "But hearing that my mother has been looking for me makes me a little sad."

Becky grabbed his hand, "Mel, I wouldn't worry too much, if she knew where you've been and that you're okay, I'm sure she'd be happy for you."

"I guess." Mel replied. After a few moments of silence, he realized they were holding hands. He smiled blissfully up until he saw John walking toward them, with an angry stride. Mel released Becky's hand with a quick jerk.

"What's going on here?" John bellowed.

"What are you, my father?" Becky asked snidely.

Uncomfortable beyond anything he'd ever experienced, Mel decided his best move was to move on rather than confronting John. "I'd better get going. I shouldn't be late for my lecture."

"I'll see you later, Mel. Thanks again!" Becky offered her most alluring smile to the young professor before turning to her brother with an irritated glare. "What's your problem?" she hissed, not wanting Mel to hear them argue.

John stood over her, trying to be intimidating. "I didn't bring you here to flirt with my friends!"

"Flirt?" Becky stood up so she could be face to face with her brother. "I was not flirting, he's a nice guy."

"Becky, I know how you are," John calmed down just a bit.

"What are you talking about?" Becky became even more defensive.

"Never mind," John huffed. He wasn't in the mood to argue. Honestly he knew that part of it was that he just didn't like seeing her with guys — any guy — even his friend.

"Fine. Whatever." Becky began to storm off.

"Where are you going?"

"To Mel's lecture and be around someone who isn't a jerk."

John was about to follow her until he was interrupted by Ryan and Sally's arrival.

"Hey guys, good morning," said Ryan. He wore the same style attire as John, but his shirt was a steely dark blue. "How are you doing?"

"I was doing fantastic until John came to pester me," Becky sniffed. "I'll see you two later. I need a change of scenery."

"Becky! Wait!" John called as she stalked away.

"What was that all about?" asked Sally. She wore loose-fitting wide-legged tan pants with a snug-fitting blue shirt. "Is she all right?"

"She was holding hands with Mel. I guess I'm too overprotective."

"John, she'll be fine," said Ryan. "You can trust Mel."

"Yeah," Sally agreed. "And your sister can take care of herself."

"You're probably right." John exhaled.

"Want to come for a walk with us? Maybe take your mind off things?" asked Ryan. "We want to take a look around before we hit a lecture."

"Sure," John felt bad about arguing with his sister. He needed the comfort of his friends.

They toured walkways outside, and crossed the small drawbridge to a smaller courtyard. They heard squeaky, high-pitched voices coming from the far cobbled wall and noticed a dozen different colored basketball-sized balls lined up next to a small tree.

"Look!" Sally squealed in delighted recognition. "Snuffballs!"

As the trio drew closer they could hear an argument taking place between the little colored balls.

"I'm not taking 'er!" a pink-cotton-candy colored snuffball with a squeaky voice wailed. "Put Channy on your team!"

114

"No way!" a pale yellow snuffball bounced. "Channy will slow us down! You take 'er!"

"Well," a vivid purple snuffball proposed bluntly, "If no one wants you on their team Channy, you will just have to leave."

"But I want to play!" a tiny, fist-sized turquoise snuffball pleaded. "Come on. *Please*?"

"No!" the other snuffballs exclaimed.

"You're too small Channy," a coral-colored snuffball pounced on Channy. "No one wants you here! Now leave!"

"Yeah leave," a crimson snuffball rolled in and pushed Channy, sending her flying. She slammed hard against a tree trunk and rebounded against Sally's foot. The rest of the snuffball contingent rolled out of the courtyard.

"Oh dear!" Sally quickly bent over to pick Channy up. "Are you all right, little one?"

Channy quivered profusely in Sally's palm.

"Are you all right?" Sally repeated, petting it. "That was so mean of them not to let you play."

"It's okay, Miss Sally," Channy cried. "I am used to never being picked to play in games."

"You may be small, but that gives them no right to be so mean to you," Sally remembered being a child and also being picked last or not picked at all, and the damage the experience had done to her self-esteem.

"Thank you, Miss Sally," Channy rolled around her hand. "But no praise can help make me grow or change the truth. I am just not like the others."

"Don't think you're the only one who has been teased or bullied." She stroked the snuffball. "I was just like you once."

"Really?" Channy bounce in her hand. "I would never have believed the great prophet Miss Sally would ever," Channy paused taking a deep breath, "Be like me."

115

"Yes, I was once a lonely girl," she whispered as she looked up at Ryan. "But then one day I fell in love and found some really good friends."

"And you also saved our world." Channy rolled off her fingers and circled them with excitement. "Do you think I could ever be like you? A hero?"

"Of course, little Channy." She bent down and patted the snuffball lightly. "Even the smallest of things can make a big difference!"

"Oh thank you, Miss Sally!" said Channy, rolling around swiftly, making tracks in the snow as she traversed the courtyard.

"Wait! Where are you going?" Sally asked.

Without a word Channy rolled away, exiting the snow-filled courtyard in the same direction as her larger counterparts.

"I think you just acquired a new fan," John said, chuckling.

"Don't tease, John."

"I wasn't." John sounded defensive. "Chill out. I was serious."

"Good, because that is terribly sad," she looked at them openly. "No one should be treated liked that. Especially not an adorable little snuffball."

"It'll be fine," Ryan reassured her. Sally appreciated his attempt to understand a feeling he'd never known. He'd always been one of the first to be picked when teams were forming. "I'm sure it'll grow into a large snuffball in time."

"But it's so cruel." Sally began to follow the snuffballs. "No one deserves that kind of treatment. It's so damaging to one's self-worth."

"Sally," Ryan caught up to her. "Just stay out of it. You don't need to save everything that's small and helpless."

"Ryan, what if you were that snuffball, what if you were unwanted? Don't you have any empathy?" Sally took a look around, but no snuffballs were in sight. "I guess you're right. There's not much I can do. But I have to keep trying."

Ryan comforted her with a hug. If it was up to Sally, she would help everything lost and unwanted.

When they picked up their tour, the first thing that drew their attention was a small garden lush with intricate purple, blue and pink flowers. Sally knelt down to take a closer look at the bell-shaped blossoms, which nodded on long silvery stems.

"They are so beautiful!" exclaimed Sally. A light ringing sound vibrated from one of the flowers. The volume increased from the bell-speaker as a song began to play. "They're like little music boxes." Sally clapped her hands. "I wonder what they smell like."

"No! Don't smell them Miss Sally! Get away!" Channy yelled, rolling up to her. It was too late. The flower coughed, spraying a flatulent, gassy sewer odor directly into Sally's face.

"Oh no! The Stinkerbells got Miss Sally!" Channy yelled.

"Ugh," John quickly covered his nose. "Farting flowers." He laughed in spite of the putrid odor that made his eyes water.

"Sally!" Ryan had pulled his shirt over his nose. "Are you okay?"

"It got in my eye!" Sally rubbed it then forced herself to put her hands down. Maybe rubbing would make it worse. "Why does this always happen to me?"

"Don't rub, Miss Sally," Channy confirmed. "Come with me, hurry!"

"Sally!" John, holding his breath, managed to gasp out, "You smell like a rotten sewer!"

All three followed the bouncing turquoise snuffball.

"We must hurry before it goes deep into her skin," Channy talked as she bounced. "If that happens she will reek for at least a week and be shunned by everyone."

117

"What's the cure?" Sally asked. She could barely stand the smell herself.

"You must fully immerse in the moat outside the castle. This will fully cleanse you," Channy explained.

Channy led them swiftly to the water barrier, its shore lined with a stone walkway. As they reached it, Sally abandoned all caution, wasting no time in submerging in the bright green colored water. As she splashed her arms and kicked her legs, she dove under water, making sure her entire body was cleansed from hair to toenails. The rank smell of Stinkerbell pollen rapidly receded.

"It feels so good!" Sally's wet head emerged from the water. "It's like a hot tub. Come on in you guys!"

"I'm fine here," said John crossing his arms in a show of stubbornness. "Left my swim trunks at home."

"Don't be a wimp." Ryan shoved John in from behind before diving in himself.

"Ryan, you jerk!" John splashed his friend. "I didn't want to go swimming."

"You'll be fine." Ryan splashed back. "You needed a bath anyway. You were starting to smell as bad as Sally."

"Ryan, zip it!" Sally dunked her boyfriend under. She surreptitiously sniffed an armpit, just to verify that the awful smell was gone. She was rewarded with a tantalizing, calming whiff of lavender and mint. "Yes! I'm clean! Thank you, Channy!"

"You're welcome, Miss Sally," said the little ball ashore. "I have been purposely tossed into the Stinkerbell bushes many times. I know the feeling."

The kids swam around, splashing each other lightheartedly. Sally was enjoying the sensation of being in the hot water while gazing at the snowy backdrop when she realized she felt strange. She felt puffy.

"Ryan," she said, treading water. "I think I'd better get out. Something's not right. I feel really bloated."

118

"Oh brother," John wisecracked. "If I only I had a dollar for every time a girl said that."

"Put a sock in it, John," Ryan said firmly, swimming toward his girlfriend.

As Sally inspected her arms, a progressive feeling invaded her entire body, as if her skin was being stretched like a sausage. She touched her rapidly plumping face and neck. Ryan looked at her pudging cheeks with alarm.

As Ryan watched in horror her face and head grew twenty times larger. She whimpered as her body began to inflate to the same balloon-like proportions.

"Channy!" Ryan yelled. "Help! What's happening?"

"Uh-oh," Channy said. "I didn't think this would happen."

"Uh-oh is right, you stupid ball!" John was freaking out as his body also began to inflate, as poufy as a beginning swimmer's blow-up water-wings. "We've got to get out of here," he hollered to Ryan. "It must be something in the water."

Before they could make their move, their bodies had been transformed into huge floating beach balls. Their arm and legs disappeared, small hands and feet poking from their hideously swollen torsos. They rolled powerlessly on top of the water, bobbing aimlessly.

"Channy!" Ryan yelled before his head rolled underwater and emerged again. "Help us."

"Oh yes, Mister Ryan. I do apologize, dearly. I did not know this would happen to humans."

John spit out water. "You knew this would happen?"

"Why yes, but not to you! I come here many times to expand myself into a bigger snuffball."

"Well, go get help!" John yelled. "NOW!"

Channy did not waste any more time, hastily rolling back to the castle.

"Sally," Ryan tried to see her face, but rolled the other way. "When your head is about to submerge, take a deep breath."

Sally spit out some water and replied, "I did. Don't worry."

They heard loud laughter on shore. When the rolling John was right-side up again he spotted their audience. Brian, Russell, and David were gawking at the ridiculously inflated trio.

"Are you going to help us or just sit there with your fingers up your noses?" John had no patience at this point.

"What have you kids gotten yourselves into this time?" Brian asked rhetorically, snickering. "Hang on. We can help."

The three Knights held out their arms and closed their eyes. Rope lassos materialized, strategically positioned loops around the poofy midsection of each floating teen.

"You three should not be roaming about without chaperones." Brian cackled, handily pulling Sally onto shore. "You never know what trouble you can get into."

As the hapless teens were fished out, David held out his staff and recited:

"Spongy potion, curse of Elves;
Deflate these chubbies back to themselves!"

A blue beam shot from his staff, engulfing them in its light as they quickly shrank back to normal.

"Thank you, thank you, thank you!" Sally babbled, feeling her arms, legs, face and body to make sure everything was in the right size in the right place.

"Whose brilliant idea was it to curse this water?" John asked.

"Not too bright," Sally agreed. "And why would you have those disgustingly smelly flowers in your gardens?"

"You'll have to ask your friend Mel about both of those, uh, shall we say, innovations," replied Brian, trying not to grin too broadly.

"I believe they are part of his strategy for the castle's defense." David added. "Marvelous idea if you ask me. Of course none of us smell the flowers or swim in the moat."

"I truly apologize, Masters." the returned Channy said contritely. "I truly did not know this would happen."

"It is quite all right, little Channy," Brian said. "We all know you were only trying to help."

"Easy for you to say," John huffed. "I never want to go through that again."

"And you won't," said David. "From now on, you all will be accompanied by Buttercup."

The comely young fox maiden stepped out from hiding behind a small blue bush and bowed, clearly eager to chaperone and assist the prophets.

"I don't need a babysitter!" John was adamant.

"How about you accompany me?" Dyad floated in to join the group. "I promise that I won't babysit you." She settled on his shoulder. "You can come to my next lecture."

John's pulse fluttered; his heart beating faster. He didn't object. "As much as I'm not a fan of school, I guess I can make an exception."

"That's a great idea," Sally looked at Ryan. "I also want to attend some classes."

"It would be my honor to accompany you, Miss. Please follow me," said Buttercup. The bells from the clock tower chimed. Buttercup started back to the castle. "School is now in session."

Chapter VI
An Enchantian Education

Becky sat fascinated at her assigned desk watching Mel present his lecture, pacing with energy as he spoke, engaging every student in active learning. He was a terrific instructor, much better than any of the teachers back at Willington School.

The desks positioned in a circle surrounded Mel and his lab display featuring an impressive array of beakers filled with a variety of solutions. Hanging out in a chemistry-like classroom made Becky very happy.

She sat next to a tiny girl as small as a typical kindergartner. Half Becky's size, the tot-sized lass wore a celery-green dress, her dark-brown curly hair flowing down to the middle of her back. The girl took copious notes and asked a vast amount of questions throughout the lecture. This annoyed Becky because most of the questions seemed irrelevant, even silly. Undoubtedly, the girl was a suck-up doing it for attention.

"Now after we include a dash of bunger spice," Mel deftly sprinkled the correct amount of blue powder into his concoction, "We place the flumpkin juice underneath the burner to evaporate any excess toxins."

"Professor," the tiny girl beside Becky interrupted again. Almost everyone in the class sighed. "What about the lixy dust? When will you put that in?"

"Patience now, Cully." Mel was always attentive and kind to his students. "That comes right after."

Becky rolled her eye and butted in. "Professor? Can I ask an intelligent question?" Becky glanced over at Cully, giving her the slightest, barely detectable sneer. "Rather than stopping you every five ticks for something senseless?"

"By all means, Becky." Mel smiled. He knew she was annoyed by Cully's tiresome questions. "But remember, the only bad questions in my class are the ones that aren't asked."

"That's debatable," Becky said under her breath and then continued. "Why would you use flumpkin juice? Right here in the ingredients book it states that the juice brings your heart to a comatose state. When you used essence of bliffle jam a few steps back, that does the same thing. It seems to me that if you were trying to make this work you wouldn't need it."

"Good question." Mel took a deep breath. "Flumpkin juice, if distilled, produces the opposite-from-natural effect in the potion, which enhances certain necessary ingredients. I could spend a tock or two explaining in detail the chemical effects, but we do not have enough time. Does this answer your question?"

"Yeah," Becky nodded. "It's interesting."

"Any other questions?" asked Mel, as he continued. "Again, thank you Becky. I truly enjoy being challenged."

"You shouldn't contradict the Professor," Cully hissed in an aside. Apparently their irritation was mutual. "It's really rude. He's a smart man!"

"Well you shouldn't be such a brat," Becky began, but the clock tower bells interrupted her harangue.

"And finally, class, the crowning element: lixy dust!" Mel concluded, with pride. "Now you can all say that you know how to concoct my infamous tickle-me potion! Remember, rules prohibit it from being used on any of your instructors or peers. And make sure you're near a bathroom if you use it on yourself." He cautioned, noting in an undertone, "That's a good way to have an accident."

Becky was anxious to compliment Mel but as she approached Cully cut in front of her. "P-p-professor," Cully stuttered. She seemed more nervous than earlier now that she was speaking to him without an audience. "Can I ask you something?"

"Sure Cully, what is it? Actually, if it's about grading your exam, I will have to do it after the festival. Real busy you know."

"It was actually regarding the Ball," Cully said.

"Oh right, the Ball! Thank you for reminding me, Cully," Mel looked at Becky. It was so gratifying she couldn't help but smirk, but remembering he was looking at her, too, she put on her game face. "Becky, are you going with anyone to the Enchantian Ball?"

"I just heard about it last night," she said. "What is it exactly?"

"It's a dance. It's like a dance." Mel felt like smacking his own forehead. God, he sounded like an idiot! But she made him nervous.

Becky was enjoying the panic-stricken look on Cully's face. "Are you asking me to go with you?"

"Yeah," Mel lit up. "I am."

"I'd love to go with you, Professor." Becky slipped her arm through his, shooting Cully a contemptuous smile.

Cully gritted her teeth, but didn't say a word.

"Great!" Mel began to pack up his demonstration materials in a series of velvet-lined leather cases. The labs and lecture rooms were locked when not in use but some of the ingredients were too volatile or potentially toxic for him to feel comfortable about leaving them out in the open. "I'm sure I'll see you later at the games. I'll save a seat if I get there before you."

Mel then looked at Cully. "I'm sorry to keep you waiting, Cully, did you need something?"

"No professor," she said, in her tone neutral. "It can wait."

"That was so wicked of you," Cully snarled at Becky after Mel left. "You knew I was going to ask him to the Ball."

"What are you talking about?" Becky retorted, feigning innocence. "I'm not a mind reader."

"Whatever," Cully whirled toward the door, but before storming out of the classroom she dramatically declared, "You had better let me have at least one dance with him. Or you *will* regret it."

"Not a chance," Becky said, grinning. "Bite me."

***

After a hearty "see you later" smooch for Ryan, Sally entered her classroom of choice enthusiastically, quickly choosing a seat. She normally preferred the front row in all of her classes, but since the desks were positioned in a circle there was no need to worry about an unobstructed view.

She was early, first in the classroom. She was watching everyone including Buttercup file in, trying to figure out who the instructor might be when she was completely distracted from her guessing game by a petite woman in a voluminous long green dress and pointed hat. As she entered the classroom, flashing a kind smile, Sally jumped out of her chair, rushing to envelope the little gnome in an affectionate embrace. "Seara! Boy, is it good to see you!"

"Same here, Sally," Seara squeezed her a little harder. "When I heard the three of you had arrived, I was hoping I'd run into you sooner rather than later."

"Well, I'm real glad you did," Sally sat down. "Are you in this class?"

"I'm teaching it, my dear," Seara said proudly. "When the Knights requested that I be an instructor at the new Institute, I was so honored. And I found it fitting to be asked to be a history professor, as Gitchy was the previous Herald."

"Yes," Sally said sadly, remembering her old friend Gitchy, Seara's mate, who had passed away during their first visit. "He would be very proud of you."

"Thank you, my dear," Seara whispered. "I should probably start the class now. We can chat later."

Seara set a glass down on the desk in the middle of the room. "Welcome, again, everyone, to history. We have a special guest today. Please say hello to Miss Sally. You, of course, all know her as one of our prophets. Please welcome her."

Everyone in the room applauded. Sally smiled and waved, uncomfortable and embarrassed at being the center of attention.

"Today we will discuss the last chapter," Seara said, immediately launching into her lecture, "The rise and fall of the Enchantian Fairies."

How exciting, Sally thought. What a perfect day to attend this class.

"First, can someone tell me how a fairy is born?"

A blue raccoon raised his paw.

"Yes, Scooter."

"Aren't fairies grown, not born?"

"Yes, that is true in a sense, but I probably would not say that in front of them. They prefer not to be known as grown," Seara explained. "The fairy race has one mother, a Fairy Queen, if you will, who had the gift of planting fairy seeds in the great flumpkin patch outside of Cumberlake Valley.

"Understanding this fact is key to understanding why there are only four fairies now. Does everyone know their names?"

"Pixy, Nymph, Sprite, and Dyad are the last of the fairy kind, Professor," Buttercup responded promptly.

"Correct," Seara continued. "Sadly, none of them can become a Fairy Queen. Meaning they do not have the ability to give life to new fairies, so their species are near extinction.

"Yet the fairies were once one of the most prominent species in Enchantas. Their numbers flourished and brought happiness to all of the realms. Fairies are, of course, one of the first mythics of Enchantas." Seara specifically looked at Sally to offer clarification. "Mythics, Miss Sally, are Enchantians who have the natural gift of magic."

Sally nodded. She remembered hearing that during her first visit.

"Many ages ago, after the Knights established our society, the fairies began to explore other realms and build more villages and towns. Our history books state that during one of these expeditions a young Knight had accompanied the Queen and in the midst of their exploration, they fell madly in love.

"When the two came home after their expedition, they asked the Knights for their blessing to be married and start their own family.

"At the time, there were many concerns related to such a union, including if it would be possible for the couple to produce children and if so, how that might affect the fairy species. The drawbacks, the Knights felt, outweighed a personal love story.

"Though their concerns about the relationship were legitimate, the Queen and her Knight decided to marry anyway."

"What happened to them?" Deeply involved in the story, Sally spoke at the same time she raised her hand.

Seara beamed at her friend before continuing. "Well Sally, after they declared their marriage to the Knights, the two of them were banished from Enchantas and sent to your world.

"It wasn't until cycles later that the two returned to Enchantas. The Queen had given birth to a child and they believed raising this child in Enchantas would be much safer than in your world."

Sally nodded. She agreed with the decision.

"After hearing their pleas, the Knights decided to put their love to the ultimate test. If the two were truly in love, they would agree to allow the Queen, her husband, and another Knight to be struck by cupid's arrow. If their love was true, they would be spirit-mates forever."

Sally, contemplating how she would feel were she and Ryan put to the same test with some other girl. She felt horrified.

"With confidence the Queen and her husband agreed to the test. It was no secret at the time that the other knight forming the love triangle for cupid's arrow, Sir Brian's brother, had once also been secretly in love with the Queen. Upon her return he realized those old feelings had never faded. So he had his own strong reasons to put himself to the test."

"The three of them were shot with cupid's arrow." Seara paused for what seemed like forever. "Not long after, the Queen realized who her true love was — and it was not her husband.

"Devastated and heartbroken that the Queen could not keep her vows, the Queen's husband took his child and left Enchantas forever."

"What happened to him?" Sally felt his pain. "Did he ever fall in love again?"

"No one knows." Seara said.

"What of the Queen and Sir Brian's brother?"

"They had left Enchantas soon after their wedding. It was said that they had left to find the Queen's child," Seara continued, but her tone grew darker. "Ages later, during the crusades of the Witch and Warlock, the Fairy Queen had been summoned back to Enchantas. Summoned by the Witch and Warlock, that is. It was the plan of the Witch and Warlock to bring back the fairy species."

"Wouldn't that have been a good thing?" Sally asked, trying to justify her mother and father's actions. It had been some time since she'd thought about how wicked her parents used to be and what they'd been like when they lived in Enchantas.

"Yes, it would have. But the Witch and Warlock wanted the Queen to raise fairies bred to do harm — an evil fairy army, if you will. She of course refused. The Witch and Warlock cursed her and the Queen has been lost and locked away ever since."

"Where is the Fairy Queen now?" Sally hung on every word.

"Nothing is known for sure," Seara continued. "We cannot even confirm that she is still alive. Legend has it that there is a book — closely guarded by the Knights — that shows the Queen's location.

"But it is theorized that if found, the Fairy Queen will be enraged from being trapped and kept from her loved ones, that she will raise an army of thousands of wicked fairies and release their wrath onto the land."

"So what happened to all of the other fairies?" Sally wanted to change the subject as guilt from her parent's actions surged through her body.

"All but four had been killed during the crusades. And with the curse of the Queen, there was no chance of breeding more."

Sally felt awful. She stood quietly. "Excuse me," she said. Biting her bottom lip, she walked out.

***

Ryan couldn't decide what class to partake in. He finally settled on a course titled 'The Art of Spell-Casting'. What better way to learn magic than starting with the basics? He'd always been intrigued by how the Enchantians came up with their clever and effective rhymes. He doubted his abilities, but how cool would it be if he could learn how to create and cast a spell?

He was surprised and disappointed to find that Dyad's sister, Nymph, was the instructor. If he could have left the classroom without being noticed he would have. Ryan didn't feel comfortable around Nymph. It wasn't just another girl hanging all over him; he was used to dealing with that even though he didn't like it. There was something different about Nymph. He couldn't put his finger on it.

Anyone with eyes would admit that Nymph was stunning, to be sure, but he loved Sally so much that he would never cheat on her. Nymph didn't seem to respect that. He felt like she was trying to lure him into becoming something he was not: unfaithful. Ryan didn't trust her and worse, he didn't trust himself around her.

Nymph morphed into a larger form rather than a small fluttering fairy to deliver her lecture. Ryan sat apprehensively in his chair as she paced the circle constantly, watching him and smiling. Her strawberry-blonde hair flowed down her back and her long legs were curved to perfection.

Ryan tried hard not to stare but he couldn't help the feelings of desire that seemed to engulf him. He was confused by this because he knew that Sally was his spirit-mate. He could not help but wonder what Nymph was up to.

"Ryan," said Nymph, gliding to him, "How about you try? You seem very distracted today."

"Huh?" Ryan jumped out of his daze. "Try what?"

The classroom broke out in giggles. Ryan was suddenly embarrassed, hoping no one knew why he hadn't been listening.

Nymph smiled and lightly touched his cheek. His heart pattered for a moment.

"We were talking about basic spell casting and how it works." Nymph placed a bark pen on Ryan's desk. "Take this pen for example. If I wish to levitate it, I must come up with a quick verse and concentrate hard on what I would like it to do. You must rhyme. Your imagination and rhythm are the key elements for the spell work. The better it flows and rhymes the more powerful the spell.

"Please," Nymph turned toward him, putting him on the spot. "Ryan, use this wand and try it."

Ryan's mind was racing, but not with spells. He had to force himself to find any words, let alone words that rhymed.

"Umm, how about:

Little thing, little pen;
Get picked up, and float in the air?"

Ryan flicked his wrist, but nothing happened. Titters again filled the room. He was not making a good impression.

"That's fine for a first try, Ryan. But I think we can do better." Nymph brushed his hair flirtatiously and recited a spell:

"Wind, rain, and stormy weather;
Make this pen float like a feather!"

The bark pen seemed weightless as it gracefully levitated. "Not to worry, Ryan. Some do not have a knack for spell casting; their talents lie elsewhere. I do know you are a very strong warrior," Nymph winked at him.

Ryan was clammy with sweat; his guilt at putting himself in this situation consumed him.

"Moving on," Nymph continued, "I would like to talk about magical ethics. As we all know, our definition of magic is very broad. However, the point of casting spells and enchantments is to make objects or beings do our bidding. Being the one in control is our ultimate goal," Nymph began to pace again. "Logically, this can become concerning if the wrong one conducts magic. That is where our ethics come in.

"Each and every one of us must promise to take the responsibility seriously, appreciate the power of magic and not use it for evil or our own personal desires."

Ryan gulped; it felt like a frog was stuck in his throat. The way Nymph said "desires" made him squirm in his chair.

"A great example is the power of temporary enslavement," Nymph moved behind Ryan and rubbed his shoulders. "To put another in a trance and make them do your bidding."

Nymph turned Ryan's desk so he was facing her. He looked up at her wide-eyed, wondering what was going on.

Nymph gave him a mischievous grin and recited:

"Spirited fairy, playful bliss;
Take me Ryan, and gimme a kiss!"

Before Ryan could object, their lips came together. Sparks of excitement flooded his veins. He closed his eyes for a moment, yielding to the energy of her sensuality. When he opened his eyes he saw Sally standing in the door, eyes filled with tears, arms crossed in anger.

Ryan quickly pushed Nymph away and rose to go to his spirit-mate, to explain. Sally wasn't in the mood to talk. She moved swiftly ahead of him down the hallway.

"Sally!" Ryan begged. "Wait! Stop!"

He glanced back into the classroom shooting Nymph a fiercely disgusted look. Pointedly ignoring him, she airily continued her lecture as if nothing had happened. "Class, I hope you've all learned a good lesson here today. Ethics are a very important part of magic. You never know who you will hurt by a carelessly cast spell.

"Fairy bright with wings that soar,
Give us peace and shut the door!"

At that the classroom door promptly closed, leaving Ryan alone in the hallway.

Chapter VII
Prophet's Day Games

John sat between his sister and Dyad in a large booth overlooking the Institute Arena. Not too far away from them sat the Knights and Firp. The arena had been built miles from the castle only because the castle could never accommodate the vast amount of Enchantians who wanted to attend the games. John's only framework of comparison was a football field, but he was sure the arena was much bigger than that.

Thousands of Enchantians from all over the land came to celebrate the day of the four prophets. The thought of having a holiday named after him kind of made him ill. But out of respect, he kept his thoughts to himself.

John could not believe how many different types of Enchantians were there. Foxes, dogs, cats, rabbits and wolves sat together, while other valley creatures grouped together in other sections. In the far distance John could see gremlins and imps sitting next to trolls and griffins. Bands of dwarves, leprechauns and goblins had also arrived.

Dyad was surprised by this, because they were known to be solitaries. "Most creatures from the other side of the Enchantic

Mountains do not concern themselves with our society," she remarked to John.

It seemed that everyone was here, except for three out of the four guests of honor: Ryan, Sally and Mel. They'd yet to show. And I'm known as the rude one, John thought. Go figure.

Becky and John had made up before they left the Institute grounds. John loved her too much to hold any grudges and understood that she was old enough to make her own decisions. He was not happy, however, that Mel had asked her to the Enchantian Ball and was hoping to have some 'big brother' words with him beforehand.

Festival events had been in full swing since classes let out around midday. Flying ships, those sky-sailing vessels that had played such a major role in the last major battle for Enchantas, were used to transport revelers to the arena. John was hoping to see Max, the pirate captain that he'd bonded with during their previous visit, but the sea-dog evidently had naval business at the academy. Max, a one-eyed Border Collie, enjoyed a robust fight and was fair to his crew — one of many reasons that John admired him greatly.

John noticed that Becky was fully engaged in the fun and pageantry of the festival. A parade of representatives riding magnificent floats from each city, village, and town kicked off the festivities. Accustomed to tissue-paper flowers and high school marching bands back home, Becky and John had never seen such an elaborate parade. They were stunned by the sheer grandeur.

John's favorite float entry represented the military academy. Enchantian troops dressed as humans pretended to battle the armies of the Witch and Warlock.

Becky's favorite was the Foxtown float featuring a perfectly replicated, working miniature rollercoaster.

All in all, the parade was very different from what they were used to. The peculiarities of the procession included a spin on the usual candy tossing to the crowd from the floats. Instead, spectators hurled screaming vegetables at the floats.

Becky had told John about the incident with Burf. He wasn't at all sympathetic to her trauma. He only laughed and told her to get used to it. The way Becky was partaking in the veggie-throwing, John figured she had. They made a contest of it. Ten points for head-shots, five points if you hit a body. Becky won, but wasn't sure if her brother let her win, or if it was on her own.

After the parade the sky above the arena transformed into a massive snuffball racetrack ten times larger than the track he'd seen on Max's ship; the losing snuffballs on the ship had been sent flying into the spectacular pink sea to drown.

This race was staged on a much grander scale. Colossal glass slides and loops created an obstacle course designed to provide an outstanding and exhilarating show. Rather than throwing the losing snuffballs into the abyss of the sea they were ejected into the crowd, where they could bounce themselves off fans. John was reminded of rock concerts he'd attended where beach balls were tossed around and the crazier fans threw themselves into crowd-surfing. This was tons more exciting as they could hear the cheerful screams of the resilient snuffballs each time they were volleyed into the air and ping-ponged across the wave of spectators.

At one point there was roughly one snuffball for every twenty fans being punched high and hard across the jubilantly shouting spectators. It was great fun for everyone, including Becky and John.

Before each race you could bet on a snuffball. John usually picked a red competitor; Becky chose randomly. The stakes were decided between those who wagered. Becky and John decided that the loser would have to do something to really embarrass the other once they returned home. At the moment, John was in the lead by one. He was not sure what he would make his sister do, because Becky did not embarrass easily.

"Hello John," an unfamiliar voice said.

John was snapped out of his reflective state by the sight of a large green rabbit with long, floppy ears wearing a blue-buttoned silver coat. Next to the rabbit he saw Buttercup and another pretty female fox. Both were wearing long purple dresses with a flounce on the bottom and a vent that allowed their lushly furred tails to plume ornamentally behind them.

"Hi," John said to Buttercup, nodding to her companions.

"Do you remember me?" the rabbit spoke again.

John looked inquisitively at the rabbit but no name came to mind. "Well, this is awkward," he said.

"It's me," the rabbit smiled, buck teeth jutting out. "Peaches."

John continued to study the rabbit without recognition and then took a guess. "You're the rabbit who helped me escape Foxtown, right?" John found it ironic that Peaches was with two foxes and hoped they did not take offense. He sensed no tension; it was another situation that must have changed since he last visited Enchantas. "Peaches, I'm glad to see you again."

John wished Sally and Ryan would show up. He still felt weird as he didn't know Peaches as well as they did. Sally would talk about Peaches every now and again back home. He tried the standard ice-breaker: "So, how are you?"

"I'm doing great," Peaches sighed. "Busier than ever, I'm a family rabbit now. Yep, there are the bunnos now," Peaches pointed to a full section of the stands that was overrun by wild little rabbits in a variety of primary and pastel colors wreaking havoc and annoying nearby spectators.

"Daddy!" they all screamed when they saw him pointing, hopping wildly in a frenzy of childish enthusiasm.

"Oh boy, I'm being summoned," Peaches grumbled, but the twinkle in his eye spoke volumes. "Being a father is a lot of work.

Hold on bunnos! Daddy's coming! Can you believe it; these little rascals never give me any time to hunt anymore."

"How do you keep track of their names?"

"I don't," Peaches laughed. "That's what my wife is for. I just number them." Peaches' eyes narrowed as he raised his voice and yelled, "Sit down Number 252!"

Becky gave out a loud snort. Apparently, she found that very amusing.

"I was hoping to see Ryan and Sally," Peaches spoke quickly with one eye on his bunnos. "Are they here?"

"Nope, not yet. Hopefully they'll show up soon."

"Pity. I'd love to see them," Peaches said. "Well maybe they will turn up before the bunnos overtire themselves. Oh, and where are my manners? I believe you know Buttercup. This is her mother, Linah."

"Hi," said Linah, sticking out her paw. "Pleasure to finally meet you."

"Likewise," replied John, extending his hand. He felt beyond uncomfortable, not surprising considering he'd killed her husband. As he was wondering if he should apologize or at least acknowledge this disturbing fact, Linah took charge.

"Let's get going, my little Buttercup," she instructed. "We should find a seat, if there are any left." Linah laughed. "That's if Peaches' family didn't take them all!"

"Hey!" Peaches pretended to be insulted.

"Yes mother," Buttercup lovingly grasped her mother's paw. "Nice seeing you again John," she said softly.

"You too," replied John, then he looked at Peaches again.

There was an awkward silence as Peaches stood there, clearly dawdling, with his paws in his pocket.

"Daddy!" his children screamed.

"Peaches," a stern female voice caterwauled over the cheering crowd. "Get over here!"

John looked over to see a larger red rabbit, the shade of a cherry Popsicle, in the middle of the smaller bunnies.

"Yep, that's the wife, the better half, the old ball-and-chain," Peaches attempted to lighten the mood with a feeble attempt at humor. "Better get going. Fatherly duty calls. It's nice to see you. Tell Sally and Ryan I send my regards and hope we can catch up soon. If, that is, I ever get a day off."

"No problem, will do," John said, again offering his hand.

As Peaches hopped away, John leaned over to his sister and whispered, "I didn't know him that well."

"I could tell," Becky laughed. "I always know when you're uncomfortable. I enjoy it."

John looked to his right just over Becky's shoulder and saw Mel moving toward them, scooting past the Knights.

"Hey guys," Mel sat next to Becky, ignoring John's ominous look. "Sorry, I'm late. I had some business to take care of at the Institute."

"You should be," Becky smiled at Mel flirtatiously. "You're definitely going to have to make it up to me." John shot him a black look; it was clearer than if he'd actually said 'don't touch.' "

Mel wasn't going to let an understandably protective brother get him down. "I'm glad I didn't miss the best event," he addressed both of them.

"And what would that be, Mel?" Becky asked. "I don't see how you can beat these snuffball races."

"The gladiator battle is by far the top event." Mel rubbed his hands together in anticipation. "It's honestly the most compelling contest to watch. The veggies get *really* into it."

"Veggies?" Becky gasped.

"Don't worry," Mel assured, handing her and John binoculars. "It's pure entertainment."

A few tiers below them from a raised dais draped with ceremonial bunting, Firp stood up to address the crowd.

"Welcome all!" Firp's magic-enhanced voice needed no microphone or bullhorn as it echoed through the stadium as strong as a public-address system. The crowd hushed as the snuffballs herded themselves out of the arena, the veterans corralling the wildest bouncers.

"Welcome to the final event of our fourteenth annual Prophet's Day Festival."

The crowd applauded enthusiastically at his stirring pronouncement as drawn out as a boxing-ring announcer's.

"It is my pleasure to present to you all our special guests." Firp turned to greet the prophets and promptly registered that Ryan and Sally weren't there. He continued anyway. "Please welcome our four prophets who gallantly brought peace back to our lands!"

The already loud crowd kicked their roar up a notch. John experienced a quick flashback to the Battle of Enchantas when they were about to be tortured to death in front of the army of the Witch and Warlock. Chants of "Skin 'em, Shred 'em, Smash 'em up; Cook 'em, Boil 'em, and Eat 'em up!" still haunted him.

"Each cycle," Firp continued to address the crowd, "Our gladiator battles have brought us much pleasure, reminding us how bravely our warriors fought that fateful night. There is much to be grateful for and we are reminded of this during our annual feast after the battle."

"Firp's referring to the losers of the gladiator battle," Mel whispered.

Becky flinched slightly. "How do you know who wins?"

"The vegetable species that remain standing, no matter how many there are, are permitted to live in freedom for the rest of their existence," Mel pointed toward the ground as large bay doors at the western end of the arena began to open. "Last cycle a group of forty red peppers survived. Such a bummer. I love red peppers."

As the large doors slowly opened, thousands of little vegetables strutted out. Radishes, turnips, carrots, onions, beets, and cabbages rallied at the left. Stalks of celery, garlic bulbs, jauntily capped mushrooms, and flamboyant green and red peppers massed to the right. Finally, legions of broccoli, cauliflower, potatoes, eggplants, and corn took their places in the center. The warrior vegetables were armored with old silverware, sharp kitchen knives and small pot lids, colanders and fine-mesh strainers for shields.

"So do they just slaughter each other?" Becky scowled. "That's not entertainment, it's cruelty to vegetables."

"Not all are forced into this, Becky." Mel explained. "Many of these competitors hail from Gardenopolis or Cropville. They are passionate volunteers who want to live the rest of their lives as heroes."

"Veggies, take your positions," Firp bellowed. "Ready!"

Loud clangs from the arena floor echoed through the stands, the vegetables stared at each other in challenge, clashing their sharp kitchen knives against metal pot covers. The crowd fell silent.

"Fight!" Firp boomed.

Prodded by an ear-splitting buzzer — not unlike a super-sized oven timer — the legions of vegetables began to battle. Knives swung from every direction, machetes chopped and shredders shredded as the vegetable clans diced, sliced and julienned themselves into pieces. Screams of horror thundered below while the crowd cheered elatedly.

Becky intently followed an onion and carrot engaged in a dreadful, savage duel. Both of the well-trained opponents deftly blocked each other's strikes. Then the more agile carrot jumped over the onion and sliced it in half with one swift stroke.

"My eyes!" Becky could hear the carrot scream. Blinded by the vapor of the sliced onion, the carrot was defenseless as a radish swooped in to finish it off.

"That carrot had no chance," Mel murmured, gripping his binoculars tight, obviously caught up in the action.

The radish's victory dance was premature, providing an opening for an advancing potato to shred it to ribbons.

"I can't take this anymore." Becky dropped her binoculars and leaped from her seat, making her way toward an exit.

"Becky, don't go." John rose to follow.

"I got this, John," Mel stood up. "You stay with Dyad."

John, about to object, had a welcome revelation at that moment, finally understanding that he didn't always have to be the one to protect or console his sister and that at times his interference was actually harming their relationship. With wisdom beyond his years, he acknowledged that Becky would most likely reject his support anyway. They'd mended their earlier tiff and had been getting along so well; he'd hate to ruin the truce just as it was progressing to a deeper, more permanent level.

"I'm glad you decided to stay with me, John." Dyad held his hand. She transformed into her larger self for the occasion. "We needed some alone time anyway."

"You're right," John agreed. "I'm her big brother and I always want to protect her, but she's in safe hands." Wincing slightly, he amended that to, "She'll be all right. Mel is a good guy."

***

Mel caught up with Becky outside the arena where she was sitting under a small lixy fruit tree. There were no leaves during this season, but the succulent pink cubed fruit still hung from its branches.

"Becky, are you okay?" He sat down next to her.

"Yeah," Becky replied, sighing. She lit a cigarette and took a huge drag before chuffing out a cloud of smoke. "I'm fine."

Mel lit his pipe. They puffed in companionable silence, although he could almost feel the wheels of her mind turning.

"It's just that whole thing is — sadistic!" Becky blurted out. "That's the word I've been searching for to describe that so-called contest. It's sadistic!"

Mel stared at the ground momentarily, not sure how to respond. Then it hit him, "Becky, let me try to help you understand this from their point of view." Mel turned toward her.

"Okay."

"You know, I thought the same way you do. Living in Enchantas helped me to realize that it's a way of life here." Mel took her hand, holding it in a way he intended to comfort. "I mean, of course you'll never look at vegetables the same way, but in this world, they are at the bottom of the food chain."

"It still doesn't change the fact that they talk and have families and feel pain," argued Becky. "Which humanizes them. So when they're being cooked or slaughtered or just tortured for sport it's very upsetting."

"True," he said. "But think of this this way," Mel looked into her compelling, vibrant eyes. "Before your brother, Sally, Ryan and I arrived; the food chain went all the way to the top. The carnivores ate the herbivores; the herbivores ate the vegetables and the omnivores ate anybody they could get their paws or claws or hands on. We've seen firsthand how the foxes eat the rabbits. And knowing the Enchantians personally gives you a whole new outlook on their eating habits." Mel looked up and continued. "You see this tree right here? This is a lixy fruit tree." Mel plucked a cubed pink fruit from above. "This fruit has been the foundation of Enchantas since the beginning. This fruit helps Enchantians cultivate, create magic and most importantly, prevents them from getting hungry and killing each other." Mel handed her a fruit. "Here, try it and think of whatever food you are craving."

Becky thought for a moment and took a bite. "Buttered popcorn!" Becky took another bite as its juice spilled over in her hand. "Wow, if they can eat this fruit that tastes like anything they crave, then why have these merciless gladiator games?"

"Because," Mel put his arm around her. "Enchantians are still animals who have strong instincts to kill or be killed. Without a way to channel this innate inner need many of the inhabitants would regress to existing as brutal, insensate savages consumed with killing and foraging. This way, they have a chance to remain a civil society."

"You have some valid points, Mel." Becky patted him on the back after taking another satisfying puff on her cigarette. "I guess you're not so bad after all."

"Thanks," Mel didn't really know how to take that gesture. He hoped it didn't mean that they were just friends.

The reverberating decibels of a strong gong echoed from the arena as Firp's voice rang out.

"And the winner of this cycle's gladiator contest is: The *Potatoes*!"

The crowd's roar was so strident that it rumbled like rolling thunder through the arena into the landscape beyond.

"Darn," Mel teased. "I guess that rules out any tater tots at the feast."

"Shut up," Becky laughed, playfully slugging him in the shoulder.

Mel was so unsure. Was she just a friend? Or did she have feelings for him? If she felt anywhere near the same tingles as he did, that would truly be earth-shattering. It would make the vegetable battles look like a walk in the castle.

"What's next?" Becky asked.

"First the feast, and then the Ball," he said. "And let's get the true confessions out of the way. I don't know how to dance."

"Mel!" Becky jested, stubbing out her cigarette so she could put him in a friendly but forceful headlock. "You can't ask a girl to a dance if you don't know how to dance, ya dork!"

Mel would have made a smart remark, but Becky was blocking his airway and he was having trouble breathing.

"I'll just have to teach you." Becky pulled him to his feet. She knew Mel liked her. And she liked to be in charge. Ever since Carl she'd been determined to be involved on her own terms. She wasn't going to fall for just anybody. She wasn't going to get hurt again.

Chapter VIII
The Enchantian Ball

Sally sat alone in the ballroom of the Institute. The room had high arched ceilings with lights that sparkled like bright fireworks and then reflected onto the floor dancing as they hit the hard surface.

Sally was clearly not in the mood for any festivities as she and Ryan had been arguing since the kiss. She didn't really blame Ryan as much as she did Nymph, but her anger and frustration had been building up since the football game. Seeing Ryan and Nymph enjoying a kiss had been the nail in the coffin.

Buttercup stood on stage waving a large wand that emanated colorful streams of sparkly blue, yellow, pink, green, orange and lavender. The magic light beams floated around the room like animated ribbons, sinuously twisting in time to the beautiful orchestral sounds that flowed along with them and through them. The music consumed Sally's entire being for a fleeting moment in which she felt nothing but rhythm and joy.

Then the jealousy returned. Sally could not get rid of the painful thoughts cycling in her mind: the girls at school who constantly threw themselves at Ryan; the girls at the football game and now, even here she wasn't able to have a moment of peace. Thanks to the captivating, beautiful fairy who'd been trying to seduce him since they arrived and finally pulled a fast one in public, in *class*. It was wrong on every level. It was just too much for anyone to handle, she thought, becoming more irate by the moment.

Sally observed the dance floor with envy, watching couples dressed in their finest having a blast. Mel and Becky had the giggles because he couldn't seem to stop tromping on her feet. Becky looked ravishing, Sally thought. She wore a short, sparkling navy blue dress with matching dark, patent leather high-heeled boots that reached her knees. Her long, straight shiny black hair swirled as she twirled, her blue eyes shined as she laughed at Mel's clumsy maneuvers.

Not far from them, John and Dyad were also having the time of their lives, gliding as gracefully as if they had been dancing together all their lives.

And there was Ryan. She hadn't seen him since she kicked him out of her room before the feast. He looked dashing as usual, wearing a dark blue tuxedo. His hair looking neat and messy at the same time, just the way she liked it.

Her heart softening, Sally was about to go to him, maybe even to apologize, when Nymph swooped down from the ceiling and in a twinkling burst, transformed into her larger, more human self.

Sally swore out loud as anger boiled within.

Nymph looked gorgeous in a thigh high palest-pink dress. In seconds she had dragged Sally's boyfriend onto the dance floor, that seductive wench, her wicked hands caressing his body as they danced. Sally was furious!

"I can't handle this," she muttered, again cursing out loud as she stomped toward the nearest exit.

Makeup stained the bodice of her bright yellow dress as tears gushed, running down her face in a non-stop waterfall of misery.

She sat down to hide herself, lick her wounds and get under control in what she thought was a secluded stairwell.

But she wasn't alone. Below her, unclear as to how many flights down, she could hear whispering. Straining to listen, keeping as quiet as she could, she was able to make out four distinct voices.

"Come on," a young voice commanded. "Ye said ye wanted to try it. Now just do it already."

"I dunno, Bart," another sounded apprehensive. "It sounded like fun at first, but now, I don't know."

"I didn't steal this bottle of Rittleroot Rum from me father fer nothing!" The one called Bart argued again. "Now drink!"

"Yeah, come on, Gilroy," another voice piped in. "We're all doing it." Sally could hear someone take a chug and cough. "Here Mart, your turn." Sally heard another swig and cough.

"I just don't know," Gilroy stuttered. "I don't want to get in trouble."

Sally stomped down the stairs, calling out authoritatively, "What's going on here gentlemen?" She was right, there were four of them. Four young Enchantians — a fox, a wolf, a coyote, and a leprechaun — standing there stunned, caught in the act and trying to look innocent.

"Nothing Miss Sally," replied the leprechaun in a voice she recognized as Bart's. "We just standing here, talkin'."

"Right," Sally snorted. "Hiding at the bottom of the stairwell and being all secretive?"

"Exactly," the coyote answered with a cocky attitude. Sally recognized him as Mart. "Just getting our courage up to dance."

Sally looked at the wolf and noticed his paws behind his back. "All right guys. Give me the bottle."

The four stood there giving her their best innocent look. "What's his name?" She asked the fox.

"That's Flick, Miss Sally."

"Flick." She turned back to him with a stern look and extended hand. "Give me the bottle. Right now."

Flick slowly handed the half empty bottle to her, glancing down, shamefaced.

"Oh, great!" said Bart. "Now we're in trouble. And me hardly even got to have any."

Without another word Sally lifted the bottle, took three huge swigs, one after the other, wiped the rim with her hand and handed it off to Gilroy, the fox.

"There. Now everyone's doing it, so you can't say you won't."

"Wow," Mart was amazed. "Nice chugging, Miss Sally!"

Sally fought the urge to choke or worse, and plopped down on a stair step. She was instantly dizzy and she hated the taste, but her anger was beginning to subside.

"Are you all right?" asked Gilroy, leaning over her.

"Yes, yes," Sally waved her hand dismissively. "I'm fine, just hurry and drink your turn so I can have another one."

Gilroy took a sip and passed it on.

The bottle made its rounds back to Sally. She lifted it high above her head proclaiming, "Screw men! Screw 'em all!"

"Hear hear!" the others cheered, not really understanding what she was referring to but eager to go along with the respected prophet.

Fueled by the "talking water," it didn't take long for Sally to open up and share her woes. Soon the five of them were laughing all the cares away. Sally felt like she was finally able to breathe. For now her problems were gone and she was finally having fun.

***

Ryan entered the ballroom late — he hated to be behind schedule — and thoroughly exhausted from arguing with Sally for the better part of the day. He understood her anger and frustration

150

and did everything he could to validate her feelings and offer reassurance. But he couldn't help but feel abused from both sides. He'd never played the victim in his entire life and he didn't like being placed in that position now over events he couldn't control. He'd been considered boyfriend material since he was old enough to date. His above-average looks and athletic ability helped out with that. His reputation for being smart, kind and non-snobby about his family wealth also earned him popularity points. But the hike to varsity football took the invasion of boy-crazy girls to a whole new level. Although he literally felt stalked at times, it went against his nature and his upbringing to be rude. They all knew he was with Sally, but the flirting and pestering only got worse as the weeks went on. They'd all been taught at school that *no means no*. Well, Ryan always told them "no". What part of that didn't they understand?

He thought Sally knew how much he tried to ignore and discourage the too-attentive females that seemed to be constantly buzzing around him. But she wasn't hearing him when he told her. She was so insecure. It hurt him to watch her going through such needless turmoil. Since his words didn't change things, he started trying to hide the truth. Ryan never told her about the countless phone calls and secret love notes he received on a weekly if not daily basis. If Sally knew, she'd be devastated.

Ryan was furious with Nymph. It wasn't just disrespectful to him and Sally, it was totally inappropriate for an instructor to kiss a student — especially a visiting student — in the classroom in front of an audience. Ryan knew that he could probably have laughed at the situation and politely let Nymph know her behavior was unacceptable if the timing hadn't been so horrible. Then again, he was increasingly uncomfortable with hiding these blatant come-ons from his spirit-mate; the dishonesty didn't sit well with his conscience. If she wasn't so irrational, if they could talk about it, maybe they could come up with a strategy for handling the flirting in a way that made both of them feel solid in their relationship.

In the case of Nymph, he was pretty certain she'd used more than natural charm. He'd been bewitched and that was not his choice or his fault. However, he knew she'd tapped into some kind of not-so-innocent feelings lurking in his subconscious, primal urges or whatever. Ryan felt utterly confused and alone and he wanted to talk to Sally right away to make things right.

Ryan's eyes quickly swept the ballroom and homed in on Sally, standing alone, looking absolutely lovely in a simple, beautifully draped, buttery yellow dress. He'd started toward her eagerly when Nymph landed in front of him cutting off the direct route to his spirit-mate.

"Hey, Ryan." She tried to grab his hand but Ryan batted it away.

"Not now, Nymph." Ryan attempted to move around her but she blocked the way.

"Are you angry with me?"

"Angry doesn't even begin to describe how mad I am at you, Nymph. I don't cheat and I don't appreciate your inappropriate, disrespectful behavior." He spoke quietly but forcefully, not wanting to make a scene but determined to get his point across and get to Sally.

"I do apologize." Nymph latched onto his hand, pulling him toward the dance floor. "Come, have one dance with me and then I'll let you go talk to your girlfriend."

Ryan couldn't break free. "What the heck, Nymph. Let me go." He was not in control of his hand, nor could he stop his other hand from grabbing her hip and squeezing. "Have you lost your mind? This is completely unethical. Stop it, now!" His raised voice was attracting attention.

"Shush," Nymph caressed his back and pillowed her head on his chest. "Just let me enjoy this moment."

"Nymph. No," Ryan looked desperately over at Sally. She'd obviously witnessed the encounter and was in the process of bolting out of the room. "Great. Sally just saw us. How can you be so wicked?"

"Ryan," Nymph stared at him intensely, her vibrant emerald green eyes like lasers, looking into his heart. Ryan felt her power. It was very much like being hypnotized. "Oh Ryan, I know you and I are meant to be together. Can't you feel it?"

"I don't feel it," Ryan argued. "Sally and I are spirit-mates. That's what I feel. We belong together. You need to stop interfering with our relationship."

"But I want to be with you, Ryan." Nymph rubbed her soft hand on his chest, breathing in fluttery little palpitations as if excited beyond control. "I've never felt this way about anyone before. I've wanted you for my own ever since I first saw you on the battlefield all of those cycles ago. We are meant to be."

"That's whacked!" Ryan shouted, abandoning his attempt to keep the conversation courteous. Though the music played on, most of the surrounding dancers stopped to stare. "Nymph, get a grip. Get it through your head that I don't want to be with you! Sally is my girlfriend. More than that. She's my spirit-mate. Forever." Ryan looked around, hoping Sally had heard him, had come back, even if it was only to yell at him again. But she was gone.

"Fine! Have it your way!" Clearly livid and probably humiliated, Nymph instantaneously returned to her normal, tiny self, buzzing up toward the high ceiling. Whirring like a frenzied insect, she shot out of sight.

Dyad and John had moved closer to them as the scene was developing but hadn't heard anything but the parting shot and the furious buzz. "What's going on?" Dyad asked.

"Your sister has some real issues, Dyad."

153

"I know, I am truly sorry," Dyad apologized. "Nymph can be a bit-"

"Obsessive?" Ryan finished angrily. "Unreasonable?"

"Yes," Dyad sighed. "She's a volatile spirit. It does take some doing to get her to see clearly sometimes. She is very stubborn. I'll go talk to her." Dyad turned small and blew a kiss to John before flitting after her sibling.

"Come on, Ryan," John said encouragingly. "All is not lost. Let's go find Sally. I think she went this way."

Ryan followed John through several hallways and corridors. The castle was a maze; they didn't bother to keep track of the twists and turns. The only thing Ryan cared about was finding Sally. He needed to make this right.

After searching just a few passageways, much to their surprise and gratification, they found Sally sitting alone on some stairs.

"Sally!" Ryan ran up to her. She had been crying and from the smell of her, drinking. "Are you all right?"

"I don't get it Ryan," Sally sobbed. "I thought you loved me."

"Oh Sally," Ryan quickly sat next to her, encircling her shoulders with an arm. "I do love you with all of my heart."

"Then why do you do this to me?" Sally looked up at him with red, puffy eyes. She'd cried all her make-up off. "Why do you make me hurt?"

"I didn't mean to Sally!" Ryan held her in his arms tightly. "I don't want to hurt you! You're my spirit-mate, remember?"

Sally smiled a little and touched her nose to his. "Are you sure? Promise?"

"Oh Sally, I promise!" Ryan kissed her passionately. "Forever and ever!"

"Oh Ryan!" Sally pulled him closer and held on to him tightly. "I love you Ryan."

Ryan's heart pounded fervently as they kissed. He wished the feeling would never end. His pulse raced faster and faster. This was how it was supposed to be. This was that one, perfect love.

John, standing over them, averted his eyes and turned his back. He could still hear them, though, as he twiddled his thumbs with unease. "*Okay*, I guess that's my cue," he chuckled. "I'll catch up with you lovebirds later. Glad you're making up."

John headed up the staircase, glancing at the landing door to double-check what level he was on. There was Sally, bottle in one hand, a tight fist in the other. "Ah, Ryan?" John tried to get his buddy's attention but he was too deep into the kissing to be pulled out with anything short of a fire hose. Desperate times call for desperate measures, John thought, still not sure which Sally was which.

He descended the steps, delivering a swift kick to Ryan's backside. "RYAN!" John yelled, still staring up at the other Sally.

Ryan flinched. The kick wasn't hard but it was completely unexpected. He whipped his head up to yell at John when he too noticed the other Sally standing on the landing. Ryan's eyes darted back to the Sally he'd been so ardently and thoroughly kissing.

Nymph flashed a poisonous smile. Before he could react, Sally charged. Thankfully she had to get through John, first. His athletic conditioning stood him in good stead as she punched, pummeled and pushed to get around him. John grabbed her in a bear hug. He kept his tone very calm.

"No, Sally. You don't want to do that. That's just sinking to her level."

"Yes I do, John!" Sally tried to wriggle out of his strong grasp, bawling hysterically, but John was stronger. "Let me go!"

"Nymph!" Ryan drew back in total shock and repulsion. He felt assaulted in every possible way: mind, body and soul. "How could you do this? You're truly twisted."

"Thank you, Ryan. And I'm not sorry." The unrepentant Nymph turned small, "I will never forget our moment together." She flew out the window into what had been meant to be a glorious, celebratory night.

"Sally!" Ryan was up the short flight of stairs in two strides, arms outstretched, panicked pleading in every line of his handsome face.

"Don't touch me. Let me go, Ryan," Sally stumbled to the floor just as Mel & Becky appeared. Ryan tried to help her up, but she pushed his hands away. "I said don't touch me!"

When their friends didn't reappear, Mel and Becky had decided to track them down. No magic to it, as Mel noted. All they had to do was follow the shouting.

"What's up?" he asked. "They can hear your yelling back home."

Sally dramatically raised the bottle and chugged for a good five seconds. Managing to open the door, she eased through it, still hanging on to the rum.

"Sally wait," Ryan started to go after her. Becky stopped him.

"Hold on, Prince Charming." Becky joked, smiling earnestly to let him know she meant no harm. "This situation calls for some girl talk. Trust me. You'll be glad I helped."

Ryan didn't object. He wasn't relishing the same cycle of guilt, blame, tears, shouting and no resolution. He was ashamed and felt like the most idiotic, clueless guy in the world. "I didn't know," Ryan told John and Mel. They nodded sympathetically. He blinked; Sally wasn't the only one ready to shed tears over the betrayal. "I didn't know it wasn't Sally. How could I not know?"

***

It wasn't hard for Becky to find Sally. She only needed to follow the sounds of sobbing.

156

She found Sally was sitting alone on the floor in a bathroom taking small but nearly continuous sips from the rum bottle.

"Hey Sally," Becky said softly, sitting beside her.

"Please get away." Sally said, head between her knees.

"Sally," Becky put her arm around her. "You should know I'm not that easy to get rid of. So I'd stop being stubborn and start talking. What happened?"

Sally lifted her head. Becky was watching her with sincerity and concern. She found it comforting.

"It's just Ryan. Ryan and his girls again. Or should I say fairies? I caught him kissing Nymph. Twice. Today."

"What?" Becky stood up, flashbacks of Carl with her best friend spurring her into action. "That dirty dog! He won't get away with this!"

"Wait! Wait!" Sally clumsily tried to grab Becky's arm. It took two swipes to grab her. "It wasn't his fault. I didn't tell him that, but I'll tell it to you." Her words were slurred.

"How so?"

"Well," Sally took another sip. "The first time he said he was under a spell or something. I didn't really believe him, 'cause he looked like he was enjoying it. When I caught him the second time, tonight, just now, Nymph took the form of me. It was like watching myself kiss him. It was too messed up."

"That is messed up for sure," Becky said. "Sounds like there's a slutty fairy around here who needs her wings pulled off."

"Well yeah, okay, but that isn't the real reason I'm angry." Sally rubbed her wet cheeks.

"Go on. Tell me, girlfriend."

"Ever since we've been together, I never felt like I was good enough for him."

"Sally, that is just not true," Becky moved closer. "You're the most beautiful and intelligent girl I know. Other than myself, of course," She laughed. "Why would you think you're not good enough?"

"I don't know." Sally took another sip of rum. It was a miracle that she hadn't thrown up. Becky was glad they were in a bathroom, just in case. "Ryan is so popular, he's a star football player, and I'm just," She paused playing with the bottle as she tried to find the right words. "Just me. Sally. A nobody."

"Sally," Becky lit a cigarette. She needed one for this conversation. "Stop selling yourself short."

"I'm reminded each and every day how desirable he is when I see all these girls flirting with him, sending him love notes, calling him, touching him. It just pisses me off! I can't stand it!"

"Does he ever go after these other girls?"

"No, but I still can't stop wondering if he is better off with someone else," Sally took another drink. "I don't know. But I do know we shouldn't have come back here. Everywhere I go I have to be reminded that I'm not good enough for him."

"Here take a drag of this," Becky handed her the cigarette. "Trust me, it helps. For as much as I know the two of you, I know you're right for each other. It's chemistry and it's there, plain and simple, for everyone to see. I wouldn't worry about being good enough for him, because he will never be good enough for you."

"Think so?" Sally took a drag and coughed uncontrollably.

"There you go. That helps doesn't it?" Becky lightened the mood with a chuckle. "I really do think so. Are you better now after taking a drag of my cigarette?"

"No," Sally couldn't stop coughing. "Take it away. I'll stick with the rum, thank you very much."

"I'm with you there," Becky put her cigarette out. "Here, let me have a swallow."

Becky took a large drink and almost spit it out immediately. "Oh geez! What the hell is that stuff? Battery acid?" She'd never thought of her dad as an upscale brand kind of guy but this crap

158

was beyond bitter. *Somebody's head is gonna be thumping in the morning,* she thought.

"It's supposed to be some kind of rum. I got it — okay, stole it — from some students. I was talking to them, but they must have gotten annoyed because they left pretty quickly after I started talking."

"Well, don't worry," said Becky. "You're with me now."

"Thanks for being such a good friend, Becky. I really did not need to be the only girl on this trip this time."

"No problem, Sally." Becky snickered. "Us girls have got to stick together, you know?"

"Yeah, we do."

Becky took another drink and it was a little easier to swallow this time, but she still made a face. "Man, you had better check your chest tonight."

"Why's that?" Sally asked, not sure where Becky was going with this conversation.

"As my dad would say to John, 'it'll put hair on your chest, boy!' "

The two of them laughed loudly.

Becky stood up. "What do you say we go back, huh?"

"Okay, I think I'm better now. I should go talk to Ryan."

"Actually," Becky smirked. "I was thinking you shouldn't be too much in a hurry to work things out with Ryan. Let him sweat it out for a bit before you talk with him. Remember you're a woman and you have the power. Men like the challenge. It's that whole hunter and prey thing."

"Will it work?"

"It worked for me and Carl, but after he cheated on me I never let him stop sweating."

The two of them giggled, pausing to share sips of the rum as they meandered slowly back to the Ball.

Chapter IX
The Quest

The Enchantian Ball was finally coming to an end and everyone with partners was out on the dance floor. Sally did not take Becky's advice; she made up with Ryan immediately, throwing her arms around him and planting a kiss on his contrite, sweetly familiar face. Sally was very tipsy from the rum, so the relieved but still cautious Ryan made sure her feet were on top of his while they danced.

Becky watched happily while her brother and Dyad danced slowly to the last song. She had never been so pleased for him. He'd finally found someone who he cared about that was worthy of him.

Becky cheerfully continued to teach Mel how to dance and found it adorable that he was so clumsy. He was silent the whole time so he could concentrate on his steps. After a while Becky began to find the silence deafening.

As Becky examined the waning crowd, she noticed Cully pouting with her arms crossed, sitting by herself. She had been watching Mel closely for the past few songs, obviously waiting for her chance to cut in. Becky had no intention of letting him go. That little brownnoser wanted to cash in on a better grade. Tough, Becky had no respect for teacher's pets, not at home and not here in Enchantas.

When Becky glanced over a few moments later, trying to keep her eye on the interloper, Cully was gone. Before she could scope out the rest of the room she realized all she had to do was look behind Mel, still silently counting out his one-two-threes to himself.

"Professor," Cully said shyly. "Could I have this last dance?"

Mel stumbled for a moment, his concentration broken. "Well hello there, Cully." He looked at Becky for permission; she silently moved her eyes indicating that he should say no. "Actually, Cully. This is the last dance and it's almost over. If you would have only asked me earlier." He hesitated then said. "I'm very sorry."

"Okay, Professor. Sorry to bother you." Cully moved away with humble sadness.

"Oh, now I feel bad," said Mel. "The poor kid. Who's gonna dance with her now?"

"Don't worry," Becky teased. "You wouldn't have been able to lead. It would have been a disaster. This way she gets to keep those tiny little feet."

"Very true." Mel conceded, permitting himself a laugh before returning to concentration on his footwork.

"You know, I think she has a little crush on you."

Mel smiled, "I suspected as much. She *is* my best student. Very clever."

"Kind of a suck-up if you ask me."

"Of course," Mel joked. "All the best students are."

Becky was laughing with Mel when they heard Cully yell. "Professor Mel! Look out!"

They froze where they were as Cully catapulted through the air, hitting her professor full in the chest, tackling him to the floor.

A shaft of an arrow protruded from her back as she lay still on top of him.

Cully was dead.

Dyad and John, rushing to Mel, were diverted by a strange noise in the rafters. They spotted a large green lizard jumping to another beam and disappearing.

"Weapon!" John declared. "Somebody give me a weapon! Now!"

But no one was armed on this occasion and the guards had been stationed outside the ballroom.

"Do not worry, John." Dyad flew after the culprit swiftly. "I will get him!"

Mel slowly rolled, displacing Cully's body, which tumbled to the floor on its side. The entire crowd was in shock, none had made a move to help Mel extricate himself from under her diminutive weight without assistance. He stood up, shaking.

"Come now! Collect yourselves. We must collect evidence and properly respect the fallen." Mel stared at Cully's body, still shocked that she was dead.

"Cully!" Seara was the first to rush forward, kneeling next to the small lifeless body. "*NO!* Who did this?" The gnome keened in shock and grief. Mel dispassionately recognized the symptoms of shock in himself. He couldn't move, or think, or speak.

Sally and Ryan rushed to the small group that was forming around the body. Spotting Seara, Sally immediately went to her, enfolding her in a consoling hug.

"She's my daughter, Sally!" Seara cried. "My daughter!"

Sally cried with her. Seara had been burdened with too much death for one lifetime, first her husband Gitchy, and now her daughter. Sally knew all too well what it felt like to lose a loved one.

"How did this happen?" Seara managed to ask. Her ability to pull herself together for the safety of the community was awe-inspiring. Mel could do no less even though he was overcome with emotion.

"She, she, she," he stuttered. "She saved me. She jumped in front of the arrow," Mel paused again, bowing his head. "For me."

Survivor's guilt consumed Mel. She was so young, this ardent student with her life ahead of her. Thoughts of remorse also came unbidden, not only for her death, but for having rejected her. The last dance, the last she would ever have had in her life. The look of hurt on her face when he refused her would haunt him forever. It seemed so petty now. How could he have been so selfish and hurt her so?

Mel felt his own mortality at that moment, looking at Cully's lifeless features. She'd saved his life by sacrificing her own. He had to figure out how to defeat these assassins, how to radically restore balance and peace to Enchantas.

He wanted to avenge her death.

Becky also felt guilty as she forced herself to look at Cully's lifeless body, the blood pooling on the floor next to her, horribly real. Becky did not like the little gnome, but would never have wished for this.

Mel turned, marching away with military precision. If you didn't know him, you would never have recognized his barely controlled rage, Ryan thought, watching his friend with admiration as he quickly began to formulate a strategy. Underestimating Mel, the playmaker thought, could definitely work in their favor.

***

Mel burst through the council chamber doors to find Brian, Russell, and Robert already heavy in conversation.

"You said this was a good idea!" Mel shouted, unleashing the full force of his fury behind closed doors. "Now we have a dead student in the ballroom. That is unacceptable!"

"Yes, we know that." Brian stood up, gesturing Mel to a chair. "Professor, please, I know this is a shock. Please, sit. We need to talk."

"No," Mel began to pace. "I will not sit down! I need to do something! This is an outrage!"

"Mel, calm down," said Russell. "We're devising a plan. We need your clarity."

"I don't want to devise a plan! I want action! All we do in this room is talk, talk, talk! Nothing ever gets done."

The others had found their way to the conference room. Mel had his back to them. Russell indicated they should find seats, which they did, in nearby chairs so as to not interrupt Mel's tirade.

"If it were up to me, I'd find that witch and kill her myself!" Mel swore, which was so uncharacteristic it jolted everyone in the room. The Knights remained wide-eyed and silent as they let Mel vent.

"I'd go alone, scour the lands until I had her head on a plate!" When he had finally started to wind down after a lengthy diatribe detailing everything he planned to do to the Banshee and her minions, Robert felt it was time to broach a more proactive topic.

"This is wonderful to hear, Professor." Robert smiled. "Particularly the head-on-a-plate concept. It's exactly what we're proposing."

Mel shut up and sat down. He was consumed with raw emotion. But his intellect was a thread leading him back to reasoning, to planning, to facilitating and successfully executing a solution.

"We believe the Banshee is trying to draw the four of you away from the Institute, luring you into a trap," Robert explained. "Ultimately the outcome of this trap would mean death to you and the end of Enchantas as we know it."

"What would you like us to do?" Ryan didn't question the theory. For him it rang true.

"I have an operative in Gnelfton," Russell replied. "He has been tracking the Banshee's movements for a few cycles now. He would be our best bet to find out where she is."

"When do we leave?" John was eager for a fight. He savored another chance to stop Lexis for good. He remembered the Battle of Enchantas and how damaging she could be. She was even more of a menace now that Enchantian society had evolved into a peaceful, education-centered civilization that promoted magic for good and not evil. Sometimes, John knew, there was no getting around it. You had to fight fire with fire.

"You leave immediately," the deep tones of the Great Owl's voice reverberated in the chamber as he entered without preamble. The fact that the Sage wasn't announced with great ceremony more than anything telegraphed the urgency of the situation.

"The assassination attempt on the Professor was not the only objective tonight," the Owl said. "The Banshee had other motives in mind and her mission to that end was successful."

He paused, clearly shaken.

"Our Herald has been kidnapped."

"Firp?" Sally screeched. "Oh no!"

"Yes, my dear," the Owl continued. "I am not quite sure what her exact agenda is, but Honorary Herald Firp holds a vast amount of knowledge about our defenses and our secrets."

"The Sage is right," Russell agreed. "We must act quickly."

"I will take a transport back to the academy to begin rallying our troops," Robert smiled coldly. "If a war is what the Banshee wants, war is what she will get."

"I do not believe war is what the Banshee desires, Sir Robert," the Owl's voice became deeper, ringing out a warning that terrified the group. "She wants our annihilation. Our new way of life destroyed."

***

166

John knocked on Becky's bedroom door, waited a moment and knocked again. "Becky, are you dressed?"

"Yes, yes," Becky sounded like she was in a hurry. "Come in."

John opened the door slowly, looking at her strangely as she donned his black leather jacket. "We should hurry; everyone is waiting for us on the balcony."

Becky nodded.

"Do you want this back?" she asked, sitting down to slip on her running shoes. She'd changed back into her own comfortable clothes.

"No," John grinned. "That's okay. It looks good on you."

"Good answer." she zipped it up. "Because I don't think I'm capable of giving it back. Not willingly, anyway."

"Becky," John sat on her bed. Made of griffin feathers, it was exquisitely cushiony and soft. His bed was comfy too, but it would probably be quite some time before any of them got to sleep. "I have something for you," he told Becky, producing a small wooden box containing two geometrically rendered bracelets made of sparkling gold. "Here take one."

"These are beautiful." Becky chose the bracelet that shown with a nickel-sized cerulean blue gem at the center of the wristband. The sturdy bracelet, shaped as a lightning bolt that wrapped the wrist, was sharp at each point of its arrow-like ends. John picked up the other bracelet, a V-shaped design with a luminescent green emerald at the center. Each wristband was encircled with engravings, the facets of which added extra sparkle and brilliance to the extremely striking but very practical jewelry. "What are they?" Becky asked, her forefinger tracing the engravings on her zig-zag cuff.

"Enchantas is a very dangerous place, Becky, and I want you to be protected even if I'm not around." John clasped his bracelet onto his left wrist, raising his arm. "These bracelets are a source of

167

magic, health and protection. Mel says they have a lot of functions, but for now, all you need to know is that your bracelet will help you stay alive."

"Wow. Okay," Becky said, blown away by yet another unbelievable, magical situation beyond anything she had ever imagined. "How does this magic bracelet work?"

"It's easier to show than tell," John said. He stood up, holding out his arm as a long spear expelled from his hand. "In times of danger, your persona weapon will emerge. Mine is a spear, as you can see."

"Awesome!" Becky stood up to check out his spear, but he pulled it back in. "Careful. It's not a toy."

"What's my weapon?" she was eager yet nervous. What if it was something she couldn't handle?

"I'm not sure," John stepped closer to her. "But don't worry. The choice will absolutely be the correct choice for you. It creates itself. Try."

"How?" Becky put the bracelet on. She wobbled for a second as she felt a rush of blood go directly to her head. When she opened her eyes she didn't feel dizzy anymore and the effects of the rum she'd had with Sally were completely gone. "Wow, that was weird," she exclaimed, shaking her head again. "Now what do I do?"

"Just concentrate real hard and imagine you're in danger. You need help. Something's coming after you. Go!"

Becky closed her eyes, pretending something was coming after her. She opened them after a couple of seconds feeling a heaviness in her right hand. Looking down, she saw she now held a large platinum dagger.

"A knife?" Becky was disappointed, "What the hell am I going to do with this?"

"That looks like a throwing dagger to me," John teased. "Don't worry, that can come in handy in a fight. Anyway, I'm just glad you have this for protection."

"Whatever you say, bro," Becky swung the dagger around, making mock slices in the air, until it retracted and disappeared.

"I need to talk to you about something else," John sat back down on the bed, "Mel."

"Mel?" Becky blushed slightly. "Why?"

"It's obvious from the way he looks at you and is acting that he likes you."

"So?" Becky turned, giving him the cold shoulder. She really didn't want to have this conversation with her brother.

"I'd like it if you," John paused. He wanted the words to come out right. "Well, if you — didn't lead him on."

"Lead him on?" Becky was offended. "What the hell are you talking about?"

"Come on, Becky," John smiled to show he meant no insult. "We both know how you are with guys. You flirt with them until you get what you want and leave them on a whim."

"That is so not true," she argued.

"Yes it is." John contended. "Mel is one of my best friends and I don't want to see him get hurt, especially by my sister. I won't be in the middle."

"I can't believe you think so low of me," Becky said softly. "Mel is a cool guy, why would I ever hurt him?"

"I don't know, but ever since Carl, you haven't been nice to guys."

"Don't ever bring that pig up again, John!" Becky clenched her teeth. "You don't even know what happened, how he hurt me!"

"I may not know the whole story, but I still have to look out for my friend."

"Why don't you mind your own business, John? It's not like you've cared much about me the last couple months." Becky would not let that go.

"That's not fair, Becky! Listen to yourself," John tried to retaliate. "What would Mom think of you right now?"

"Mom?" Becky tried to laugh but it sounded more like a sob. "Mom left when I was a kid, remember? I didn't know her! You did! You were older! You always say how great she was — is — but here's the hard truth, John: Mom was not that great! You wanna know why? Because she left us! She left us with *him*! With dad!"

The conversation had blown up in his face. The argument was intensifying thanks to his thoughtless comment about their mother and now there was no taking it back. John knew her point was valid; there was no arguing the fact. He'd struck out at her defensively, not wanting to own up to neglecting her this school year or to the guilt that nagged at him. Totally immersed in football, new friends, or his studies he could sometimes forget about it. But the truth was that being there for her was not at the top of his priorities anymore and it should be.

"Get out, John! I don't want to look at you right now." Shaking with anger, Becky pointed at the door.

Without another word that could escalate matters, John sulkily left her room, heading to the balcony where he'd agreed to meet the others. He'd planned to take his sister with him but decided it was best to let her cool off on her own. She'd be fine. Things were quieting down for the night. If worse came to worst, she had the bracelet.

***

Mel, Sally, and Ryan stood under the blue moonlit sky on the castle's uppermost balcony. The wind was light and the cool winter breeze smelled like pine needles.

170

The trio was tired, especially Sally, even though the effects of her drinking binge had dissipated when she put on her persona bracelet. She and Ryan wore matching V-shaped cuffs accented with bright citrine-yellow gems.

"Sir Robert said they'd be here by now," Mel said, yawning. He quickly put on his bracelet, adorned with a geode-style amethyst purple gem at its center and was immediately awake and alert.

"Ah! That's better! I wonder what the holdup is."

"Who's coming to get us?" asked Ryan.

"Oh, here they come," Mel pointed to the sky. He threw his brown leather satchel over his shoulder, preparing to leave.

Silhouettes of over a dozen winged creatures glided swiftly, shadows in the moonlight that gracefully landed in front of them.

Two of the creatures stepped out of the shadows to greet them.

"Brista!" Sally exclaimed, hugging the large griffin around her neck. Brista's beak poked Sally's back. "I'm so glad to see you!"

"You too, my dear!" Brista straightened her back and ruffled her feathers. "We came as soon as Bion informed us of your need. We would have come sooner, if he had mentioned that you'd all assembled."

"Now, now, my darling," Bion kissed her on the beak, "No time for complaining."

"I wouldn't complain, sweetie, if you would just keep me in the loop."

"You can stop nagging any time, my love," he kissed her again, hoping it would shut her up.

"Oh, will you two stop!" another male griffin strutted up. Ryan noted he was different from his companions, having large bat-wings like a gargoyle, rather than feathers.

"Why don't you introduce me, Mom?"

171

"I'm sorry, dear," Brista covered her son with her left wing. "You can blame your father for that," she said, jumping in before Bion could offer a rebuttal. "Sally, Ryan, I'd like you to meet our son, Flaux."

"Hey, what's up," Flaux bowed, then gestured at the flock behind him. "These are my friends. We call ourselves the Death Devils!"

"Hi," his pals said in unison.

"So you and Bion are married? When did that happy event take place?" Ryan asked.

"Yes, Master Ryan," Brista said, beaming. "After the Battle for Enchantas many of the old treaties were restored and with that, marriages were arranged. Gargoyles and Griffins were among the first to reunite and with our unions came our children. The griffoyles are our new breed of guardians."

"Ma!" Flaux protested. "We're the Death Devils!"

"Okay, dear." Brista patted her son on the head, condescendingly. "Whatever you wish."

Sally and Ryan giggled.

"Where is Master John?"

"He's coming," replied Ryan. "He went to get his sister."

"His sister?" Brista asked. "Is she by chance, just as, shall we say-"

"Arrogant?" Ryan joked. "Maybe even a little more so."

"Ryan!" Sally punched him in the shoulder. "Be nice! I like her."

"I know, I do too," Ryan rubbed his persona bracelet remembering that instantly healing small wounds was one of its benefits. The pain in his shoulder rapidly disappeared.

"I'm here," John appeared. "Becky should be right behind me. So how are we getting to Gnelfton?"

"Flying," Mel said smugly, knowing John still had a fear of heights.

"Oh please. Not again?"

"Chicken!" Becky snuck up behind him. She, on the other hand, was excited to fly. There wasn't a freer feeling than being in the sky as the wind flowed around her. "Oh yeah! We're flying again! Woot! Woot!"

"I was afraid you got lost," Sally said.

"Not me, girl!" Becky snorted and pulled out her bracelet. "Check these out!" Two daggers emerged. "Pretty cool, huh? What do you have?"

Sally brandished her arm; a long, golden whip flicked out with blinding speed.

Becky sidled up for a closer look. "I have to say Sally, that totally suits you."

"You think?"

"Oh yeah! A bit feisty I must say!"

"It's supposed to match your personality, honey," Ryan beamed. "And you know it's true, you do get feisty sometimes." He mimicked a whipping motion, complete with sound effects.

"Ryan!" Sally instantly blushed, moving closer to him. She rubbed his firm chest seductively. "You wish," she whispered.

"Oh please, get a room," Becky laughed, offering Mel a saucy smile. She ignored John and he ignored her rudeness, knowing she was still quite angry with him. He was just relieved she'd decided to come with them.

"All right guys, are you ready?" Mel easily mounted a griffoyle as if he'd been riding one his entire life.

John stopped pouting — a poor cover for his discomfort — and tried to muster a smile as he nodded a greeting to the winged envoys. "Okay," he said. "Let's get this over with."

Flaux found John's attitude both irritating and wimpy, but kept quiet as he cooperatively bent down to make it easier for the reluctant rider to climb on.

"What the hell!" John complained. "Aren't there ever any seatbelts? I swear!"

The Death Devils rolled their eyes at Flaux. He replied a mischievous wink.

"Don't be a wimp, bro!" Becky was already sitting astride her griffoyle. "Just jump on and enjoy the ride."

"Sure, whatever," John leaned closer to Flaux's head. "What's your name again?"

"Flaux!" he was really becoming peeved.

"Okay, whatever, Flump," John whispered. "Could you do me a huge favor and fly slow and steady? I'm seriously afraid of heights and-"

"Death Devils!" Flaux roared. "Let's *move out!*"

"Wait! Wait!" John pleaded, but before he'd even gotten a decent grip, the stunt-loving fliers were diving straight down the tower wall then swooping back up through the courtyard like careening jets.

"What in the hell is wrong with you Flump?" John cried, but Flaux continued his acrobatic maneuvers.

Flaux executed corkscrew turns, upside-down figure-eight loops and barrel rolls. John screamed the entire time. Becky enjoyed the show as the others flew gracefully alongside the star performer, holding impeccably to their V-formation.

"Let me down right now!" John begged.

"As you wish!" Flaux smiled, bucking John off his back into a freefall.

In seconds the agile Flaux swooped under the tumbling teen. John grabbed Flaux's back feathers so tightly his fingers throbbed. Panting he struggled to catch his breath.

They slowed down and evened off, rejoining the group formation. Wide-eyed with shock, John's entire body was tensed and stiff.

"Oh, and by the way, everyone," Flaux shouted his announcement, "I'm not sure if my mom told you, but since we're half gargoyle sometimes we can't help but turn to stone in midflight."

"What?" John freaked out. "W-what happens then?"

Just then, Flaux's back began hardening and he and his fellow riders dropped like boulders.

"Wake up!" John pounded on Flaux's stone back. "Wake up! Wake up! Wake up!" He was screaming like a squalling baby.

The ground was looming closer and there was no change in the griffoyle. No more than a few feet from the ground Flaux morphed back to his flesh form, swooping up into the sky exuberantly. As he reached a safer altitude he stalled abruptly then plummeted beak first, in a spiraling stunt-pilot-style death dive before revving back up again just before it looked like they'd crash into the ground.

"Just kidding!" Flaux laughed hysterically and the other death devils joined in.

"Stop that, right now, Flump!" John was white. "That's not funny! I think I'm gonna be sick."

That got Flaux's attention. He immediately slowed to a level glide. "Let me know if you're really going to throw up. I don't want anybody puking on me!"

Flaux's request was too late; John was already hurling. Completely grossed out, Flaux reflexively heaved him off his back. John continued to barf during freefall. He stopped worrying about being scared or embarrassed because he had to concentrate on not inhaling the vomit.

Flaux, recovering his senses and reminding himself that he must not fail in his duty to safeguard the lives of the prophets, again caught John before he hit the ground.

"I-I," John said, securing his grip. Then he fainted.

"By the way, the name is Flaux," he huffed, soaring back into the formation. "Finally," he remarked to his flying companions. "I was getting *SO* tired of his complaining."

"Thank you so much for that, Flaux," Becky enjoyed watching her brother's discomfort, especially after his stupid wisecracks earlier in the evening. He was out cold. Vomit covered his face and shirt. It was immensely satisfying. "John was overdue for a scare."

"Good one, Flaux." Ryan agreed, although not so heartily. He felt some sympathy for his teammate. Being decorated in fright-barf wasn't a good look for anybody.

"Next stop Gnelfton!" bellowed Flaux. "Death devils, Hoo-Raw!"

Chapter X
The Empress

The dark-brownish-yellow sky was clogged with thick, smoke-colored clouds. The air reeked of pungent sulfur from the bubbling swamp nearby. Surrounding the area around the swamp were thick brown bushes bearing knife-sized thorns that if poked would cause instant seizure and death.

It was a perfect hiding place for the Empress.

Lexis stood proudly surveying her goblin minions; her piercing bright purple eyes not missing a move as they worked diligently to build her new fortress. Her straight hair, brown with light blonde highlights, had been cut so that it reached just below her chin. Her once beautiful face had also changed, aged by a few wrinkles etched deeply in her forehead, webbed around her eyes and furrowed into her cheeks. The evil had taken over her features and made her almost ugly. She wore a dark purple and black velvet dress with a tall pointed collar that reached her chin. The tight cut of the floor-length garment melded to her body, fitting her figure snugly. The flaring cuffs at the wrists revealed shiny emerald green lining of the silky velvet sleeves. The beauty of her attire clashed with her surroundings.

Lexis had come a long way since her life as a lonely young gypsy princess trapped under the care of the Witch and Warlock. From that sad and tortured young woman with no companions or friends to a leader of many, the resilient Empress was proud of her accomplishments.

"Your Grace," a small goblin approached, carrying a hammer. He was about the same height as an elf, but had the characteristic ugly green slimy skin, long pointed nose and long pointed ears that distinguished his breed. Goblins weren't good warriors like imps and gremlins, but they were masters of architecture and had built more castles and other impressive edifices than any other in Enchantas.

"What is it now, Goodrow?" the Empress snarled. He bowed, deeply.

"You instructed me to inform you when your agents arrived. They are here now in the cave with the prisoner."

"Delightful!" she exclaimed. She swiftly spun around, marching toward what appeared to be a dark tunnel. Extracting a purple amulet from a cleverly hidden pocket in her otherwise form-fitting dress, she rubbed it with her long skinny fingers. The amulet began to glow, giving her light as she moved along.

"Show yourselves," the Empress demanded, as she stepped into a seemingly empty room. "You know I despise it when you're invisible."

"I apologize, Your Grace," a green chameleon appeared. He wore a jester's hat and carried a crossbow.

"Well, where is she? Where is your partner?"

"I'm right here, Your Grace." Nymph floated into the room before expanding into her larger form. "I apologize for my tardiness."

"Do not apologize, my dear fairy," the Empress flashed a rare approving smile. "You have done more than enough for me. Tell me, how did everything go at the Institute? Have the prophets arrived?"

"Yes, Your Grace, and our plan continues to come together brilliantly," Nymph said. She withheld further details.

"So your seduction of Ryan was successful?"

"Like a charm," Nymph smirked. "Humans are so easily manipulated, madam. By now, I am sure Sally is beginning to mistrust him."

"Wonderful!" Lexis clasped her hands together. "One by one, they will be divided and then vulnerable."

"We do have a problem, Your Grace."

"What is it?"

"There is a fifth member of their party," Nymph looked concerned. "John's sister, Becky."

"I wouldn't worry," the Empress said confidently. "Things have a way of working themselves out. She is nothing to me and our plan. We will take care of her."

"Yes, your majesty," Nymph's fears were immediately erased. If the Empress saw no reason to worry about the unexpected visitor then neither did she.

"Where's the frog?" asked the Empress curtly.

"He is chained to the Rack, as instructed, Your Grace," replied the chameleon. "He refused to talk on the way here."

"That will change," the Empress sneered contemptuously, "soon enough."

As they entered the torture room, Nymph noted that Firp was arranged to be interrogated. His arms and legs spread and chained as he lay on a flat wooden bed.

"What device is this?" asked Nymph.

"This, my dear," the Empress answered pompously, "is called the *Rack*. I arranged to have it removed from my godparent's dungeon before the academy took over. It serves particularly well during the interrogation process. I always achieve the desired results."

She turned to Firp. "Welcome, Honorary Herald of Enchantas. Welcome to my lair."

"Let me go!" Firp spit blood at her. "You'll never get away with this. The Knights will be coming for me."

"I'm sure they will be," the Empress walked over to a round wooden device resembling a crank. "I hope for your sake, they come while you're still alive. That is, if you're smart enough to tell me what I want to know."

"I have nothing to say to you, now or ever," Firp responded, calling on every shred of his personal integrity to maintain and convey his dignity. Catching sight of Nymph he shot her a look of dismay mingled with hope. "Come, Nymph! This isn't you. You aren't meant to walk down this path of insanity and cruelty. Help me! Please!"

Nymph stood silently, arms crossed, staring emotionlessly. She knew Firp well, even liked him, but the allegiance to her Empress was far too strong. Her leader's personal agenda and goals were dependent on the information he would give. Nothing could help him now.

Goodrow walked in, removing his cloak with a flourish and rubbing his absurd little potbelly, completely incongruous with the imperial stance he was working so hard to convey.

"Perfect timing, Goodrow!" the Empress stepped away from the crank. "Our new friend here has just told me that he will never talk. Would you please show him what happens when he refuses to talk?" she motioned to the crank and bellowed. "Begin!"

"Yes, madam." Goodrow began turning the round wooden crank. The chains began to pull on Firp's limbs.

Firp howled in pain, a panting "oh-oh-oh" as his muscles and tendons were stretched beyond their endurance. No warrior schooled to tolerate physical and mental warfare could withstand the immense pain the Rack could inflict. Firp was no warrior either; he was quick to beg for mercy. "Stop, please, stop!"

"Are you ready to talk?" The Empress drew closer. "I'm listening."

"I will never tell you anything," a tear fell down his slimy cheek.

"I beg to differ," she signaled to Goodrow. "Pull! Again! Harder!"

Goodrow pulled the crank for about ten tacks before releasing.

"What do you want to know?" Firp pleaded.

"There we go, now you are beginning to appreciate the intensity of the Rack," the Empress continued. "For cycles now, I have been studying my old godparents' journals, learning much magic and much about their time in Enchantas. One book I found particularly interesting was from the time of the crusades."

"There are many stories from the crusades," Firp gasped in pain. "Why would I know anything different than you?"

"You are the Honorary Herald, my little froggy, you have all the knowledge. One story I found particularly interesting was about the Fairy Queen."

"There is not much to know," said Firp, trembling from his ill treatment. "It's very sad. The Witch and Warlock cursed her. She's been lost ever since."

"I think you know more than you're leading us to believe, my slimy friend," the Empress jeered. "Pull!"

"I know nothing," Firp squealed at the cruel turn, the strings of his ligaments stretched further beyond endurance. "I only know the stories told in school. I swear!"

"That's not true," Nymph fluttered over him, a malevolent accelerant that kicked his pain up a notch, the deep hurt of knowing there were seemingly limitless legions aligned against him. "You are entrusted with the deepest secrets of the Knight's

Order and their hidden past. I know you know! Do not lie. It will only prolong your agony!"

"Pull again!" the Empress demanded. "Pull again! Pull longer this time."

Goodrow pulled for twenty more tacks, Firp's pleas for his life turned to incoherent screams, his tendons and muscles and every fiber of his being ripped beyond repair.

"What interests me the most," the Empress continued after Firp stopped screaming, as if his vocal chords had also been pulled apart. "Is that I was not the only one who had been summoned to Enchantas by my godparents. All this time, they had someone who could rid this world of your kind and begin a new order. But they got scared. Frightened by what they had created. I searched everywhere for the location of the Queen. But the only journal I had found with the hidden location was missing a page." The Empress's eyes burned like purple fire. "*MISSING*! Out of *all* of the stupid books of theirs, there was only one with a missing page and that had to be it."

"I don't have the missing page," Firp panted, summoning the last of his mental faculties. "It is insanity to expect me to produce something lost cycles ago."

"You know the location of her cursed prison," a wicked grin grew on her evil face, revealing her rotting, yellow teeth. "You know where I could find her."

Firp closed his mouth indicating he would not reveal to her what she wanted to know.

"Pull until I say stop!" exclaimed the Empress. She was losing her already short patience. She waited half a tick, enjoying every tack of Firp's screams. Listening to creatures begging for mercy was her favorite pastimes. "Stop!"

Goodrow knelt down for a quick break. He was getting very tired.

"Where is the Queen imprisoned, Firp?" the Empress snarled, her patience gone. "Tell me! Now!"

"Is this why you joined her, Nymph?" Firp summoned the last of his strength to query the fairy. "Is this why you would betray us?"

"My race is dying, Firp!" Nymph retorted. "There is no other way to bring them back!"

"But you can't trust her!" Firp turned his head defeated. "You can't trust any of them!"

"Silence!" the Empress commanded. "Goodrow, pull!"

Goodrow resumed. The cracking, ripping sounds increased.

"I would talk now frog," the Empress whispered viciously, victoriously. "Or you will forever be in pain."

"I am there now, Banshee," he said. And at that, the torture became unspeakable to anyone with a heart. The Empress paced, as Firp's ululating, piercing waves of agonized cries forever marked the space. The pain that Firp endured was transmuted by his vibration into the very fabric of the walls, the ceiling, the floor, and beyond.

"Your Highness," Nymph whispered. "I think you can stop. I think he's ready to talk." Her old friend was bleeding and ruined. It didn't feel good. It didn't feel victorious. It certainly didn't feel *right*. For not the first time she realized that her hot impulses had caused severe errors in judgment. Who was she? A monster like the Banshee?

Firp gasped for breath, slowly lifting his head. The broken frog had dignity. His spirit was intact. "Don't any of you see? You cannot control the Queen. If you had read the journals and scrolls, you'd understand why. What makes you think she'll agree to join you?"

"Because my little froggy," her eyes glittered purple. "She is my mother."

"What?" Firp gulped.

"Yes!" the Empress called out, eager to tell her story. "As I read my godparents' journals, the story of the Queen seemed so familiar. She, falling in love with a Knight and then betraying him by falling in love with another, my father leaving her and taking me with him. For so long, I had wondered what drove him mad!" her voice suddenly deepened. "What drove him to lock me away in that basement!" her demeanor suddenly changed to one of cheerfulness and delight, as she continued. "But, my uncle saved me and my life was wonderful again, until I was whisked away and trapped here." Her bearing suddenly changed back to wickedness. "You see my friend, my mother will be on my side because she is family and we have both been victimized by the citizens of your world. Our hatred runs deep and our vengeance is unwavering!" She turned back to the goblin and yelled. "Pull!"

"Stop! Please! Stop!" cried Firp.

Nymph turned her head, she could not watch anymore.

"I promise you, the pain will stop once you tell me the location of her prison."

"Okay, okay!" Firp begged. "I'll tell you. I will tell you everything," he paused for a moment. "She was trapped in the caves of the Iced Mountain! Frozen forever!"

"Thank you, mister frog," the Empress rubbed his slimy sweaty head with a misplaced sensuality amusing only to her. "Now was that so difficult?"

"Will you please let me go?"

"I did say the pain would stop, didn't I?" the Empress smiled at the Nymph. "Nymph, can you please take care of our frog here?"

Nymph walked up to Firp, looking deep into his soulful black eyes. He thought all hope had left him, but he was able to summon one final, tiny glimmer.

"Oh, thank you, Nymph," Firp sighed with relief. "I knew there was still good in you."

Nymph took a moment to ponder the situation. Their plan was finally coming together; nothing was going to stop them now. If Firp was released, he'd tell the others. Their plans to rebirth the fairy race would be over. She could not let that happen. She finally realized who she was, and what was truly important to her. She was the savior of her race. Her sister fairies would be born again!

So she did what she had to do. Nymph tightened the straps around Firp's wrists and ankles.

"Wait, Nymph," Firp panicked.

Nymph ignored him. "Goodrow, pull! Pull as hard as you can and don't stop!"

"Nymph! Wait! Don't do this!"

But Nymph was beside her Empress now. Goodrow pulled the crank as hard as he could.

"You see, Firp," said Lexis. "I promised that the pain would stop. And so it shall."

Screams echoed through the tunnels until a sudden, loud snap came from the Rack. Firp's limbs had been torn off; blood splashed everywhere, and his body had fallen to the floor.

"There you go, Goodrow," Nymph cackled. "Frog legs for dinner. Enjoy."

Goodrow quickly picked them up, salivating as he began to gnaw the delicacy.

"Good job," the Empress put an encouraging arm around the fairy. "I knew you had it in you."

"Thank you, your majesty."

"Now come," the Empress pulled her outside. "We have a hunting party to break up."

Goodrow ignored Firp's still-twitching body on the floor next to him as he munched, bones and all, on his reward. Firp's eyes shifted to the goblin as he watched his own arm being devoured. His last breath was that of knowing that no one was there to care for him now or after death.

Chapter XI
Gnelfton

It was close to sunrise and the Death Devils had been soaring throughout the night, taking only short pit stops to stretch and rejuvenate their minds and bodies, filling the sky with their songs. Sally enjoyed the rhythm and melody of their music; she found it both soothing and upbeat.

John did not appreciate anything on this trip and found it even more irritating that Flaux had to find a cold lake to dive into with John on his back. Flaux justified it by pointing out that John smelled bad and needed a bath. John knew it was more about Flaux trying to get under his skin rather than washing it off, but he remained silent, knowing complaining would just make it worse.

John had never felt so helpless, weak and afraid in his entire life. Though, he knew the griffoyles were only joking around, the ride put in perspective how vulnerable he really was here in Enchantas.

John covered his ears, gripping tight with his thighs, as the griffoyles sang while they flew:

"Death Devils! Hoo-Raw! Death Devils! Hoo-Raw!
Who has come to rock the night?

Stir up trouble, pick a fight?
Death Devils! Hoo-Raw! Death Devils! Hoo-Raw!
We are formidable, audacious gliders;
Who don't favor screaming riders!
Death Devils! Hoo-Raw! Death Devils! Hoo-Raw!
Lethal, frisky, spirits of the sky;
Challenge us, be prepared to die!
We'll be watching, stalking near!
Death Devils! Hoo-Raw! Death Devils! Hoo-Raw!"

As the group began to descend, Becky leaned over her griffoyle so she could see the breathtaking, thick forest of trees with purple, blue, and pink leaves. As they drew closer the treetop canopy moved, the branches shifting to create a V-shaped path for their visitors. As they descended into the thick treetops, thousands of lanterns hanging from the tree branches became visible. The lanterns provided light for the city below and as they flew closer they could see hundreds of treehouses, wooden bridges, swings, boardwalks, balconies, and stairways circling upward. Branches intertwined through the city and thousands of animals, gnomes, and elves scampered through the trees and on the forest's floor.

The griffoyles glided to a large flat balcony in the middle of the city and landed.

"Welcome, my friends," said Flaux, "to Gnelfton. The capital of the Mystic Forest."

"Wow, this place is amazing!" said Becky. "These houses remind me of the treehouse dad made us, right John?"

"Sure," John leaped off Flaux the moment they landed and moved as far away as he could. He really didn't care about the treehouses and was not in a good mood.

"Greetings," said a short brown flying squirrel who glided down from above. He was a little shorter than the average rabbit and was wearing a dark blue trench coat that covered his fur. "My name is Riscal. Sir Robert told me you were coming here and that you needed information. Please, follow me."

"Are you guys coming?" asked Becky, turning to the griffoyles.

"No, we'll stay here," Flaux answered. "We must rest, if we are to safely transport you to where you need to be."

The griffoyles subsequently turned themselves into stone.

"Thank God!" John exclaimed in relief. "I hope they stay that way!"

The kids followed the squirrel down a narrow boardwalk leading to a web of passages overlooking the city below. They soon realized, after countless twists and turns, that they would not be able to find their way back by themselves. The city was so vast and complex, they would easily get lost.

John stayed close to his sister; he didn't dare look down. He'd had enough of heights for one day.

"Riscal," Mel struck up a conversation with the little squirrel. "What's it like being a spy?"

"Well," the squirrel sighed as they crossed a narrow bridge leading to another stairway, "I've been working for the E.I.C. for a few cycles now."

"E.I.C?" asked Sally.

"Enchantas Intelligence Committee," Riscal explained, continuing, "When I signed up, I thought it was going to be exciting and adventurous. You know, dangerous missions day in and day out. But truth be told, there's a lot of boring downtime." He looked at Mel. "Don't get me wrong, I'm happy being a spy, but I would like to go on more missions. To be stuck doing paperwork like I have been gets to be very tedious."

"I know what you mean," Mel was reminded of all the exam-grading that came with his duties at the Institute.

"I wish I were able to come with you all and go on a real mission."

Riscal stopped, motioning the five to enter a small elevator-sized wooden cage.

"What's this?" asked Ryan.

"It's a zip-cage." Riscal climbed in and held onto a rail. "It'll take us down to the lower level across the city. It's the fastest way to travel in Gnelfton."

The visitors silently examined the unstable, wobbly cage.

"Don't worry," Riscal waved them in. The cage shook as it hung from a rope above. "It's quite safe. There are hundreds of them here in Gnelfton. There goes one now." He pointed up as a cage zoomed by as fast as a freight train.

"I am not going in that thing!" John shouted, wide-eyed. "It was bad enough to be flung around like some ragdoll by those psycho griffoyle things and now you want me to get in this rickety thing? Oh hell no!"

"John, quit whining and being a wussy," his sister insisted, pushing him into the cage. It teetered, as John held on for dear life.

As he looked down, he noticed the floor had a crack, and he could see the forest's ground which was hundreds of feet below. "You have got to be kidding me!" He squeezed his eyes shut.

The group piled in, the cage shook, and the boards creaked. John was sure they exceeded the weight limit. His heart began to race.

"Could someone please pull the lever outside?" asked Riscal.

"Sure," said Sally, pulling the lever.

Immediately, the cage flew swiftly down the line; tickles arose in their bellies caused by the rapid descent. John held his fluttery stomach hoping he wouldn't get sick again. The others screamed with excitement. The wind was blowing and the squeak of the pulley above was so loud they could barely hear their own cries of exhilaration.

The cage glided over the city, the residents below were a continuous blur. They were so high up that the residents looked like blue and green ants feverishly scurrying around on the forest floor.

Sally watched other zip-cages zoom by above and below as they carried little people wearing either green or blue suits and hats. Sally remembered Mel telling them the difference between elves and gnomes. From what she had observed already, there really was no variance, except for the colors they wore.

Their ride abruptly came to an end as they slammed into a stopper and the cage tottered for a moment. "Oops," said Riscal. "Forgot the brakes. No worries. Is everyone in one piece?"

"Nice landing," John complained, pulling himself off the cage floor.

"My apologies," Riscal brushed passed them and started down another boardwalk. "Please follow me; my home is right up this way."

They climbed a few circle staircases that wrapped around the enormous trees, crossed several more bridges, until they finally reached Riscal's treehouse.

The home, nothing fancy, looked similar to all of the others they'd passed.

"Would you like a cup of my homemade acorn tea?" Riscal asked, opening his door. "You all look completely exhausted. Especially this guy right here," he pointed at John. "Are you all right? You look as if you'd recently been in a battle or some other traumatic event."

John glared at him.

"Don't be rude, bro," Becky slapped him on the shoulder. John didn't budge.

"In that case, I'll make a pot right away," Riscal hurried into another room, leaving the five unattended. "I think I need a cup myself."

Riscal's home was small and quaint. There wasn't much in it; just a few books, scrolls and maps. There were a few paintings of squirrels and chipmunks which must have been friends and family. After a few ticks, Riscal came back with a platter holding five tiny cups. Each of them took one, holding it between index finger and thumb.

"Cheers," said Riscal, raising his cup and drinking.

The rest of them followed suit. As the hot liquid poured down their throats, they couldn't help but gag at the harsh bitterness of the tea.

"Pretty good, right?" Riscal gathered their cups to return them to the kitchen. "Acorn tea is my favorite."

"Riscal," Mel coughed; his mouth felt as gritty and dry as if he'd just eaten sand. "Do you have any clue of the whereabouts of the Banshee?"

Riscal came back into the room carrying a large, rolled-up piece of paper along with a platter holding more tea. He unfurled the map of Enchantas and set it and the platter on his wooden table.

Becky was amazed by the vastness of Enchantas. This expansive land contained forests, mountains, deserts, oceans, lakes and rivers, so big, so all-encompassing that she wondered how it could possibly have remained hidden from everyone else in their world.

"My job is to track the Banshee's movements. Every time a loyalist reports seeing the Banshee, it is then messaged to me. In the past couple of cycles, she has been spotted here, here, here, and here." He pointed to places on the map as he spoke. They were all random. "I've been trying to find a pattern that may help us figure out what she is up to, but that hasn't yet been revealed through our research methodology."

Mel concentrated on the points and then shared a theory. "Riscal, everywhere you have pointed has an office of the

Institute's Library. I know, because I oversaw each of their constructions. Maybe she is searching for something in the libraries."

"Hmm," Riscal pondered, scratching his chin. "That could be, but what of these places?" He pointed at some mountains and swamps.

"She could have been seeking out past supporters of the Witch and Warlock. Not all have agreed to our new way of life. And most are on the other side of the Enchantian Mountain range."

"Very true," said Riscal. A soft but distinctive three-note chime — "Ting! Ting! Ting!" — came from his desk. "Incoming E-Mail!"

"E-Mail?" Sally asked.

"Enchantian Mail," answered Riscal, retrieving and unrolling a scroll. "It's the most efficient way to send a message. You just write it down on this scroll and it disappears as the message gets delivered. When someone sends you a message it chimes." He smiled at Mel. "It's a very good and useful idea, Professor. I truly don't know how I'd do my job without it."

"Thank you," Mel replied.

"You all should be very proud of your friend here. Since his arrival his inventions have made life so much easier for us."

"Yeah," Sally glared at Mel. "At some point, we're going to need to talk about a couple of those 'great' innovations: some flowers and a moat that you neglected to inform us about."

"Yeah," Ryan crossed his arms.

"Oh," Mel laughed. "You found those, huh?" he quickly changed the subject. "Riscal, what does the message say?"

Riscal took a moment to read it. "Wonderful, news! Nymph the fairy has just indicated to me that the Banshee has been spotted recently in the mountains of the Enchantic Mines."

Sally's jaw clenched and fists tightened as she heard the fairy's name.

"Makes sense," Mel nodded. "That's where more of the past supporters of the Witch and Warlock, primarily the imps and gremlins, have been hiding out all of these cycles." He took another sip of his tea. Although he still wasn't enjoying the bitterness it was helping him to stay awake and alert. "She must be trying to recruit them."

"Well," Sally started for the door. "What are we waiting for? Let's go!"

"Sally," Ryan grabbed her and turned her around knowing something was troubling her. "Slow down. It's been a crazy couple of days."

"I'm fine, Ryan," she snapped. "It's just that every time I hear her name I want to choke somebody!"

"It'll be all right," Ryan comforted her. "Just let it be."

"It's not going to be all right! What, are you taking her side on this?"

"No," Ryan objected. "What are you talking about? I'm not taking anyone's side."

"So you're not on my side either?" Sally's face began to turn red. "What kind of boyfriend are you?"

Ryan didn't say anything. He just wanted this conversation to be over, but it was escalating instead.

"I cannot believe you!" Sally stormed out of the treehouse and began to walk down a boardwalk. "Riscal, where are the griffoyles?"

"I believe your mission has begun," said Riscal, following the irate girl outside. "Come, follow me, everyone."

***

The trip back to the griffoyles was brief thanks to a zip-cage shortcut Riscal knew. When they reached the landing pad, Riscal promptly knocked on Flaux's stone head. His stone body transformed back to normal; the others quickly followed suit,

194

shifting from griffin-looking stone statues to skilled flying machines.

"That was quick," Flaux whistled through his beak. "Where are we off to now?"

"I am not going on those things again," John fumed. "I've had enough of them!"

"We have to get going, John," said Ryan. "Stop being so stubborn."

"No, Ryan!" John argued. "I will not! That last ride was not at all fun. I'd rather walk. I will seriously-"

John had been hit in the face. Purple juice covered him and he puckered up until he looked like a prune. John dropped to the ground quivering and curled into a little ball.

Everyone turned around to see Mel holding a slingshot with a purple diamond-shaped object in his hand.

"What?" Mel sounded innocent. "Please tell me he was annoying all of you as much as he was annoying me."

Everyone nodded, even the griffoyles.

"What did you do to him?" Becky was enjoying a break from her brother's non-stop complaining but she also wanted to make sure he wasn't truly hurt. "Will he be all right?"

"Yeah," the slingshot disappeared into Mel's bracelet. "He's fine, just stunned. I popped him with a puckerberry. He should wake up by the time we get to the Enchantic Mines."

"Becky, can you help?" Ryan tried picking John up, but his dead weight and his quivering was too much for Ryan alone.

Becky looked at John's head, it had been shriveled into a small ball, "Mel, is this normal?"

"Oh," Mel snickered. "Don't worry about that, just a side effect. He'll be back to his old handsome and well-mannered self in no time."

Becky chuckled and continued to help Ryan pick her brother up. They began to drag him to Flaux.

"No, no, no," Flaux protested. "I've had enough of that guy for one night. Give him to Borgo over there."

"Do I have to?" Borgo objected. "He got on my nerves when you were carrying him."

"Do your job," Flaux demanded. "Does anyone want a thrill ride on our flight to the mines?"

"I do!" Becky dropped her brother's body without hesitation and jumped on Flaux.

"Becky!" Ryan grunted, still trying to carry John's dead weight. Mel helped. It took a few tries, but John was eventually safely strapped onto Borgo.

The rest of them settled in comfortably as they flew up toward the forest ridge. The branches opened and the white sun gleamed brightly on them. The griffoyles flapped their wings hard, reaching high into the green sky and gliding toward a far blue mountain range on the distant horizon.

"Next stop," called out Flaux, "The Enchantic Mines! Death Devils, let's *move out*! Hoo-Raw!"

Chapter XII
The Demigons

They had been flying less than five tocks before the land below began to change. The forest was vast with a bravura array of green, yellow, red, and orange, which reminded them of another autumn day back in Willington. The further they flew the fewer the trees they saw — none were as magnificent as the ones in the grand Enchantian Forest— and the more desolate and dark the landscape became. The blue mountain range grew larger; the sun hid behind dark gray clouds giving a yellowish tint to the barren ground below.

John was still asleep, paralyzed by Mel's puckerberry shot. Sally and Ryan spoke to each other for most of the ride, arguing every now and again. Mel slowly moved his griffoyle clandestinely next to Becky, which took about a tock, but once he was next to her, he had nothing to say.

He wondered what had happened that made him so shy all of a sudden, but then he figured he was just tired. He found it soothing to watch her as her hair flew in the wind. It made him so relaxed that he soon fell asleep.

Becky couldn't sleep. She was enjoying her ride too much. Every now and again, she could not help but pinch herself as a reminder that she was not dreaming and that this was all real. Still, the reality of this new world was just too mindboggling for her to fully comprehend, but she adapted and was really enjoying herself.

Flashes of white light came from the sky above the mountains and explosions of thunder rang in their ears.

"Keep your eyes open, Devils!" called out Flaux, warily. "We are beginning to enter demigon territory."

"Demigon?" Becky leaned into Flaux to ask. "What's that?"

"Bruno," called Flaux. "Would you like to tell the lady what a demigon is?" He tilted his head back and whispered, "He's our history buff."

"Sure," Bruno soared closer as Mel slept on his back. "Demigons are a rival gang of feathered dragons who roam the great mountain range."

"Feathered dragons?" Becky was interested.

"Yeah," Flaux piped in. "Dragons live far away in a remote lagoon on the other edge of Enchantas. Nobody goes there because dragons are very unpleasant. Mostly because when they talk, they spit fireballs at you."

"Flaux," Bruno whined, "I was getting to that."

"Sorry, Bruno. Please proceed."

"Anyway, legend has it, that many, many, many cycles ago, an adventurous dragon ventured across the Enchantic Ocean to explore the other lands. Unintentionally, she met and fell in love with the lord of all birds, the Red Phoenix. Who incidentally, was a distant cousin of our Grand Sage."

"That big owl, right?" Becky asked.

"Right," Bruno continued. "They were married and lived in the caves of the mountain range. Life was wondrous for the family for many, many cycles. They birthed thousands of children, who like us, are mixed breeds. Their parents had named them the drageese. They are quite beautiful creatures, if you ask me. Their gorgeous colored feathers cover their dragon scaled hides. Their wingspans are enormous, but so elegant."

"Don't get all mushy, Bruno," warned Flaux. "You know very well how dangerous they are!"

"Yeah, I know, I was getting to that."

"What happened?" Sally piped in, also interested. "Why are they so dangerous?"

"For ages the dragon, the phoenix, and their children had kept the mountain passes safe for Enchantians to cross. That was until the days of the crusades. During the war, the Witch and Warlock asked the mountain keepers to become allies. They respectfully declined and wished to not be a part of the war, because their beliefs did not concur with either side. The Knights of course, respected their wishes, but the Witch and Warlock had become vengeful and concerned that if they were not friends, then by definition, they were enemies and had the dragon and the phoenix killed."

"That's horrible!" Becky cried.

Sally recoiled quietly as she rode behind. Guilt ravaged her insides as she wondered how her parents could have done such a terrible thing. She continued to silently listen.

"The morning after the assassination their children, the drageese, resentful and angry, stopped all travel through the mountains and began to kill all who try to fly through. They renamed themselves the demigons, the kings of the mountain."

"Bruno," Flaux interjected. "Don't forget to tell her how and why they are so dangerous."

"Indeed. Besides their enormous size, instead of breathing fire, like dragons, the demigons breathe lightning. This is much more frightening, if you ask me. Depending on how close or direct a strike is, you could be scorched to ashes instantaneously or they can stun you for torturing later. They are very ruthless."

"So why are we flying directly into their mountain territory?" asked Ryan, joining the conversation. "Wouldn't it be smarter to divert?"

"We need to get you all as close as we can to the entrance of the mines," Borgo explained. He glanced back at John who was snoring, still shriveled but not as severely.

"They don't particularly like humans, so walking through their territory is not the best idea. With any luck, we hope we can fly through unseen."

Sally rubbed her lucky earrings intently. If the demigons knew who she was and who her parents were, they would certainly torture and kill her.

A thunder clasp banged loudly, jolting John awake. His arms flailed sporadically as he caught his balance. Falling again was not an option for him.

"What the hell, Mel!" John slurred. His post-puckerberry face was still a little numb and crinkled.

"Sorry, John, but we needed — and you needed — a break." Mel listened to the thunder. It was louder. "Where are we?"

"We just flew into demigon territory," replied Flaux.

"Oh, great," Mel sighed, "Demigons."

"You know of them?" asked Becky.

Mel lit up instantly, ecstatic that she was talking to him again. "Yeah, well I've never been up close. I've read the history and seen the paintings of them at the Institute. Beautiful creatures but very dangerous."

"Right you are, Professor," Flaux said, flying faster.

The sound of thunder and streaks of lightning became more prevalent the deeper they flew into the canyons. The mountain began to rise up underneath them; the ground consisted entirely of rock.

"Where's the entrance?" Sally cried over the thunderous cracks and ominous rumbles.

"Right up there." Flaux pointed with his beak.

The cave, which resembled nothing more than a small hole from a distance, was located directly at the summit of a jagged mountain.

"You expect to fly all the way up there in this weather?" John complained.

"Shut up, John," the other four teens intoned in unison.

Streaks of lightning began to shoot from the sky near their flight path. The griffoyles maneuvered gracefully and evasively as Flaux spotted an incoming shape bulleting toward them.

"Brace yourselves!" Flaux yelled as he and the other griffoyles dove in delta position toward the ground, deftly pulling up to glide just a few feet above the rock surface.

"Oh my God," gulped John. "You can just drop me off right here."

An immense, purple-feathered demigon darted above them, spraying white lightning bolts from its nostrils. Its body, the size of a semi-truck, was covered in bright purple and light blue feathers; its feet and wings glowed vibrant red. Its spear-like teeth jutted out of its open mouth as its large, piercing eyes glared in determination.

"Evade! Evade!" Flaux pulled up, Becky holding on tight. "Pull up!"

The others followed, ascending into the yellow sky.

"We need to split up!" yelled Borgo.

"Borgo," commanded Flaux. "You take a formation this way. Bruno, take your group that way. I'll head straight for the cave. I'll drop her off and we'll regroup."

"What about-" John began to say, but the three groups had already split up.

The demigon began to follow Borgo's group, but quickly returned to tail Flaux, as he was closest to the mountain. Flaux dove, twisted and turned to outmaneuver the demigon, but it remained directly on his flank.

Becky turned and began to throw daggers at it. Her aim was off; she missed her target. "Dammit," she muttered. "I need some practice."

Flaux dove, rapidly looping in a brilliantly executed helix pattern, under then above again. He was simply too fast and agile for the larger beast. Before the demigon knew what happened, Flaux was able to escape the pursuit for a moment and land in front of the cave entrance.

"Here you go, my lady," said Flaux. Becky nimbly hopped down as Flaux launched back into action.

"Hurry!" Becky yelled as she spotted a dozen more demigons swooping into battle. "They're coming!"

Flaux regrouped with the squadron, which then split into two groups, one with riders, one without. The Death Devils arched their wings as far back as they could, giving them faster speed, but the demigons were still gaining.

Lightning bolts struck griffoyle wings but glanced off without effect. The clever Devils were temporarily shifting to stone as needed to deflect the attack. Becky could see Ryan, John, and Mel hurling spears and shooting arrows at the beasts, but nothing would penetrate their armor of thick scales underneath their feathers. This was a skirmish that couldn't be won.

The second group of griffoyles suddenly dove from above, blindsiding the demigons and causing a freefall. The distraction gave Flaux and the others a chance to reach the cave.

Moments felt like days for John as he clutched tightly to Bruno. He could see his sister waving her hands from the cave entrance. Finally, his flight was over.

The four others landed quickly and stumbled off the griffoyles. The Death Devils fled the mountain range, the demigons following.

"Thank God that's over!" John panted. "If I was still smoking, I'd have one right now."

"Don't mind if I do," Becky smirked, and lit up. "And don't get any ideas bro! I only have a few left."

"Hey! Those are mine. I left them in my jacket."

"So?" said Becky with a lit cigarette in her mouth, smoke trailing and wreathing around her eyes.

"Where to now, Mel?" Ryan motioned the group back from the entrance. "We should get inside before those feathered dragons come back."

"It's dark in there, Ryan." Sally didn't know which she feared more: whatever lurked in the unknown blackness or the murderous sky beasts.

"I got this," Mel told her. He rubbed his bracelet and chanted:
"Cave of fear, dark as night;
Torch appear, and give us light!"

A long rod extended from his hand emanating a bright green flame.

"Now that is seriously cool," Becky smiled, patting his back. "Can you teach me how to do that?"

"No problem," Mel smiled back.

"I don't know how you come up with those spell rhymes," Ryan said.

"You should try it," Mel said, happy to share his skills. "It's really not that difficult."

"I did try it." Ryan sighed. "Trust me, I'm not a poet and I am definitely not in the mood to embarrass myself, again."

"Again?" Sally grabbed his hand. "When did you try?"

"In Nymph's lecture."

"Don't say that name in front of me," she snapped, curtly letting go of his hand and crossing her arms.

"Sally, come on," Ryan tried to take her hand again, but she stubbornly refused to let him. "Don't be like that."

"Don't be like what, Ryan?" Sally gave him a heated glare. "I don't like her."

"Sally," Ryan took a deep breath. "What happened is really not my fault. Neither time was my fault."

"It's not just that, Ryan." Sally said quietly. "It happens at school, during games. It happens all the time and I hate it."

"Stop being jealous, Sally," Ryan complained. "It's beginning to be a pain."

"What?" Sally was shocked by his comment. "I'm sorry I'm such a burden on you!" she yelled, caution forgotten as she stomped farther into the cave.

"Good going, preppie!" Becky patted him mockingly on the back before following after Sally. "You sure have a way with the ladies, especially your own girlfriend," she said over her shoulder.

Ryan was baffled. "I was just being honest."

"Sometimes honesty isn't the best option when it comes to girls," said John. He and Mel walked side by side.

"How would you know?"

"I've had a few girlfriends," John laughed. "Not like our friend Mel, over here."

"Hey, be nice!" Mel didn't take it as a joke.

"It's all right," John continued. "I don't think I'll ever truly understand girls. But I do know there are some things you don't say out loud. Comments like that, for instance."

"And about a girl's weight," Mel added.

John and Ryan looked at Mel to see if he was making a joke.

Mel defended his observation, "We've all heard it. They're always worrying about how they look."

"True," John laughed. "Telling them how they look can be tricky business."

"What about telling them how you feel?" asked Mel. "When would be a good time to do that?"

John glared at his friend. "I'd say never, keep it to yourself and let them figure it out."

"John!" Ryan interjected, "Now look who's acting jealous." Ryan threw a comradely arm around the Mel. "Here's a lesson for you, Professor. You should always share your feelings with the girl you like. Don't listen to John. His reluctance to share is probably why his relationships never last."

"Suit yourself, Mel." John took the green torch from Mel and began to walk in front of them. "Don't come crying to me when your heart's broken." John got a few feet behind the girls and began to strut at the same pace.

"Yeah, don't listen to him," Ryan continued. It was a welcome diversion from their less-than-relaxing situation. "So you're interested in someone? That's good. Really good. We never really talked about it before."

"I don't know," Mel was feeling shy; he paused before answering. "I kind of like Becky. She's," he paused for the right word, "interesting."

"Interesting?" Ryan chuckled. "Yeah, I guess she is. But that's not why you like her, right?"

Mel thought for another moment. "Well, actually, it is. I like girls who intrigue me."

"I guess coming from you that says a lot." Ryan laughed again. "But think of it this way, you wouldn't want to tell her that you think she is interesting or intriguing when you want to tell her you like her, would you?"

"Why not?"

"Well, girls like to be flattered, you know, woo them with words like beautiful, gorgeous, mesmerizing."

"Pulchritudinous?"

"Sure," Ryan shot a baffled look. "That is, if she even knows what that means."

"Hypnotic, entrancing, seductive?"

"Better, but it all depends on how you phrase it in a sentence."

"Well," Mel swallowed hard as his throat was dry, "that's how she makes me feel."

"Good, good," Ryan nodded encouragement. "Then you must really like her."

"I think I do," Mel rubbed his forehead. It was sweaty. "Sally and I kind of had a feeling you had a crush on her."

"Did you?" Mel's eyes widened, face flushed. "Am I that transparent?"

"It's fine, Mel. There's no need to be embarrassed. It makes sense, really."

"How so?"

"You've been here for so long."

"Over fourteen cycles," Mel reminded him.

"So I'm sure you're lonely and besides," Ryan gave him a wink. "She is pretty cute."

"Cute?" Mel sounded appalled. "Astounding is more like it."

"There you go, buddy," Ryan praised him. "Your flattery is getting better. Keep practicing." Ryan began to walk faster toward the girls. "I'm going to apologize to Sally."

Ryan could hear Mel mumble as he practiced lines. He passed John, overtaking the girls. They were in the middle of a conversation but stopped abruptly when he arrived.

"Sally, can we talk?"

"Sure," Sally looked at Becky as if asking for permission, or reassurance. Becky nodded her head.

"Okay," Sally told Ryan. "I guess."

Becky held up, waiting for John so the couple in front of her could have some privacy.

"Sally," Ryan said sincerely, "I am so sorry about what I said. That was really rude of me."

"Yes it was." Sally said bluntly.

206

"I have no excuse for what happened with Nym-"

"Don't say her name!"

"You know what I mean, though," Ryan continued. "And I'm sorry about how you feel when we're back home."

"I'm sorry too, Ryan. I really wish I wasn't so jealous," Sally took a deep breath. "But I can't help it sometimes! Seeing those girls hang on you all day and then that stupid, sleazy fairy making her moves. It irritates me that no one respects that we're together. No one respects me or our relationship!"

"I respect you, Sally," Ryan kissed her on the cheek. "I love you so much. I don't want you to be hurting like this anymore. You are mine and I am yours, no matter what. Nothing can change that. Remember, we are spirit-mates. We have proof that we are supposed to be together. Always and forever."

"Oh, Ryan!" Sally threw her arms around him. "I love you so much!"

"Oh, get a room!" John almost snarled as he passed them up. Alone, he was feeling like the infamous "fifth wheel". He missed Dyad and he felt even lonelier when he watched Sally and Ryan, even when they were fighting, because at least they were together. He'd often felt the same way back home; there was no one in school that could fill his heart as Dyad did. Even though she was much closer now, she was still too far away and they were still separated. Though they didn't have a committed relationship, he knew as well as she did that they had feelings for each other. He didn't want to admit it, but it had really been true love at first sight for him.

Becky and Mel lagged at the back of the procession. She was more interested in Mel's stories and Enchantas facts than where they were actually headed. She noticed how excited, almost giddy, Mel would get when given the opportunity to share his knowledge. He stuttered because he talked so fast. She thought it was cute.

"These mines have been here for many ages," Mel told Becky, eager to share but fervently praying that he wouldn't get any more nervous than he already was. He hoped he wouldn't say anything unintelligent, or worse, embarrassing. "From the beginning, I believe."

"Really?" Becky sounded disinterested, but in reality she thought it was very fascinating.

"Y-Yeah," Mel stuttered. "When the Knights found out that lixy dust had magical properties, they began to train Enchantians to mine it. Today, the best miners are the dwarves and moles of these caves."

"I don't understand. I thought the dust came from the fruit that grows on the trees. Now you're telling me that lixy dust comes from here?"

"In a sense. You see, there is a cycle that it goes through before the dust can be mined. First, there are the little worms here in Enchantas that eat the cubed lixy fruit that you saw the other day."

"Oh, yeah," said Becky. "That was tasty. Like buttered popcorn."

"Yes. That's what the worms eat, too. When they're full, they find a small, dark and damp place to cocoon. A bottle tucked away somewhere is ideal. After their release, they grow into these huge worms and produce lixy dust. These worms have a tendency to become addicted to Lixyworm Wine. Some Enchantians have used the wine to lure and trap the worms in the bottles so they can make their own lixy dust."

"They're the size of a bus," John tossed the comment from up front. Eavesdropping on their conversation may have been a little rude, but it distracted him from missing Dyad.

"Exactly, John, and then they burrow deep underground and shed from time to time. The shedding of these worms is what is mined and then manufactured into lixy dust."

Mel continued, "Lixy dust used to be sold, traded and bartered around Enchantas, but since the revolution our currency is meticulously regulated. The dust can be used for many things, for example fueling flying ships; providing non-mythics access to magic; and it's also a great spice for food and drinks."

"Wow," Becky smiled at Mel, and let out a little giggle.

"What's so funny?"

"You're like a walking encyclopedia," Becky replied with a flirty grin.

"I hope that's a good thing." Mel was worried that he was being teased.

"It is," Becky playfully twirled a tendril of his curly hair before quickly slipping free the elastic holding his ponytail. As she let down his hair she realized that she was flirting and that her brother had asked her to leave Mel alone, to not hurt him as she'd hurt other guys. She thought Mel was nice, but hadn't decided how she felt about him beyond that. To avoid leading him on and having any further arguments about that with her brother, she tried to explain herself as honestly as possible. "Mel, I'm really glad we became friends. You're a cool guy. I haven't met many good guys since my ex-boyfriend."

Mel had nothing to say. His heart sank at the word *friends*. He didn't hear anything she said after that kiss-of-death declaration. Just friends. His heart was too hurt to hear the rest.

The light John held grew brighter as the group walked down a set of blue brick stairs. They came upon an opening to a large brick tunnel about thirty feet in circumference.

"Where to now, Mel?" John's words echoed, the sounds rippling, like a skipping stone, the final "el, el, el," carried down the vast, empty tunnel.

The torchlight illuminated several hundred feet of the tunnel, but there was no end in sight.

"It's this way," Mel directed, ignoring Becky as he stepped to the front of the group to take the lead. Focused on the expedition, she took no offense, simply following along with the others. "There should be a couple mine trolleys up this way."

"I think I see one!" Ryan, torn between staying back with Sally and surging forward to walk in tandem with Mel, gave in to his natural instincts, quickening his pace.

As the trolley came into clear view they couldn't help but notice how rusty and old it was.

"Another thrill ride, I take it?" asked John, who was obviously not excited at the prospect.

"Yep," Mel was the first to board. "Come on up. This is the best way to tour the Enchantic Mines."

One by one they piled into the trolley, which did not fit them comfortably. Mel released the brake lever and they slowly rolled down into the mines.

Chapter XIII
Enchantic Mines

The trolley rode slowly down the heavy, rusted iron tracks into the depths of the mine. Others might find the experience claustrophobic and boring, but it was a relief for John. He'd had his fill of thrill rides this trip; a slow cruise was just what he needed, although it would have been nice not to be crammed into a conveyance that wasn't built to hold two people — let alone five — comfortably. He could tell his sister, on the other hand, was getting restless. He tried to keep from chuckling as he watched her impatiently trying to simultaneously take a drag on her cigarette and keep it from burning anyone, or from getting knocked away. She finally got a puff in, then wrenched her head around to try to blow the smoke away without getting it in anyone's face.

Ryan and Sally, like John, seemed to relax. They held each other quietly and contentedly as Mel easily manned the trolley brake.

The smooth tunnel had given way to sharp, jagged cave walls much like the Forbidden Cave John remembered from their first trip to Enchantas. It didn't have a musty cave smell, though. The air was sweet and thick as honey and the red rock walls sparkled like rubies.

Becky took a final drag of her cigarette and flicked it at the cave wall. A wave of bright sparks flowed outward from the point of impact. Startled, she looked at Mel for an explanation. He smiled at her and threw a couple rocks at the wall causing the same effect along with producing a light, tingling sound like a wind chime. Becky scooped up a handful of little pebbles from the trolley floor and tossed them at the wall, smiling as they gently released an array of musical melodies and beautiful sparks.

Then without warning the trolley stopped; the cave had ended.

"A dead end?" Ryan braced himself, looking behind them.

"I don't think so." Mel jumped out and began to feel the jagged wall. "The entrance should be here. At least, those were my calculations when I studied the maps. Although, it has been a long time since I've reviewed them."

"Maybe you took a wrong turn," Ryan suggested.

John jumped out of the trolley, wielding a pickaxe. "Glad I decided to bring this along for the ride. There were a few of them on the ground at the head of this tunnel. Maybe it was a hint that we need to dig a little more." He raised the pickaxe and before Mel could stop him, he swung it against the wall. A horrendous clang reverberated around the cave, louder than a thousand cymbals, deeper than a thousand gongs, shaking the earth around them and spitting sparks everywhere.

"Are you trying to kill us?" Ryan grabbed the pickaxe. "Smart move, hotshot."

John was about to retort with a rude remark when the wall behind him began to open, a sort of combination crumbling, cracking and sliding that began at the point of his pickaxe impact.

The wide scope of a searchlight beam radiating through the opening, momentarily blinded them. When their eyes adjusted, to their amazement, they saw that the trolley tracks continued. A peak overlooking a vast cavern came into view as the trolley began to move itself. Ryan and John hustled to jump back in. The vast opening was deep, wide and tall, a valley landscape within the mine.

Hundreds of determined, focused little men with long beards were bustling about carrying baskets and barrels of sparkling red, turquoise, and violet rock that they were loading into a seemingly never-ending train of trollies. They all wore matching brown overalls and floppy brick-red hats. They were much more muscular than gnomes, elves or leprechauns, but just as short.

"Dwarves," Mel whispered to Becky.

High above the cavern there were more dwarves swinging their pickaxes from scaffolding and slings, tucked into every nook and cranny. The room sparkled beautifully and a symphony so magical radiated out that the dwarves couldn't help but smile and hum along. The dwarves whistled in harmony with the banging of the pickaxes as the music sprang from the mountain's walls.

Most of the dwarves did not pay any attention to the visitors, five strangers riding a trolley through their assembly line. The few who did look up from their unceasing labors glared briefly, annoyed, but quickly dismissed them as unimportant and returned to their tasks.

Their trolley suddenly stopped. Oblivious to their presence, a black-bearded dwarf began to empty his basket of red and turquoise glittery rock into it.

"Hey!" John bellowed, holding the basket upright. "What the hell?"

"Oh, I didn't know it was occupied," the dwarf replied blandly. "Foreman! We have visitors?"

The cavern fell silent. The clinging and banging of pickaxes and hammers and the music stopped completely as all heads turned toward their trolley.

"Get back to work!" A white-bearded dwarf demanded. The symphonic clanging resumed. "Mindless laborers!" he mumbled under his breath as he reached the trolley. The dwarf put on a pair of old spectacles and studied the five young people. "Humans, eh? What are you doing here?"

"Yeah," another dwarf hissed from above, "Ain't you a little far from your comfortable Institute?"

"Back to work!" the foreman barked again. "Or else you'll be workin' another double!"

"Big deal!" the hissing dwarf replied. "This is already my third double in a row. Bring it on!"

"We were actually on a mission," Mel said, trying to be as quick and courteous as possible with his explanation but knowing there was not really any way to please the perennially dissatisfied dwarves. "We're in search of the Banshee. Have you seen her and if so where?"

"Why would you think she's here?"

"We heard from sources," Mel began.

"Well, we don't concern ourselves with outside matters," the foreman said dismissively.

"Yes," Mel tried to be reasonable, "but our reports indicate she's in the vicinity."

"Can't you see we're busy?" a dwarf yelled from behind.

"Yeah," another bellowed from below, "mining your precious lixy dust!"

"So if you please," the foreman continued, "let us get back to work."

"Hey!" John stepped out of the trolley. He towered over the foreman. "All we want is some information. We heard the Banshee is here and want to know what you know."

The dwarf sighed, "Well if you're gonna be that stubborn about it, I'd probably ask the governor. He knows all that goes on

214

around here. We are just drillers, blasters, and choppers. We ain't privileged with such knowledge."

"Thanks," Mel was still trying to be polite. "Which way should we go?"

But the foreman was gone.

The brake released itself as the trolley accelerated. John quickly jumped back in. "You were right about them being cranky."

"Yep," Mel nodded, as he tried pulling on the brake to control it.

"Mel?" John was getting nervous. "Can you slow this down?"

The brake wouldn't budge. Becky grabbed onto the handle too, putting all her muscle into it. Nothing. The trolley sped on, faster and faster, as it dipped down a dark tunnel and Mel's green-flame torchlight was extinguished in the wind. "This is what we call flying blind," he remarked to no one in particular.

Becky squealed and squeaked again in surprise as her big, strong, brave older brother grabbed her arm in fear, clutching her bicep in a death grip.

The trolley took a couple of hard lefts and a few swooping rights until it finally slowed down and stopped in a small room containing a large desk, a few chairs and stacks of books arranged neatly in a long, horizontally constructed bookshelf.

"I guess this is our stop," said Mel, as he wiggled the now-working brake. "Everybody out!"

"Gladly," John said, his pulse still racing and sweat trickling down his back.

They disembarked cautiously to investigate the small room. The ceiling was low; everyone needed to slouch slightly to avoid hitting their heads. Sally and Becky went to the books and began riffling through them, pulling them off the shelves and opening pages at random.

"Sally," Ryan blurted, surprised at her aggressive exploration. Was Becky rubbing off on her? "Have some manners."

"We were just looking," Sally giggled and Becky joined in as they replaced the books they'd been examining.

Becky resisted a strong, confusing desire to pocket one of the small books. There was no reason she needed it, but her old shoplifting habits stubbornly lingered. Embarrassed, but still holding it, she glanced around to see if anyone had noticed her hesitating over the irrational impulse.

"It's all right Ryan," Mel grabbed the book from Becky. "I know the governor. He won't mind the girls checking out the library."

"Professor Mel!" a voice thick with cheer and goodwill announced. A black-haired dwarf carrying a book and wearing an immense grin strutted out of the shadows. He wore clean blue overalls and a long green stocking cap. His beard wasn't as straggly as his counterparts in the mine and his long hair was also well groomed. "Fancy seeing you here, old friend!"

"Grunky!" exclaimed Mel. "I didn't know you'd returned."

"When my father passed away I assumed the governorship and will continue to do so until the next election." Grunky gave his friend a hug so intense that Mel's back cracked, loudly echoing down the tunnels. "Honestly, I don't think anyone else wants this job. There is just something so comforting about the tedious, mindless work of mining that calms the soul, you know what I mean?"

"I can't say that I do," Mel chuckled, rubbing his back, which surprisingly didn't hurt but instead felt as if he'd received a chiropractic adjustment.

"That's true, how would you know? You aren't a miner," Grunky said. "Until you came along, I thought all humans were miners in your old world." He looked at the others curiously. "Are any of you miners?"

216

Everyone shook their heads, no.

"Fascinating," Grunky said. "Ahem."

"Sorry," said Mel. "How rude of me. Grunky, this is Ryan, Sally, John, and Becky. I'm sure you've heard about the first three, who previously came to Enchantas with me. Becky is a newcomer. She's John's sister."

"How delightful to finally meet you!" Grunky made the rounds, shaking hands enthusiastically with his strong grip.

"Grunky was a student at the Institute until just a couple cycles ago." Mel turned toward his old friend. "I was wondering what happened to you. You were one of my top students, you and Cully."

"Cully!" Grunky smiled. "How is she? I sure hope she's not still mad at me for beating her in the potion competition and then leaving before we could have a rematch. I still have my trophy, right over here."

Mel dropped the bombshell, shaking his head sadly. "I am sorry to tell you, but Cully has just been murdered."

"What?" Stunned, Grunky dropped into one of the barrel chairs with raised arms near the bookshelves. "How?"

"She was killed by one of the Banshee's assassins," Mel's voice was bleak.

"But why?" Grunky shook his head. "I don't understand. She was a student with no agenda other than to learn."

"She took an arrow," Mel paused to swallow back sobs that came unbidden. The memory of that moment was fresh and painful, as vivid as her blood, pooling around the fatally wounded youngster. He would always see it. "She took an arrow that was intended for me."

Tears dripped down Grunky's face, collecting in his beard. "Oh no! That ain't right!"

"I know. I know," Mel continued. "The attack, which was not the first assassination attempt, is what brings us here. We received word that the Banshee was seen in the mountains of the Enchantic Mines. We've come to find her and bring her to justice."

"I'm sorry, my friend," Grunky wiped his cheeks, standing up. "I have not seen that witch since the battle. If I get my hands on her," he closed his fists tightly, shaking them at the ceiling.

"We need you to think about where she might be. Is there anywhere she could hide out, maybe an old tunnel that's not being used?"

"Mel, let's get real." Grunky sniffed. "There are thousands of old tunnels in these mountains; she could be anywhere! If she's even hiding in the mines."

"Are the imps and gremlins of the old faction still roaming around your tunnels?" Mel continued. "She could be with them."

"We banned them from these mountains seasons ago," Grunky said proudly. "They were a pain, from leaving their trash everywhere to poisoning the very air with their cynical, negative, nasty dispositions. It was a relief to ban them, even though they didn't go without a fight."

"Well, that doesn't explain the E-mail message," Mel pondered, thinking out loud.

"Can you trust the word of your source? Someone could be sending you out on a wild snuffball chase. Especially considering you were sent here, a most unlikely location for an enemy of our land to find refuge. Our track record of expelling and repelling insurgents is flawless."

"My sister was the source," Dyad flickered in; John's heart fluttered in response as the group stared at the unexpected arrival. "She is trustworthy, but I have not had any luck finding her. I fear she may be captured."

John's eyes lit up as he stared steadily at his beloved.

She smiled back.

"There are countless tunnels throughout the mountains, Professor," Grunky said. "Should we split up to search as many as possible? I could send some of the workers to assist."

"It's a thought — a plausible thought," Mel answered. "But I think that the divide-and-conquer theory could come into play. We should stick together. We're much stronger when we're together. If any one of us was forced to confront the Banshee alone, we all would be vulnerable."

"My thought at the moment is that everyone needs to get some rest, to replenish and recoup from your travels and all that's happened," Dyad interjected, landing on John's — now ecstatic — shoulder, right where he needed her, with him, touching him. She went on, "If we do decide to search the mines you must all be at full strength."

"I'll be fine," said John.

"I know," Dyad breathed softly into his ear before raising her voice. "But I would feel much more at ease knowing you are rested – that you all are rested – before we continue."

"Good idea," said Grunky. "That will give me time to find volunteers. They may say they don't like working the mines, but trying to get them away from the job for a few tocks is like pulling teeth."

"We appreciate your help, Grunky," said Mel. "Where should we rest?"

"Take this trolley to the next stop, where you'll find a hallway leading to our visitor's quarters. You may all retire there to sleep and relax for as long as needed."

"Thank you, Grunky." With a friendly salute to the helpful interim ruler, Mel clambered back into the trolley. "Come on guys, let's get some sleep."

Chapter XIV
Divided They Fall

The school bell rang and Sally leaned against the lockers. She was wearing loose-fitting low-slung jeans and Ryan's favorite blue-and-white football jersey with pride. It was right before the last hour of school and only hours away from the Homecoming game. Their ritual between classes was to meet quickly for a kiss. But something was wrong, something was different this time. Ryan had not shown up.

Sally tapped her foot on the tile floor, making a mental effort to lessen her anxiety. Nothing was working. Irritated, she stormed off toward Ryan's locker which was just around the corner and down the hall.

Sally's mouth was set in an inflexible, angry line as she stomped down the hall, indifferently bumping passing students. A tall woman stepped in front her, causing her to halt abruptly.

"Well, well, Miss Sally," a familiar voice snarled.

It took her a moment to focus; she still wasn't used to contacts instead of glasses. A stunning, blond-haired woman peered down at her with imperial snootiness and an "I'm better than you" expression. It was Lexis.

"Where are you going so fast, sweetie?" Lexis narrowed her deep purple eyes, stepping even closer. "Well, well. I love what you've done with yourself. When we first met I thought I'd never seen any girl more in need of a makeover. You look marvelous!"

"What are you doing here, Lexis?" Sally was rocked by the sight of her. "What are you doing at my school?"

"If you must know, I'm substitute teaching a couple of classes."

"You shouldn't be here. Just leave me alone," Sally tried to step past her. Again Lexis blocked her path.

"Who are you looking for?" Lexis leered. "Your boyfriend?"

"As if it's any of your business," Gathering courage, Sally sneered back. "But yes, so if you don't mind, get out of my way."

"I wouldn't bother, little sister."

"Don't call me that!" Sally shrieked, causing a few students to look their way.

"Why not? Your parents raised me as their own." Lexis put a seemingly friendly hand on Sally's shoulder. Sally shrugged it off. "That should make us stepsisters, at the very least."

"No it doesn't," Sally lowered her voice and using a football maneuver — one of which Ryan would be proud — moved around Lexis, and walked briskly down the hall.

"I wouldn't bother with him, Sally. He's not worth it!"

Sally knew Lexis was just trying to get a rise out of her and she should keep walking, but there was something about her tone that made her doubt her own instincts. Sally stopped and turned around. "What do you mean?"

"I was the substitute teacher in his last class and he was getting a little too close to some girl named Jessica."

"Jessica?" Sally's eyes went cold and dark as she seethed. "That little-"

"Here, let me help you with that," Lexis snapped her fingers.

They were magically transported to the teacher's lounge, where she saw Ryan and Jessica comfortably sprawled shirtless on top of each other. Sally stood speechless, staring at the two of them while they caressed each other, oblivious to their surroundings. Ryan ran his hands through her long blond hair as Jessica dug her nails deep into his back leaving bloody claw marks from the top of his shoulders to his lower back. Their mouths clung to each other as they breathed deeply through their nostrils, moaning for more.

Sally screamed.

"You see, sister. What did I tell you?" Lexis said smugly, snapping her finger.

Sally woke up sweating in the dark. Her feet hung off the edge of the small bed. She was back at the dwarf mines — back in Enchantas.

She took a deep breath, then another, trying to calm down and restore her respiration to normal. "It was just a dream," she repeated. "Just. A. Dream."

Sally felt for the nightstand, grasping the dwarf-sized mug Ryan had brought her. She raised her head and took a drink of water, her heart still racing. She'd had nightmares of Ryan cheating on her before, but never any that felt so vivid and real. And none of them had involved Lexis. It was as if Lexis was actually in the dream with her. This is Enchantas, Sally reminded herself. Anything could happen. For all she knew Lexis could be watching them right now. She could be malevolently prowling in all of their dreams.

"Ryan, Ryan!" Sally turned over to wake her boyfriend, but he was gone. Motion-activated purple torches spontaneously lit the room, confirming no one else was there. She got up. She had to find Ryan.

As she walked along the orange brick hallways, torches lit automatically, guiding her along. Her face was still damp with sweat and her heart beat faster at each tentative step forward. After turning a few corners she realized she was lost, but kept going down the unknown corridors, passing through several tunnels. Her determination to find Ryan outweighed anything else.

Voices echoed from farther down the hall. Sally's pace quickened as she recognized Ryan's voice. And then there was another voice, too, a lilting, sensual female voice. Sally's body stiffened with anger and frustration. *It's that hussy nympho, Nymph.* She snorted. *Ha! That was the proper nickname for the philandering fairy!*

As she drew nearer Sally peeked around the corner for a closer look.

"But Ryan," Nymph in human form caressed his chest. "What I've told you is true. I think we should leave this place. We belong together."

Ryan stood there like a gargoyle turned to stone. Angrier than she'd even been, Sally stormed around the corner.

She sprang close to Ryan as Nymph hastily stepped away. Sally slapped his face as hard as she could.

***

The torches suddenly lit up in the room where John was sleeping. Someone or something was pounding at his door. Instinctively, his spear shot out of his bracelet. Rubbing his eyes, he got out of bed, calling toward the oval wooden door.

"Who is it?"

"It's Dyad," said a distraught voice. "Can I come in?"

His spear retracted. "I'll be right there," he called, finger-combing his unruly hair before he opened the door.

"What's wrong?" John asked. Dyad was in human form again. John took her hands. "Did something wake you up?"

"I wasn't sleeping," she said.

"Yeah, I have a hard time, sometimes, like the night before a big test or an important game."

"No, I mean I never sleep. Fairies don't."

"Oh," he said. "That's odd. Kind of reminds me of my mother; it seems like she never slept either. I remember getting up in the middle of the night to sneak cookies when I was just a little kid and she would always be in the living room watching TV." John scratched his head, continuing, "Come to think of it, my dad said she was an insomniac. That explains a lot."

"What's an insomniac?"

"Sorry. I'm just rambling. My brain isn't all the way awake yet, I guess. Feel free to tell me to shut up at any time." He laughed at his own blathering. "That's me, a regular motor mouth."

"That's okay." Dyad said, but she still looked troubled.

John smiled, hoping to reassure her, but it didn't seem to help so he fell silent, trying to give her time to put her worries into words.

"I really need to talk to you about something," she began.

"You know what?" John cut her off; he wanted to be the first to share feelings. "I need to tell you something, too." He took a deep breath. "From the moment I saw you, you had my heart. I could not believe that someone so beautiful and enchanting could ever exist. But then I met you. I'm in love with you, Dyad. I want to be with you. I see Ryan and Sally every day in my world. I see them so happy and so in love. If I only had the chance to express my love for you daily, those would be the greatest days of my life. Will you be with me Dyad? I don't know if you feel the same way about me as I do about you, but I am willing to take the risk and find out. I see the way you look at me, I see it even now. So what do you say? Will you be with me?"

"John," she looked up at him. "I really wish I could tell you another way," she paused, eyes lowering. "We can't be together."

"What? Wait. Why?" John's jaw dropped. He was in shock. "What do you mean?"

"John," she sighed. "I was coming here to tell you that I don't think it will work out between us. I'm truly not comfortable with us being together. We are from two different worlds. I mean you're human and I'm a fairy. It would never work."

"What do you mean it would never work?" John's voice raised a little. "We care about each other! I know that for a fact. You're just making some stupid excuse."

"John, seriously, we can't be together. A union between a fairy and a human would never work."

"I don't care what you think. My feelings are strong enough that I would rather try and fail, then to never have tried at all."

"John," Dyad sighed unemotionally. "Please stop."

"No," John was at the brink of shouting, but not there yet. "I just poured my heart out to you and this is what you tell me? You're just scared!"

"No, John. I'm not," Dyad took a deep breath and blurted out. "I don't care for you at all. I found someone else."

A stabbing feeling shot into his heart, the pain radiating throughout his body. Tears began to form. He had not cried for anyone since his mother left.

"Fine," John turned toward the door. He did not want her to see him cry so he left the room, slamming the door behind him. He strode angrily down the tunnels, at intervals slamming his fist into the yellow brick walls as he went.

The fairy smirked with pleasure as she quickly transformed back into Nymph. John had been deceived.

***

Ryan rolled out of the small dwarf-sized bed and kissed Sally on the cheek. She was snoring slightly which he always thought was absolutely delightful. He smiled as he watched her sleep remembering how vehemently she would deny that she snored and how he would give in and let her believe she didn't.

Ryan had been having a difficult time sleeping since late last school year when his parents started to take more vacations, leaving him and his brother alone. At first it was because of his fear of being alone, but later he began to take midnight walks and realized there wasn't anything to be afraid of. He'd found that those quiet dark hours were a good time for thinking, for planning and for dreaming.

At his movement the room's torches suddenly lit. On a whim, he whispered, "Off."

To his surprise, the flames disappeared. He grinned. Maybe this spell-casting wasn't so hard after all, now that he'd figured out another mysterious magical trick on his own.

Stepping out into the hallway he quietly closed the door before breaking into a jog. Most halls and tunnels ran a straight course, but there were a few corners and intersections that he followed on instinct. He warned himself not to take too many; losing his way wasn't an option.

Since summer, the pace of Ryan's midnight walks had turned into jogs. The exercise helped him sleep better once he did drop off. Ironically, after a couple of months of the routine, he found himself unable to sleep well without them. He didn't mind though. As he ran the streets of Willington he grew to appreciate the fresh air filling his lungs as the always chilly night temperatures cooled his sweating body. The town was quiet and peaceful in the early morning hours. No one bothered him; it gave him time to think.

His parents were still never around, so there was never any need to sneak out. His brother Ben didn't mind. He was either home sleeping or out with friends anyway.

"Ryan," a barely audible voice weakly hailed him as he passed a partially open door with light spilling into the hall.

Ryan found Nymph curled up in a ball on the floor.

He ran to her, kneeling down next to the diminutive sprite.

"Nymph! What's happened?"

"You're all in trouble!" she gasped.

"What do you mean?" he asked, putting his hand on her back. She jerked back quickly as if burned, grabbing his hand. She was shaking.

"The Banshee is here!" she exclaimed. "She is setting a trap for you."

"Wait a minute." Ryan stood up. "How do you know this?"

"That doesn't matter, we must leave, now."

"Okay. I'll go get the others."

"Others?" Nymph rose as well, enlarging as she tightened her grasp on his hand. "There's no time! We must save ourselves."

"I won't leave without Sally – or the rest of my friends."

"Sally?" Nymph huffed, clearly annoyed. "You don't need her."

"Nymph, she's my spirit-mate. I can't just leave her."

"Yes you can," Nymph tugged on him. "I'll be your girlfriend. I'll be your spirit-mate."

"I don't think you understand relationships entirely well, Nymph."

"What do you mean?" Nymph drew him closer. "I've seen the way you look at me."

"I don't know what you're talking about." Ryan freed himself from her grasp, taking a few steps back.

Nymph advanced on him, eager for possession. "I would never treat you the way she treats you."

"What are you talking about?" Ryan was confused and impatient. He had to get to the others. "We're great together."

"I see how jealous she gets," Nymph said. "The way she looks at and talks to you. It's pathetic. I would never treat you like that. You deserve better."

"Jealous?" Ryan almost laughed. "You're the one who makes her that way. Why do you keep kissing me in front of her? That's not cool. And why do you think it's okay to trick me into kissing you? It's manipulative and it's not real!"

"Whatever," She moved in, her lips inches from his. "You're better off with me. I can give you everything. She holds you back."

"She keeps me in line," Ryan pushed her away again. "Which I appreciate."

"You would be free to be the man you are destined to be, Ryan," Nymph contested. "I can give you anything you want, everything you've ever dreamed of."

"I do have everything I want! I love a great girl who loves me back. I've got great friends. I'm the captain of my football team. What else could I ask for?"

"Me," she kissed him.

Ryan pushed her away and wiped the kiss off his lips with his hand then rubbing it on his pants. "Come on, stop it! Can't you take a hint?"

"But Ryan," Nymph stepped closer to him; her eyes gleamed with lust as she caressed his chest. "What I've told you is true. I think we should leave this place. We belong together."

Ryan tired of her circular conversation. There wasn't much more he could say to get through to her. If only there was something he could do to prove to Nymph, to convince her that he was in love with Sally and that that would never change.

Sally came at him from around the corner. Her slap was sharp, powerful and startling.

Nymph abruptly disappeared, leaving the two alone.

"What did you do that for?" Ryan rubbed his face which was already swelling into finger-shaped welts that would definitely cause a bruise.

"You! I can't believe you wouldn't stick up for your own girlfriend! I thought you loved me."

"What are you talking about?" Ryan tried to hold her, but she pushed him away. "I do love you. Didn't you hear-"

"Stop making excuses, Ryan!" Sally yelled at the top of her lungs. "I see the way you look at her!"

"I don't know what you're talking about," Ryan was beginning to get very angry. "There's no reason to hit me any further. Please just stop!"

"I will not stop!" Sally began to sob. "You need to stop making yourself so available to all those girls who flirt with you! I'm sick of it!"

"I am not making myself available to anyone!"

"Shut up, Ryan!" Sally was ready to leave. Ryan stopped her.

"I'm not sure what you heard, but Nymph was right about one thing. Your jealousy needs to stop."

"My jealousy?" Sally was offended and hurt. "You make me this way!"

"No, I don't," Ryan said defensively. "I'm not sure where it comes from, but I'm not sure how much more I can handle. It's ruining us." Ryan took a deep breath. "It's like a roller coaster with you. One minute you're fine, the next you spaz out. What's going on?"

"Whatever Ryan," Sally said sternly. "If that's the way you want to be then forget it! Forget us!"

"That's not what I'm saying Sally," Ryan's voice was suddenly sincere. "We need to work on this. Something has got to change."

"Something is changing, Ryan. It's over! If I'm not the one for you, then go off with that fairy!" Sally broke free. "I see you

230

looking so longingly at Nymph, that skank, every time she's here. Well, go ahead and have her."

"Wait, Sally!" Ryan started after her; she began to run, crying hysterically.

"Goodbye Ryan!" she screamed. "It's over!"

Ryan stopped chasing her. Shame, regret and sadness overtook him as he let her go.

In the shadows, Nymph silently clapped her hands, smiling with glee. Her mission was succeeding.

***

Becky was awake too. The demigon's attacks repeatedly looped through her busy mind, preventing sleep. She was especially obsessed with her own shortcomings. She'd fought so poorly with the daggers she'd be surprised if her bracelet still worked. She knew that the adrenaline and stress of the life-threatening situation were factors in her poor aim and failure to hit the target. *But dammit*, Becky thought, *I was a number one softball player two years in a row. I should have done better.*

Practice makes perfect. Since she couldn't sleep anyway, Becky arranged several glass bottles she had found lying throughout the miner's halls on the patio railing that overlooked a cavern ledge outside her room. She threw several daggers, but again her aim was off and she missed each time. Grunting in frustration, she gave up focusing on aiming and just flung the next round of daggers as rapidly as possible without thinking. She shattered only one of her targets.

"Nice job," said Mel.

"Not really," she sighed. "More of a lucky throw than anything. I don't understand why my aim sucks so bad. I used to be the best softball player in my class."

"Well," Mel said, laughing, "For one thing, these aren't softballs. So they shouldn't be thrown like one. Also, you're not throwing with your bare hand. May I?" He gently extracted a dagger from her grasp. He threw it sideways without looking and hit a bottle dead on.

"How'd you do that?" Becky pulled out another dagger, lifting it over her head.

"And two," Mel grabbed her hand and stood behind her. His heart thumped every time he was this close to her. "Remember that these are magic daggers, so they quite literally have a mind of their own. And they sense your emotions, which can interfere with their vibrational field. So if you concentrate too hard they won't work. Just take a deep breath, relax and throw. Let your instincts do the work." Mel let her go. "Here, try it."

Becky closed her eyes and took a deep breath slowly releasing it. She did this several times. After a few moments, her body was almost limp, her mind perfectly clear. She opened her eyes, focused on a purple bottle and threw.

The sound of shattering glass echoed throughout the cavern.

"I did it!" she cheered, hugging Mel without thinking.

Mel was surprised but quickly seized on the opportunity to hug back.

"Sorry," said Becky, letting go, suddenly remembering that she wasn't supposed to lead him on. She was embarrassed about acting so childish. Giving him what she considered her most mature, sophisticated smile, she tried to keep her voice calm. "I apologize for jumping you. I just got a little excited."

"That's quite all right," Mel grinned. The hug truly made his day. "Actually, there was something I wanted to talk to you about."

"Oh yeah?" Becky turned back to her target practice, almost ignoring him. She threw another dagger and broke a bottle with ease. She snorted, pleased with herself and asked without turning around, "What did you want to tell me?"

Mel mumbled under his breath for a moment, almost as if he was practicing what he was going to say. Then he tapped her on the shoulder. As she faced him he launched into his explanation: "I'm a little new at this and I didn't want to go about it nonchalantly. I wanted it to have a special meaning, some feeling, so I made up a spell. Would you like to hear it?"

"Sure," Becky said, thinking he must have invented some magical spell he wanted to share.

Mel inhaled, exhaled and continued:

"Diamonds are delight, your beauty is divine;
This flower's so bright, it'll make you shine.
My heart skips at your sight, so please show me a sign;
That my feelings for you are right, and that you will be mine."

Suddenly a bright pink-and-purple sunflower emerged from his bracelet. Becky stared silently as Mel handed her the flower. Nervous, he fidgeted from foot to foot, awaiting her response.

"Mel," she began with a smile. "I have to be blatantly honest. That was really corny." Her smile grew as her heart swelled in unison. "But so corny that it fits you." How could this be happening? She was falling for him. Right now, at this moment she was falling for him. She didn't tell him how she felt, she showed him with a hearty kiss. When they came for air she shared what was in her soul.

"Thank you, Mel. You're the nicest guy I've met in a long time, maybe even the nicest guy I've ever met. It would be my pleasure to be *yours*." She still couldn't believe it. *He's really the one*, she thought to herself, kissing him again. "This is really beautiful. How'd you know sunflowers are my favorite?"

"I didn't, that was part of the spell," Mel glanced at the flower, as it changed color to light blue. "It's a mood flower. It changes color according to the emotions surrounding it."

"I love it, Mel," she kissed him again. "Thank you."

233

"Okay!" John barked angrily, stomping toward them. Becky and Mel immediately drew away from each other, trying to act as if nothing happened. John stood between them. "I can't handle this anymore! Mel, please don't kiss my sister! And Becky, please get away from my friend. I really don't want you two to be together."

Mel took a step back quietly, feeling a little ashamed about kissing her, but feeling guiltier for feeling ashamed.

"John!" Becky shoved her brother as hard as she could. John almost lost his balance. "You don't have any right telling me what to do or who to like!"

"Yes I do," John stepped forward. "I'm your brother, Becky! I am here to protect you?"

"Protect me from what?" Becky laughed. "Mel? What's he going to do? No offense, Mel."

"None taken," Mel replied softly.

"Mel is my friend," John pointed at him. "And I am here to protect him, too."

"Protect him from what, John?" Becky shook her head. She couldn't believe her brother was acting like this. "Me?"

"Yes, you!" John's voice rose. "You're just going to end up breaking his heart like you do with every other guy you meet!"

"That's not fair," Becky's voice also rose. "That's not what I do!"

"Yes it is!" John looked at Mel, concerned. "Mel, you should really know what you're getting you yourself into." John looked back at Becky and continued. "You've been jumping from guy to guy all school year!"

"I have not, John!" Becky slapped him. "Guys come on to me."

"And that's supposed to make it better? Please!" John's face began to turn red. "Don't think I haven't heard rumors about you just because you're in middle school and I'm not. It's a small town. Word travels."

"What is it with you, John?" asked Becky, her eyes welling with tears. She'd never seen him this upset. "You never cared who I went out with before."

"This is different," John looked back at Mel. "This is my friend!"

"You're just like Dad!" Becky sobbed. "Maybe even worse!"

"Shut up, Becky!"

"I'm so sick of you! Fine, you want me to not be with him? Then I'm going home," Becky took off her brother's leather jacket, throwing it at him. "Here, take your stupid jacket and leave me alone!"

"Becky," John called after her. "Wait!"

But she was already gone.

Mel remained silent, uncomfortable at witnessing the vicious argument and sorry for the part he'd played in it. They'd gone from zero to one-hundred on the temper scale in an instant. He stared at John, wide-eyed and speechless.

"I'm sorry Mel," John said, gasping from hollering for Becky to come back. "I couldn't help it."

"What's the matter? I've never seen you like this before," Mel noticed John was crying just as hard as his sister. "It's not like you."

"She's right! God, I sound just like him," John looked up. "And I try my hardest not to be like him. Like my father. I see it sometimes and it scares me."

"That's okay, John," Mel comforted. "I know how protective you are of her. For all that you've been through, it only makes sense. But you should know that I would never hurt her. I really do like your sister a lot."

"That's what scares me, Mel." John squeezed him with his arm. "I don't want her to hurt you, either."

"You know," Mel smiled, "for me, Becky is worth taking that risk."

John turned to look at his friend; seeing the sincerity in his eyes put a smile on his face. "I guess you're right. If she is to be with anyone, I'm glad it's you. You really are a great guy."

"Thanks," said Mel, but could tell there was something else. "Is there anything else that's bothering you? I mean, you really went overboard."

John wasn't one to share his feelings, but maybe it would help to get it off his chest.

"Dyad just told me she didn't want to be with me," he said, the tears starting again. "She said there's someone else."

"Someone else?" Mel was confused. "Who? I see the way she looks at you and for the fourteen cycles I've been here she's never stopped talking about you, it's 'John this' and 'John that' every time I see her. I don't get it. Are you sure that's what she meant? Girls, even fairy girls, can be so weird with their mixed messages and all those hormonal highs and lows and whatnot."

"Yes, I'm sh-sh-sure," John gave in and let a sob out. "Sh-sh-she was serious."

"You should go talk to her, figure things out."

"Later," John turned toward the hallway. "I need to talk to Becky, too. Fix things with her first. After all, she's my little sister."

"Wait," Mel suggested. "Let me go talk to Becky. Just give me a minute and then come. Let her calm down a little."

"All right," John felt hopeful at the thought of having someone else on his side – on their side. "I guess I should get used to you taking over the role of protector, huh?"

"Not fully," Mel winked. "She'll always need her brother."

After Mel left, John leaned up against the railing of the cavern, thinking over the situation. He was ashamed of blowing up at Becky even though most of what he said was true. He feared for both her and Mel, but knew it wasn't his place to tell her who to like or what to do. In retrospect he realized that telling her that she couldn't be with Mel probably only attracted her to him more. He was like that himself. Just tell him not to do something and well, that's what he wanted to do. He just hoped she liked Mel for his own sake.

"John!" Ryan ran onto the patio. "Where is everyone?"

"Mel and Becky are gone," John paused, avoiding the details. "Long story. What's up?"

"Have you seen Sally?"

"No. Did you misplace her?"

"Long story," Ryan retorted. He didn't want to get into it, either. "We have to round up everybody. The Banshee is here and setting a trap!"

"How do you know?"

"Another long story!" Ryan said. "No time. Come on!"

John followed without question.

***

Lightning bolts illuminated the sky, strobing behind thick, dark yellow clouds. The peaks and summits of the treacherous terrain were viewed by Sally as she sat on the mountain side. The air was dry and warm, unlike the thick, damp air inside the caves.

Thunder roared, shaking the ground underneath her as she sat sobbing with her feet dangling over the edge, deep in thought and still so very angry. Fear of the demigons lurking above did not deter the rage she felt inside.

"Hey, girl," Becky hailed, coming to sit beside her. "How's it going?"

Sally turned her tearful face toward her.

"That bad, huh?" Becky said sympathetically. "Guy problems?"

"How'd you guess?" Sally sniffled, noticing Becky's eyes were red, too. "You?"

237

"Yes. Guy problems. Brother problems," She shook her head in disgust. "All kinds of male problems."

"I'm sorry," said Sally.

"It doesn't matter, they're all jerks anyway." Becky said firmly. "No matter what role they play. Father, brother, boyfriend, even uncles. Kinda makes you lose hope."

"I know what you mean," Sally blurted. "Why can't they just understand?"

"Trust me girl, it's a waste of your time to even bother with that question." Becky put her arm around her. "Just ask yourself if it's worth working on the relationship."

Sally was quiet.

"Is he worth it?" Becky asked.

"I don't know," Sally said, sadly. "I used to think so. I used to believe that he and I were supposed to be as one in this world. But lately we've been arguing so much that it makes me wonder. He just lets these girls control him and that brings out a jealous streak in me that I didn't know existed. I get so mad that I can't see. It takes me back to a weak place, to a 'less than' state of mind. I've worked really hard to boost my confidence and claim my own sense of self-esteem. I don't want to feel 'less than', I want to feel secure and empowered. And I hit him tonight. That's abusive and it can't happen again."

"Well I'm sure that fairy situation doesn't help."

Sally's voice got hard. "Oh, you mean Nymph the nympho? She's a real piece of work."

"I'm not sure how to handle that," Becky said sympathetically. "I once thought as you did. You meet a guy and think 'he's the greatest,' but then in an instant when you're least expecting it, your world just comes crashing down."

"Yeah," Sally knew exactly what she was talking about.

"If you are going to learn anything from my experience, Sally, it's to search yourself, deep down. Your intuition and your heart will tell you if he's worth the effort or not. I knew Carl wasn't," Becky paused and her faced turned dreamy. She threw a rock down the cliff. It seemed to take forever before they heard it clatter on the rocks below. "But I don't know, maybe this time will be different."

"What do you mean? *This time?*" Sally watched as Becky blushed.

"Mel just asked me out!" Becky couldn't hold it in anymore. She was truly excited. "John's not crazy about the idea but I don't care."

"Oh my God!" Sally suddenly became just as giddy. "Really? When?"

"Just like five minutes ago," Becky said excitedly. "Or is it ticks, or tocks. Whatever, it just happened."

"What did he say? What did you say? Tell me everything!"

Becky scooted closer to Sally. "It was the corniest thing ever, but it was so adorable I couldn't say no. He was so nervous. He recited a super-sweet spell and then gave me this flower."

Becky handed the flower over to Sally. It turned a shade of greenish-gray.

"I'm so happy for you," Sally said, as the flower began to turn darker green in her hands. "Ryan and I knew that Mel had a crush on you."

"Yeah, that was obvious," Becky agreed.

"But I didn't think you were interested," Sally gave the flower back to Becky; in a twinkling it turned back to a light, airy blue. "Or that he was your type. You seem so," she paused, trying to think of the right word, "Strong willed. And he is a little timid at times."

"I wasn't so sure about him at first," Becky grinned. "He is kind of a dork, but the more I got to know him, the more I realized that he's cool — and smart and easy to talk to. Not to mention, kind of cute, too."

"I'm really happy for you," Sally said, touching a petal on the flower. It turned red. Alarmed, she pulled her hand back.

"Sally," Becky put her hand on hers. "I think you want to be happy too. Is Ryan worth it?"

Sally nodded with a wince of a smile.

"Well then go get him girl! What are you doing sulking out here? You're spirit-mates and that's not something to be taken lightly. Go to him!"

Sally gave a great smile, encouragement from a close friend was something new to her. Something she had always needed. *Where has this girl been all these years*, she thought.

Becky winked and boosted another grin.

Sally wasted no time, quickly taking off back into the cave.

Becky looked at her flower; it was once again light blue. She smiled dreamily.

"How sweet," said a mocking, malicious voice. "The Professor has a dear little girlfriend."

Becky swiveled where she sat, shifting her gaze from the mountain ranges to the cave behind her, where a statuesque brunette woman stood atop a boulder, hands on hips, in a wide-legged, conquering stance. She was beautiful, in a menacing, imposing way. Her purple eyes blazed with hatred and her essence reeked of pure evil. Becky stood quickly, dagger at the ready.

"And a feisty one, too," the woman's voice lowered. "Charming."

"So, you must be the notorious *Banshee* everyone's talking about." Becky wound up her arm ready to throw the dagger.

"Don't insult me with your puny weapons, little girl!" the Banshee pointed her finger, shooting a violet lightning bolt that knocked the dagger from Becky's hand. "And don't call me that distasteful name. I am the Empress!" Her eyes smoldered feverishly, as if purple embers burned within.

"*Ooooh*, intimidating," Becky said, pretending to shiver with fear. "Did you want to show me your big, bad teeth, too?"

"I am not here to fight you, my dear," the Empress levitated smoothly off the rock, descending to ground level. "I am here to offer you a truce; only you though, not your friends. They made their choice a long time ago."

Becky bravely stepped forward. "All right, tell me about this truce."

"Our pact, our truce, will bring freewill back to Enchantas. As champions of this ideal you and I will fight together to restore the old order, to restore Enchantas to the magnificence and majesty of what it always has been and always should be."

"Huh," Becky grunted. "I really don't care about the ideals of your world, which strike me more as something in your head than a real thing. I don't know why you'd think I'd want to fight on your side. I don't even know you. And from what I've heard, I don't even want to know you." She tossed her hair. "Trying to get me to join you is a waste of your time."

"You're a bold girl for speaking your mind," the Empress's voice grew deeper, forbiddingly defiant. "But I warn you: If you don't join me you will die."

"Yeah, sure." Becky said casually as she swiftly deployed another dagger. The Banshee deflected it effortlessly.

"Becky!" Mel yelled, running out of the cave.

"There's our dear Professor Mel!" the Empress declared, levitating back to her position on the boulder, where she could look down on them. "There's our great and powerful wizard prophet."

"Lexis," Mel nodded his head deferentially, holding on to every semblance of calm he could muster. "We've been looking for you!"

"Really? You flatter me, Professor. Now I truly feel special!"

"Let's drop the pretense, Lexis. Your assassins killed an innocent child. You will have to answer for that," Mel informed her.

"As I hear it, Professor, the alleged assassin failed to kill you because this foolish student of yours got in the way of the real target. Therefore you are to blame for that sad tragedy."

"You're not going to get away with this," Mel told her. "You're no Empress. You're just a spoiled, nasty, ugly Banshee who will soon be in a place where you can never hurt anyone again."

"You think so, huh?" she laughed.

"Mel!" Ryan yelled as he and John joined them.

"Becky!" John started toward his sister.

"Enough of this playing around!" Lexis snarled, launching into her curse. Her fingertips shot purple lightning, crackling in twisted flashes as she clenched her fists tightly and chanted:

"Curse the Dead, Curse the Bone;
Turn this Brat into Stone!"

She took direct aim at Mel, but before the lightning bolt reached him, Becky stepped into the crossfire.

"I love you, Mel," Becky cried as the gray stone covered her face.

"Becky!" John screamed in terror and hatred as he charged Lexis.

"I don't think so!" the Empress snapped her fingers, throwing him with brutal force into the rock wall.

Mel controlled his natural urge to charge, rapidly cycling into his cursing spell:

"Empress witch, cursed to stone;"

"Not this time, Professor!" the Empress interrupted him with a triumphant scream and slithered swiftly as a snake to Becky's statue. With a powerful kick, she sent the girl's stone body tumbling off the ledge into the abyss.

"*NO!*" Mel flung himself at the ledge, trying to intercept Becky's inert form. John was right behind him, both diving for her, both praying that with their combined muscle power they could hoist her back to safety.

They missed by mere inches. Horrified, they watched Becky descend. The fall to the barren, rocky floor below took several agonizing tacks. The stone that had once been a living, breathing, laughing, loving girl in her prime slammed into the unyielding ground, breaking into millions of pieces. Beautiful, flamboyant, spirited Becky was now a scattered pile of rubble.

"Pathetic!" the Empress let out a prolonged, keening laugh, then vanished in an acrid cloud of dark purple smoke.

"Where did she go?" John screamed, charging the cloud with his spear, ready for battle. "*WHERE IS SHE?*"

Mel stood in utter shock. It felt as if everything was far, far away.

"Mel!" John yelled, sobbing, shaking him. "Bring her back! Bring Becky back!"

"I-I can't," Mel stuttered.

"What do you mean, *you can't*? You're a professor for god's sake! Finish your spell." John began to shake Mel even more ferociously. "You know the magic to fix this! Do it. Do it now! Do your job!"

"I-I can't," Mel began to cry, heaving guttural sobs. The worst part was knowing there was nothing else he could do. Becky was gone. A pile of stone debris scattered below. "Not anymore. It's too late."

"Stop messing with me Mel!" John suddenly threw his friend to the ground and began to punch him repeatedly. Mel tried to block the first few punches but his body, paralyzed with shock, wasn't cooperating. So he just remained prone, sobbing, allowing John to pound him.

"John!" Ryan began the task of pulling John off Mel. "Stop it! Stop it! It's not his fault!"

"Not his fault?" John, pried away, stood up, panting. "It's entirely his fault! We wouldn't be here if it wasn't for him!" John looked down at Mel's battered face. "She wouldn't have taken that curse, if it wasn't for him!" John narrowed his eyes at Ryan. "We wouldn't be here either if it wasn't for you! Always trying to be the hero! And now my sister is dead."

"John," Ryan tried to calm him. He put his hand on his friend's shoulders, but John pushed him away.

"I'm through with all of you! I'll find that Banshee myself."

"John," Ryan said, "We want to help you. We have a better chance of finding her together."

Mel could only groan, but his sentiments were clear. They were still a team with a shared mission that had taken on a new urgency.

"You will do no such thing, my friends." Nymph materialized in her daintiest form then expanded into her larger, human-looking persona. There was an odd expression on her face.

"My Empress does not want you following her and ruining *our* plan."

"Your plan?" Ryan narrowed his eyes.

"This should keep you three busy," Nymph laughed and chanted:

"Empress ally, which you have crossed;
Will curse you three, and get you lost!"

A licking green flame encircled the trio, swirling higher around them as they disappeared. Nymph's eyes darted around the ledge, looking for Sally. No such luck. Sneering, with a flick of a bright green light, Nymph disappeared, too.

Sally arrived back at the ledge moments later. The wind had picked up, whipping her hair around her face.

"Hey, where did everybody go? Becky?" she glanced around, confused. "Ryan? John? Mel?"

As Sally edged closer to the ledge, fearing the worst, she noticed a petal glistening on the ground. She recognized it from Becky's magical sunflower. When she picked it up it turned black, slowly disintegrating into ash.

"Guys?" she called again, louder. Her echoes resounded over the mountain, but her only reply was the howl of the wind. "Where did everyone go?" she asked herself, out loud.

Then it hit her; she was all alone. They were all gone.

Chapter XV
The Mirror of Reflection

The ambient golden aura of the sun behind the clouds began to dim as Sally sat alone watching the lightning strikes far in the distance. Ryan and the others should have shown up by now. Something was wrong. Her mind reeled with possibilities.

It had taken her much longer than anticipated to run back to the room, only to find Ryan wasn't there. It had taken twice as long to find her way back outside. The labyrinth of the mining caves was not at all easy to navigate without a map.

Sally continued to sit alone with her rampantly running imagination, waiting, unsure of what to do. She was not a natural leader by any means, not like Ryan. It always seemed that he knew exactly what to do in any situation. She didn't mind being the follower. It was easier that way and besides, she'd always feared that any decision she made would be the wrong choice.

"Sally." Dyad called out from behind.

Sally gripped a rock outcropping next to her, using it as a handhold as she rose to her feet and pivoted to face Dyad. The fairy was flying toward her.

"Where are the others?" Dyad transformed to her larger self as she landed, gesturing to Sally to sit back down and sitting herself. "I was helping Grunky rally a few dwarves to help with the hunt," Dyad explained, "but I lost track of time. Thought I better find out what you all were up to."

Sally didn't try to hide her concern. "I don't know where anyone is. Ryan and I got into a fight. Then I ran into Becky and we talked out here. I decided to go back and work out things with Ryan, but he was gone." Sally paused for another breath. "It took me a long time to find my way back and when I got here she was gone. I haven't seen Mel or John since we went to bed. I don't know where anyone is, Dyad. I've got a feeling that something's wrong."

Dyad surveyed the scene. Her eyes narrowed as she used all her senses to tune into the energy of the area. "You're right. Something has happened. Something is not right here."

Dyad floated up in fairy form, circling the rocky clearing at the mouth of the cave. She glowed with a silvery light from within as she chanted:

"Mystic past, not so clear;
Show us now, what happened here."

A blue, translucent, beautifully curved young female shape materialized before them, armed with her daggers, a fierce expression on her exquisite face.

"It's Becky!" Sally excitedly moved toward the specter.

"Wait," Dyad cautioned. "Stay back." She wafted closer to the Becky image. Becky's mouth was moving, but no words came out. "This is only a hologram of what transpired here, Sally, a recorded shadow. She is talking to someone." Dyad glowed brighter, illuminating the night and in essence creating a stage for the hologram to play out. Another shadow-shape materialized, taking the form of Lexis. "The Banshee was here!"

Sally's fists tightened, remembering her dream. "Why can't we hear what they're saying?"

"A hologram is a silent showing," Dyad explained. "Nothing more."

Mel, John and Ryan specters materialized on the impromptu stage. Sally and Dyad watched events unfold, gasping as Becky was turned to stone and crying out as Lexis kicked her over the edge.

"Oh my God!" Sally screamed, bursting into tears.

The translucent play of events continued, the two of them watching as John pounded Mel to a bruised and bloody pulp. Dyad sighed, feeling shame for John and wishing she could have been there for him.

Suddenly, Nymph appeared, looking vengeful and victorious. Dyad felt true rage as she watched her duplicitous sister appear, cast a spell, the boys vanishing, then disappearing herself. Moments later, the blue shadow of Sally's specter came out, looking for the others in vain.

"Well," Dyad paused, trying to hold her feelings in. Moments such as this called for calm and strength. "At least we know now what had happened here. The Banshee set a trap for us. And she was aided and abetted by my traitorous sister."

"How do you know?" asked Sally.

"She was the one who informed us that the Banshee was here," Dyad said, barely containing her fury. "It's obvious she has allied herself with the Banshee and fully participated in the set-up. I am beyond disappointed," Dyad proclaimed. "I have no idea why she would do this."

"Where did the boys go?" asked Sally.

"I am not sure," Dyad considered the possibilities. "But from what I know of my sister and the scope of her powers, she likely would have used the spell that transports them to anywhere in Enchantas. It is completely random. She has always liked that spell. When she was young she would cast it on animals in the valley, for no reason. I guess she's always been vindictive and willing to hurt others. Why did I not see it before?"

"Dyad," Sally said, "Don't blame yourself. You couldn't have predicted she would turn against you and Enchantas."

"I should have known, Sally!" Dyad snapped out in frustration. "I should have known by the way she was treating you and Ryan. That was a sign, but I thought she was just having some harmless fun." Dyad's angry red glow matched her voice. "She will not get away with this, Sally!"

"You're right." Sally agreed. "We'll find her. But we have to find the boys first."

"Agreed. We should find the boys first," Dyad said grimly. "But I have a feeling there's no time. This was planned. The Banshee and Nymph wanted us to be divided."

"For what purpose?"

"That, I do not know." Dyad floated a few paces and continued. "But we must stop them right away!"

"You mean, not go look for the boys?"

"We don't have time to scour Enchantas looking for them. They literally could be anywhere."

"Well, I don't agree with that." Sally balked. "I need to find Ryan, first, before I do anything else."

"I do not agree with you. We should not be divided. However, there is no time to argue. Whatever the Banshee and Nymph are planning is going to happen soon," Dyad said. "I must continue with the mission. I must focus on the greater good of Enchantas. If you must find Ryan before you are willing to do anything else, then you are on your own. I hope you find the prophets. I am sure all four of you will be needed."

"Where do I begin?" asked Sally. "I don't even know how to get to my room without getting lost."

Dyad morphed to her human size, handing Sally a small blue purse. "Here is an E-Mail scroll and a tracking compass. The compass is much like Fate's Compass, which you will remember using the last time you were here. This compass, however, will not point you in the direction that Fate wants you to go, but will instead direct you to the nearest towns and villages. It can also be used for more specific destinations. Try it out."

Sally opened the compass, which was inscribed with three locations: Enchantic Mines, Bearton and Gnelfton.

"How is this supposed to help?"

"It will not tell you where the boys are, but you will be able to search the nearest settlement and ask questions. Also, if you say the name of a destination, it will point you in the true direction." Dyad looked at the compass and said, "Enchantian Institute of Magic."

The letters 'E.I.M.' glowed yellow on the right side, with a helpful glowing arrow icon pointing the way.

"That's cool," said Sally, figuring she'd best learn everything she could about various functions that could help her track her friends and spirit-mate. "What about this?" She pulled out the E-Mail scroll which was sealed in a cylindrical canister.

Dyad took it, explaining as she unrolled it, "You can use this to stay in contact with me; we can let each other know our progress."

A tear came down Sally's cheek. She was frightened and sad. "I feel so bad for John." She wiped her eyes. Up until now, she hadn't processed Becky's death. The tragedy had so many ripple effects. "And for Mel. I can't believe Becky is gone!"

"You all have my utmost sympathy," Dyad comforted her. "Losing a sister is very difficult; I have lost many over the ages. Now it looks like I've lost another. But come — we have work to do before we can truly mourn." Dyad was too focused and determined to be sentimental for long. "I am going now, Sally. I advise you to get going, too."

Sally nodded, wiping the last of her tears. She knew it was not a time for weeping. She had to be strong; she had to be like Ryan, she had to be a leader.

"Where should I start?" asked Sally.

"Find Grunky. Have them search the tunnels for the boys. Then search the nearest settlement. Instruct Grunky to E-Mail you and me if he finds anything."

"Excellent idea."

"Good luck, Sally," Dyad smiled.

Sally rubbed her diamond earrings. She recalled how Ryan had chosen them for her; it was one of her favorite memories. Her determination and longing to find him was strong. "Thank you. Good luck to you, also, Dyad. Take care."

Dyad's form vanished into a pinpoint of bright blue light. Sally hurried back into the cave.

***

The dwarves were not eager to change their hunting party into a search party, but Grunky gave them an ultimatum. Working triple shifts was not a favorable option for any of the crabby laborers.

Sally walked with Grunky as he led his company in combing the upper south tunnels of the mines. So far, there was no sign of the guys.

"So, how far is it to the next exit?" Sally asked Grunky, who was busy arguing with the complaining dwarves.

"Sorry about that, Sally," he turned back to her. "The next exit is right up here. And it's safe from the demigons."

"That's a relief."

252

"Yes, the good thing about them demigons is that we don't get many visitors." Grunky smiled. "Only, it makes transporting the lixy dust very difficult."

"I said split up and search every tunnel!" Grunky yelled at his crew. "Hurry it up!"

The dwarves mumbled colorful curses as they followed orders.

"Sorry, again," Grunky chuckled. "We really are pleasant when we have a day off, a mug of beer and a large amount of well-cooked food in front of us." Suddenly, his demeanor turned sad. "Though, those times have become fewer than we have wished the past few seasons."

Sally wasn't really listening; she had Ryan and the others on her mind.

"My apologies," Grunky frowned. "I keep going on and on about our problems, I forget you have bigger concerns than I. So where did Dyad suggest you go?"

"Dyad said my best bet is proceeding town to town, looking for any signs of the boys." Sally looked at her compass, "This says the closest settlement is Bearton."

"Bearton?" Grunky shook his head. "No no no, it's not safe to go there. Those bearbarians aren't friendly at all. They hate humans. Besides it's at least twenty sprints away."

"Sprints?" asked Sally. She wasn't sure what he was referring to.

"Oh, umm a sprint is a hundred dashes, which is a hundred leaps." He looked at Sally for confirmation; she was still dumbfounded. "Okay, let me break it down. There are ten paws a leap and ten claws a paw. That's how we measure distance." Sally still looked mystified. "Anyway, let's just say Bearton is too far away to reach by walking. Did Dyad provide you with some type of flying conveyance?"

"No. And she neglected to tell me how far the closest town is, too."

"Ha, fairies," Grunky snorted. "They always miss the details. They can zap themselves everywhere with ease, so they figure everyone else can, too."

"Yeah," she agreed. "It does seem that way, doesn't it?"

"I'm sorry we don't have any flying machines or creatures you can use. We dwarves prefer life on the ground. In fact, we like the ground so much that we love being under it!"

"That's okay. I'll manage." Sally, used to walking, was in good shape. She thought of Ryan again and how she'd occasionally join him on his midnight rambles.

"So tell me: What's this about dangerous bears?"

"After the crusades the bearbarians revolted against the Witch and Warlock. It was hopeless for them and many bruins died. Ever since, they have not taken kindly to humans. They remain secluded in their tribes. If I were you, I'd skip Bearton and try the next village."

"But what if the boys are there?" Sally argued. "I can't just leave Ryan or Mel or John there, especially if it's dangerous."

Before Grunky could answer, the floor opened underneath and a shocked Sally slid down into the gap.

"Sally!" Grunky cried from above, hollering and peering down the hole. She was gone.

Sally slipped along on a smooth hard stone surface resembling a slide as she descended down another tunnel. She could not tell how fast she was going in the pitch black. The slide twisted and turned and her body bumped hard into the sides, almost knocking her unconscious.

Finally, she landed on a flat, smooth stone floor. Torches flared with bright red flames in a small room. At the far end, a large oval mirror glowed bright yellow and a voice resonated around the room.

"Sally! Can you hear me?" the voice called, a very familiar woman's voice.

"Hello?" Sally answered.

"Oh, good," the voice echoed again. "You can hear me. Come closer to the mirror so I can see you."

Sally walked cautiously to the mirror. As she approached, the glare of its projection disappeared, allowing her to see into it with total clarity. The mirror did not reflect an image of her. Instead, Sally stared in amazement at her mother.

"Mom?" Sally smiled. "Is that you?"

She saw her mother looking straight at her. Behind her mother was what appeared to be their bathroom back home. Sally knew this room all too well; this was the room where she'd done all her crying back in the day. Her grandmother would always find a way to coax her out and cheer her up, usually by bribing her with a scrumptious home-cooked meal.

"Oh Sally dear!" her mother sounded relieved. "I'm so happy to see that you're safe!"

"Mom, what's going on?"

"This is a communication mirror," her mother explained. "They are stationed throughout Enchantas. I'm contacting you from our bathroom, back in our world."

"Oh," Sally replied, trying to adjust to the shock of so many changes all happening so fast. Her senses were on overload.

"Where are the others?" her mom asked. "Where's Ryan?"

"I don't know," Sally looked sad. "They were zapped by Lexis and Nymph the fairy. I'm looking for them now. Becky is dead."

"Becky? Who's Becky?"

"John's sister," Sally sighed. "She was a real good friend."

"I'm so sorry, dear," her mother looked agitated and anxious. "I told Brian to let you go home! Those knights never listen to me!"

"Mom! Calm down. It was our choice to stay," Sally assured her.

"I'm sorry. There's been enough anger in my life and yours. There's been a lot of loss, too, and I can't allow that pattern to continue."

"I wish you were here," Sally was close to tears again. "I don't know what to do."

"Honey, I would come if I could but it's not possible. Our truce with the Knights forbids us from ever returning. Even if you are in trouble."

"How long have you been talking to Brian?"

"We've been in contact with the Knights and the Sage for about a month," she replied calmly. "We'd given our advice to the council on numerous occasions. I am not convinced that they listened, but at least they were able to accumulate other points of view. Brian informed us that you all were there. I didn't worry much until he told me of your quest."

"We were fine up until Lexis showed up."

"I really worry about you being there with Lexis on the loose. She is very unstable."

"Mom, what happened to her? What did you guys do?"

"Sally," she became very sad. "You must understand that nothing we did made Lexis who she is. When she came to us she was already unstable. She had a horrible past that I will not get into. Her social skills were touch-and-go, her temper treacherous. We took it upon ourselves to take her in and keep her away from all other Enchantians. For their safety."

"About that, Mom," Sally didn't want to tell her mother about their horrible reputation and all the stories she'd heard about the Witch and the Warlock. But she knew she had to have this conversation for her own sake. "I've heard over and over the many evil things that you've done, that you and dad did. How can you justify all that pain and violence and what it did to Enchantas? It makes me sad and ashamed every time the topic of 'the Witch and Warlock' comes up."

Sally's mom stayed silent for a moment. "Sally, I have my regrets. Many, many regrets. We did some terrible things. But all we truly wanted was to come home to you. For us to be a family again."

Sally didn't know what else to say. Their past would forever mark them, but she still loved them for the good, young, and innocent people they had been before Enchantas and the good people they were now, older, kinder, and so much wiser.

"The best thing for you to do now is to show Enchantians that you are good and to tell them that we regret the things that we've done."

Sally nodded, silently appreciative of her mother's advice.

"I have to find the boys, Mom." Sally told her. "I need help."

"Well, I'm glad I found you," her mom smiled again. "And I can surely help you find them. Where are you now, exactly?"

"The Enchantic Mines. I fell down a hole into this room and then there you were, looking at me in the mirror."

"Perfect! I have something for you to use — that is, if I left one there. I think I did," her mother mused half-talking to Sally, half to herself. She tore off a piece of paper towel and began to write on it with a lipstick. When she was finished she raised it to the mirror for Sally to read. "Recite this verse."

Sally squinted for a moment; as it finally came into focus, she read out loud:

"Witch's spell, glare of mirror,
Give me a ride, and escape appear!"

Suddenly a long crooked broom ejected out of the mirror, hovering in front of Sally like an eager, obedient dog awaiting further instructions.

"There you go, dear," her mother declared. "Now you're free to travel Enchantas in style. You know, this was my ride of choice. My broom took me everywhere."

"Thanks, Mom," Sally said, startled and perplexed. "But I'm kind of stuck in a cave. How do you propose I ride a broom down here?"

"Don't worry, dear," her mother waved at her, then blew a kiss. "I'll let you go now. Just fly into the mirror and it will take you on the correct route to your next destination."

"*Okay,*" Sally stared at her broom, still feeling uneasy.

"All-righty dear, I love you! Have a safe trip and come home soon." With that, her mother vanished, leaving Sally alone but for her own reflection and the eager-to-serve broom.

Doesn't anything come with an instruction book around here? Sally thought as she grabbed the pole and threw a leg over the broom, mounting it Halloween witch style. "Here goes nothing," she said to herself. The mirror flashed and a mountainside with a dark forest not too far in the distance appeared in its depths.

She leaned into the broom moving it slightly forward. She bobbled for a moment, almost losing her balance.

"All right, Mom," she mumbled to herself. "If you say so." Sally kicked off, lifting her legs from the ground. Her body wobbled until she grasped the broom tighter. Then the broom jolted forward, skyrocketing faster as she smoothly entered the mirror. She was off!

Chapter XVI
Bearbarians

Ryan shivered, slowly opening his eyes, and sat up in the cold air. He glanced around the moon-silvered landscape, brushing off an accumulation of colored snow. Thick walls, composed of impenetrable blue pine trees, completely enclosed the small area where he lay. He felt trapped. He rubbed his aching head as he tried to recollect what had happened. He remembered the fight with the Banshee, Becky falling, and Nymph cursing him here. Wherever *here* was.

Nymph, he snorted, he should have known there was something off with her. It all made sense now; she had been conspiring with Lexis the whole time. Nymph had tried to separate him from Sally just as the Banshee tried and succeeded in dividing the group. Ryan knew Mel was correct. They were strong when they were together. This of course was the Banshee's fear.

Her plan had worked, with much of the credit going to that awful Nymph. Ryan felt lost and wondered where John and Mel were, and most of all, Sally.

He whispered her name quietly. Where is she? He had not seen her since the argument.

"Sally!" yelled Ryan. He knew there was little to no chance Nymph's spell had sent her to the same place as him, but he couldn't resist the urge to call for her. "SALLY! Are you there?"

There was no answer — of course — only the frigid wind howling through the trees. Still shivering, Ryan stood up and began to walk, having no idea where he was going. He squeezed through two of the blue pine trees. The needles were sharp, cutting his face and arms. He rubbed his bracelet and the wounds healed.

It took a few ticks for him to worm his way through a resistant opening in the copse of tightly spaced trees and by then he was already tired. He dropped to his knees struggling to catch his breath.

"Great!" he sighed with relief after escaping the thicket until he glanced ahead and realized there were more walls of blue pine trees as far as he could see.

"Wonderful," a voice growled from above, "isn't it?"

Ryan looked up in wonderment as a large yellow bear standing on its hind legs lumbered up in front of him. About twice his size and extremely muscular, the bear wore rusty metal armor that covered its back, belly and limbs. A metal helmet covered most of its skull as well as its snout.

"Look here, boys," the bear pointed a long spear at him. The head of the weapon was as large as Ryan's torso. "We've got ourselves a human!"

Two black bears, wearing similar armor stepped out from the shadows, armed with axes.

"What should we do with it, boss?"

"Yeah," the other black bear drooled. "Should we eat it, Grizz?"

"No," Grizz replied. "Let's bring it back to the village. The chief will know what to do."

Ryan's sword appeared in his hand as he swiped the bear's spear away from him and charged at Grizz. His attempt to defend himself was futile as the two black bears pointed their axes at Ryan's neck, stopping him dead in his tracks.

"A persona bracelet?" Grizz ripped it off Ryan's wrist. "I don't think so! Put these on instead and follow me."

Grizz tossed a pair of cuffs to Ryan and having no alternative, Ryan put them on and followed Grizz. The two black bears stayed close behind, ready to attack if he tried to escape. Ryan knew better, though, and wasn't about to try to run. With their size, they were sure to catch him.

"Now," Grizz looked back at his captive, "what would a Knight from Minerton be doing on this side of the mountain range? And in our territory?"

"I'm not a Knight of Minerton," Ryan replied.

"You're a human, right?"

"Well yeah, but-"

"Then you're a Knight!" Grizz bellowed, dismissing Ryan's argument. "We do not concern ourselves with the logistics of your kind. You are human, so you are the enemy!"

"I am not an enemy," Ryan argued.

"Yes you are," Grizz replied calmly. "And you will be tried for breaking the treaty. Which will amuse me greatly!"

"What treaty?" Ryan didn't have time for this nonsense. He needed to find Sally. "I have no idea what you're talking about. I was transported here, against my will, cursed by a fairy."

"Save your excuses for the chief!" Grizz snarled. "I don't want to hear them!"

"Let me go!" Ryan tried to break the cuffs, but his attempt was useless.

"Don't try it human!" a black bear grunted.

"Yeah, if you run, it'll just give me a good reason to eat you," the other licked its chops, "without getting into trouble."

Ryan quickly shut up.

They squeezed through a few more dense blue pine thickets. Ryan was now covered in scratches deep enough to draw blood. His skin burned and stung. He wished he had his bracelet back to heal the wounds.

They came to a wide-open area with large bonfire pits scattered around the flatlands. Scores of bulky brown clay huts had been erected unsystematically, standing tall with walls made of stick and thatched roofs of long, yellow grass.

Dozens and dozens of bears came out of their huts when they smelt the human. They approached Ryan and his captors with aggressive curiosity. Ryan observed a group of black bears donning their helmets. They looked at him scornfully. Another group, comprised of arrogant white polar bears, sharpened their swords. This was not looking good for him, he thought. Not looking good at all.

His captors paraded him through most of the village, the procession of bears trailing behind them multiplying. They finally stopped at a large three-story hut decorated with blue symbols unrecognizable to Ryan.

An immensely fat panda bear waddled down a flight of stairs, holding aloft a staff topped with a bear skull. Dignified despite his grotesque girth, the obvious ruler or dignitary wore a showy cape of large, shimmering purple and blue demigon feathers.

"Chief Featherslayer!" Grizz roared, falling to one knee.

The entire tribe of bears followed suit, kneeling and bowing their heads in deference. A black bear jabbed the back of Ryan's knee with the butt of his axe, forcing him to kneel as well. "Bow to our chief," it growled.

"I've come before you tonight," Grizz continued, "to inform you that we have an intruder. A possible spy from the Minerton humans."

Ryan raised his head, shouting defiantly. "I am not a spy!"

"Silence!" Grizz snarled, glancing to the back of the gathering, where a commotion from the villagers was beginning to grow. Ryan knew it wasn't a good sign when he heard the words "dinner", "snack", and "spices". If they were going to eat him he hoped they'd put him out of his misery first.

"Grizz, my mightiest warrior!" the chief went to him, setting his staff lightly on one shoulder, and then the other, as if knighting the beast. Grizz rose. "You never cease to amaze me. Just the other night, you presented us with that delectable herd of snuffballs for our feast and now a human? What an amazing combination of luck and skill you possess, my gifted young apprentice!"

"Thank you, Your Grace," Grizz smiled, fangs glimmering in the light of many fires. "We found him just on the edge of pines. I am unsure how he got there."

The chief waddled over to Ryan. He was gigantic, much larger than Grizz, and his heartless black eyes glared frighteningly. "What brings you here, boy? I thought our treaty was clear: No influence or communication from the outside. We are to be left alone."

"I apologize," Ryan said softly. He wasn't sure what to say, but continued anyway. The truth would have to do. "This intrusion was not on purpose. I was transported here by a fairy's curse. A fairy acting on behalf of the Banshee brought me here."

"A fairy, eh?" the chief bent over to take a closer look. "Well bad luck is upon you, boy. This is not the place to be transported. Especially for a human."

"If I could just leave," Ryan began to say but was interrupted.

"Leave?" the chief bellowed with laughter. The crowd surrounding him laughed as well. "There is no leaving for you! I just don't know what to do with you." The chief scratched his chin as he contemplated, "We could keep you as a slave?" there was a small cheer from the bears. "But humans are much too weak for labor with their skinny little arms and legs. Or we could have you as an appetizer for our next feast!"

The crowd's cheer became deafening. Ryan was suddenly reminded of the battle for Enchantas when they were offered as a meal for the legions of gremlins and imps.

"We shall see." The chief made his ungainly way back to his hut and turned to give his orders. "Until then, put him in the cage! I will decide in the morning!"

With that said, Grizz and the two black bears hustled Ryan to a small hut fashioned with large bamboo bars facing a campfire.

The villagers spat on him as he walked past. There was clearly no love for humans in this village.

"Get in!" Grizz prodded him. The floor was damp and muddy. Grizz locked the bamboo-barred door, striding away. Ryan shook the door, but it didn't budge. He was trapped.

***

It had been well over three tocks, and Ryan couldn't sleep. He was not as worried about himself, his main concern was Sally. Where had she been sent? Hopefully she was not somewhere more horrible than this awful place.

He shifted position so that he was leaning against the wall on his dry side. Covered in mud and blood, he was wet and cold to the bone. This was not how he'd imagined his return to Enchantas. He wondered why the bears hated humans so much. He figured it must be something historically heinous proportions for their prejudice and hatred to be so extreme. Not that it mattered at this point; his fate now rested on the whim of a gargantuan panda. *Life could not get any more bizarre*, he thought.

Then he felt something move in his right pants pocket. Ryan jumped, thoroughly startled, trying to grab it and get it out of his pants before it could bite him or worse. He patted it squeamishly, trying to grasp the moving target as it burrowed further into the interior of the fabric, but it kept squirming like a baby kangaroo in its pouch. If it wouldn't have brought a guard running, he would have shrieked like a girl.

"Ouch!" a delicate voice squealed. "That hurts!"

Frantically digging deeper, Ryan finally got a grip, extracting a squishy, round object, a ball of some sort. He quickly lobbed it against the rear wall.

"Wheeeeee!" it giggled, bouncing and rolling back to him. "That was fun!"

Ryan squinted, bending down. It was a small, turquois snuffball. "Channy?"

"Hey Ryan!" The spirited snuffball rolled toward him excitedly. "Is it safe to come out now?"

Ryan stared at Channy curiously. "How long have you been in my pocket?"

"Oh, since we left the Institute," Channy said innocently. "And boy, being on an adventure with you guys is such a blast! Wait'll I tell the others! They'll be so jealous!"

"Channy, you can't be here," Ryan tried to keep his voice down. "It's not safe."

"Boy, you sure got that right! Demigons, the Banshee. And who knew Nymph was evil? Although I always did think she was a little off."

"Yeah, well you should get out of here while you still have a chance."

"I don't want to leave; I wanna be a hero, just like you and have my name remembered forever!"

"Channy," Ryan sighed. "This is no time for fun and games, this is real! There are vicious bears out there."

"Oh. Yeah. Sorry," Channy whispered. "Snuffballs don't like big bad bears. That's why we don't go in their territory. They eat us."

"Yeah," Ryan picked Channy up. "That's why it's not safe and you need to go. You should be small enough-" Ryan suddenly had an epiphany. "Channy, did you just say you wanted to be a hero?"

"Yes!" Channy squealed with excitement. "Just like you and Sally! I want my name remembered, a statue of me and most of all," Channy sighed and quietly said, "All the other snuffballs to like me."

Ryan smiled, petting the adorable little snuffball. "Well I've got a very, very important mission for you!"

"Really? Really?" Channy pounced off his hand and bounced off the walls. "What is it? What is it?"

"It is a very important mission," Ryan kept whispering, hoping Channy will take the hint and quiet down. "Not only will you be saving me, you'll be saving the entire land of Enchantas as well!"

"Tell me! Tell me!"

"Shhhhh, Channy. We must be quiet so we don't wake up the bears."

"Right," Channy whispered. "Tell me. Tell me."

"This must be covert. Do you know what that means?"

"Just like the famous black snuffball, Bubbles!" She puffed herself up proudly. "He's my hero, too!"

"Right," Ryan scooted closer to the bar door and pointed at another hut. "I need you to sneak way over there, steal the key for this cage and bring it back."

"You mean," Channy gulped, "steal from the big bad bears?"

"Yes," Ryan said gravely. "This is a very dangerous mission and you must be very brave and very quiet and very skillful to do this. I'll understand if you don't want to."

Channy took a deep breath and sighed. "I will do it, Ryan! I will be your hero!"

"Awesome!" Ryan petted her some more. "Now if you have any problems, come back right away. Oh, and if you see my bracelet, could you get that, too?"

"Okey dokey," Channy shivered nervously but began to roll cautiously out of the cage and toward the fire.

"Covert! Covert!" Ryan whispered, reminding Channy.

"Oh, right," Channy whispered back, "Sorry." She rolled back toward the hut, slipping into the shadows.

She was too small and too well hidden for Ryan to track her progress. He crossed his fingers, wishing the adorable snuffball the best of luck. Their lives depended on it.

Channy hopped over a large black armored chest and rolled past a doorway. A few bears stumbled out, spilling mugs of beer on the ground, but they were too drunk to notice little Channy.

Channy passed a few other huts, still unseen, before reaching the hut that Ryan had indicated. As Channy rolled in, she noticed a pile of armor lying alongside a stone bed where Grizz snored loudly. The sound rumbled through Channy as she carefully rolled on top of the bed. Next to the bed was an end table that held both the key and bracelet.

Channy rolled over the bear's hide and hopped on the table without making a sound. As Channy rolled on top of the key, she sucked it inside herself. She then did the same with the bracelet.

Channy let out a burp and giggled. Grizz growled loudly and turned toward Channy. Stunned and afraid that Grizz might awake, Channy froze for a moment and waited to make sure he was still asleep.

Urgently, Channy rolled back to the cage following the same path back to Ryan.

"Any problems?" asked Ryan.

"Nope!" Channy spat out the key and bracelet. "That was easy! Am I a hero now?"

"Not yet, my friend." Ryan said, trying to unlock the door. It opened. "We have to get out of here first."

Ryan stepped out, his clothes still muddy and wet. He put on his bracelet, rubbed the gem and his wounds healed immediately. Ryan sighed in relief.

"Come, let's go this way," Ryan crouched down, pulling out his sword. Channy followed without question.

They went alongside a hut draped in protective shadows. Ryan searched for another shadowy path to hide them, but there were too many fires illuminating the well-lit village.

"This is not going to be easy," Ryan muttered under his breath as he darted toward another hut. Regrettably, this time he was seen.

"Hey you!" a drunken bear yelled. "It's the human! It's escaping! Sound the alarm!"

A loud horn blew and before they knew it, they were surrounded again by bears. Grizz came out of his hut, huffing and puffing with anger.

"Where do you think you're going, little human?" Grizz howled.

"We're leaving!" Channy yelped. "I'm a hero!"

"Oh, are you now?" Grizz laughed with his fellow bears. "Looks like I've got a little appetizer before the main course."

"Not if I can help it, you grizzled grumps!" called out a voice from above.

A large wooden sailing ship hovered above, a one-eyed Border Collie gnashed his fangs and called threats over the edge as he looked down.

"Max!" Ryan yelped with joy.

"Pirates!" Grizz growled. "I hate pirates!"

"*Yar*, yourself," Max growled back as a rope ladder was hastily deploying, dropping down from the ship. "Hurry now,

Ryan, grab it!" bellowed Max, brandishing his black pirate captain's hat.

"Get the human!" Grizz ordered, but the charge was too late.

Ryan, had a firm handhold on the ladder, which was being rapidly hoisted up by deckhands. The chunky, clumsy bears jumped in vain, unable to reach him.

"Ryan!" Channy cried, still on the ground. "Come back! Come back!"

"Max, wait!" called out Ryan, "We have to get Channy."

Grizz snatched the little snuffball, calling out, "Don't forget your snuffball, human! Come and get it!"

"Ryan," Channy called out, "tell everyone what I did! Tell Sally-"

Suddenly Grizz threw Channy up in the air like a piece of popcorn and caught her with his mouth, swallowing her whole. "Yes, Ryan, tell Sally-" Grizz began to mock, but then his stomach made a massive gurgling noise, like the burbling of a stopped-up drain when it finally lets go. His gut lurched, expanding and contracting under his belly fur.

Uncontrollably, Grizz spat Channy out high into the air, up onto the deck of the ship. Ryan climbed up the ladder as quickly as he could and the sailors continue to assist in dragging him over the railing onto the ship.

"Channy," he cried, picking up the wet snuffball. "How did you get away?"

"Yuck," Channy shook the wetness off. "Bear tummies are gross!"

Ryan laughed and then heard screaming below. He and Max dashed to the ledge and looked down. Grizz was on a rampage, burping fire with a nauseating retching sound as he scrambled to find water. Huts began to burn. The village was in flames.

"Why it's *Professor Mel's Dragon's Breath Super-Duper-Hot Fire Sauce*," Channy squeaked out a giggle, spitting out a vial of red liquid. "It's the most powerful repellent we have."

"You didn't!" Max chuckled, rubbing his good eye. "I had that aboard once; nearly burned down the ship. You're a clever little one aren't you?"

Channy replied with another giggle, "That'll teach them to mess with *Channy the Savior*."

"Yes, that will." said Ryan, holding his pocket open. "You truly are a hero, Channy."

With pride, Channy jumped back in Ryan's pocket, safe and satisfied.

"And you! Am I glad to see you!" Ryan embraced his rescuer in what he would never again refer to as a *bear hug*.

"Hey, now," Max pushed him off gently and laughed. "Come on. Not so close, you'll give me a bad rep with my crew."

"Sorry." Ryan withdrew, heartily shaking the pirate's paw. "I can't thank you enough. Can you fill me in on what's been going on? Where are we off to, Cap'n Max?"

"Back to the academy, our forces are assembling."

"Are the others there? Is Sally?"

"No," Max replied grimly. "You're the only one we found, matey."

"Can we look for them?" Ryan feared the worst. "They've got to be out there somewhere!"

"I'm afraid not, my friend. Our mission was to find who we could and go directly back." Max stood next to him on the starboard railing of his ship. The Storm Glider was pristine and seaworthy, unlike their last cruise. "I'm disappointed, but our orders were time-specific," Max added.

Ryan leaned over the edge, silently watching the trees below as Storm Glider plied the skies. The air warmed as they soared toward the moon and over the clouds. He thought of his companions, especially Sally, somewhere under the same moon, fervently hoping that they weren't too far away and that somehow, they all would be reunited.

Chapter XVII

The Pyramid of Prophets

The scorching white sun beamed from the cloudless light green sky onto the desolate pink sands below. The desert radiated with increasing heat. Mel slowly woke up, face bruised, head pounding, and very thirsty.

He spit out a mouthful of sand and surveyed the landscape ahead: nothing but sand dunes as far as he could see. He thought maybe he could make out canyons in the distance, but it was too far to walk in this heat and anyway, it could easily be a mirage.

Mel swiveled for a full 360-degree view. He rubbed his bloodshot eyes, astounded by what he saw. It was still there when he looked again, a massive red pyramid, standing alone in the middle of the desert. Directly ahead was an entrance, and more importantly, shade.

Mel rubbed his bracelet, but it wasn't working. His body was too banged up and dehydrated for him to be able to move quickly. He touched his face, feeling the welts and dried blood. He suddenly remembered why he felt this way and what had happened.

Becky, Mel thought, *such an amazing person.* A girl who he could see spending the rest of his life with. But not anymore, now she was gone, forever.

Mel would have cried, but there wasn't enough moisture left in his body for tears. He wondered how John was doing, John, whose wrath in grief was unlike anything he'd ever witnessed or felt before.

Ryan had told him about the infamous first day of school incident that brought them together and how over-the-top angry John had been with Sally for accidentally breaking his bike. At that time his temper had been way out of proportion to the situation. What Mel had done to John was much, much worse. Mel knew he didn't deserve to be beaten, but acknowledged that he might have done the same thing if he was John. The feelings of anger and denial must have consumed him, breaking his spirit and causing him to react uncontrollably.

Becky's death was also devastating for Mel. He could only imagine how John felt, losing his only sister, a sister he'd loved so dearly all his life. The two of them were always there for each other. Mel never had that. He grew up mostly an only child. His stepfather had children, but Mel wasn't close to them. They were adults and did not live with Mel, his mom, and stepfather.

Mel had this one, fantastic chance to have someone who cared about him and someone he cared about. Becky was the one, but now she was gone, forever.

It occurred to him that he must be suffering from a double dose of survivor's guilt. In the span of one day two young, vibrant beings — one the possible love of his life and the other an adoring pupil with a strong case of hero worship — had sacrificed their lives for him. He was not worthy.

Mel staggered toward the pyramid, seeking shade. He ran his swollen tongue over his lips, tasting nothing but dryness, salt, and grit. His arms and legs were weak and his clothes smelled of his sweat. He dug in his satchel, finding nothing but his octahedron shaped puckerberries. Eating those would only make his thirst worse.

Mel toppled down a large dune and rolled into a shaded area of sand. It was much cooler there. His eyes became heavy, but he knew if he slept he'd die.

Struggling, Mel finally got up, forcing himself to walk faster. Though wobbly and unstable he made it into the pyramid. It was surprisingly much cooler. It felt like it was air-conditioned. He leaned up against a wall, glancing around to orient himself. To his astonishment he spotted a fountain sparkling with fresh blue water.

Mel threw himself at it, desperately gulping as much as he could then forcing himself to stop as he remembered that drinking too fast wasn't a good idea. He slowed down, enjoying every last sip until satisfied, then threw himself on the ground, spent and breathing heavily.

He noticed a painting on the wall, a startlingly lifelike portrait of John, Sally, Ryan, and him near the abandoned well not far from their high school that served as the conduit for their first journey to Enchantas. John and Ryan were fighting as Sally and he looked on. Examining closely, Mel noticed that John and Ryan were actually pushing and punching; he could follow their movements like a silent film that captured that moment and held it in instant replay for all time. He wondered who or what was activating it. Possibly there was an iris detection sensor. Still musing on various theories (he really did love to learn and it distracted him from the traumas he'd recently experienced), Mel kept walking. A little further along he found another painting. This one showed the band of travelers in the Forbidden Cave, depicting Sally finding the compass. As Mel continued he saw more and more paintings, a complete and comprehensive retrospective of their adventures in Enchantas. Some were familiar to him: meeting Gitchy, their trip to Rabbit City, the Owl's home, and Minerton Castle. Others weren't. There were surprising images of John talking to a Leprechaun and bravely battling foxes in a caged arena. And there were disturbing images of Lexis, as well as of the Witch and Warlock.

It suddenly became clear to him that these moving paintings were actual recordings of their Enchantian exploits. Mel paused at the battle for Enchantas, remembering how frightened he was. He had come a long way since then, living here, learning magic, and becoming an Enchantian himself.

As he continued, new scenes were depicted and displayed including Sally, Ryan, John, and Becky in a parking lot talking to Dyad. Others featured landmarks and events including Beaverton Bridge, the Enchantian Ball and the demigon attack.

He continued moving along, noting the chronological order until he reached the sequence detailing Becky's death. Mel investigated it carefully for any overlooked details, to verify that it really happened, and to determine if there was truly anything more he could have done to prevent it. There was nothing.

Becky's fate was sealed from the beginning. Lexis was solely to blame. It didn't make his heart hurt any less. He would mourn her for the rest of his life. But the logical side of him needed to know the facts in order to put his mind at rest. It made it possible for him to move on with concentration and deliberation, allowing him to put forth his best to save Enchantas from current and future threats.

As Mel moved along, he saw Sally talking to her mother in a mirror, then Ryan being captured by bearbarians.

Finally, there it was: a painting of this exact moment. Mel stood in front of it watching himself watch himself, over and over again.

Mel moved his arm up to wave; his image in the painting waved, too. It reminded him of a childhood game that could fascinate him for hours. He'd position himself between two large mirrors, one of his bedroom closet, the other on his bathroom door, mesmerized by his repeating reflection, refracted over and over again.

An image of Cully appeared behind him in the painting, as if she had actually stepped behind him. Spooked, Mel jumped away from the wall. There she was.

"Are you surprised to be here, Professor?" said Cully.

"Cully?" Mel's boomerang emerged. "Is that really you?"

"No, Professor," Cully transformed into a sphinx with the face and head of Cully, an Egyptian-style crown befitting Cleopatra wrapped around her head and face. She had the body of a lion and stood twice as tall as Mel on all four legs. "I am Destiny."

"Destiny?" Mel walked closer as the painting behind him recorded the event. "I haven't seen you since-"

"Before the battle for Enchantas, yes," Destiny replied. "At that time, I took the form of a rat. I take many forms as you can see."

"What am I doing here? Did you summon me?"

"No. I did not. Nymph's spell brought you here, which I find very convenient. I was hoping to speak to you."

Mel sighed. "It's been a very confusing time. Since my friends came back, so much has happened. I feel so lost."

"I know. I have recorded all of the events," Destiny gestured. "As you can see."

"Those paintings are amazing." Mel couldn't help but examine the current painting again. He watched himself talking to Destiny. "What is this place? It's not at all familiar to me."

"This is my home, Professor." Destiny began to walk down the hallway. "You were here before, the last time we met."

277

"This is the same place?"

"Correct." Destiny nodded.

"But where is it?" Mel looked curious. "I never saw it charted on any map."

"It's hidden in the great Enchantian desert on the far west side of the main land. Not many know it exists, the Sage and a few Knights, mostly. I call this place, the *Pyramid of Prophets*."

"I can see why," Mel was referring to the moving portraits. "But why did the paintings not end after the battle? I just saw one from a few tocks ago. And another painting of now. I thought we fulfilled your prophecy?"

"Only parts of the prophecy have been fulfilled, Professor. Enchantas has grown and peace has been restored, but the prophecy is truly not fulfilled until Lexis has been stopped. She is endangering the land each day, planning to awaken the Fairy Queen, to unleash her own breed of dark fairies."

"So that's her objective," Mel felt a new resolve. Now that they knew what she was after, it would be easier to form their own plans. "Yes, she must be stopped."

"She's intent on starting another war. She hopes to destroy everything that we have been working so hard to accomplish."

"I agree with you, but tell me," Mel took a deep breath, "I don't understand why so much evil has been allowed to happen. So much has gone wrong."

"You must always remember that I *do* have a plan for you, my wise but oh-so-young prophet," Destiny looked at Mel sincerely. "Everything has happened for a reason."

"Do me a favor and spare me the clichés. For a reason?" Mel's face became scornful. "There was no reason for Becky to die. Cully's slaughter was also senseless."

"Trust me," Destiny assured him. "Death is but another journey in my plan. And you, the prophets, are now being tested to prove how strong you can be."

"This is a test?" Mel complained. "You're testing us? If that's what this is all about you can call it off right now. I've had enough of your deadly tests killing the innocent around me."

"I am not testing you, Mel, any more than I am testing John, or Sally, or Ryan. You are all testing yourselves. Testing your own self-reliance. You proved on your last journey that coming together, despite different pasts, different personalities and different kinds of friends, family, and beliefs allowed you to overcome any challenge. Now you must overcome yourselves and come back together, stronger than ever."

"That's a little manipulative don't you think?"

"You may think so now," Destiny patted him on the back. "But soon you will see that everything truly does happen for a reason. If each of you prophets can overcome obstacles alone, imagine what you can do together."

Mel could understand her logic, but he still didn't like it.

"I don't think I can do it by myself, Destiny. I still need the others."

"You will all be reunited, in time," Destiny said calmly "Do not worry." Destiny opened a heavy stone door, one sunk into the wall, which Mel hadn't seen before. Inside, Mel spied the old Witch and Warlock's castle, surrounded by a beautiful purple, blue, and green forest and thousands of marching troops.

"It has already begun. My plan is falling into place. It is time to once again play your parts as saviors and fulfill my prophecy," Destiny gestured for Mel to come to the door. "Enchantas' future is in your hands. You must go. Now."

"But what about-" Mel began to ask as Destiny gently ushered him through the door, transporting him to his next endeavor.

"You will find out soon enough," said Destiny, to herself, firmly shutting the door and walking down the hall of her lonely home with its ever-expanding, ever-changing art collection.

Destiny stopped at a new painting that depicted Mel climbing the stairs to the entrance of the fortress. She rubbed her lion paws together with eagerness. Finally, after all these ages, her prophecy might be completely fulfilled.

***

The tunnels of the mountain were frigid and wet, dripping with ice melted by Nymph's heat as she burrowed passageways throughout the glacial mountain searching for the trapped Fairy Queen. The mountain itself was a gargantuan berg, perhaps the largest glacier ever created in both surface and volume. Its icy summit pierced the clouds, reaching toward the green sky above.

They had been at it for almost fourteen tocks, legions of imps, gremlins, and goblins stood guard outside Iced Mountain. The imps and gremlins standing guard were outcasts from their own kind. Unlike their brethren, they remained loyal to their Empress.

Finding anything in this monstrous mass of ice was worse than trying to find a needle in a haystack, but Nymph and the Empress were more than persistent, they were irrevocably determined. Finding the Queen was the most important mission ever undertaken for both of them.

Legend had it that the mountain had been formed by a curse made a long time ago, but the why and for whom had been largely unknown, until now.

"How's it going, my fairy friend?" the Empress asked, appearing on site to check out the progress. She was wrapped in a snug, long, black bear furred coat, but underneath her legs were bare.

"Still no sign of the Queen, madam," Nymph replied, heating more of the ice as she sculpted a rounder tunnel. "We have been at it for tocks, Your Grace. What if the frog has lied to us?"

"Impossible. He was in too much pain to be duplicitous. The *Rack* never fails."

Nymph nodded briefly as she continued to search. The ice surrounding them was like foggy glass and light from the rising sun refracted in rainbow prisms all around.

"Your Grace!" Nymph spotted an irregular blue-brown shimmer. "I think I found something."

The Empress shoved the fairy out of the way, eagerly peering into the ice and saw through the translucent ice a tall, brown-haired woman kept in stasis, held fast in the icy heart of the mountain.

"At last!" the Empress cheered. "It is her. It is the Queen! It is *my mother!*"

"I will melt the ice and get her free, Your Grace."

"Be careful, Nymph," the Empress rubbed the steaming ice. "I want her unharmed. Conduct your excavation delicately."

"Yes, Your Grace," Nymph agreed. She needed the Queen as much, if not more, than Lexis did. Putting aside distracting, but exciting thoughts of resurrecting the fairy population, Nymph concentrated hard on her magic, delicately melting the ice around the Queen in tiny increments. Finally, all but a paper-thin sheet of the ice coated her. She wore a long baby-blue dress that matched the color of her wings. Like Lexis, she had very straight brown hair, but hers was very long unlike Lexis' drastically shorter cut. She was a little taller than her daughter, and looked comfortable and peaceful — a state few, if any, had ever seen Lexis in — with her eyes closed and arms crossed. The Queen was as undoubtedly beautiful as the similarities between mother and daughter were undeniable.

"Look, Nymph," the Empress circled the frozen Queen. "This is my mother after so many long ages. She is finally here standing in front of me."

"Yes, Your Grace," Nymph wanted to cry with happiness. "At last, my kind can flourish once again."

"Yes they will." the Empress's eyes narrowed. "They will flourish, and legions of fairies will follow our cause. The Knights and their way of life will be no more!"

"Yes, Your Grace," Nymph bowed. "How are we to unthaw her?"

"Leave that to me," the Empress pulled out an old wrinkled sheet of paper. "The curse can only be broken by one who shares the Queen's bloodline or one who loves her dearly. That could be you, me or even my father, but I shall do the honors." She rubbed her purple amulet, chanting:

"Queen of fairies, mother of mine;
Frozen and buried, frozen in time!
Undo this curse, so wrongfully accused,
Awaken mother, to be rightfully excused!"

A purple hue enveloped the frozen body, the ice glowing lavender for a tack before growing dim and eventually fading to pitch black. The Empress's sparkling purple eyes were the only light that remained and it too was subsiding. But just as that light went out, the white sun broke through, and the Queen was released into the light, rising and then gently settling on the wet, cold floor. She lay curled on her side, her body quivering. Nymph and the Empress covered her in soft blue blankets.

"W-where am I?" the Queen's soft and pure voice trembled. She looked at the two standing in front of her. "How long have I been here?" She focused on the Empress, "Who are you?"

Lexis remained silent, awestruck by the sight her mother.

"You have been frozen for many ages, my Queen," Nymph replied, helping the Queen to her feet. "I am very glad you are back."

"Nymph?" the Queen gave the fairy a hug. "Where are the rest of your sisters?"

"They are gone," Nymph said sadly. "All but four."

"Oh my!" the Queen exclaimed. "How?"

"The crusades," Nymph replied, not bothering to disguise the outrage in her voice. "The Witch and Warlock."

"What?" the Queen covered her mouth in shock. "Where is my family? My husband-"

"They are dead," the Empress said coldly. "Killed by the Knights of Minerton!"

"What?" the Queen fell to her knees. "This can't be true. My husband was a Knight!"

"I'm afraid so, my Queen," Nymph sat beside her. "The Knights have turned to evil ways for their own shadowy motives."

"It is told here in this journal." Lexis handed her an old scroll. "After the Witch and Warlock cursed you, your husband came searching. The Knights had him killed for asking too many questions."

"Then I am all alone," the Queen moaned. "I have no one."

"That is not true," the Empress took a big breath. "Your family is here."

Nymph smiled affectionately, worshipfully as the Queen regarded her.

The Empress smiled also. "Most importantly, you have a daughter."

The Queen studied the self-proclaimed Empress. She touched her own face and then Lexis's. Identical features became apparent: nose, chin, cheekbones and lips. The Queen's bright blue eyes widened in surprise, as she gasped, "Alexis! Is that you?"

"Mother!" Alexis leaped into her mother's arms as feelings of pure joy rushed through her. "I thought I'd never find you!"

"Oh, Alexis!" the Queen squeezed her daughter, her feelings of anguish and despair transformed into joy and happiness. "I thought I had lost you forever."

"I thought so, too."

"What about your father?" the Queen anxiously asked. "Did he hurt you?" Then, in a voice more frantic, "By all that is sacred, tell me he didn't hurt you!"

Alexis remained quiet, with her head down, ashamed and forever scarred by those awful, abusive days and nights locked in the basement of what once had been a happy home. She replied in a monotone voice, "I survived."

"Oh, my dear child!" the Queen held her daughter once again. "I feared for you when I left him."

"Mother," Alexis exclaimed in pain, reliving those nights. "He blamed you when he hurt me. He said it was your fault."

"That is not true," the Queen looked at her sincerely. "I was afraid of your father, too. After we were married, something changed within him. I am unsure where it had started, perhaps with jealousy or maybe with mistrust. But whatever it was, he was never the same afterwards. He changed from the man I fell in love with to a manipulative beast. For years, I feared for my life when he abused me and threatened me. We decided to come back here, back to Enchantas to start over. He wanted me back here so that I could never be tempted by the sins of your world. I secretly wanted to be here so that I would be protected from him. Protected by the Knights." Her voice became softer, a little smile grew. "And then, I met your stepfather and we fell in love."

"But what about me?" Alexis cried. "Why did I have to be left with him?"

"Your father took you without my consent, my dear," the Queen cried. "He hid you from the rest of us. Believe me, we searched everywhere, but could not find you! You are my daughter, my lovely innocent little child. I would never have willingly left you with him. But I had no choice; you were taken and lost to me."

"Not anymore," Alexis gave her mother another hug. "We are together, at last. We can be a family!"

"Alexis?" the Queen sniffed. "You say the Knights killed my husband?"

"Yes," Alexis replied gravely.

"He will not have died in vain." The Queen's eyes rippled, wavered, transformed to a fierce, dark blue. "Too much has happened in my absence. First my dear fairies have been killed, then my family! Revenge is in order," she looked at Nymph. "Are you ready to bring back our race?"

"Yes," Nymph was ecstatic at hearing those words. "Yes, I am."

"We have work to do," the Queen raised one arm, waved it back and forth, igniting orange-tipped blue flames. A tunnel appeared, opening into a large room in the mountain that contained thousands of sapphire blue, pumpkin-sized pyramids scattered throughout. "These flumpkins have been here since the crusades. The Witch and Warlock wanted me to create an army for them to use against the Knights. How ironic that I now agree with them. No one will hurt me or my family again! Let us begin!"

Chapter XVIII
Purgatory

The wind gusts herded dried leaves toward John, where they piled against the small of his back. He awoke, startled and anxious. The trees surrounding him were leafless, lifeless, the dried, dark gray remnants of foliage covered the ground, clotting around the hundreds of tombstones scattered throughout the forest. He rolled over on something rocky, a gravestone under him. He withdrew, repulsed and frightened. The engravings on it were not legible.

John jumped up, the quick movement causing his head to throb, which made it even harder to recollect why he was here and what had happened. Scenes of Becky's death flashed through his mind. His stomach lurched and his heart ached in despair as he relived her fall to death, the way Lexis had laughed after she sent Becky over the edge. Retaliation and revenge was all he could think of.

His body stiffened with anger as he wandered through the graveyard. John, in shock, blamed himself. He was supposed to protect her. The cost of his failure was her life.

She couldn't be dead, He thought to himself, cycling into denial. *This was just a trick, in the same way that Nymph could shape-shift.* As he walked past the broken headstones the realization of her death kicked in again. Who was he kidding? Pretending wouldn't bring Becky back.

In the silence he heard something moving. Then he saw it, traveling slowly in the distance.

"Hey," he yelled, running as fast as he could. "Wait up!"

John ran, passing grave after grave as he went along. The figure continued moving as if it did not hear his call.

"Hey! Stop!" John caught up to it and pulled at its shoulder. Shocked, John took a step back. The creature bore the face of a dead dog, its skin and fur partially decomposed. Its teeth were visible with no flesh to conceal them. It was missing an eye. Its once-floppy ears were bloody and half-eaten. Its shredded shirt was soiled with dirt and blood.

"Oh my God!" he gasped. "What happened to you?"

The dog just moaned, staring at him with one eye. He looked as though he was starving. His drool dripped from his snout and his tongue hung out of the side of his holey mouth. The dead canine-thing stumbled forward with a limp, reaching for him.

"Get away from that, John!" A voice called.

Firp was behind him, Firp the frog herald with his scepter shining.

"Firp! What the hell is that?"

"I am unsure, John," Firp wielded his shining scepter, keeping the creature at bay. "But, I believe it's a dog. A dead dog."

John gulped. "Where are we?"

The dog's moan turned to a growl as it lunged at them and tried to bite. More of the dead — a rabbit, a turtle, and a fox — appeared from behind a tree, slogging toward them, moaning with hunger. The rabbit's green fur was decomposing and the turtle's shell was completely broken, oozing with puss. There was no fur left on the fox, only muscle and bones. Flies swarmed around the three animated corpses and their stench emanated throughout graveyard.

"I was wondering that myself. Come." Firmly brandishing his scepter and directing a repellent force field around them. Firp began to walk faster, motioning to John to stay close to him as they passed the zombie animals. "But then it occurs to me, there are legends of a place that you go to when you die. Purgatory, a place where Destiny makes the final judgment based on the choices you have made during your life. This is the place where the dead wait until judgment is rendered."

"Are you saying," John gulped. "That I'm dead?"

Firp placed his scepter on John's chest, close to his heart; it glowed brighter at each beat. "No, you are not." Firp put it on his own heart and nothing happened. "But I am."

"Firp!" John yapped, taking a step back. "What happened?"

"I was kidnapped by Nymph and the chameleons," Firp recounted with a matter-of-fact tone, "I was then tortured and killed." Firp thought for a moment, he looked down, sad that his life was over and continued. "Well, regrets about the past are pointless. If this truly is Purgatory, I am curious as to why you are here, John. If you are still alive, which for all intents and purposes you appear to be, then why?" Firp scratched his slimy chin with his long webbed pointer finger. "Hmm. What do you remember about what happened immediately before you found yourself here?"

John winced. He didn't want to think about it. Flashes of his sister's stone body falling and smashing into pieces still haunted him.

"I watched my sister get pushed off a cliff by the Banshee. I couldn't save her." He took a deep breath trying to stuff his anger in. "She's dead, too. Then Nymph cast a spell on me which must have brought me here."

"Hmm," Firp responded, with all the logic and intellect he had possessed in life. "If there is a spell to bring you here, it only makes sense that there must be a way to transport you back."

"Well, great!" John began getting excited. "Let's figure it out. Maybe there are others here who could help."

But the only presences in the immediate area were more slobbering, smelly zombie animals, lumbering slowly toward them.

"It is too late for me, my friend," said Firp. "But not for you."

A shining white light radiated from a nearby tree trunk. Firp stopped, staring into it with complete concentration, as if it was speaking to him. The zombies, now more than two dozen strong, shifted their course, lurching toward the tree.

"That doorway is for me," Firp announced softly. "It's my time to go."

"Wait, Firp!" John urged the frog to stay. "You can't go now. You just got here. I don't know what to do or where to go. I need you! I don't want you to go." Tears came to his eyes, unbidden. He'd never felt so lost or lonely.

With a deliberate effort, Firp snapped himself out of his trancelike state. He spoke rapidly, urgently, as if there was little time. "Find a way back to Enchantas, John. Go back as fast as you can and warn the others. I know what the Banshee and Nymph are planning. They are going to awaken the Fairy Queen and convince her to join them. They plan to assemble an evil fairy army to unleash against the Knights. It will be devastating."

"Where do I start? Who do I tell?"

"First, go to the academy and rally the troops. Tell the General that the Banshee can be found at Iced Mountain. They will know what to do."

John nodded as he acknowledged the instructions, but revenge was first on his mind. If he found a way out of here, he'd find the Banshee first and make her pay for what she did.

"Promise you will do this, John," Firp's tone was serious. "We need to go about this the right way. I know you have thoughts of revenge. I can see it in your eyes."

John just looked back with a blank stare. No emotion.

"Promise me."

"All right," John sighed. "I promise."

"Thank you," Firp said, as the moldering zombies drew closer to the light, like moths to the flame. "I believe I must go before the light fades. I don't think it's their time yet."

The closer they got, the louder the zombies groaned.

"How do I get out of here?" John asked, desperate to not be left alone.

"Goodbye, friend." Firp hopped with great dignity toward the light. "Tell everyone I said goodbye."

John waved, watching as Firp's body was absorbed into the shining opening. It slammed shut, the light cut off as if by a kill switch, just as the zombies reached it. They beat their broken, rotting arms against the tree in frustration.

A raccoon grabbed John's shoulder from behind. He turned instinctively, his spear ejecting from his bracelet, stabbing up though its jaw and into its head. It quivered for a moment, excreting bloody puss from its decomposing mouth.

John flung the carcass away. Other zombies were moving toward him. He ran and kept running until he was a fair distance from the greedy ghouls. Although he was still in the cemetery, which seemed to go on forever, he could see the zombies wandering aimlessly in the distance.

Desperate to get out of this *dead* place, he continued to run in the endless cemetery until he spotted a mausoleum with a red flamed lantern above the doorway, imposing music rolling from its interior. Curious, he drew close enough to read the engraving above the entrance: "The Crypt".

He knew he wasn't going to get anywhere by being a wimp, so bracing himself, his bracelet at the ready, took a deep breath, and pushed open the heavy wooden door. The music was almost deafening. But it wasn't a creepy web-filled crypt at all. It was a bar, much like the pubs his father frequented back home. The smell was even the same: cigar smoke, liquor, and bodies in need of a washing.

A smoky haze covered the ceiling. The Crypt wasn't as busy as the Husky Sled Saloon he'd visited during the previous trip to Enchantas. There were only a few occupied tables, different animals tossing back a few cocktails, but for the most part the watering hole was empty. A turtle sat at the bar by itself while a skeleton cat served him drinks.

John stepped down a small flight of stairs into the bar and was about to ask a question when an eerily familiar voice yelled from the back of the room.

"Well now, me lad!" A leprechaun stood up. "Me be waiting for the next time me see ya!"

"Liddy!" John recoiled.

"And me see ye still be wearing me jacket!"

John zipped it up. "This is still mine, leprechaun!"

"Ahh," Liddy walked up, patted John on the back and gestured him back to his table. "No hard feelings, me hopes. T'was a very long time ago."

John followed but with caution.

"What are you doing here, Liddy?" John cracked a smile. "Are you dead? I sure hope so."

"Me?" Liddy asked with his mischievous grin. "No, me ain't dead."

"So then why are you here?"

"Me just enjoys it here," Liddy replied, waving his cane around. "Me enjoys the company."

"Right," John didn't trust the leprechaun, especially after what had happened last time. "So you like sitting here with the rest of the stiffs, huh?" John joked; he couldn't help it. "So, what about those things outside? You enjoy their company too?"

"Oh those just be the *roamers*, very unsociable," Liddy sat down at a large circular table surrounded by a large cushioned booth covered in brown leathery material. He placed a deck of playing cards in front of him, motioning John to join him at the banquette. "They just be waitin' fer their chance to leave. Me like it in here, in The Crypt. 'Tis where the dead go when they give up, lose all hope of ever leavin' an' movin' on. Me like it, because these be the ones who can handle the truth. Bein' strong enough to handle the truth can make ya quite a fine card player. That's why, me boy."

"If you're not dead," John said, feeling a spurt of encouragement, "Can you leave?"

"Me comes and goes as me pleases," Liddy said proudly.

"Really?" John tried not to show his excitement. He knew the unscrupulous wheeler-dealer would only ask for more if he knew how badly John wanted to get back to Enchantas. "Can you take me with you when you leave? I can make it worth your while, I promise."

"Well now, me boy," Liddy giggled, shuffling his cards. "Don't get hasty. Me won't just do any old service for free. There be a price."

"I figured," John said, sighing as he shucked his jacket, holding it out on one finger. "Here. Go on and take it so I can get out of here. Please."

"Me don't want ye grubby ol' black jacket," Liddy began passing out his cards. "Me wants a rematch."

"Is that all?"

"Yes," Liddy snarled. "Ye cheated me the last time we played!"

"No, I did not cheat," John argued. "You cheated, but you messed up and I still got the better hand!"

"No one calls me a cheat!" Liddy stood up with his chest puffed, obviously insulted.

"I just did!" John also stood up; he'd never back down from a fight.

"Chill out, bro," Becky peeked over the top of the booth.

John thought he would faint. Then he felt a surge of relief unlike any he'd ever experienced. John ecstatically jumped over the booth, right over the top, and tumbled into his sister's adjacent seating booth.

"Becky!" John hugged her tightly. As he held her, he felt the coldness. Death had consumed her. Her eyes were slightly bloodshot, with dark circles underneath. Her bluish lips were a tell-tale sign. "Oh, Becky," he said, tears springing again to his eyes. "What are you doing in here?"

"What are you talking about? Having a cocktail." She lifted a petite hurricane-glass drink filled with creamy green liquid and took a sip. Stirring her small pink umbrella with confidence, she looked at him and asked, "What about you?"

"Just glad to see you! You know you're dead, right?"

"Am I?" she asked, feeling her face. "I don't feel like it. That explains the zombie animals I guess," she chuckled. "I just thought it was a normal thing, here in Enchantas. Are you dead too?"

"No," John thumped his chest, "I'm still ticking."

"So how did I die?" she asked nonchalantly, as if it didn't faze her.

"The Banshee," John began to get angry, remembering those moments. "She turned you into stone and then pushed you off the ledge."

"That witch!" Becky swore. "Is Mel okay?"

John was silent, remembering how badly he'd beaten him up.

"John?" she slugged him lightly. "Answer me."

"He's alive, if that's what you mean."

"Good. That's good." she smiled.

"What do you mean *good*?" John was irritated. "If it wasn't for him, you'd still be alive!"

"John!" Becky snapped defensively. "It was my choice to save him. I don't regret it. Even if I am dead because of it! You should feel the same!"

"Well I don't."

"Of course, the same old John," Becky moved out of the booth in a huff, plopping down next to Liddy. "Selfish." She looked at the leprechaun and changed the subject. She was not in the mood to argue. She'd had enough of that when she was alive. "So who's your friend, John?"

"He's not my friend."

"Me name is Liddy, me dear," Liddy kissed her hand.

John looked at him with a clear warning in his eyes.

"Fine." said Liddy. "Hands off, me takes it. Then let us have that rematch, shall we?"

"No," John got up, grabbing his sister's hand. "I changed my mind. I'm staying here."

"John!" Becky resisted. "You can't stay here if you're still alive! You need to avenge me."

"Avenge you? No, Becky! I need to stay here and protect you!"

"Stay here and what?" she snorted. "Rot like the rest of us! No, you need to get back to the living world. Find that Banshee chick and make her answer for what she did. Besides, you can't protect me. I'm already dead."

John knew there was truth in what she said; there really was no reason to stay. But it was so hard to leave. Hard to let her go. He just knew he'd miss her all over again.

"So, are you going to play or no?" Liddy broke the silence.

John's self-control snapped. He picked Liddy up by the neck, slamming him into the round table.

"Can't you see that I'm talking to my sister?" John screamed; spit flying into the leprechaun's face. John's spear emerged from his bracelet, touching Liddy's neck. A flashback of what he had done to Mel flashed through his mind.

Liddy lay shaken, he was not expecting this to happen.

"Sorry, me boy," Liddy stuttered. "Me meant no offense."

"John!" Becky pulled at him. "You need to calm down. You can't go around the rest of your life beating people up."

John shook his head. For a moment it had felt like he blacked out.

"I'm sorry." He rubbed his forehead. "I don't know what came over me. I've always had this temper. But after you died I couldn't control it. There has got to be a way to bring you back to life." He glanced at Liddy who was straightening his green jacket and mustering his pride. "There has to be."

"Sorry me boy," Liddy cleared his throat and headed to the bar. "There ain't."

"You see," Becky complained. "That's where your temper takes you! Just like dad!"

"Don't compare me to him, Becky!"

"Well it's true. I bet you beat up Mel, too."

John didn't say anything.

"John!" Becky slapped him in the face, hard. "He's your friend. Why would you do that?"

"I couldn't help it. I was so angry!"

"You really need to get help! He's one of your best friends. You should feel ashamed."

"That's what I need you for," he said. "I mean that in a good way." She may not have known it, but Becky had always made John a better person, a good person, to himself and others.

"What am I supposed to do now?" John sat down with his head down.

"John," Becky sat next to him, her head resting on his shoulder. "Go live your life! I don't want you to be stuck here with me." She looked around. "Wherever we are. I hope this isn't heaven. It's gotta be hell."

"No. It's Purgatory."

"Whatever," she laughed. "You deserve more than this."

"So do you Becky," tears dripped down his face. "You shouldn't be dead."

"I know," she squeezed him. "But it's too late for me. But not for you, though."

"I have nothing to live for now," John wiped his face.

"What about Dyad?" asked Becky.

John shook his head.

"What happened?"

"Nothing," John said sadly. "It doesn't matter anymore. I have no one. Not even dad."

"You've got your friends, John."

He looked at Becky doubtfully. How could they like him anymore after what he did to Mel and for blaming Ryan for her death, too?

"They'll forgive you," Becky kissed him on the cheek. "Trust me. They're your friends. Just accept my death, make amends with your friends and avenge me." Her voice sounded cheerful and encouraging. "Come on John!"

John smiled. Becky always knew how to cheer him up and get him motivated.

"That's my big bro!" she kissed him again, a cold kiss but one he welcomed as he knew it was one of the last he'd ever receive from her. He understood he was lucky to have had this unexpected time with her.

Liddy returned with a fresh beverage. John sat across from him, wordless, wearing his most stoic, unreadable, intimidating poker face. Becky sat between them.

"My brother apologizes for going crazy on you," Becky talked for John as he stared blankly at the leprechaun. "He accepts your challenge of a rematch, but I will be the dealer. This will prevent any cheating. Agreed?"

"How will me know ye will not cheat?" asked Liddy, staring back at John suspiciously, taking sips from his large brandy snifter.

"Because I have nothing to lose," Becky lit up the last cigarette from John's pack. It seemed so long ago that she stole it. "If he loses, he stays here with me. If he wins, he can avenge my death. Either way, I get what I want. So there's no motive for me to cheat. Agreed?"

"Agreed," Liddy sneered.

Becky took a drag and dealt the cards, winking at her brother roguishly.

Chapter XIX
Cupid's College

The cold breeze blew against Sally as she flew hastily through the dark Enchantian sky. Small blue and red snowflakes floated down erratically as she passed over a forest of dark blue pine trees. Not too far in the distance smoke billowed from the woodlands. Flames climbed into the sky as a rapidly growing fire scorched the landscape.

Sally pulled back on her crooked broom slowing it down until she was hovering over the blue forest. Curious, she gradually descended, scouting until she found a safe spot to investigate.

As she landed she referred to her compass, the dial twirled around and blinked 'Bearton,' indicating her location. There was definitely something wrong in this community: it was on fire.

Sally crept underneath a small bush, hands submerged in rainbow snow, watching horrified as hundreds of large bears lumbered frantically toward escape routes. Their large, burning huts created huge flames that ran rampant toward the forest thickets encasing the village tight as a vise.

"Sally?" a dark black poodle stood over her, clad in red shorts, carrying a quiver of arrows. "Oh, hurray, it is you!" the poodle yapped excitedly.

"Butch?"

"Yeah, it's me!" the poodle gave her a hug with his forepaws. "It's been a long time! When did you get here?"

"We arrived a couple days ago, although in some ways it feels longer than that," Sally smiled, remembering her trip on the good ship Storm Glider. Butch was Captain Max's first-mate. "How have you been?"

"Doing great!" Butch sat next her. "I made a bit of a career change."

"Oh?" she looked at him curiously.

"Yep," Butch turned his back toward her showing her his feathered wings. "I'm a cupid now!"

"Really?" Sally was surprised. She recalled how enthusiastically Butch embraced the pirate life, boldly facing the attack of the Cat Vikings, and so quick with his sword. "That is quite the change!"

"A wonderful change too," Butch smiled. "So how is Ryan? Last I remember you two were getting quite chummy, if you know what I mean."

"We're okay," Sally's demeanor dimmed. The last time she'd seen Ryan they argued. "I need to find him."

"Hmmm. I'm sensing some trouble in the love department," Butch said. Intuition came with the job.

"What's going on here?" Sally changed the subject. "This fire is out of control."

"I'm not sure what happened," replied Butch, taking another look. "I was here on a job when I heard the screaming. When I got closer, the fire was out of control."

"Is there anything we can do?"

"No. But I trust the firefighters will be coming soon from the Enchantic Ocean. They're skilled at snuffing out wildfires. Anyway, you shouldn't be here. It isn't safe for humans to be in this territory."

"I'm looking for Ryan, Mel and John. We were separated back at the Mines."

Butch thought for a moment, brightening, "Well, we just may be able to help you. Come back with me to the cupid's training center."

"I don't know," Sally looked at her compass, still twirling and blinking. "I don't want to get off track."

"It won't get you off track. Besides, it's a quick trip, so you won't lose any time. It's right above us." He pointed a paw.

Sally looked at the large, orange cloud high in the sky, "That looks like Cloud Island!"

"Correct!" Butch said. "We acquired it from the Griffins a while back after they returned to duty."

Sally remembered the grand island with its distinctive orange hue and ground as soft as pillows. Even the buildings were puffy. But it wasn't all pleasant memories. On that island they'd been betrayed by the Griffins and handed over to Lexis. Thankfully, all had been resolved. The Griffins had made amends and once again protected the Knights, ensuring peace over the lands. Until Lexis came back on the scene, that is.

"Okay, Butch," Sally sat astride her broomstick. "Lead the way."

Butch began to flap his cupid wings, ascending with effort. Sally followed him with ease. The broom was much faster, so she had to slow down a few times.

Far off in the smoke hazed horizon, Sally noticed a large group of creatures flying toward them. "Are those demigons?" Sally was on high alert.

Butch scanned the scene with his superior vision. "Nope. That's the firefighter's brigade. A little late, if you ask me."

In an instant a pod of pink dolphins was upon them, sparkling with lixy dust. They arced gracefully in formation, using fins and tails as steering rudders as they swam through the air, fast as bullets. Closing in on the village they dove, spitting streams of water on the flames. The dolphins were flanked by a contingent of enormous dark-purple sperm whales who soared above the cupid poodle and Sally before swooping down to drop their water loads on the conflagration. Smoke from the extinguished blaze threatened to blind Sally. She stared hard, trying to keep Butch in sight. He was panting, so she slowed down as much as she dared. She was finding her finesse with the controls, managing to keep the broom at a smooth cruising speed by applying steady pressure with her left hand.

"Thank you," Butch's tongue was hanging out. "I'm not in shape yet. I just graduated, and got my wings, last season." They coasted in companionable silence until the poodle recovered from his exertions.

"Tell me, if it won't tire you too much, why you decided to become a cupid," Sally was curious.

"I'm good," he assured her, still panting a little. "This is the perfect speed for me. As you may know, for cycles I had always believed the pirate's life was for me. You know, a new adventure every day, sunny days on the open water or in the open skies flying the Storm Glider as Max's first mate. It was everything a dog could wish for.

"But then one day, I met Gracie, the love of my life. Her fur was a silky white and as soft as a chinchilla." His eyes lit up and sparkled with adoration as he continued, "She was the most beautiful, beguiling Enchantian I'd ever seen.

"We spent cycles together with Max at the academy. Not only was she the most amazing dog I'd ever met, she was quite the warrior. Better at sword fighting than all of the crew. Even me!"

"We spent many wonderful nights together on the open sea. Life was great," Butch stopped, a tear beginning down his snout.

"What happened?" Sally felt his sadness.

"While we were on a transport to Cursed Island bringing a shipment of inmates to the Enchantian Prison she became very sick. No one knew what it was. She was in so much pain," Butch paused, taking a breath to regain his composure. "We returned to our home, where she was bedridden for almost a season until she finally succumbed to the illness and died."

"Oh, Butch," Sally cried with him. "I am so sorry. I know how it feels to lose someone you love."

"My life was never the same," Butch continued. "For a long time I lived day in and day out feeling nothing. Everything that I had ever loved before Gracie was never the same. I argued with everyone, even with Max. Being a pirate and warrior did not appeal to me anymore. I felt alone and lost. I came close to taking my own life once."

Butch smiled, "That's when the Cupid found me."

"You mean the pig we brought aboard your ship, right?"

"Yes," Butch brightened. "He showed me a different life, a cupid's life. At first I resisted. The thought of helping others find what I had so tragically lost was a devastating concept. But he taught me a better way to look at it. He said, 'It's not what is lost that matters, but what you had while you were together that does. The gift is the memories you will keep and cherish for the rest of your life.' Those words have stayed with me. Now I'm living a life of giving happiness to others. Delivering love is the best thing that's ever happened to me. It has given me a chance to be a better dog."

"That's a wonderful story, Butch." Sally beamed at her poodle pal.

"Yeah, and being a pirate helped."

"How so?"

"I've had many years of practice with a bow and arrow. I'm the best sharpshooter in my class, if not the whole land."

They reached the cloud. As they penetrated it, Sally was momentarily blinded. Then they emerged.

There it was, as grand as ever with its fluffy cloud buildings. Winged animals busily walked or flew about their business. The bright full moon cast its beams on the orange city illuminating it with a peachy-tangerine glow.

"Are they all cupids?" asked Sally.

"Not all. Most are in training, but some are retired and just living here." Butch flew faster. "Headquarters is up this way."

They proceeded up an avenue in the center of the city until they reached a large orange cloud shaped like a skyscraper.

"Welcome to Cupid College, Sally," Butch climbed higher. "We'll just take a shortcut."

As Sally followed the dog, her ears finally popped, relieving the pressure building up inside her head. She noticed more winged animals in the building and even jumping out the windows of various rooms as they flew to their next job.

Sally and Butch reached the top, landing on the soft, cushiony floor. As they walked Sally's shoes sunk in slightly and as she lifted them she bounced.

"Well then." Butch stopped abruptly. "I'd better get going Sally. Lots of work to do. Love never takes a holiday!"

"I thought you said you could help me." Sally looked at him quizzically.

"Yes. Yes we can," Butch gestured to a small figure headed toward them. "I'm leaving you in better hands. Good luck and it was nice to see you again." Butch flew away.

"Miss Sally!" a cheerful voice squealed.

"Oh boy," she said, less than bowled over by being placed in these better hands. Better hooves were more like it, for it was Cupid, the drunken pig they first encountered on their last visit to Enchantas. For a time a sad, lonely, depressed beggar, Cupid had reinvented his life as the contented cupid he always wanted to be. The pig wore an arrow quiver, red shorts and a necktie underneath a white goatee, which Sally thought was odd, but must have meant he was important somehow.

"It's been so long," the pig oinked. "How have you been? How's Ryan? How's your world? How long are you here?"

"Oh boy," Sally said again. "That's a lot of questions."

"My apologies. Please come, walk with me," Cupid said as he trotted along. "Let's just go straight to the important stuff. How are you and Ryan?"

"All right I guess."

"You guess? What's wrong? Tell me. I was hoping that you two would be married by now, family, kids. You know, the works."

"Married?" Sally laughed in spite of her impatience at his gossipy chit chat. "We're still in high school."

"Hmm," the pig scratched his hairy chin. "Not sure what that means, but it sounds bad."

Sally laughed again; the pig sure knew how to cheer her up.

"But please, tell me. I hope everything is going well, as you two are my first spirit-mates. My match-making reputation rides on your romance. Go ahead and tell, but nothing too juicy, I may get sick."

"Well, there isn't much to tell," Sally looked down, almost in shame. Cupid looked at her inquisitively. "Cupid, are you sure those arrows work? I mean, that they truly help find your spirit-mate?"

"What do you mean, child?" Cupid stopped to look at her. "Of course they work! Are things not working out?"

"I don't know," Sally didn't know where to start. Their relationship had been rocky for a while, at least in her mind it was. "All we do is argue, it seems. Ryan says he loves me, but I find it hard to believe sometimes especially when there are other girls around. All they do is flirt with him. It pisses me off."

"Oh, I see," Cupid said calmly. He sat down, took a deep breath and continued. "One thing you must remember about relationships is that they are not easy. Not for friendships and especially not for spirit-mates such as you and Ryan. Those need the most work and very special attention. Being spirit-mates means that the both of you are meant to be with one another, that somehow, Destiny brought you two together to make each other a better person and to live a happy life. Now this doesn't mean that you will live happily all the time or *happily ever after*. No, this gives you the chance to strive for it. Many go through life never finding their spirit-mate that one perfect special someone that completes you. You two are just ahead of the game."

"But why does it seem that our relationship is going downhill?" Sally asked, her frustration evident.

"Sally," Cupid put his hoof on her shoulder. "Even though you and Ryan are meant to be together, even though you're proven spirit-mates, it doesn't mean that the relationship will always be perfectly blissful and never need to be worked on. An old Cupid once told me, 'Even if something doesn't come that easy, it doesn't mean it has to be that difficult.' The trick to any relationship is that both parties need to find a happy medium and compromise once in a while. If you have a problem with the other girls flirting with Ryan, he needs to step it up a little and you need to give him a little more slack. Trust me Sally; compromising is the most difficult concept, but one of the most important. I see many relationships end this way, spirit-mates or not."

Sally thought for a moment and knew the pig was right. They had a lot to work on and giving up was not in her plans.

"Thank you, Cupid," she said gratefully. "Your advice means a lot. I know exactly where to start." She would take Nymph's antics straight to the source, telling the flirting fairy that Ryan was not on the market, would never be on the market and that she needed to back off.

"Wonderful!" Cupid stood back up. "Now why has Butch brought you here? How can we help?"

"I'm trying to find Ryan, John, and Mel. We were separated on the hunt for the Banshee. Part of it was Nymph's fault," Sally noted, and the pig snorted in agreement.

"Terrible wench that fairy is," the Cupid commented. "I've tried hard to match her suitably, but she's so gosh-darn demanding nobody can stand her. I won't even begin with the troubles of the Banshee."

"Yeah," Sally remembered what her mother said, "She is. Anyway, the guys disappeared after I had a fight with Ryan over Nymph coming on to him. Dyad was going to help me look, but she has a larger mission to think about. I was going to search every town until I found them and bring them back in time to assist in defending ourselves against the Banshee. At least that was my plan. Now I'm thinking I should do something different."

"Oh?" Cupid's eyebrows rose.

"I have to confront Nymph." Her teeth clenched even saying the name. "I need to stand up for myself, if Ryan and I are ever to have a future together, I need to be stronger. You're right Cupid, I need to take action. My compromise is going to start with taking charge."

"All righty, then," Cupid began to fly slowly. "Follow me. We have a devise that assists us in finding Enchantians, but you must promise not to share the knowledge with anyone, as it has been a secret within the cupid community for many ages. If fallen in the wrong hands, it could be used for warfare. We use it for love-finding purposes only. Hope this makes sense."

Sally nodded in agreement as she followed him carrying her broom. They had come to the building ledge, where Cupid rubbed his tie whereupon it began to glow bright red.

"Good, then let us begin." He took a deep breath, closed his eyes, and recited:

"Magic scope, appear tonight;
Give us hope, and give us sight!"

A large telescope appeared, pointing out at the starlit night. It was three times as long as Sally's arm.

"This telescope can show you anywhere in Enchantas," Cupid peaked into the eyepiece. "All you need to do is say a name or town. Try it."

Sally stepped up to the eyepiece, rubbed her earring and said, "Ryan!"

A red fog temporarily covered the lens, obscuring her vision as she peered into the telescope. And then, there he was. Ryan was pacing the deck of the Storm Glider, laughing with Captain Max. "He's okay! Ryan's okay!"

"Good! Good!" the pig clapped his front hooves. "Is there anyone or anywhere else you'd like to search?"

"Yes," Sally's eyes narrowed as she looked back into the telescope and grunted, "Nymph!"

A red fog blotted the lens once again before Nymph appeared, surrounded by shining white ice. She was with the Banshee and another, taller fairy with brown hair.

"Cupid! I found her, too!" Sally lifted her head, motioning him over. "Tell me. Where is this?"

Cupid stared into the telescope, "I believe this is Iced Mountain. It's a long way from here, at least a thousand sprints."

Sally barely registered the distance; she didn't care about the details. There was a vendetta with a certain fairy that needed taking care of. Now. nothing was going to stop her.

"If it's so far away, I'd better get going," said Sally, mounting her broomstick.

"Do you know how to get there, my dear?"

Sally pulled out her compass, quietly requesting "Iced Mountain." The dial twirled for a moment before lighting up with the location name. "I do now. Thank you for all your help, Cupid!" Sally hovered skillfully; she was finally getting the hang of the broom.

"You're welcome, Sally." Cupid waved a hoof in farewell. "Good luck and I hope I am invited to the wedding!"

"You will be!" Sally said, zooming off with her broom at top speed. Far in the distance the white sun began to rise above the horizon. She did not know exactly how long it would take, but she didn't care. She was going to get even. She was going to get her Ryan back.

Chapter XX
The Academy

The air was moist and warm in the forest, its trees a vivid combination of blue, purple, and red leaves. John emerged out of the deeply shaded grove, facing a small valley thick with violet grass. An orange brick trail ran through the middle of the valley leading to a tall, black castle tower. He recognized it immediately; it was the old castle of the Witch and Warlock, Sally's parents. The scenery was a dramatic change from the dry, dead and desolate landscape that once was. The once barren valley had been lushly filled with life in full bloom encircled by serene and majestic turquoise-capped mountains.

In the distance he heard troops chanting as they marched in unison around the castle. The cloudless green sky was filled with hundreds of flying pirate ships.

John made his way confidently down the orange brick trail. He was not the boy who had left the mines, so spiteful, vengeful, and negative. Now he felt a little more at peace. Saying goodbye to his sister had helped. He was still angry at the Banshee for killing her. But he felt closure, calm and clarity.

John had said his goodbyes to Becky quickly. Though he knew he would miss her terribly, he did not want to drag out the inevitable.

John smirked as he recalled his poker game with Liddy. He'd beaten the leprechaun handily, again. This time his hand was nothing more than a pair of fives, a real embarrassment for Liddy. John figured he wouldn't be seeing the humiliated leprechaun for a while.

John finally reached a few lines of troops: foxes, imps, badgers, and gremlins armed with swords and axes. They stopped to watch John strut by. He didn't recognize any of them, but the way they stopped and whispered made him wonder if they knew who he was.

John passed a company of skunks, weasels, porcupines, turtles, beavers, squirrels, chipmunks and rabbits. They, too, stopped to watch John as he sauntered toward the castle. Some bowed to him and he nodded back in greeting.

"John!" a deep-yet-squeaky voice shouted. An ebony-colored snuffball rolled up, a large one a few inches taller than him. "Hey, it's been a while. Remember me?"

John studied the snuffball for a tick. Then he remembered that there was only one who was black. "Bubbles? Is that you?"

"You betcha!" Bubbles replied, bouncing in jubilation. At that, dozens of other snuffballs rolled up to say hello, in all different sizes and colors. A few were larger than Bubbles but most were soccer-ball size. "I was just telling my troops here about the Foxtown breakout."

"Oh, right," John didn't like thinking about his encounters in Foxtown during his first visit to Enchantas, but he certainly was very grateful Bubbles had come to the rescue. "That was quite exciting. Thank you again for your help!"

"No problem." Bubbles rolled closer. "So you're here for the assembly?"

"What assembly?"

"The Knights have called a meeting; I believe it's beginning soon. We're all preparing for battle out here. Do you know exactly what's going down? I hope we're not fighting on the water. Can't swim."

"I just got here. I'll fill you in when I know more, okay?" John quickened his pace; he didn't want to miss anything and had some intel from Firp to share. "Have you seen Ryan, Mel, or Sally here?"

"I saw Ryan and the Professor a bit earlier, but not Sally."

A pang of guilt tightened John's gut as he remembered what he'd done to Mel. How was he going to make up for beating on him? Becky was right; Mel was his friend and didn't deserve that.

"Where are they meeting?"

"Upstairs, in the war room." Bubbles rolled faster. "Come, I will show you."

Bubbles left his group, directing them to roll a few laps around the valley. The two hurried toward the castle.

John was okay with running, he was used to it by now from football practice. He would never have been able to run this far if he had kept smoking, though. He was so glad he'd quit.

"So rumor has it that Sally's parents decided to have the Knights take their old castle and make it into the Enchantas Military Academy," Bubbles said. "No matter who thought of it, it was a great idea. These training grounds are ideal for all branches of our forces, the navy, air combat, intelligence and infantry, alike."

"So do all Enchantians join the military?" John slowed down to a walk so he could focus on the conversation.

"Not all," Bubbles continued, matching speed so they could move in tandem. "Most of us who do are those who don't wish to attend the Institute, but still want to make contributions to our communities. A lot of us don't want to use magic — or just can't."

"Does anyone from the Institute join?"

"Only a select few graduates from the Institute are sent to the Sorcerer's Academy. The ones with the touch."

John looked at him, waiting for an explanation.

"'The touch' is a phrase we sword jockeys use for those with particularly strong magical powers or those who are gifted with particular skills in a rare type of witchcraft or sorcery. The majority of elves, gnomes and leprechauns study at the Sorcerer's Academy. Only a few other Enchantians have had what it takes to gain admission. But here, at this academy, we mostly focus on hand-to-hand combat training and war strategies. Our infantry program trainees consist of gargoyles, imps, gremlins, foxes, dogs, and wolves. Enlistment is open to anyone, really, and the program is only one cycle long prior to assignment."

John found it interesting that the military network was so similar to the armed forces structure back in his world. Last year a recruiter came to school to talk to the students. John thought about joining if he ever got his act together and graduated. Leaving his sister had not been an option. Now that she'd left him, his future plans could change. He felt guilty for thinking about what other changes could impact his life plans now that there was only him and his father. His father, he thought for the first time, how was he going to tell him about Becky? Maybe he'd be too drunk to notice or care.

"There have been a few deserters," Bubbles continued as they reached the large black gates of the fortress. The doors swung open into a massive room with a vaulted, cathedral ceiling. "The penalty for desertion is death. Most of the runaways are gremlins and imps, which makes sense as their kind has been split in allegiances. They come to feel, as the rigors of training increase, that the grass is greener on the other side. So they leave the way of life created by the Knights and side with those of their kind who follow the Banshee. Sometimes I wonder about the loyalty of those who have enlisted with us." He paused. "I guess we shall see where their true allegiances lie when the battle begins."

John followed Bubbles into the empty room, his footsteps echoing with each step. The flat-black brick walls created an eerie, almost sinister atmosphere.

They continued to a long flight of stairs at the far end of the room, wrapping around the interior of the castle tower.

"Here we are, my friend," Bubbles stopped. "This is where I leave you. Take the stairs to the war room."

"Thanks, Bubbles," John started the climb. "It was nice to see you again."

"Don't say your goodbyes yet." Bubbles rolled backward. "I may be seeing you on the battlefield."

"True," John smiled, saluting the snuffball. "Until we meet again, then."

"Until we meet again," Bubbles echoed. "Now stay right there. No need to exert yourself. Stairs," he commanded. "War Room."

The stairway began to move, just like an escalator, rapidly progressing upward along the tower wall. As John reached a landing, he was surprised that the floor took over where the stairs left, off, conveying him along smoothly on a tour of the castle. He was carried swiftly through many corridors filled with paintings and doors. He did not have enough time to examine the details of the artwork, but noticed that most were death-riddled bloody battle scenes.

John was carried along a few more flights until the mover finally stopped in front of an enormous, intricately carved arched wooden door. The sound of an interior commotion bled out into the hallway.

With no hesitation John stepped into the fray.

The room fell silent as all heads turned toward him.

315

Everyone was sitting comfortably in tall chairs grouped around a long, rectangular, highly polished wooden table strewn with maps and books. Mel was closest to the door. John gave him an apprehensive look; Mel looked back coldly. John didn't take offense. He knew he deserved worse.

"John," Brian stood at the other end of the table. "I'm happy to see you here in one piece. Please, join us." He indicated an empty chair.

John sat next to Ryan, across from Mel. He nodded to Ryan, but was too ashamed to look at Mel. When he looked down to the other end of the table his eyes rested on Dyad. John hadn't had time to think about, much less process, their last conversation. His heartbreak was still raw. She smiled at him. Staring at her with unwavering steadiness, his gaze neutral, he didn't smile back.

"We were just discussing strategies," Brian explained. "The Professor has provided us with intelligence that indicates the Banshee and Nymph are planning to raise a dark fairy army against us. They plan to do this by awakening the Fairy Queen and enlisting her help."

"Yes," said John. "I've also heard this. I spoke with Firp in Purgatory, and he said the same thing."

"So Firp is officially dead?" asked Brian.

John nodded sadly.

"You see," Brian looked at his fellow Knights. "That is confirmation then. We must act quickly."

"If you believe so," Russell broke in arrogantly. "But that's not what I have heard."

"Russ, your department has been compromised," said Robert. "I would not trust anything you hear until a full investigation of your operatives is completed. We do not need another infiltration."

"Are you challenging my department's competency?" Russell seemed defensive.

"Brothers," Brian stood up. "Please, we need not argue amongst ourselves. We have bigger problems."

"Agreed," said Randall. "Robert and I can get our ships ready within the tock. Daniel, how's the infantry coming along?"

"I have everyone waiting outside as well as troops flying in from other towns and villages. We are ready as well."

"Brian," Randall continued, "We need to hammer out an agreed-upon strategy and move forward from there. We know where they are: Iced Mountain. We know that the Queen is hidden deep underneath the surface, virtually encased in a glacier. Extricating her will not be fast or easy. The Banshee should be searching for a while."

"Agreed," said Brian and addressed the counsel. "Are there any objections before we proceed?"

"I object to something," said Mel, glancing at John. "I don't think John should be accompanying us on this attack. He is unstable and may endanger the mission."

There was a long silence as once again all heads swiveled in John's direction. He sat quietly, without objection. He understood why Mel believed that and any outbursts, whether hot-headed or mild, would only prove the point.

"I disagree," said Brian. "John is essential to this mission. He may be our only hope when it comes to preventing the Queen from unleashing her army."

"I disagree," said Mel. "Clearly he has a taste for revenge. Do you think it would be wise to have him turn vigilante in the heat of battle with the mountain under siege?"

It had seemed as though Brian was about to elaborate on his reasoning, but for whatever reason, he decided against it, remaining silent.

Suddenly a chime came from Dyad's direction; she unrolled her scroll and quickly stood up. "I've just received an E-Mail from Sally. She is heading to Iced Mountain to stop the Banshee!"

"We have to go!" Ryan exclaimed, jumping up. "We have to get there before she gets hurt!"

Memories rushed back, flooding his consciousness as alarm bells went off in his brain. He remembered Sally's foolhardy bravery during the battle for Enchantas. If the Witch and Warlock hadn't turned out to be her parents, the outcome may have been different. Once again, she was making reckless decisions.

"We should leave immediately," Brian said, standing up. "We do not know if they have found the Queen or if they have, how close they are to accomplishing their goal."

"I agree," said Randall.

"Hear hear!" the other Knights chimed in, slapping their palms decisively on the table.

"Randy and I will prepare our ships," Robert quickly rose, ready to spring into action.

"I will assemble the infantry," said Daniel.

"And I will follow up with intelligence," Russell stood up. "At least with the ones I trust. We can prepare for what they may have waiting for us."

"Good," Brian said looking at the prophets. "You three have your own orders: Please head to the tower. Your rides will be waiting. I would like you to lead the siege."

"Fine," said Mel. "As long as the majority believes it's for the best."

"It is fitting that the prophets have come back together at this time. Destiny is on our side." Brian looked around; all the Knights were nodding in agreement. "This meeting is adjourned," Brian banged his gavel. "Let's do this!"

The room quickly emptied. Dyad hesitantly floated up to John, but he deliberately ignored her. Sadly she slowly flew away.

"You should really talk to her," whispered Ryan.

"I will," said John, looking at Mel. "I need to talk to Mel first."

"Okay, I'll meet you guys upstairs."

Ryan left, leaving John to clear the air with Mel. Mel slowly picked up his books, pretending to be totally involved in gathering his materials, almost as though he was the one most dreading the talk.

"Hey, Mel," John said kindly, contritely, walking closer to his friend. "I just wanted to say I'm sorry." He swallowed a lump. "I'm sorry for blowing up on you back at the mines. I don't know what came over me. And I understand why you think I shouldn't be with you guys on this mission."

Mel looked at John. They were both grief stricken. "I'm sorry too, John." His voice broke. "So, so sorry! I wish there was something I could have done to save her."

"It wasn't your fault Mel. I know there wasn't anything you could have done to save her." John voice cracked as he tried to control his emotions. "I just don't know what came over me. I know that I used to always be like that. You know, always angry and fighting, but after watching her fall and break into pieces I went into shock. Honestly, it's like I blacked out. Went crazy."

"It's okay, John. I forgive you. To be honest, I was afraid of you. I never saw you like that before."

"Yeah," John sighed. "I call it the curse of my father. I'm not sure if I ever told you this, but after my mother left us, my father became a real bad alcoholic. He was horrible; he beat me and Becky all the time. At times, especially when I'm stressed or angry, it feels like I've turned into him."

"You're not like him." Mel said. "It's okay. You had every right to be upset. Your sister was a wonderful person. I miss her, too. I think I could have loved her forever," Mel's voice broke again and his eyes welled up with tears.

"You know," John smiled slightly. "I saw Becky."

"What?" Mel lit up. "Where? When? How?"

"When we were transported by the spell I ended up in a place called Purgatory."

"Really? And Becky was there?"

"Yeah, she was being a brat as usual." John sighed and let out a quick laugh. "She was funny though. It almost seemed as if she didn't care about dying."

"What did she say?"

"Well, her last words to me were for you."

"Really?" Mel took a huge breath, fighting for control. He was close to breaking down.

"Yep," John continued. "She told me to tell you that she will miss you. And that she really enjoyed the time you guys spent together. She will always remember your kiss," John began to laugh, "And said you need to work on it because it was a little sloppy."

Mel laughed and cried at the same time. His eyes had turned red and tears streamed down his cheeks.

"She also said that she hopes you will someday find someone that makes you happy. That you're a great person and you deserve that."

His tears continued to pour. She could have been the love of his life, she could never be replaced.

"She also said to never stop being yourself. What she loved most about you was that you were mischievous. She said that it is a part of you and don't ever give that up."

"Oh, John!" Mel gave him a hug, squeezing tight. "Your sister can never be replaced! Oh my God, she was so beautiful, so unique, so amazing. I miss her so much! I miss what could have been."

"I know," John held Mel tightly. He was crying, too, and it was okay. Their tears were healing their friendship. "I know," he said again. Then he wiped his wet face on his shirttail. "Now let's go kick some Banshee ass."

Mel laughed. "Well said, my friend, well said!"

They let go of each other, slowly but decisively moving toward the tower, moving forward toward their future.

***

As John and Mel stepped out on the roof, a rip-roaring wind hit them at full velocity, blowing hard against their backs. The winds had been building all day, as if echoing the growing tension between opposing factions now coming to a head. John didn't dare go near the edge of the tower roof, let alone look down. He'd had enough of heights on this journey already.

Dyad stood alone, in her largest incarnation, staring out at the mountains like a lovely, lonely Rapunzel awaiting her prince. It seemed to John that talking to her might be the bravest thing he had to do all day. Her rejection had been devastating. After all the hopes and dreams and fantasies spanning fourteen cycles, it seemed cruel and unfair that she did not want to be with him.

"Dyad," John called out to her as he came close. She turned around, so fresh and lovely that he couldn't be anything but grateful to be in her presence.

"John," she cried joyously, jumping into his arms. "I'm not sure if you spoke with Ryan, but I need to tell you something."

"I just wanted to say-" John began, but Dyad silenced him with a kiss, a long, passionate kiss.

"Whatever you think I said before," she pulled away for a brief moment, wanting to look into his eyes to make her point, but they were still closed as if he was dreaming and didn't want to wake up. Her voice and her touch would have to convince him. "John, that wasn't me. It was my sister pretending to be me."

At that John's eyes opened wide. He grinned, not even attempting to hide his full-out joy. He was elated and was incapable of pretending otherwise. "So you didn't find someone else?"

"No!" she laughed. "That was just a ruse by Nymph to separate us."

"So you do want to be with me?" John just wanted to make sure. "Really?"

"Yes, you dimwit!" She kissed him again and then good-naturedly slapped him against the back of his head.

"I'm so glad to hear you say that, Dyad!" John kissed her again.

"Come on lovebirds," said Ryan. "We have to go. Sally could be in danger."

"How are we leading this convoy, anyway?" asked Mel, joining the group.

As if on cue, their dear friend Gusto cruised into view, rising up to tower level in a perfectly level, impressive show of stability and levitation. Following him was a rose-red carpet trimmed with black and yellow, of the same size and dimensions. Both allowed themselves another moment of aerial showboating, smoothly swooping and looping before assuming boarding position in a steady hover at just the right height.

"Gusto!" Ryan was overjoyed to see the loyal, competent carpet. "Who's your friend?"

"Dartly?" Dyad asked, carefully extending a hand, as if to a strange, sniffing dog, then receiving some signal that it was permissible to pet the red carpet. "This is your brother?" She looked at Gusto as she stroked Dartly's nap, gently rubbing his fibers. "Who knew?"

"Are you actually talking to Gusto?" asked John.

"Well, yes, of course," Dyad looked at John curiously. "Can't you hear him?"

"No," all three of the guys shook their heads, mystified.

"Odd," she clambered aboard. "I can hear them clear as a bell."

A sound overhead drew their attention. Scores of ships were moving toward the mountains.

"It's time," Dyad announced. She patted a spot on the carpet next to her. "I know you're afraid of heights, so I decided to go with you this time. It'll give you confidence."

"I don't know," John said hesitantly. He wasn't going to lie about his phobia. "I still don't want to be on this thing."

"Don't worry, sweetie," Dyad winked. "I'll keep you occupied."

"In that case," John quickly jumped on Dartly. "Let's move out!"

Mel and Ryan chuckled as they situated themselves on Gusto. The four flew swiftly into the air passing the armada of ships. They slowed down once they took the lead. The boys looked at each other with conviction, their persona weapons already emerged. They were ready for a fight.

Together, they were unstoppable. Together, they were strong.

Chapter XXI
The Siege

Sally flew as fast as the broom could go over the forests, valleys, and hills of Enchantas, following the direction of her trusted compass. She didn't notice or enjoy the beautiful lands below as she had only one thing on her mind; confronting Nymph. After that she could find Ryan and fix their relationship.

Deep down Sally knew she was strong. She had proven it before, but somehow she'd always revert back to that lonely, shy girl she'd once been. This time was going to be different. This time, she would be strong and stay strong.

Sally read her E-Mail from Dyad urging her to regroup with the others. Though she was elated that Ryan was safe and had missed him dearly, she couldn't bring herself to see him until this one last mission was finished.

Sally flew over a light blue valley and gorge, and then over the crest of a large hill. As she skirted the treetops she finally saw it: Iced Mountain.

The mountain's enormous white peak was intimidating. Sally strained her neck trying to see the top, reaching high into the green sky, poking through the clouds above. The wall of ice reached as far as the eye could see in both directions. There was no easy way around it; the traveler's only choice was up and over.

Sally leaned forward as she accelerated then slowed as she spotted a mass of troops standing guard on the slopes below. From her height they looked like millions of small insects marching in columns, but she knew better. This was the Banshee's army and they were prepared.

Sally's whip immediately extended from her bracelet, dangling and flashing fluorescent gold. She pulled back on her broom to stage a plan of attack. There were a few cave openings in the far distance, but the entire mountain was too well guarded. There was no safe way in. Suddenly a horn blew from below. She noticed the troops turning in her direction and marching faster. Attempting to evade their line of sight, she put the broom in reverse. A strong gust of wind blew down on her from all sides, a turbulent effect that sent the broom spinning. Dizzily she looked up into the clouds. Several single-masted flying ships were descending in her direction. Gangplanks were deployed from their keels as hundreds of flying black cats on brooms were ejected out the port and starboard sides of each ship, meowing their war cries. It was a trap.

Before she could react, Sally was surrounded. The fearsome black cats with sharp fangs snarled and hissed with hatred. Spears, arrows and swords were aimed at her as the cats waited for the call to strike. Imps from below jumped high into the air and hovered over her, joining their allies. They held their spears tightly as their oily, brown, scaly skin sweated profusely emitting a noxious odor that stung her nostrils. The hovering enemies slowly moved aside as their leader flew in to greet them.

"Excellent work, everyone," a fat black cat said, applauding. He wore shiny armor and a horned Viking-like helmet. A long sword hung from his side. As he moved closer, Sally noticed he was missing his left leg and right paw, they had been replaced with a wooden prosthetic and a curved metal hook. "Hello there, prophet girl. Remember me?"

Sally looked curiously at the plump feline. She didn't recognize him.

"I am Commander Hisser!" he snarled. "Our forces fought you at the battle for Enchantas, a defeat I am reminded of each and every day." The commander shook his hook at her.

"Pity," Sally tossed her head. "We all have to live with our choices, good and *bad*, right or *wrong*." She was going to show them how strong she was. She was not afraid.

"I wouldn't challenge me, little girl!" the cat commander hissed. "If the masters didn't want you alive you would be pleading for your life as I sank my teeth into your limbs. I'd be making you squirm like the pretty little stuck-up princess you are as your insides were spoon-fed to my troops."

Sally gulped. The terrible images raced through her mind. She knew that showing fear would only render her powerless, so she gathered every ounce of courage she could call upon, gritted her teeth and replied, "I would never give you the pleasure!"

"Never pretend to be brave, little miss," Nymph fluttered up, glowing green next to Sally. "We all know who you are on the inside, a wimpy little dishrag. That's why Ryan doesn't love you anymore."

"Shut up, Nympho!" Sally's anger fired her bravado but just as she let another stream of curses flow, her mouth was sewn shut. She threw her hands to her lips in shock, trying to pry them open. The more she pulled the tighter her lips locked. Sally squealed helplessly as the fat cat cuffed her hands behind her.

"There. That will shut you up!" Nymph laughed. "I never liked you, Sally. I don't see why my sister has such an interest in you humans. Fairies are far superior! Humans are all so weak. That is, except for the Empress," she laughed, adding, "But then again, she is only half human! And half fairy!"

Sally's eyes widened with surprise.

Nymph laughed again. "You probably didn't know that. The Empress is the daughter of our Fairy Queen! She was meant to rule Enchantas!"

Sally wiggled, twisting her wrists, trying to free herself. It was useless.

"We know your friends are coming," Nymph flew in close to Sally, whispering. "They're coming straight for the trap set for them. Once they arrive, my sisters will be born again and will wipe out every one of the Knights and their pathetic army. Plans to stop us are futile."

Sally squirmed frantically, mumbling curses behind her stitched mouth.

"Take her down below," Nymph said to the Commander. "And make sure everyone can see her when they arrive. They need to know they are doomed."

Nymph zoomed back down into the mouth of a cave, one of several entrances, as Sally was corralled and herded by a horde of bloodthirsty cats. She shivered on her broom; despite her best intentions she was more afraid than she'd ever been in her life.

***

The fluffy clouds whizzed by as Gusto and Dartly led the Enchantas armada. John and Dyad held each other tightly on Dartly, while Ryan and Mel prepared themselves for battle on Gusto.

"I really hope she's all right," said Ryan. "Why is she so reckless?"

Mel chuckled, shaking his head. "I'm surprised you don't already know."

"What do you mean?"

"She's trying to impress you, Ryan."

328

"What for?" Ryan was baffled. "She doesn't need to impress me. I love her for who she is."

"Ryan, you know her much better than I do. So I hope this isn't a shock. She has always been very timid. Especially when we first met her. That's just been who she is and how she sees herself. And being with you, *the big, popular Ryan*, made her feel like she has something to prove, to justify to herself and to others, but mostly to you, that she is good enough to be with you."

Ryan considered what Mel had to say. "I guess you're right. I just never really thought about it like that. I think she's just like me. I understand that she is naturally timid, as you say. But there's more to her than what's on the surface. I've seen it, deep inside. And she can grow and change, confront her fears. We all do. That's a part of life."

"That may be, but when you see her don't be mad at her. I think more than anything she needs you to be there for her. Help her out."

"Gee, Mel," Ryan laughed. "Just a while ago, I was giving you advice about girls. How the times have changed." Then he realized what he'd said. A reminder of losing Becky might be a little too soon. "Oh my gosh, I'm sorry!"

Mel's eyes welled with tears. He blinked and a droplet slowly traced a path down his face, which seemed to have aged in the last few days. "Well I may have only had a girlfriend for a few ticks, but losing someone that you care for puts what should be appreciated in a certain perspective. Time you spend with them is precious." Mel smiled at Ryan. "Just appreciate what you have, Ryan and cherish every moment with Sally."

"I will," Ryan hugged him. "Don't worry, I will!" Ryan was determined to put his relationship with Sally back together. The last time he saw her they'd had yet another heated argument. They needed to break the pattern. They needed to fix it.

John quietly eavesdropped on their conversation as the rug brothers flew side by side with grace and serenity. Listening to them talk about love and loss and relationships kept his mind off the anxiety of flying, a welcome distraction from his phobia of heights.

Dyad laid her head on his shoulder.

John admired the way the wind blew through her straight black hair. She was so beautiful. He appreciated being with her like this, so peaceful and easy. He wanted to savor these moments before the conflict ahead.

"Right, now," John told her, "I couldn't be happier."

She kissed him on his cheek. "Were you listening to them, too?"

"Yeah," John took a deep breath. "I really wish my last days with Becky were different. And I wish I hadn't been so stupid about her and Mel. He's one of my best friends. They were good together. I was just too stubborn to realize."

"No regrets, John. Remember, Destiny has a plan for all of us."

John shook his head. "Sorry Dyad, but I don't buy it. Please don't get all religious on me. That was one thing I couldn't stand last time we were here. All that talk about Fate, Chance, Luck, Freewill and Destiny. I just don't believe in that stuff. No offense."

"That is all right," Dyad kissed him again. "You don't need to believe. I know what's true."

John kissed her back, a neutral nonverbal reply. Deep down he did wish that some sort of higher power would magically turn his life around, but he knew that would never happen. Not even in Enchantas. As far as he was concerned, his mother leaving, his father being a drunk, and his sister's murder was proof that life was hard and then you died, having grabbed whatever small bits of joy were available. If there was a higher power looking over him, it was a cruel one who didn't care about him or worse, was enjoying the show. Everything good in his life had happened on his own accord because he made it happen.

"Dartly says the mountain is right up here," said Dyad, an interruption John welcomed. He turned his attention to the horizon as they flew up and out of the cloud banks. Before them was an imposing white peak, jutting far above where the eye could follow.

"Wow," Ryan said amazed. "So the entire mountain is ice? No rock or metal?"

"Correct," Dyad replied. "It was formed by a curse Sally's parents made a long time ago."

"Thank you!" Ryan called over from his perch on Gusto. Dyad looked at him inquisitively. "Thank you because Sally would appreciate that you didn't call them the Witch and Warlock. They weren't always evil. "

"I knew them when they first arrived," Dyad explained. "And I knew all along that they were compassionate people and caring parents. I did not agree with the Knight's decision, but that is all over now. We move on and learn from our mistakes. I wish my sister would learn hers."

"I'm sure you'll have a chance to talk to her. If anyone can get through to her it's you," John told her. He could tell Nymph's treachery was bothering her a lot.

"John," she said grimly. "The time for talk is over, I'm afraid. I may very well have to fight and kill my own sister."

John thought about being in the same situation. Could he have killed his sister? No way.

"Let's focus on more pleasant things while we can," Dyad said, caressing his windblown hair. She admired his sea-green eyes with adoration for a few more precious moments. A deadly battle was ahead, and these moments must be cherished.

Dyad then let go of his venerating gaze and gently pulled on Dartly, slowing him down as the ships behind them closed in. Dyad cupped her hands over her mouth, magically letting all of the ships hear her. "Troops!" Her voice rang out loud and clear on every ship, although the enemies below couldn't hear a sound. "As we are all aware, what lies below these clouds may very well be a trap. Be prepared, as they will be too. May Destiny's plan be with you all." She paused for a few tacks, looked at the boys and asked, "Who wants to do the honors?"

"I will," Ryan said proudly. He was getting anxious to find Sally.

"Very well," Dyad cupped her hands over Ryan's mouth.

"CHARGE!" Ryan trumpeted, then steering Gusto straight down. Mel quickly gripped the carpet and readied his boomerang.

"Let's do this!" whooped John, aiming Dartly down through the thick fluffy yellow clouds his spear in hand, ready for another battle.

They emerged just above the mountainside. Hundreds of ships and legions upon legions of troops awaited, swarming below.

Large ice boulders thundered by, as cannon fire boomed from the distance. Viking ships soared toward them, smoke rising from the cannons.

"Pull up!" Ryan yelped to John.

John pulled up and Dyad fell off Dartly.

John quickly turned Dartly around, rushing back toward Dyad.

"I'm fine, John," Dyad quickly reassured him and took out a bow. "My wings will take me to battle."

The next thing John knew, she was gone. He tried not to worry, reminding himself that she was a warrior too and that both of them needed to focus on the business at hand.

Ice boulders continued to rocket past them, crashing into the pirate ships as they flew closer to the ground. Screams of horror resounded from above. A few ships with large impact holes plummeted from the sky, troops aboard tumbling out, falling to their deaths. Some ships began to list, tipping on their sides from fatal fire. They also plunged into the icy ground. Cannon fire rang from the falling ships, valiant crews of the doomed vessels attempting to take out as many enemies as they could before they crashed.

Ryan was first to spot the mass of broom-mounted cats pouring out of their ships, flying eagerly toward them, purring loudly, tails twitching.

"Mel, John," Ryan puffed his chest, gripping his sword tight. "Are you ready for this?"

"Oh yeah, baby, bring it!" said John. *"Hello kitties!"*

Mel stayed silent, concentrating on locating the best route for his boomerang.

"Count us in, bro!" Flaux and his Death Devils swooped in from each side, flanking the prophets. "You didn't think we'd miss this, did you?"

"I was hoping you wouldn't." Mel laughed.

"Just don't my tell mom, okay? She'd be mad if she found out we crashed the battle. She's way overprotective."

"Deal," said Ryan. He was happy to have reinforcements to deal with the flying cats.

"Death Devils! Follow me!" Flaux cried and pulled back his bat-like wings. "Hoo-raw!"

The other griffoyles followed into the swarm, blocking cat strikes by turning to stone. They used their pecking beaks to brutal perfection, as well as their beating wings, unseating countless felines from their brooms.

John aimed his unlimited spears with precision, knocking dozens of free-falling cats out of his way. Mel threw boomerang after boomerang. The black cats never knew what hit them as they, too, fell to the icy ground.

A cat broke through the ranks. Ryan reflexively swung his sword, slicing its head clean off. Blood splattered on him, but he didn't mind. Better that than his own blood. As the headless cat wobbled on its broom, Ryan kicked it off and took its place. "There," Ryan said to Mel, settling himself on the broom. "We can cover more air this way. Follow me."

Ryan, John, and Mel veered from the cat fight, leaving the griffoyles to clean up the strays. They headed toward the still-flying ships trailed by flocks of imps and more cats in hot pursuit.

As they reached the *Storm Glider*, they could see that Max and his shipmates had it under control. A smaller contingent of cats and imps were attempting to board but Max and his crew held their ground, killing all enemies who came within range.

"Don't worry boys!" Max yelled, simultaneously running a sword through both a cat and an imp. "We got this. Get down there and stop the Banshee!"

"Roger that," confirmed Mel, pulling back on Gusto. That was when he saw the Viking, Commander Hisser, jump down onto *Storm Glider's* deck.

"She is the Empress!" Commander Hisser exclaimed with a feral snarl. "And she is –"

"Hisser," Max shook his head in mock sorrow as he marched up to the cat. "Won't you ever just lie down and die?"

"Not before you, you scurvy mongrel!" Hisser brandished his hook at the dog. "I'll see you in your grave, my old adversary!"

"Sorry to burst your bubble, but that ain't happening!"

"We'll see about that!" Hisser hobbled toward his target with surprising dexterity, nimbly swinging his long sword.

Max easily feinted then blocked the attack, stepping aside with a bullfighter's flourish. "Won't you ever give up? I'm surprised you didn't learn your lesson during our last entanglement."

"The only lesson I learned was that old dogs are full of tricks," Hisser charged again.

Max exchanged the briefest of glances with his audience: Ryan, Mel, and John. It gave Hisser the opening he'd been waiting for. The crafty cat swung his sword again, slashing Max's furry black arm. Blood trickled from the wound as Max fell to his knees.

"Finally!" Hisser cried, meowing in triumph. "Vengeance is mine!"

"Prophets!" woofed Max, panting from the pain. "Get going! I'll be fine. You need to get to the mountain."

Ryan nodded, "Come on, he's right."

The three of them took off, hoping it wasn't the last time they'd see their old pirate friend. A screaming, careening, meowing cacophony of flying enemies launched assaults as they descended toward the most likely looking entrance to the mountain interior. They were beginning to tire, but knew there was no time for rest. The fate of Enchantas was hanging in the balance.

"Look!" yelled John, ramping up Dartly's speed and pointing toward the opening. "There."

Ryan, close behind, scanned the mountainside. They couldn't afford an ambush. There, on a bare rock face to the west of the entrance, was a small silhouette, a human shadow-figure tied up arms and legs spread apart. To his horror and dismay Ryan recognized Sally. "I see her!" he cried, instinctively diverting to a direct course for his staked-out spirit-mate dangling like bait off the ledge. John kept Dartly on track for the entrance.

"John," bellowed Mel. "No! You have to come with us, we need your help!"

"No you don't," John yelled back, resolute in his determination. "I have to do this guys. I have to find Lexis!"

"John! Come on! We need your help with Sally, the Banshee can wait," Mel continued to plead even as he saw there was no convincing him. John had a one-track mind.

"It's okay!" he yelled from a distance, offering a thumbs-up. "Get her and meet me. I'll see you inside!"

At the mouth of the entrance John pushed down on Dartly as hard as he could, swooping into the cave.

"That jerk!" Ryan complained as he sidled up to Gusto. "Let's just hope he doesn't get himself killed."

"Forget it," Mel said. "We've got to focus on the immediate task. I'll follow you in."

Flying as fast as he and the broom could go, Ryan was making headway in his effort to reach Sally when dozens of gremlins climbed out of an icy passageway, completely surrounding her.

"Pull up! Pull up!" Mel yelled.

Ryan bristled at the directive, hesitating, but knew that he had no choice. There was no way they could retrieve her without reinforcements.

"Dammit, John!" Ryan swore. "If we had three of us, it might be do-able."

"I don't know about that," said Mel, "But we need to refine the rescue plan. Where's Dyad?"

"She's too busy acting out on her sibling rivalry." Ryan was furious. Seeing Sally strung up, so helpless made him feel angry and powerless. Then it occurred to him.

"Wait a minute, we do have reinforcements!" Ryan grinned as he dug in his pocket, pulling out his trusty sidekick. "Hey, Channy, how you doing?"

"Wheeeeee! This is fun, Ryan!"

"Glad you think so, little one!" Ryan petted the little turquois snuffball. "Are you ready to be a hero again?"

"Where did that come from?" Mel wondered. "Do you always carry a snuffball in your pocket?"

"Only on special occasions, for very special hero missions," Ryan said.

"Am I, am I? Yes, I'm ready to be a hero! Again!" Channy was giddy, jumping out of his hand and bouncing around in a happy little dribble dance on Gusto. "What do I do? What do I do?"

"I need you to help us save Sally."

"SALLY?" Channy zipped around Gusto and back into Ryan's hand. "Oh boy! It would be my pleasure!"

"Wonderful, Channy! Now listen closely. Here's what we're going to do," Ryan explained. "I'm going to throw you as hard as I can at the troops guarding Sally. I want you to knock those nasty gremlins out like a pin-ball machine!"

"Pin-ball?"

"It's a game, Channy."

"Game? Channy loves games!" She bounced excitedly.

"Yes," Ryan couldn't stop himself from laughing despite the dire situation. "In this game, you're the star, the brave little ball ricocheting in the pin-ball machine," he traced a zig-zag motion with a forefinger. "Your goal is to save Sally by bouncing off as many gremlin heads as you can to get the best score. You get more points for knocking them out. Got it?"

"Got it, sir!" Channy bounce-pounced her version of a snappy salute.

"All right. Ready? On the count of three." Ryan gripped Channy firmly, like a baseball player going for a World Series strikeout. He glanced at Mel to ensure he was turning Gusto around, preparing to charge. "One, two, three — GO!"

Ryan threw Channy as hard he could at a gremlin, hitting it directly between its beady eyes. The gremlin flew backward off the mountain, taking out a few other gremlins with it.

"Never fear! Channy is here!"

Channy bounced herself rapidly off the heads and bodies of the enemy troops. She was a non-stop blur of boinking action, knocking out the unsuspecting gremlins or rendering them so off-balance that many tripped and fell off the mountain ledge. Within ticks Sally was alone, except for a few unconscious gremlins. Most of her captors had plunged to their doom.

"Sally!" Ryan jumped off his broom and began untying her. "Are you all right?"

Sally mumbled incoherently. Ryan saw that her lips were sewn shut. "Hang in there, Sally," he said, calling to Mel, "Look at her mouth. Can you do something?"

Before Mel had even dismounted from Gusto, Ryan cleared his mind, closed his eyes and recited:

"Fairy seamstress, evil freak;
Remove these threads, so Sally can speak!"

Blue smoke covered Sally's mouth for an instant. When it cleared her lips were back to normal.

"Hey! I did it! My first spell!" Ryan cheered, but then was puzzled. "How did I come up with that?"

"Good job, man!" said Mel, patting his buddy's back congratulatory. "I knew you could do it! The persona bracelets also help with creativity when it comes to spell-casting."

"Nice!"

"Oh Ryan!" Sally wasted no time throwing her arms around, and kissing her long-lost spirit-mate. "I'm so glad to see you!"

Channy jumped on Sally's shoulder. "Miss Sally! You're saved!"

"Channy?" Sally laughed. "Is that you?"

"It's me! Your savior!" Channy bounced enthusiastically.

"Thank you for saving me, Channy!" Sally kissed the little snuffball.

"She kissed me! She kissed me!" Channy hopped with excitement. "I'm a hero! I have to go tell the others."

Suddenly, Channy rolled down the mountain towards her fellow fighting snuffballs. "I'm a hero everyone! I'm a hero!"

As Channy rolled down the white hill, she began to build up speed, collecting ice on the way. Before she knew it, she was snowballing out of control, growing larger with each revolution of her round little being.

By the time Channy rolled down the hill onto the battlefield there was no stopping her. She resembled the largest snowball ever created. Armed with a crushing weight of ice and unstoppable forward momentum, she continued rolling over the enemy, flattening hundreds of goblins, imps, cats and gremlins. The battling snuffball troops bounced in triumph, a boinging flurry every color of the rainbow, as Channy's snowball finally came to a halt. The friction from smushing the opposition had softened the outer icy shell encasing her. With a few well-aimed bounces, her fellow snuffballs cracked the coating, cheering as they broke her out. The littlest snuffball stood joyous in victory reveling in the acceptance of her kin.

"So you see, Ryan!" Sally kissed him. "Proof positive that even the smallest of things can make a big difference."

"You're right, sweetie," said Ryan, as he picked her up gently, placing her on Gusto next to Mel.

"Thank you too, Mel." Sally kissed him.

Ryan gave them both a funny look.

"What was that for?" Mel scooted back, in shock. "Trust me Ryan, I wasn't planning on that."

"Don't worry, buddy," Ryan kissed his friend on the cheek. "You deserved it."

"Sheesh," Mel rubbed his face. "That was disgusting. Don't ever do that again." Mel kept rubbing his face, and then snickered. "That only goes for Ryan. Sally can smooch me anytime!"

"If you say so," she said, kissing his cheek again.

"Hey, come on guys," Ryan laughed, pulling on Gusto's back. "You're pushing it here."

"Sorry," they said simultaneously.

"Where to now?" asked Mel. "Do we track down John or go back into battle?"

Ryan looked down to the ground, watching in sorrow as Enchantians continued to slaughter each other. Pools of blood

339

covered the ice. More troops descended from the ships above as cannons fired on each other in the sky.

"Nothing has changed has it?" Sally said sadly. "I thought we fixed it. I believed we'd brought peace back to Enchantas."

"Nope," Mel said. "War is almost inevitable if there is still evil in the world."

Sally looked up, smiled, and pointed. "Well hopefully, this will be the end of it."

They all looked up at the bright green sky as a large orange cumulous cloud glided in. Swarms of animals began to drop from the bottom of it, spreading across the battlefields above and below.

"Who are they?" asked Ryan, as he mounted his broom.

"Cupids," Sally giggled. "What better way to stop a battle than to cover it with *love*. I E-Mailed Cupid on my way here."

"You saw Cupid?"

"Yes, goof!" Sally punched him. "Now let me finish my story. I'll tell you everything that happened a little later."

"Sorry babe," Ryan kissed her. He forgot how much he missed listening to her.

"Anyway, I E-Mailed Cupid and suggested that they come join the fight."

"Very clever Sally!" Mel was impressed. "Gee, why didn't I think of that?"

"Think of what?" asked Ryan.

"Cupids use a particular type of magic to bring out happiness and goodness in those touched by their love-arrows." Mel was nodding and gesturing expansively as he explained, caught up in the brilliance of the idea. "Their love-arrows are extremely potent. If used in battle there can be no fighting. Their magic simply overrules hatred and violence. With the help of the Cupids, this war can end immediately, with no more casualties. Not like last time." Mel looked at Sally. "It's the perfect solution. Why didn't I think of it?"

"I don't know, *Professor*," Sally said, laughing. "Maybe it's because all you men have competition and aggression on your minds. It takes a real woman to think outside of the box, to choose love, not war." Sally chuckled again. "Actually, to be honest, at first I wasn't sure they would join the effort. They said –"

"We do not condone such violence," the Cupid pig hovering next to them completed the sentence. He had an arrow poised to shoot. "We are lovers, not fighters."

"Hey Cupid, how's it going?" Ryan hailed the jovial pig.

"Hello Ryan! I'm very, very glad to see you two back together! Seeing what my arrows do for spirit-mates such as yourselves is the reason I do what I do."

Ryan looked at Sally curiously. She remained silent, obviously not wanting to go into details about her conversation with the Cupid.

"Are those love-arrows?" asked Mel.

"Not exactly, more like very potent friendship-arrows. Almost the same effects, but not as passionate. Also, they last a little longer. Like a week or so." Cupid looked down at the battle, which was now beginning to die down. "Uh-oh, someone must have accidentally shot a couple of our regular love-arrows! Look!"

Cupid pointed down. They all watched in awkward silence as Max and Commander Hisser began to passionately kiss. Butch sat a few leaps away, laughing so hard he had to hold his furry sides.

Sally smiled. "Looks like Butch got his old boss a good one," she remarked.

"That is so wrong!" Ryan gasped.

"But so funny!" Mel busted out laughing.

"BUTCH!" yelled the pig with a squealing oink. Butch quickly flew off into battle shooting more arrows.

"I must go back to work now, my friends." Cupid shot an arrow at a cat behind them and began to descend. "Nice seeing you again, Professor."

341

"Likewise!" Mel shouted, leaning over Gusto. "And thanks again!"

As the three of them watched the cupid army swarm the battalions, shooting rounds of arrows, it surprised them how many warriors resisted the cupids' siege. It was clear to them that many still had hard feelings and prejudices toward their fellow Enchantians. Even though peace had seemingly been restored for fourteen cycles, it made them wonder how authentic the truce had been.

Some troops began to fight the cupids, but for whatever reason nothing could hurt the flying matchmakers. The armies tried but failed. They dropped like flies as they were struck by cupid-arrows. Their bodies shuddered in shock as they resisted the effects, but it was not long before they succumbed to the magic. As they stood up their eyes glazed over with blissful fellowship. They began shaking enemy hands as if greeting long-lost buddies. Some hugged each other, while others sat down and carried on friendly conversations.

"I don't think we're needed out here anymore," said Mel. "Let's go get John and stop Lexis."

Ryan and Sally nodded in agreement as they flew down into the cave of the Iced Mountain.

Chapter XXII
The Fairy Queen

The iced cavern was quiet and bright. The walls and ceiling flashed in colored sequences of blue, purple, pink and green. On the iced floor countless numbers of small sapphire pyramids glowed as well. In the center the Fairy Queen raised her arms, concentrating on awakening her kin.

"Mother," Lexis said impatiently, striding into the room. "How long is this going to take? Nymph said the Knights and their army have arrived."

The Queen took a deep breath and opened her eyes. The sequence flashing stopped and the room grew dark for a moment. "Patience, child," said the Queen as she resumed. "This is a very delicate process."

"So will they all be my sisters?" Lexis asked. She did not like this much silence. She'd spent most of her life behind locked doors. She craved noise, excitement, conversation in which she was the center of attention.

"Biologically, no," the Queen said, stopping again. She decided to take a break so she could talk with her daughter, help her to understand. "Fairies are not born like humans. I gave birth to you, but my fairy children are awakened by me giving them a part of my essence. My grace, if you will. Each fairy is born from each flumpkin. So they are not biologically your sisters, but you may call them that if you wish."

The Empress smiled. For so long had she wanted a real family. Now it was finally here. She had found her long-lost mother, who had left her father. She forgave her instantly as she, too, knew how insane he was. The thought of a large family, with thousands of sisters, filled her with satisfaction.

"Are you sure they will be like us?" she asked. "I mean, the Knights can't get away with what they have done to our family and to yours."

"Yes," the Queen narrowed her eyes. "The fairies will listen to me. And we will get back at the Knights, for they killed my family and they will pay."

The Queen walked back to the center of the cavern and said, "Their mood when they awaken is related directly to the mood I am in when I awaken them." She ground her teeth, closed her eyes and began again. "And right now, I feel particularly malevolent."

"As do I, mother!" Alexis snarled. "We will kill them all!"

"Not if I have anything to do with it!" John yelled. His voice echoed throughout the cavern.

The Queen glanced at him briefly, dismissed him as unimportant and went back to concentrating.

"John!" the Empress laughed. "How's your sister? I hope she enjoyed the fall!"

"She's doing well, no thanks to you!" John threw a spear at her. She blocked it.

"Alexis!" The Queen called, distraught at the continued interruptions. "Who is this person?"

"Just an annoying brat, mother." She zapped a cutting purple beam at him. He dove out of the way. "Don't stop, mother, we

344

need the fairies as soon as possible. I'll take care of this little problem."

"You're going to pay for what you've done!" John continued to fire spears in her direction with deadly aim, as fast as he could. "She was innocent."

"No, John." the Empress slowly walked toward him with a menacing glare. "She was just like you and your friends. *So pathetic.*"

"Becky didn't deserve to die. You do!" John charged her. A large golden shield ejected from his arm, effectively blocking any magic she might choose to throw his way.

The Empress-Banshee panicked. She tripped over a flumpkin, falling backward onto the floor. John jumped on her, pinning her arms with his knees. She was helpless against his fury. John had the upper hand. He began to punch her savagely. All rational thought left him as feelings of revenge raged through his veins. He felt immense relief with each blow.

At last John held up his spear, staring into the Empress's bloody eyes and bruised face. "This is for Becky, you psycho witch!" John swore, preparing to plunge his blade into the wicked creature beneath him.

"Becky?" asked the Queen. She stopped her summoning, her attention drawn to the name uttered by the two combatants. "Who's Becky?"

"Mother, don't stop. I've got this!" the Empress turned her battered face toward the Queen. "Don't stop!"

"No, Alexis! Tell me who Becky is," the Queen demanded.

"I don't know. It's this boy's sister! Some brat from Willington! Who cares?"

At that John increased the pressure on her arms. She groaned.

"John?" the Queen asked. Her voice had softened.

John hesitated. He didn't know why, but there was something soothing, something that compelled him to listen to the older fairy's voice.

"John! Stop it!" the Queen abandoned her resurrection preparations, drawing closer.

John saw the Fairy Queen shining a sparkly blue, like Dyad but not Dyad, her long brown hair flowing delicately as her face came into focus. He blinked, not believing what he saw. He blinked again.

As the blue light glowing around the Queen lessened, recognition dawned. "Mom," he whispered the word, like a reverent prayer.

"John?" the Queen's voice trembled. "Is it really you?"

"Mom!" this time it was a shout. His spear disappeared as he ran to her, hugging her sparkling body, touching her face, her hair. "I can't believe it's you!"

"Mother?" the Empress stood slowly, painfully, brushing herself off. "What curse have you put this boy under?"

"Alexis," her mother said. "It's no curse. This is real. This is really your brother."

"What?" both the Empress and John exclaimed, glaring at each other with pure hatred.

"No! This can't be true!" Alexis raged, her eyes turning the blackest shade of purple, livid against her white face now marred by bruises and blood. "He is *not* my brother!"

"Well, he would be your half-brother, actually," the Queen noted mildly.

"She killed Becky, mom." John shook his head. "She can't be my sister. My sister is dead because of her!"

"Becky is dead? *My* Becky is dead?" the Queen's voice was shaky, horrified. She fought for composure. "Explain this to me, Alexis. You told me the Knights killed my family."

"I-I," Alexis stuttered. "I wasn't sure exactly. That was the most likely explanation. I just wanted us to be a family."

"Alexis! What have you done? You nearly led me to wage a war on false pretenses!"

"But we are supposed to be a family, Mother!"

"Shut up!" yelled John. "You can't have a family! You're too crazy!"

"John, calm down," said the Queen trying to defuse the situation.

"Mom, seriously, she killed Becky!"

"She didn't know what she was doing," The Queen tried to defend Alexis, but was also clearly confused and deeply distraught.

"And that gives her the right to kill her? Look at her mom, she's nuts!"

Alexis zapped John clear across the cavern with all her might.

"Stop it you two!" yelled the Queen. "Just give me a minute to think!"

"Mother! I can't believe you're siding with him!"

The Queen sat down on a throne like armchair, rubbing her forehead.

"Mother," Alexis knelt beside her. "We can still be a family, just you and me. Forget about everyone else."

"Dad's not doing so good, Mom." John said, slowly staggering to his feet. "He hasn't been doing anything but drinking since you left."

"Shut up, John!" Alexis screamed. "She's *my* mother. You're ruining everything!"

The Queen stood up. "Alexis, calm down. If this is going to work, we have to work through our challenges together, as a family."

"Oh no!" she yelled, crossing her arms defiantly over her chest. "I will not be in allegiance with him or any of his friends. You're my mother! No one else's. Mine!"

"Alexis, you're sounding like your father!" the Queen rubbed her head again. "Please stop!"

"No, mother! I will not stop! We are going to be together and no one is stopping us! Not him! Not-" suddenly Alexis dropped to the ground quivering, curled into a ball. Her face began to wrinkle like a prune; her fingers curled inward.

"Alexis?" the Queen knelt down. "What's happening to her?"

"She'll be fine," said Mel, entering with his slingshot in hand, at the ready, pointed at the Queen. "She's just stunned. And will be for a couple tocks."

"John!" yelled Sally, running fearlessly up to him for a big hug. Looking the Queen up and down, she asked him, "Who's this? Is everything okay?"

Ryan strolled in, displaying the unconsciously cocky walk he tended to favor after winning a football game. John had secretly dubbed it his "Superjock Strut".

"The battle is over." Ryan announced, holding up his arms and flexing his guns.

"Whoa, bro! Not yet it isn't," Mel kept a puckerberry aimed at the Queen.

"John, who are these kids?"

"Mel, you can put that down now. It's safe." John said.

"Are you sure? Because she looks anything but harmless to me. It looks like she was in the process of raising a fairy army."

"She's my mom." John smiled at the Queen, feeling peace in his heart and soul.

"Your mother? Really?" Mel scrutinized the Queen more closely. "I see a resemblance," he said, wonderingly, adding, "Actually, she looks more like Becky."

"But I thought she was the Banshee's mother." Sally was confused at this latest development.

"Who's the Banshee?" the Queen wanted to know.

"He means Lexis," Mel corrected. "Sorry, but that's one of her less-than-flattering titles." There was a twinkle in the former high school class clown's eye.

The Queen also had a sense of humor. "Well, that would make me the Banshee's mother." She bowed to Mel rhetorically, laughing at the ridiculous idea before explaining, "John is the so-called *Banshee's* half-brother."

"Wow." Sally put her hand to her mouth. "She killed Becky. She killed her own sister." A heaviness permeated the atmosphere. Sally was sorry to bring it up, but it had to be said.

John nodded, "And I thought my family was already dysfunctional. This takes it to a whole new level."

"There is always room to heal, John," said his mother gently.

Immediately, John was reminded of being a child. His mother's words of wisdom had always soothed him.

"Tell me about your father," the Queen asked. "You said he isn't doing well?"

"Sorry to break up the family reunion," Mel interrupted. "We are being summoned back to the Academy. We must be there for the peace treaty ceremony."

"Where's Dyad?" asked John. The last time he saw his lovely girlfriend she'd been diving into battle.

"She's taking care of her sister, Nymph," said Sally. There was a hint of satisfaction in her voice. Thought Sally had not been able to confront Nymph as she wanted to, she knew justice would be served.

"Dyad?" the Queen smiled. "She was always a good fairy, one of the better sisters of the bunch."

"Speaking of sisters," John wondered. "Does that mean Dyad's my sister?"

"No," the Queen answered. "Why?"

John blushed and Sally answered. "They're dating."

"Oh my," the Queen grinned. "My boy is all grown up."

"We should go," Mel reminded them, leading the way toward the cavern exit.

"What of Alexis? What will happen with her?" the Queen looked at her shriveled, puckered, very un-empress-like daughter writhing on the ground.

"She'll be picked up soon. Then there will be a trial, for both her and for Nymph's crimes against Enchantas," Mel explained. "She will be treated humanely, unlike the way she has treated others."

"Very well," the Queen said sadly, thinking of her daughter's tortured life and the sorrows that had warped her into a creature so hated that she was known as the Banshee.

"I will accompany you. The Knights will be interested in hearing my story." She looked at John. "Especially your Uncle Brian."

"Uncle?" John's eyes opened wide as everything began to make sense. That was why Brian said that John might be the only one who could prevent another costly battle for Enchantas. It wasn't because of his vengeful heart, it was because he knew John was the Queen's son. Now he understood. Certain nuances came back to him, like pieces of a puzzle clicking into place. John recalled from their last trip to Enchantas that Brian occasionally referred to his brother, James. John's father was named Jim, which was short for James.

There was an extra almost-snuffball buoyance to John's step as he followed his long-lost mother and his friends out of the cavern, and onto the carpets. His sister was gone, but his spirit embraced this new beginning.

Chapter XXIII
A Last Farewell

John and his mother stepped off Dartly onto the colorful snowy ground. Winter was hanging on strong in the land of Enchantas. The night sky was hidden, then revealed, then hidden again by the gray clouds scudding by in a brisk northerly wind. The moon made the most of the clear, crisp, icy air, shining with clarity, sharply defined. They stood in a clearing surrounded by a thick forest. The center of the clearing stood an enormous redwood tree that towered magnificently over them. An arched door larger than any garage door John had ever seen was set in the middle of its trunk. John had remembered stories told by Ryan and Sally about the size of the Sage's home, but he did not ever imagine its true grander.

Earlier that day they watched the concurrent trials of Alexis and Nymph. Both were charged with high treason and sentenced to imprisonment for life.

John's mother pleaded for her daughter to be banished, but the Knights didn't believe that their old world would be safe with Alexis there. The Queen's ex-husband, Alexis's father, was already incarcerated for imprisoning his daughter all those years ago.

They arrived at the opinion that her insanity was likely genetic and that for the safety of both worlds, prison in Enchantas would be the best course of action. This way, they could keep a close eye on the Banshee.

"So what are we doing here, Mom?" asked John. He wasn't as eager to get home as his friends were. That would mean leaving Dyad. He wondered why his mother had insisted on bringing him to this place.

"The Sage asked us to come by before we go home." She smiled, looking up at the majestic, immensely verdant tree they stood in front of. "I haven't seen the Owl in years. I mean cycles."

"Where's everyone else?"

"Brian said he'd be here already, but I haven't seen him since the trial," she looked around. "I'm not sure about your friends."

"They're taking their time, as usual," John said, trying not to be snide or sarcastic but failing miserably, which made his mother smile. So many things ran in the family.

"John, I have to be honest. It's been a long time since I've seen your father and I'm nervous. How is he, really?"

"Like I said, he's terrible," John said. Telling the truth was getting to be a habit. He just needed to work on his delivery, maybe choosing his words more carefully. "Ever since you left he's been drinking like a fish. I don't think he knows what reality is anymore. He's lost all hope."

"I'm so sorry for leaving you." His mother was also embracing honesty.

"It wasn't your fault," John assured her. "I know you were trapped here."

"By Sally's parents," the Queen still held a grudge. "There is no way for me to get back those years that I've missed. You've grown so much. I never got to see your sister grow up; that makes me even sadder. What was she like?"

"She was really smart: smart brain and smart mouth." John was happy to talk about Becky. It was cathartic. "She did well in school when she felt like it. I just feel bad that I wasn't a better role model for her. She was so beautiful, all the boys loved her. It was hard to rein her in when she wanted to do what she wanted to do."

"But I am sure you were there for her."

"Yeah, but she was there for me even more."

"I'm glad you had each other."

"Me too."

"Elizabeth!" They both turned to see Brian standing with his scepter in hand.

"Brian," Elizabeth, the Queen, smiled, "There you are. Where is the Sage?"

John felt awkward because he hadn't heard his mother's name in years. His father called her Lizzy. She hated it, but John thought it was unique.

"He'll be here soon, he's flying from Gnelfton. He said he had to pick something up." Brian looked down at John. "So now you know the truth, nephew. I'm your uncle." He smiled broadly.

"Yeah," John replied. "You could have told me before."

"I could have, but I didn't want to confuse you or give you any hope of finding your mother. I know your father hasn't been doing well, to put it mildly. When we severed contact with your world and closed the Forbidden Cave, I knew he was not happy.

"I don't mean to be so formal, but it hurts me to speak of Jim's fall from grace. We were very close once, best friends really. That's how twins usually are."

"Twins?" John didn't think he was capable of dealing with any further surprises. "But you don't look alike at all."

Brian laughed. "Nope, we aren't identical. I am the older one, by a few ticks. Or minutes, I should say."

"Jim took the looks I think," said Elizabeth, winking.

"And I took the brains," Brian laughed.

"Okay, okay, I'm slowing down," Ryan's voice could be heard from above.

Gusto descended thoughtfully, coming to a well-leveled hover at a nice height for Ryan, Mel, and Sally to disembark.

"Thanks Gusto," Sally said, rubbing his nap one way then the other in a pattern she knew he liked. "I'm going to miss you all over again."

"He says he is going to miss you too," Dyad fluttered up, instantaneously changing to her human self.

"Dyad!" John's happiness was complete as he saw her healthy and whole. "I haven't seen you since the battle."

"I am so sorry I didn't get back to you sooner, John," she hugged him ardently, unafraid to show her affection. "Or should I say, 'I apologize, my prince'?"

She was right, John thought. If his mother was the Fairy Queen, then he was a fairy prince. But he had no wings that he knew of.

"Greetings, my Queen," Dyad quickly knelt down in front of Elizabeth. "It has been many cycles; we have all missed you dearly."

"Please rise, my child," Elizabeth bent down. "No need for any formalities. I left that title behind long ago. I see that you and my son have taken a liking to each other?"

"Ah, yes, Your Grace." Dyad was trembling. Her feelings for John could not be hidden. The calmer she tried to be, the more she shook, from knocking knees to tiny tremors that rippled through her wings.

"No need to be nervous." Elizabeth gave her a hug. "Out of all of the fairies that I have blessed with my essence, I am proud that he has found you."

"Thank you." Dyad blushed, looking at John lovingly. "I could not ask for more."

John kissed her.

"Must you leave, John?" Dyad whispered.

John didn't say anything. He couldn't.

"So when are we going back?" asked Sally. "I'm sure my parents and grandma are worried."

"Soon," said Brian. "I informed them you'll be home soon. I told them not to wait up; as I'm sure it is after midnight. I also let them know the outcome of the battle and your part in bringing peace. They told me to tell you that they are very proud of you."

Sally blushed.

"Welcome my young prophets, friends and family," said the Sage, descending from above. His wings caused a strong wind to blow down on them, making it difficult to stand up straight. "You are all probably wondering why I have summoned you here tonight on the eve of your departure."

They all nodded in agreement.

"First, I would like to thank you all for coming back to our world and bringing peace to Enchantas once again. For I am sure if it weren't for your bravery, we would not be where we are today. Thank you."

"Yes, thank you," Brian added, bowing formally.

"I would also like to give you one last gift of appreciation," the owl opened a small box and set it on the cold, snowy ground. "I give you these four keys."

Each prophet moved forward to choose a key. The golden keys were of normal size, but each bore a sparkling green gem on its rounded end.

"These keys will open any door in your world and make a safe transport to ours. Likewise it will grant you safe passage from our world to yours. They were forged by your father, John."

John looked at his key in awe.

"Your father was a very skillful magicsmith," his mother told him.

"Yes, and he made the first persona bracelets too," Brian added.

"So we can come back at any time?" John asked.

"You are all welcome back, always and forever," the Owl looked at Mel with a droll expression. "Even you, Professor."

"You're coming back with us?" Sally squeaked.

"Yeah," Mel laughed at the sound of Sally's excited voice. "I figure that my time in Enchantas is over, for now anyway. I want to pursue the future waiting for me back in our world. I have plans to go to college, to become a physicist and chemist. Besides, even if I don't miss my mom's weird cooking, I sure do miss her. She deserves to know that I'm still alive."

John, Sally, and Ryan started laughing. It took several tacks for them to stop.

"I'm real glad you're coming home," said Ryan, when he could talk again. "Besides, with this key, we can come back and visit any time." Ryan looked up at the Sage. "Thank you."

"You are welcome," the Owl regarded John and his mother. "I am truly sorry for your loss. Becky did seem like a sweet girl with a lot of potential. She will always be thought of with respect here in Enchantas."

"Thank you," John and Elizabeth replied.

"Which brings me to my final gift," said the Owl, pulling out a large sack and an old book from under his wing. "For cycles, the Knights and I have been discovering and collecting magic that is too powerful for most Enchantians. In the interest of preservation, we have faithfully and accurately written the information down in this book. One of the spells we found may be of interest to you. It concerns bringing life back from the dead."

John's eyes opened wide, his ears on full alert. "You mean?"

"It is a resurrection spell, John. We may be able to bring Becky back to us," the Owl intoned.

"How?" Elizabeth asked, just as eagerly as her son.

"This magic is very powerful. It comes with a price," replied Brian. "Which as much as I am not in favor of, our Sage is." He bowed his head, indicating that the very thought went against his morality and ethics on every level.

"Yes," the Owl added. "The spell consists of a potion which I have here. It requires a sacrifice. A life for a life, which we also have available to us."

"Life?" asked John. "Whose life? I'll do it." He would give anything to bring his sister back to the living.

"Thank you, my boy," said the Owl. "But I have already decided that it will be *me*. As I have said many, many times, this body is becoming too old. I have lived a long, rewarding, and plentiful life. I've lived in this world; watched it grow and endured its triumphs and shortcomings. It is my time and my last wish is to reunite a family that I too have loved. Elizabeth, I have known you for many, many cycles. John, you are one of our prophets and I would be honored if you would grant this one last wish of an old wise Owl."

"We do," they said simultaneously.

"My only issue is that," Brian interrupted. "With our Sage gone, we will need an Enchantian to take his place, someone born to this world and just as old and as wise. We, the Knights, were hoping that you, Elizabeth, would do the honor of becoming our Grand Sage?"

"I would," she was humbled. A tear came down her cheek. "Even if it weren't under these circumstances, I would be honored.

What a privilege. I pray to do it justice, in accordance with the wisdom and blessing of our Grand Sage."

"Wonderful!" the owl hooted. "Now without further ado, I will cast the spell. I bid you all a gracious farewell. My time on this world has been adventurous and grand. Now my new adventure begins. May Destiny bless me with a safe journey to the *world beyond*."

Brian opened the sack, dumping the collected rubble that comprised Becky's remains out on the snow as the spectators stared in shock. Brian noticed their discomfort. "John, would you please pour this potion on your sister's remains?"

John dribbled a veil of purple potion over the shards. Purple smoke rose from each drop.

The wise owl then chanted:

"Death behold, this one was taken;
Take me instead, and mend the forsaken!"

The owl's body slowly evaporated into a blue mist as the rubble began to put itself back together.

John watched in amazement as he saw his sister's stone body reconstruct.

"It's Becky," he cried.

At the sight of the full statue of Becky, Mel remembered his last moment as she saved his life.

Suddenly her stone body was consumed by a cloudy violet haze and then she became flesh again.

"Becky!" John rushed to her. He was followed by Mel.

"What the hell?" Becky looked around. "Come on, I was just beating that stupid Leprechaun in poker, too!"

"Becky!" John hugged her. "You're alive!"

"What?" Becky looked around; she noticed Sally, Ryan, Mel, Dyad, and Brian. "How?"

"Magic, sis! Magic!"

"I'm so glad to see you!" Mel hugged her, too.

358

"So, does this mean we're still together, Mel?" Becky hugged him back. "Because I have to say that was the shortest relationship ever. I've had one-night stands that lasted longer." She laughed. "Naw, I'm just kidding. That's a total exaggeration."

"I'm willing if you're willing," he laughed.

She smiled and kissed him hard. "Oh yes!"

After the kiss, Mel stepped back so John could bring their mother to her. Everyone was nervous. They didn't know how she'd react. They'd never been around someone so recently resurrected from the dead.

"Becky," John pulled her close. "I'd like to introduce you to someone."

Elizabeth sauntered toward her daughter, giving a look of sorrow.

"Hi," said Becky. She felt awkward as she felt all eyes were fixated on her. "I'm Becky."

Tears began streaming down Elizabeth's face, she couldn't stop herself as she pulled her daughter into her arms.

"Becky," John began to cry, too. "I'd like you to meet *Mom*."

"Mom?" Becky pulled the sobbing woman away for a moment to look at her and then at John. "*Our mom*?"

"Yes, you dweeb! *Our mom*!" John hugged them both.

"How is this possible? Was she dead, too?"

"No dear," her mom squeezed her hard. "I will tell you all about it later, just let me hold you!"

"Okay," Becky said, as she began to cry. She didn't remember her mother that well, but now she felt who her mother was, in the flesh, and was realizing everything she missed.

"After all these years," said their mother. "We are all back together as a family."

"Wait," Becky pulled away remembering her father. "We aren't all together just yet. We need to get Dad."

"You're right," said Elizabeth. "We need to bring him back here."

"We have to do it right. This may be a little too much for him to handle," said Becky. "But I think I know where he might be."

"Well, what are we waiting for?" John was too excited to stand around. "I've got a plan." He looked at his friends. Are you guys ready to go back home? I think we may need your help."

"Count us in, John," said Ryan.

"Yeah, we're always here for you," said Sally, wiping her own tears. This family reunion made her wish for one of her own.

"All right guys, follow me," said John, walking up to the redwood's arched door. Everyone but Dyad and Brian followed without question.

"Good luck," said Brian.

"Thanks, Uncle Brian," John replied. "That has a nice ring to it." Then he looked at Dyad. What could he say?

"I love you, John," she blew him a kiss. "I'll be here waiting for you."

"I love you, too, I really do!" He knew she understood as he fitted his key into the door of the owl's home. The door opened and a beaming white light flooded the forest. Six strong, they walked in with no regrets, returning to their other world.

Chapter XXIV
Healing with Hope

The coals in the fireplace sparked lightly as he slumped on his torn and dirty recliner. His long, greasy black hair shone with the oil of missed showers and his beard reeked of liquor. He sat comfortably with his rifle on his lap sipping on a bottle of cheap whiskey. He had been there for hours just staring at the sparking fire, thinking.

The log cabin was small and quaint, and filled with dusty taxidermy. The highly prized stuffed animals, heads and furs lining the cabin walls, showed what an excellent hunter he was, or at least used to be.

An old, cobwebbed soapstone sink filled with slimy, grimy dishes, now cockroach bait, sat against one wall. On the opposite wall coals burned in the sizable fireplace, a cobblestoned edifice that retained its beauty despite the neglect. There was a table, scattered with gun parts, placed next to a window that faced the dark forest outside. Owls hooted and the cold autumn wind howled, a tangible presence felt through the cracks in the old lathe-and-plaster façade that covered the mud-chinked log walls.

The closet door slowly opened as Elizabeth stepped out wearing a short aqua-blue dress accented by a freshwater pearl necklace and black patent leather high heels. She slowly moved toward him, surprisingly not making a sound despite her stiletto heels.

Jim mindlessly lifted the bottle of whiskey to his lips and began to guzzle. Elizabeth paused as a surge of sadness shot through her body. She wondered if this was really the husband she knew years ago.

Back then their life had been wonderful. Though they had a small house and not much money, they had each other, and that was enough.

She watched her husband carefully as he set the bottle down on the table beside him and lifted his rifle to his mouth.

"Jim! No!" she leaped toward him.

Jim jumped out of his chair instantly aiming the gun at her.

"Who are you?" he screamed, afraid he was having another attack of delirium nightmares. That's why he wanted to kill himself. To stop the bad dreams that more and more often invaded his waking life.

"It's me," she said softly, a little scared now. She held her hands up in the classic gesture of surrender. "It's me, Lizzy."

"What?" he rubbed his eyes and his sweaty head with his forearm. He squinted and wobbled, still drunk. "Lizzy?"

"Yes, your wife!"

"Oh my God!" he squinted again. "I'm hallucinating." He lifted his gun into aiming position and said, "My wife is dead! Who are you?"

"It's me, Jim!"

"No, it's not! Who sent you? I'm not going to jail!"

"Please put down the gun!" she began to shake. She was now thinking this wasn't such a good idea. "You're not going to jail. I'm here to take you home, back to Enchantas."

"Enchantas isn't real! Who are you?"

"It is real, Jim. That's where we met."

"Shut up! You're an imposter! Get out or I'll shoot."

"Jim, please," she said, stepping back.

He fired a warning shot into the ceiling. Elizabeth jumped almost as high as the bullet, truly terrified. She retreated a few more steps back toward the closet. How could she reach a man in such agony? Her lover, *her spirit-mate*, was nearly unrecognizable to her in both appearance and behavior.

"John?" she said hesitantly. "Becky?"

"Those are my kids," he pointed the gun at her again. "What did you do with them?"

"Help!" she cried.

John, Mel, Ryan, and Becky quickly came out of the closet, tackling Jim. Shots rang out as he pulled reflexively on the trigger, but the bullets, thankfully, hit no one.

"Elizabeth! Come here!" yelled Sally, secreting them both away in the closet.

Elizabeth jumped in. "That is not my husband! What happened to him?"

"It'll be okay," Sally tried to reassure her, but she, too, was afraid. She hadn't pictured John's dad being so freaked out. "Trust your son; he'll take care of it."

"Johnny!" his father yelled, trying to wiggle out of their grip. "What the hell do you think you're doing?"

"Becky!" John yelled, holding his father's arms down. "Get this gun out of here. Take it outside. Dad, stop it!"

Ryan and Mel each grabbed one of Jim's legs, holding on as hard as they could.

"No!" his father swore as Becky took hold of the gun and ran with it. "Becky Sue! Give that back! I need to kill that imposter."

"Ryan, give me the bracelet!"

"No! No!" his father cried hysterically. "No more bracelets! Leave me alone. You're not real! None of this is!"

John was finally able to get a firm grip on his dad's arm by kneeling on it, just as he'd held the Banshee in place, although in this instance he hoped he wouldn't do any lasting damage. He clasped the bracelet on his father's arm, then let him go.

Jim began to convulse, foaming from the mouth. "Oh crap!" John cried as Mel and Ryan quickly let go of Jim's legs.

"Mom, you come out, it'll be all right," John called, although he wasn't completely convinced himself.

"Are you sure?" Becky asked, hesitantly walking back into the cabin, watching her father as he frothed and quivered. "He doesn't look all right."

Her mother hated that they had to see it but confirmed that all was going as it should. "This is normal, my darlings. He needs to replenish his soul. It's safe and it's self-induced. Your father made this bracelet many years ago."

"This was Dad's?" John wondered if he'd ever be done being amazed by all the turns of events.

"He knew a long time ago that there was a need to assist Enchantians who had lost all hope and fallen into the abyss of depression. This bracelet has helped so many and it is fitting that it will help him now."

It took a few seconds for the seizures to subside. They surrounded him, watching closely to make sure he didn't choke or otherwise injure himself.

Jim opened his eyes and looked around calmly. He looked at his children, then at his wife and began to cry.

"I am so sorry!" he heaved with sobs, laying his head back down on the dirty wooden floor.

Elizabeth fell to her knees, clasping her husband tightly.

"It's okay, Jim. We're here. All of us!"

"John, Becky," their father cried, "I am *so* sorry!"

John and Becky hesitated, thinking about all those awful years with him, the beatings, the neglect, the squalor. Trust needed to be earned. But they could begin now. They knelt down with open hearts, helping their mom help their dad to his feet.

"I am so sorry, kids," he repeated. "I was on a downward spiral and there was no way back. I want to make it up to you."

"You can," said his wife. "Let us be a family again. Come back to Enchantas."

"Enchantas?" he looked at his children. "You two know about Enchantas?"

"Yeah, we do dad," said John. "Come back with us. We're willing to start fresh if you are. There's nothing for us here, only bad memories."

Jim nodded, knowing his son was right. There was nothing here.

"Are you guys all right?" asked Ryan.

"Yeah, I think so," replied John, looking at his father, mother, and sister.

"We wish you the best of luck in Enchantas," said Sally softly, walking over to her boyfriend.

"Be sure to visit," said Becky. "I'll be pissed if you don't."

"We will," said Ryan, "Just to make sure you've cleaned up that potty mouth." He smiled. "Take care."

"Oh, Mel!" Becky grabbed him and kissed him as hard and long as she could. He squeezed her back, tightly, never wanting to let her go. "I'm expecting to see you!"

"Don't worry, you will." Mel kissed her cheek. "You finally have your family back, and I'm going back to mine. I need to, but I'm gonna miss you like crazy."

Becky smiled at him as she joined her reunited family.

"Come on Becky," John motioned, leading the way back to the closet door. He grabbed her hand. Their mother and father were right behind.

John turned his key, returning them to the world of Enchantas. Mel, Sally, and Ryan watched gleefully as they disappeared.

Their family was whole again. Only time could heal their wounds and what better way to spend that time than in the *Land of Enchantas*...

EPILOGUE
The Curse

Spring was in the air and it was lunch time. Sally, Mel, and Ryan raced across the parking lot of the school, hoping they wouldn't be spotted by any teachers or staff. It was their daily ritual to spend their lunch period with their friends in Enchantas. They had done this ever since Alexis and Nymph were imprisoned.

Not much had changed since their departure. Peace still flourished and the Enchantian Institute was thriving. It had become much larger and almost all the youth of Enchantas were enrolled. Magic, once a commodity used by the privileged, was now available to all.

"Hurry up, Mel," said Ryan. "We don't want to be late for John's Inauguration."

John was to be Knighted and his friends and family were bursting with pride.

Mel was a little disappointed, knowing that if he had stayed in Enchantas, he would also be knighted by now. But he did not regret his decision to come back. His mother was so happy, like a new woman. He had never known how much she loved him. Mel's stepfather had backed off from his constant lecturing; he believed his pestering was the reason Mel ran away.

Mel was back at school, at the top of his class, much to the surprise of some instructors who had previously written him off as a buffoon. A couple of teachers remarked on how much he had changed since he returned. Nobody asked too many questions about where he had been. It was as if they were too afraid to hear the truth. And his truth, well, they would have found it impossible to believe.

He was currently attending senior level classes as he tested out of everything else. His plan for the next year was to commute to Willington Community College so he could challenge himself more. High school was just too easy for him. Maybe after college he would go back to Enchantas and marry Becky. At least, that was his plan.

Mel enjoyed his visits to Enchantas; he missed Becky whenever he wasn't with her. They'd become very close. Thanks to the keys, she could also take trips to visit him, which she did every once in a while when she thought she could get away with it. There had been many nights when she would sneak through his closet door and wake him up. They'd leave his house and go for long walks. Other nights, if he couldn't sleep, he spent in Enchantas, staying as many days as he could before coming back to his world just in time to wake up for school.

Mel understood Becky's decision to remain in Enchantas. He knew how much her family meant to her now that they were whole again. Their wounds had finally healed and they were moving forward, living harmoniously there.

"I'm coming." Mel panted. He was not in great shape like his athletic friend.

They passed the parked cars and the baseball field which led to a walkway to the football team's clubhouse's metal door. They used this door because it was secluded yet in close proximity to the school.

Sally dug in her pocket feverishly looking for her key. "Ryan, do you have your key?" She checked her back pocket. "I must have left mine in my locker."

She didn't notice that she had just dropped it. The key was directly under her right foot.

"Don't worry," said Mel, pushing his into the slot. "I've got mine."

"Ryan!" a voice bellowed from the parking lot.

They all turned to look, but didn't see anyone.

"Who is that?" asked Mel.

Ryan squinted to get a better look. "Oh crap! That's my brother. Hurry let's go!"

Ryan's brother Ben sprinted toward them from behind a parked van. His brother's wavy blond hair bounced with perfection.

Mel's key was stuck. It took a moment before it finally turned and the door opened. A bright purple light emanated from the opening. The three of them jumped in, transported back to Enchantas.

The door slammed shut loudly, just before Ben reached it.

"Ryan!" Ben screamed, banging on the door. "Let me in! You're in big trouble now! I know you're in there!"

Ben slammed his open hand on the door a few more times, but got no response. He put his ear against the door, but couldn't hear anything.

"You're never going to use my car again if you don't open this door!"

Ben felt something underneath his foot. Curious, he lifted his foot to find a golden key with a sparkling green gem on its rounded end. Quickly, looking around to make sure no one else was there, he inserted the key in the lock. He was surprised that it fit, although the handle seemed to be stuck. He jiggled the handle a few more times until he heard a ruffling sound behind him.

"Hello," Ben said casually worried that someone had come up behind him. Slowly turning around as if he hadn't a care in the world. "Is there anyone there?"

Sitting in the grass, a few feet away, a gray and white rabbit stared up at him. Blood trickled down its back, white foam oozed from its mouth. Its eyes were a bloodshot, fiery red. It let out a deep, long growl, very uncharacteristic for a rabbit.

"Whoa! What the hell?" Startled, Ben wiggled the handle frantically. He had nowhere to run. He needed to get away from that creepy, demonic rabbit. He jiggled the handle hysterically and twisted the key hard. Finally the door opened and without hesitation Ben jumped into the purple light. He wasn't alone, though. The rabid rabbit had scrambled in, too, leaping for his life.

After so long, Mumbles was finally going home. But he was not the same little light-blue, plump happy-go-lightly bunny who had played merry games with his friends and occasionally gotten into mischief. No, Mumbles has changed and was now, very sick. He was infected and bringing this disease, this *curse*, back with him. Back to Enchantas…

ABOUT THE AUTHOR

Corey M. LaBissoniere is a resident of Houghton, Michigan in the northwest part of Michigan's Upper Peninsula on the shores of Lake Superior. He is a graduate of Houghton High School, Gogebic Community College and Michigan Technological University. When he is not writing, he works as an Adoption Specialist at a local Agency, enjoys a good game of billiards with his father, delights in extreme sports, likes outdoor activities, loves to travel, and appreciates a good story.

www.coreylabissoniere.com

www.ingramcontent.com/pod-product-compliance
Lightning Source LLC
Chambersburg PA
CBHW051445260626
47162CB00001B/265